Born in the UK, **Becky Wicks** ~~has had an~~ interminable wanderlust from a ~~young age. She's~~ lived and worked all over the w~~orld, from London~~ to Dubai, Sydney, Bali, NYC and Amsterdam. She's written for the likes of *GQ*, *Hello!*, *Fabulous* and *Time Out*, a host of YA romance, plus three travel memoirs—*Burqalicious*, *Balilicious* and *Latinalicious* (HarperCollins, Australia). Now she blends travel with romance for Mills & Boon and loves every minute! Tweet her @bex_wicks and subscribe at beckywicks.com.

Denise N. Wheatley loves happy endings and the art of storytelling. Her novels run the romance gamut, and she strives to pen entertaining books that embody matters of the heart. She's an RWA member and holds a BA in English from the University of Illinois. When Denise isn't writing, she enjoys watching true crime TV and chatting with readers. Follow her on social media. Instagram: @Denise_Wheatley_Writer, Twitter: @DeniseWheatley, BookBub: @DeniseNWheatley, Goodreads: Denise N. Wheatley.

MELTING THE SURGEON'S HEART

BECKY WICKS

ER DOC'S LAS VEGAS REUNION

DENISE N. WHEATLEY

MILLS & BOON

First published in Great Britain 2024
by Mills & Boon, an imprint of HarperCollins*Publishers* Ltd,
1 London Bridge Street, London, SE1 9GF

www.harpercollins.co.uk

HarperCollins*Publishers* Macken House, 39/40 Mayor Street Upper,
Dublin 1, D01 C9W8, Ireland

Melting the Surgeon's Heart © 2024 Becky Wicks

ER Doc's Las Vegas Reunion © 2024 Denise N. Wheatley

ISBN: 978-0-263-32148-7

01/24

This book is produced from independently certified FSC™ paper
to ensure responsible forest management.
For more information visit: www.harpercollins.co.uk/green.

Printed and Bound in the UK using 100% Renewable Electricity
at CPI Group (UK) Ltd, Croydon, CR0 4YY

MELTING THE SURGEON'S HEART

BECKY WICKS

MILLS & BOON

Dedicated to the Icelanders,
who always made me feel at home.

CHAPTER ONE

THE SNOWSTORM SEETHED with the ferocity of a wild beast as Mahlia strode with her face down, her hair whipping violently around her face. Flakes of snow the size of boulders flew past the rim of her hood like an unrelenting army under the sinister sky and she shivered, knowing her chapped lips were probably turning a deathly shade of blue. No sign of the northern lights tonight, she thought. If they were up there somewhere, they were hiding away in fear of this storm.

Even as an experienced search and rescue paramedic, it was hard for her not to fear the unknown out here in Iceland. She was fast becoming a snowman. A snow*woman*. One who could easily merge with a snowdrift and never be seen again.

Leaning into the wind, she trudged through the snow, wrapping her arms around herself, shivering. Just over a month in the country and already the New Zealand sun felt like a distant memory.

'Almost there,' her search team leader Erik called from ahead, where he was walking with Ásta, their search technician.

Mahlia's breath caught in her throat as a row of buildings suddenly emerged from the snowy mist. She quickened her pace, thoughts of hot chocolate and heat and light propelling her forward. The cold had long ago permeated through her thick coat and thermal trousers, and they'd only been following the compass from the road for fifteen minutes. The chopper would be with them as soon as it was safe to fly, and then they could recommence the search.

Inside the warm hut, she drew back her hood and shook out her mass of corkscrew curls. She caught a glimpse of her reflection in the window and frowned. Her lips were indeed an eerie shade of alien grey.

'Drink?' A small, hunched woman beckoned her forward to the worn wooden table and chairs.

'Yes, please…thank you,' she said gratefully through her chattering teeth, taking a seat by the fire.

The flames reached upwards like spindly hands from the hearth, their bright orange light spilling over the walls and across the wooden ceiling. It was snug in here, cosy, like a warm hug after all that walking. She grasped her mug, sipped her drink, and was vaguely aware of the murmurs of her crew and the kindly villagers who'd taken them into the community centre.

They all knew about the search. There were places like this set up for the volunteers all over the Thingvellir National Park now. But the raging snowstorm outside only served to heighten her discomfort and sense of dread. It was nearly two days since the Cessna plane carrying a male pilot in his mid-forties and two Swedish tourists in their thirties had gone missing. Over three hundred search and rescue volunteers had taken part in the search yesterday and over a hundred more had got on the case this morning. Everywhere they searched, all they seemed to find was silence.

Hopefully it didn't show on their faces, but everyone here shared the same unspoken worry—what if this mission ended in failure? With each hour that passed, the chances of finding the missing people alive were getting slimmer and slimmer. It was almost impossible to believe that anyone could survive in freezing conditions like these for so long. Iceland's weather was brutal, unpredictable, and in the middle of storms like this one it felt like the kind of savage cold she imagined her mother must have felt consumed by during the darkest patches of her depression. Thank goodness she was better now, Mahlia thought; well enough to survive the thought of her only daughter being all the way out here.

Mahlia was still deep in thought when the sound of the helicopter's thrumming blades burst through every crack in the hut like a torrent of falling water. The storm had subsided, and Sven had finally been able to land. She ran to the door ahead of the others, flinging it open.

Sven, their pilot, whom she'd been working with for three weeks already, was stepping from the cockpit, the blades above him spinning their way to a standstill. He squeezed her shoulder on his way past, motioning that they both had to get inside. The kind old lady was already waiting with more hot drinks. But there was another pair of feet on the ground now—someone else who'd just jumped from the helicopter and slammed the door behind him. Mahlia stared at the new winchman and felt herself draw a long, deep breath from some place inside her she hadn't known was there.

Was this Gunnar? He'd come to join their crew after Elias, Ásta's husband, had fallen awkwardly and broken his left femur yesterday. The poor guy was still in hospital in Reykjavik. Ásta had stayed on the search, at his insistence.

Mahlia realised she'd been holding her breath almost too long. *What?* She kept her eyes on him, pulling her jacket more tightly around herself. The man was striding straight towards her now. He was tall and broad-shouldered, with a determined jawline. Ruggedly handsome, she found herself thinking. Mid to late thirties, like her. Maybe even early forties, but he wore his skin and features well, not like some of the other Icelanders around, who seemed more weathered than the mountains.

He was blocking the snowdrifts now, stepping up to her in bulky snow pants and a heavy jacket, his hair shaggy and unruly, sticking out in all directions from under his woollen hat. He stopped in front of her, not too close, but close enough that she could feel the intensity radiating off him.

'I'm Gunnar,' he said, pulling off his gloves. 'You must be Mahlia.' He studied her face for a moment in silence, sizing her up. 'You look just like they described you.'

Mahlia was amused, even as his eyes bored into her, unsettling something deep in her belly. How had they described her? A Kiwi girl? A fragile, five-foot-five half-Maori woman, completely in over her head?

'That's right,' she said, picturing the first time Javid had looked at her like this. If only she'd known back then to run a mile. 'I'm a rescue paramedic. I've been here a month already. Good of you to join us.'

He huffed a laugh. 'I go where I'm needed.' His hand was big and strong and heat emanated straight from his palm right into her own. 'It sounds like you must have something special,' he said, cutting through the snow with her to the hut and opening the door for her.

His words made Maliah smile; she wasn't used to such compliments. Then he spoilt it.

'But you look tired,' he added. 'When was the last time you slept?'

She bristled. If there was one thing that annoyed her most it was people thinking she wasn't up to the job for any reason. 'We're all tired. But we go where we're needed,' she said, mimicking his earlier words. He bit back a smile, which seemed to settle something between them and send her heart flapping at the same time.

He pulled the creaking door shut behind them, shutting out the snow-covered mountains as well as her reply, then walked to the table, shaking off his jacket to a chorus of, 'Gunnar Johansson!' and 'Gunnar, my man!'

Everyone seemed to know him. Some jumped up from their seats, enthusiastically shaking his hand, and he reached out to them with a nod here, a friendly smile there. Some were old friends, no doubt. The women all threw their arms around him. Several seemed to hold on just a little longer than necessary. There were a couple of guys, though, in the far corner, who were frowning now, throwing each other knowing looks, nodding his way and huddling in to talk about him.

Her instincts were primed. They didn't like Gunnar. Why?

She watched him and Erik hunch over the map he'd pulled out, their fingers tracing circles. The outermost ring followed natural boundaries—a river, a mountain ridge, a coffee-coloured lake. They'd been methodically erasing possible scenarios from the list all day. Gunnar caught her eye again across the table and Maliah's heart lodged tight in her throat. Something about him made her feel simultaneously excited and cautious at the same time.

Someone had said earlier that he was a big deal, or his family were a big deal in Iceland—not that she'd been listening, really, and she hadn't the time to look him up. He was a trained renal specialist and surgeon. And he was taking some time off, like he did every year, to volunteer on the search and rescue teams.

Her radio flickered to life. Someone with a drone had just spotted an orange item of clothing, out by one of the lakes.

'We should get going,' she heard herself saying, just as Erik said the same thing in unison.

Her crew were already on their feet.

* * *

Maliah saw it first. The orange crumpled heap of something that looked a lot like a jacket tangled in the branches that swept the ground. 'Someone's here!'

'I see it,' Sven said, steering them back towards it.

The lake was iced over, a sheet of white, thanks to the fresh snow from the storm. From up here in the helicopter, the fjords held the look of giant serrated teeth around the perimeter. The iced-over craggy tops of the mountains on the horizon told her just how stranded they'd be without each other. Helpless. Like the people they were looking for.

Having flown in from New Zealand, she was only in her third week of the four-month contract she'd taken with this SAR team, but already Erik, Ásta and Sven were her family by proxy—the ones she had to rely on, day in, day out. As for Gunnar, she thought, shooting him a glance. Time would tell.

'I think I can land here,' Sven called back now.

His words were barely audible over the din of the helicopter's engines and rotors, but Gunnar was beside her in a second, his face pressed to the window, assessing the situation. Erik and Ásta checked the terrain through the opposite windows.

The trees below were sparse, a few broken stumps poking up through the snow. It was impossible to tell if it was a person's jacket from here or not, now that she thought about it.

'Hang in there,' she said under her breath to the people who were lost out here somewhere. One of the Swedish tourists had been wearing an orange jacket—they all knew it.

'Sven's a pro, in case you hadn't noticed,' Gunnar said, sensing her concern. 'I've known him since school—he wouldn't put anyone in danger.'

'It's not his flying I'm worried about,' she replied, but her cheeks grew hot at the way he was looking at her, closer than close. He smiled as the chopper lowered to the ground. His teeth were slightly jagged at the edges, milky white, still baby-like in their perfection.

'You're a tough one, aren't you?' he observed in his thick Icelandic accent.

'Is that a compliment?' she shot back, and one thick blond eyebrow shot up to his hat.

He sounded slightly American, despite his accent. She was about to ask him where exactly he was from when Sven slid the chopper almost to a stop and Gunnar sprang into action, opening the door before they were even completely stationary.

Her eyes traced his movements as he skidded down a bank and onto the frozen lake, motioning at them all to stay where they were for now. She watched from the open door with her heart in her mouth as he picked his way carefully across the ice. He crouched where the fuzzy fir trees began and started to carefully remove snow from around the object with one hand, clutching a branch with the other.

'It's a coat,' he called back to them, and her heart skidded at the confirmation.

In seconds she was on the ground, crunching over the heavy snow in her boots towards the base of the bushy tree.

'There's no one here,' he said grimly.

'Are you sure? I'll help you dig.' This was her job—to make absolutely certain there was no one here who needed their help before turning back.

She slipped, and Gunnar lunged forward with gloved hands outstretched.

'I'm fine,' she insisted, swerving his grip.

He didn't look too sure. But when he saw she wouldn't relent, a determined fire lit his ice-blue eyes and he reached out, wrapping his gloved hands around her elbows. He drew her close to him on the ice, till their faces were only inches apart.

'Careful. One wrong movement out here, one slip-up. is all it takes…'

'I know,' she interjected, taking in the severity etched in his ice-blue gaze. 'You don't have to tell me that! I've done this before in New Zealand, remember?'

His face softened and he nodded at her, amusement flickering on his mouth for just a second. 'OK, then. Sorry.'

His voice was deep and strong, his speech measured and in control, but there was a hint of gravel in there, like a trapped cough, as if he'd been screaming and had only just stopped. What was his deal? she wondered. He seemed pretty protective of her, and he barely knew her. She knew nothing about him at all, but suddenly she wanted to.

Together, they continued to remove the snow from around the coat but, just as he'd said, there was no one with it. Gunnar stood up and took off his hat, running a hand through his hair. Mahlia watched him silently from her haunches, feeling the disappointment settle in her own chest. Maybe they'd just been too late.

'We're running out of time,' she heard herself mutter. Exhaustion was seeping through her bones now.

He fixed her with an understanding gaze. 'We won't give up. We'll keep searching, no matter how long it takes. We won't abandon them.'

His voice resounded with utter conviction and it threw her, then sent her heart into a spin. Erik and Ásta were on the edge of the ice now, zipping up thick, padded parkas.

'We'll split up,' Gunnar said firmly. 'Mahlia, you and I will take that ridge over there. Erik and Ásta will take this one here.' He gestured to an icy slope. 'That way we can cover more ground, faster.'

Mahlia turned to the sky. It was difficult for an outsider to understand how swiftly the weather in Iceland could take a turn for the worse, but she'd grown pretty used to it over the last few weeks.

Even when Sven radioed in from the chopper, saying, 'Don't go too far, guys…' Gunnar didn't look fazed at all. He was already striding purposefully across the frozen lake.

Mahlia hurried after him. The snow crunched beneath Gunnar's boots ahead of her as he made his way slowly and carefully towards the trees at the other side of the lake. Mahlia watched his eyes scanning his surroundings like a hawk, matching his stride as best she could, aware of the distance between them and the chopper. That was how far they'd have to carry someone injured back to safety, if they were lucky enough to find anyone alive.

Suddenly he stopped and crouched down, motioning her over with a wave of his hand. 'Here!'

'What is it?'

Cautiously, Mahlia made her way towards him, till she got close enough to see what he'd spotted: fresh footprints in the snow, leading away from where they were standing.

New hope and excitement surged through her. 'You don't think…?'

'Maybe they made their way out here from some hiding place, and headed back again when the storm hit,' he said, whipping out a flashlight. Technically, it was daytime. But now, in mid-March, after a storm, they needed all the help they could get.

Together, they traced the footsteps, slowly heading deeper into dense, dark forest. The crackle of fallen leaves and twigs crunched underfoot now, and Gunnar made sure to keep her slightly behind him at all times, like a bear watching out for its cub. This whole over-protection thing would have annoyed her usually, but out here, coming from him… It was weird, but she actually felt comforted by it.

'We shouldn't go too far,' she warned him, her eyes darting around vigilantly.

The air felt brittle and cold, and the wind whistling through the trees sounded a little too much like voices. This was like New Plymouth in some ways, but in so many others completely different. Alien. Full of elves, trolls and fairies, apparently, always watching. She was almost starting to think the lady from the homestead back in Reykjavik might have been onto something with all the fantastical stories she'd pretended to believe. Mount Taranaki was famous, and was swarmed with visitors in New Zealand, so picture-perfect it barely looked real. But it was more than something pretty to the Maori people; it was an ancestor...a living thing. No one was even allowed to climb to the very top.

She almost wanted to turn back, suddenly fearing the Icelandic tales might be real, but something about Gunnar's steadfast demeanour kept her going. This man was clearly a force to be reckoned with; she was safe with him. Whoever he was. She'd known him less than an hour and here she was, alone with him in an Icelandic fjord. Javid would have a fit.

She caught herself. Javid's feelings were not her concern—not any more. No more manipulation, no more sly asides or cutting passive-aggressive remarks. No more gaslighting. He was probably going out of his mind now that his control over her had been broken for good. She was just wondering what might have happened to her wedding ring after she'd slid it into an envelope and pushed it through his letterbox on her way to the airport—the bravest thing she'd ever done!—when Gunnar stuck a hand out behind him to stop her. She almost slammed into his back.

A small hut was visible just ahead, tucked away amongst the trees. The footprints cut through the snow, heading towards it, and Gunnar picked up his pace. Mahlia held her breath as he eased open the creaking door and followed him cautiously into the cabin, her eyes adjusting to the darkness.

'Look,' she whispered, touching his arm as her heart leapt to her throat.

She could just make out a shape in the corner. A person. Moving closer, she could tell the figure was a man, lying on his side. He wasn't moving, covered in dirty blankets that he must have salvaged from this tiny abandoned squat. The remains of a burnt-out fire sat charred and black in the hearth.

'He's alive, but injured,' Gunnar said, pulling out his radio.

He spoke to Erik while Mahlia knelt down beside the man, gently touching his shoulder as she spoke softly, so as not to alarm him. 'Are you OK? Can you tell us what happened?'

No response. Mahlia shuffled out of her backpack. She could see the extent of the injuries now—scrapes along his neck, cuts on his forehead and beneath a rolled-up trouser leg, and one of his ankles was swollen to twice its size.

'Can you move?' she asked him.

He was stirring now, unable to do more than emit a pained groan. Taking off his coat, Gunnar carefully wrapped it around him and offered his hand for support as the man attempted to push himself up into a seated position. Together, they managed to sit him upright, but he winced in agony when they tried to move his arm.

Mahlia assessed his wounds, trying not to focus on how cold she was. She unzipped her backpack and pulled out the necessary supplies: sterile cotton swabs, antiseptic solution, gauze pads and bandages. Gently she cleaned his wounds, taking care not to cause him any further discomfort, feeling Gunnar's eyes on her the whole time.

Outside the wind was howling again, bending trees at its whim, their branches and leaves crackling like fireworks.

Sven was radioing in. 'Hurry up, guys. Get back here as fast as you can. The weather's turning.'

The man's skin was cold and clammy to the touch, but thankfully his pulse was steady and strong. Mahlia wrapped a bandage around his neck wound. She would have to treat the gashes on his head in the chopper. Gunnar helped support him as she moved to address his injured ankle.

'It's not broken, but it could be dislocated,' she told him.

'Erik's on his way across the lake,' he replied, helping her wrap a tight elastic bandage around the man's ankle for support.

This was definitely the pilot; he matched the description they had of him. But where were the Swedish couple who'd been in the plane with him? Where was the plane? All this would have to be resolved, but for now all they could do was get this guy back to the chopper as fast as they could.

Mahlia slung his arm around her neck and asked him to put his weight on her, while Gunnar held him up from the other side. 'This is probably going to hurt,' she warned him. 'But we need to get you mobile. The chopper's not far.'

The pilot winced in pain, but with their support he was able to stand. His breath was laboured and heavy as slowly they made their way from the cabin, back out through the snow and across the lake where, to her relief, Erik and Ásta were ready to help him back to the helicopter.

'No sign of the others?' Erik asked hopefully, as he and Gunnar lifted the man inside.

Mahlia felt ill with worry. The two Swedish tourists couldn't have gone far, if the orange jacket was indeed a sign that at least one of them was around somewhere, but the snow was picking up again now. They had no choice but to abandon this location for the meantime and get the chopper out to a safe location, where their injured pilot could be transported to Reykjavik.

'We did all we could,' Gunnar told her, as the air turned grey around them and the rotors churned like a machine gun above. Soon they were flying blind through a haze of snow, but thankfully Erik was the pro that Gunnar had told him he was, and all that mattered now was getting the man to safety.

Mahlia pressed her lips together; she was soaking wet and freezing. 'But maybe we overlooked something, guys. The other two are still out there.'

'We'll find them,' said Gunnar, fixing his blue eyes on hers, making her pulse quicken. 'Someone will find them.'

She watched his lips, waiting for a word like *eventually*, or two words like *dead or alive*. He seemed to know without her saying that she didn't think they'd find the others alive, because he folded his arms and shook his head wryly, even before Ásta spoke.

'Miracles do happen out here sometimes. We can never stop hoping for them, anyway.'

'We'll start again in the morning,' Erik said. 'First thing. We all need sleep,' he added, before turning directly to her. 'Mahlia, you've been on your feet since six a.m.'

The look in his kind eyes moved her. Gunnar, who'd stayed quiet, fixed his concerned gaze on her again. Suddenly it mattered what he thought of her.

'I'm used to being tired,' she said, to Gunnar, not Erik. 'I'm fine.'

Then she turned back to the pilot, who was slipping in and out of consciousness with hypothermia. It was taking every last ounce of her energy to stay awake in the biting cold.

When they touched down at the hangar just outside of Reykjavik, the bitter wind whirled snow into her eyes and she felt her eyelids droop, even as the doors sprang open on the waiting ambulance. The medics rushed out to assist with transferring the pilot onto a stretcher, and she watched as they ushered him into their care.

Gunnar was pacing the ground, talking on the phone. Sven, Erik and Ásta said their goodbyes and piled into a Jeep together. Mahlia made for her own vehicle, thankful yet again for the snow chains on the tyres. Sleep was all she wanted now. Sweet, beautiful sleep.

'Hey, would you mind giving me a ride?' Gunnar asked suddenly, hurrying up behind her now, shoving his phone back into his pocket.

The presence of his bulk behind her sent a tingle down her spine. He gestured to the pockets of his snow pants, now pulled inside out. Then he pointed to his SUV, alone in the car park, slowly gathering another layer of thick white snow.

'I must have lost my keys somewhere on the lake,' he said. 'I have spares back at my place.'

Mahlia sucked in a quiet breath, realising how gorgeous he actually was up close, even if she couldn't really read him most of the time. Well, maybe if she drove him home she'd find out more?

CHAPTER TWO

THEY RODE IN SILENCE, the heater on full blast and the car filling with hot air that only intensified her exhaustion and the sting of her lips. Mahlia felt as if she was looking at everything through a foggy lens, but she had to stay awake. She still had to email the solicitor about the divorce papers, which Javid was still refusing to sign.

She kept biting her chafed lips, feeling the roughness of them against her teeth and with her tongue. Eventually the silence got a little awkward.

'So...' they started at the same time.

Gunnar grunted a laugh, catching her eyes in the mirror. The sound made her pulse quicken even more than it had earlier, when he'd looked at her as if...as if he admired her.

'So, Mahlia. What do you do all day when you're not on a search and rescue call?'

'You mean back in New Plymouth, where I'm from? I'm a paramedic there too, but I'm contracted here for a few months. I'm kind of exploring another idea too, actually.'

She paused. There was hardly any point in telling him she was trying to get as far away from her controlling ex-husband as possible—that she'd left him six weeks ago, still begging her to take him back.

'I'm a mountain biker,' she continued.

He nodded with interest.

'And I'm in the process of developing a new e-bike for the market. It has an electric motor, and various danger-detection capabilities, so it'll help get people with mobility difficulties out and about more on all kinds of terrain.'

Gunnar turned to her, his attention focused fully on her face now. He listened, studying her eyes and her face as she spoke, and she found herself inserting more passion into her tone with each sentence, like she always did, without thinking, when she started on this topic.

She told him how she was meeting soon with Inka, who was a wheelchair user and the programme analyst here at the Icelandic Wilderness Association. In a similar mission to the one Mahlia had started in Egmont National Park, she was keen to gather updated data on various wilderness trails to determine their safety. Together with Inka, she hoped to combine her mission with locating the best places for the bike to be trialled and enjoyed by users.

Gunnar smiled warmly, running a hand through his hair, sending it spiking up even more. Adorable... 'My brother Demus has multiple sclerosis,' he said. 'I've always wished there was a way to give him his freedom back. He used to ride motorcycles with me all over the place when I lived in the US.'

'Then he's exactly the kind of person I want to help,' she said, tucking away the information that Gunnar had used to live in America. 'My bike can be used by both able-bodied individuals *and* people with a physical disability. It's specifically designed to be adaptive, so you can customise it to your ability level. A good friend of mine at home was paralysed from the waist down a few years ago.' She paused, picturing Jessica, hooked up to all those machines after her accident. 'She was told she'd never cycle again, but she wasn't going to let anyone's opinion hold her back. She was the one who inspired me to do something to help, so we could ride together again someday.'

Gunnar was looking at her with such interest now, even as he answered his chiming phone. Pride swelled her heart. A new feeling, she noted. Javid had always hated hearing anything about her side project.

Gunnar spoke in Icelandic as she chewed her lips. Damn, she needed a tube of lip salve so badly. She'd meant to buy one yesterday, but with everything going on with the search she'd clean run out of time.

'Listen, that was Erik, calling about the pilot...' Gunnar said when he'd hung up.

'Yes?'

He paused a moment. His face was too grave now for her liking and her heart bucked.

'He has severe hypothermia, but the doctors say he'll survive. He's heavily medicated and they're going to keep him sedated. He did mention the Swedish couple, though.'

She nodded, feeling her hands ball into fists on the steering wheel.

'It's not good news. The plane went down in the lake. The pilot got out through the window. When he came up it was already sinking. The divers will go down first thing in the morning for the...for them.'

A rush of nausea flooded her veins as she pictured the scene: those poor people, trying to get out, realising all hope was lost. The orange jacket must have floated out of the lake. Maybe the pilot had left it as a sign for them to look for him there. Maybe he'd already known then that he'd be the only survivor.

Gunnar's gaze was on her again. 'Sorry,' she said quickly, realising her eyes were wet. 'I don't usually get emotional, but...'

'You haven't slept. It happens...it's OK.' His voice was still measured, but his words were coated with kindness now. 'I'm sorry, Mahlia.'

'It's not your fault,' she replied, swallowing down her emotions, realising he hadn't bought her previous claim that she wasn't tired at all.

He swept a hand across his jaw. 'Take the next right.'

'Which hotel are you?' she asked, doing as he asked, hitting a right through a flurry of snow till the modern Hallgrimskirkja cathedral with all its organ key angles came into view in the headlights.

The streets were empty. The grey skies and snow seemed to smother the city, and the crowds of tourists who usually flooded this area had been left with nowhere else to go but home.

'I have a place here,' he said, simply. 'Just here—pull over.'

She did as he asked, just as her phone rang from its place in its holder on the dash. *Javid.* She grimaced, flicking it to silent.

'You're not going to answer that?' he asked.

She shook her head, embarrassed, noting the modern apartment building, the copper and glass encased in a gleaming stone wall, the dragon pillar with its mouth open, holding a lamp to light the steps. His place. This looked like a very expensive place to live—not that anything in Reykjavik was cheap. He obviously earned good money as a surgeon, but she remembered now something about his family being in banking.

He opened the door, but hesitated, turning back to her again, eyes narrowed as they studied her mouth in a way that made her stomach flip. 'Wait here.'

She gaped in response as he slammed the door shut and sprinted up the steps to the entranceway. Tapping her nails on the steering wheel, she yawned, and ignored Javid's second call—why would he not stop calling her? Wasn't leaving him for Iceland enough to drum it home that she was gone from his life for good?

What was Gunnar doing? Who was Gunnar Johansson, even? If she weren't so damn tired and shaken she'd ask him all kinds of things. But all she wanted to do now was sleep.

Suddenly he was back. 'Here.'

In a whirl of snowflakes that rushed in with his hand he deposited a small cylindrical tube into her palm. 'Get some rest,' he instructed, before she could respond. 'I'll see you soon. We're on the same team now.'

'I guess we are,' she said, looking away, wishing her heart would stop making her all doe-eyed over him. 'But aren't you due back in surgery? I heard you're a renal specialist?'

'I oversee Iceland's only kidney transplant programme for most of the year,' he said matter-of-factly, with no trace of ego. 'November through April is the best time to take my break. More people need me out here on the search teams.'

A real hero, she thought, impressed.

'Wait,' she said, before he could shut the door again. 'I'll see you tomorrow, right? I'm still coming. Just in case...'

'Just in case we *do* find them alive?' He frowned.

'Just in case,' she repeated, as firmly as she could. It didn't seem right to just give up. 'I'll tell Erik when he calls me.'

He held her eyes a moment, sizing her up again in a way that made her nervous. Then he bobbed his head and shut the door again.

Mahlia stared at the object in her hand. A brand-new, un-opened tube of lip salve. Cherry-flavoured, no less. With relief, she applied it to her lips in the mirror, feeling the soothing balm calm her instantly. How had he known? Did she really look that terrible? Or, more to the point, had he been looking at her lips long enough to notice that she needed this?

The tiny dead creature in her stomach fluttered back to

life—the one that Javid had stomped on again and again. Her ex had done his best to convince her that all her friends were bad for her; that she most certainly did not need to speak to a therapist about her spiralling lack of self-worth whenever she was with him; that she did drink too much on company nights out; that she didn't need to work as hard as she did because it made him look like a miserly provider. And every single time he'd told her any or all those things another part of her had shrivelled up and died.

Now, though…

A light flicked on in the apartment two floors up as she pulled away. Glancing in her mirrors, she swore she saw Gunnar in the window, watching her go.

Gunnar was right, of course. There were no more survivors.

Mahlia watched the last of the scuba divers surface from her place in the helicopter. The wind howled like a banshee wail, stealing words from her freezing cold lips and blasting them away as Gunnar was lowered from the chopper towards the ice, swinging on the winch like a tiny figure in a giant snow globe.

His orange jumpsuit was the brightest thing for miles, a beacon against the grey-white tundra as he touched down on the life raft on the frozen lake. The divers had set it up in case the ice broke and took the crew down, too.

She held her breath next to Ásta as Gunnar set about bringing the two Swedish tourists up through a carefully cut hole in the ice, and she kept her eyes on him, watching him master the buckles and straps and clips and harnesses, all while the weather did everything in its power to halt his expert mission.

She found herself concerned for him, even though he clearly knew what he was doing. This was her team, her crew, and she'd held out hope till the break of dawn, till arriving here back at the lake, that things would turn out differently. But she'd also been thinking about Gunnar, specifically. And about what she'd learned about him this morning on the Internet, at five a.m. over coffee.

She couldn't help feeling a little sorry for him now.

Gunnar's father, Ingólfur Johansson, had spent five years incarcerated in Kviabryggja Prison. after some privately owned commercial banks had defaulted. Ingólfur, Fjallabanki Bank's former chief executive officer, had been convicted of market manipulation and fraud and, from what she'd been able to gather online, a lot of people in this very small country had turned against Gunnar's whole family because of it.

She watched Gunnar now, on his ascent with one of the bodies. It was hard to look, knowing that someone in that thick black bag had set out for a day of excitement and adventure and wound up like this. She'd been on search and rescue teams on and off around her work for years, but if she was quite honest not even New Zealand's harshest winter could have prepared her for this.

'The ambulance will meet us at the road when we've finished here,' Erik told them, readying himself to help Gunnar, who was still swaying perilously on his steel wire, navigating the way towards them slowly but surely with his load.

She cleared the last of the room in the chopper for the unfortunate victims while her heart roared in her chest, almost louder than the rotors.

A little later Mahlia found herself watching Gunnar talking to Erik and the police as she waited for them, sipping on a much-needed coffee. The hangar was still a foot deep in snow outside, despite the shovelled snowdrifts to the sides. All the cops here had guns on show, she mused, rubbing her eyes. They were all exceptionally good-looking, too.

She pictured Javid, the night he'd dressed up as a policeman for Halloween. It must have been two years into their seven-year marriage. He'd put in as little effort as possible and had berated her for having too much of herself on display in her Cat Woman costume. He'd forced her to leave early with him. That was the same night he'd told her to give up on the adapted e-bikes project, that it would never go anywhere. It had only been a flicker of an idea at the time. She'd continued with it largely to prove him wrong.

Did he miss her? Or was he calling her incessantly to re-mind her that he didn't need her in his life? It still made her anxious, remembering how she'd finally told him it was over, face to face in the park, right after he'd told her she needed to walk straighter or she'd have a hunchback by the time she was forty-five. Something had snapped then. Years of his catty, snarky comments, made without a trace of humour, had all suddenly come to a head. She'd ditched him right by a gang of burly motorcyclists, all of them bigger than him, so he wouldn't dare go after her.

'You know, I don't think I did,' Ásta said suddenly.

Ásta was a tall, fierce-looking native Icelander with a back-ground as coach of Iceland's all-women rugby team, but now she was wondering out loud if she'd fed her cat Twinkie that morning, what with her husband still being in the hospital.

'Hmmm…' Mahlia responded, distracted.

Gunnar caught her eye from across the road. He was still in the orange jumpsuit, looking the sexiest anyone had ever looked in a jumpsuit, no question. His hair was as sticky-outy as yesterday, the opposite to Javid's closely shaven stubble. It had always felt a little like sandpaper to her…

She dragged her stare away quickly, forcing her mind to get back to where she needed it. She was psyching herself up to go home, to her rental apartment, and get on with her presentation for Inka. Working on the e-bike trial with some keen, physically challenged participants they'd sourced together would hopefully take her mind off the sight of those body bags...and Javid.

Funny, though, how her persistent mind kept going back to Gunnar, and what his father had done. It hadn't really felt right to probe the Internet for too much information on his past, but just finding out what little she had about his family made her heart go out to him. Iceland was a place where everyone knew *everyone*, and everyone's business too. Suddenly the looks on those men's faces last night in the community centre made much more sense.

All those years ago market manipulation and fraud had had a domino effect on the entire country, and on the way everyone outside it had viewed Iceland back then, too. She'd been twenty, so Gunnar had probably been only a few years older than that when his father had been held accountable and stripped of his ill-gotten gains. Gunnar's life must have been only just beginning when everyone had turned against his family. She'd read about his parents' divorce, too. Kaðlín Johansson had been an iconic TV news anchor when it had happened, and now...she wasn't.

The prison in western Iceland where his father had spent time looked awful! It stood alone on a windswept cape overlooked by a dormant volcano. It looked like a hellscape to her, surrounded on one side by the hostile North Atlantic and snow-covered lava rock on the other. Had Gunnar ever visited his father there during his sentence? she wondered. Or was that when he'd moved to the US?

'Earth to Mahlia?'

Ásta waved a hand across her face, just missing her nose. Ugh, she'd zoned out again, thinking about Gunnar! Why did his life suddenly seem more interesting than anything else she had going on in her own? *Focus!*

Erik and Gunnar were striding purposefully towards them, and the sight was shooting adrenaline through her again.

'I think something must have happened. I guess Twinkie's going to have to wait for her food a little longer.'

Sure enough, Erik's radio was buzzing. 'Road accident out on the Svalvogavegur. We'll go ahead in my car,' he said to Ásta, who sprang into action.

'Mahlia will follow in the search and rescue truck, with me,' Gunnar added.

Her heart leapt at the sound of her name coming from his mouth, gruff, but loaded with purpose that somehow made her feel extra special and essential to the mission. She was used to feeling unseen and unheard in Javid's company, so this was new. And why was he so keen to have her with him? Had he been thinking about her too? She kind of hoped he had...

He met her eyes as he scrunched up his paper coffee cup in one hand and tossed it into a trash can. 'I'd let you drive, but this is a dangerous road, and if the weather changes it's not a great place to be behind the wheel.'

No point arguing with that. 'Then let's go.'

She scrunched up her own cup with new determination, tossed it hard, and missed the trash can by a mile. Hurriedly she picked it up, placed it into the trash can carefully, and followed him.

He smirked at her as she slid into the passenger seat of the sturdy truck, loaded with all the supplies and equipment they might need on land. 'Basketball not your thing?'

'Very funny,' she said, clicking on her seatbelt as heat rushed to her cheeks and made her blood race.

Gunnar drove them quickly but steadily behind Erik's vehicle along the winding road. He reassured her on the way, talking about the top-mounted floodlight system and the twelve-thousand-pound front-mounted winch—which, to be fair, no one had bothered explaining to her until now. He knew his stuff. Which was comforting and also hot.

Despite her guilt for knowing more about him than she should at this point, she found herself wondering even more about Gunnar Johansson—like how long he'd watched her car from his window last night, and whether he'd noticed yet how her lips were much better.

CHAPTER THREE

THE ACCIDENT SCENE was a mess. The cops who'd called Erik were already on site as Mahlia sprang from the truck. She assessed the black skid marks on the road, the debris strewn everywhere—broken glass, frayed wires and pieces of metal that had clearly used to be various parts of a motorcycle. Then she saw the rider.

Rushing over, she knelt on the freezing ground in her padded snow trousers. A man in his mid-twenties sat on the snow-covered roadside, cradling his head in his hands, dressed in torn leathers. His helmet was cracked beside him on the ground—a reminder of what might have befallen his skull if he hadn't been wearing it. Miraculously he didn't look too hurt, but there was blood on his left knee, seeping through the leather.

'This is Arni Sturlson. He swerved to avoid a car,' one of the policemen told her, coming up behind her with Erik.

'Where's the car?' she asked, pulling out gauze and antiseptics and making a tourniquet for the man's leg. All she could see were black lava fields on one side and trees on the other.

'I heard them shouting for help,' the motorcyclist told her, wincing in pain as she snipped at his leathers some more. 'They're alive down there.'

'Who was shouting?' She kept calm as she hurried to curb the bleeding.

Gunnar raced past in a blur of orange, and suddenly she knew what Arni meant...why they'd been called as the closest emergency crew.

Gunnar had stopped at the edge of the road. Another cop was pointing downwards, craning his neck to see down deep into the ravine.

'Wait here and try not to move. The ambulance is coming,' she told Arni now.

She rushed over to Gunnar, but his arm came out to block her. 'Careful!'

Her heart wedged in her throat as she peered over his arm and over the edge. It was pretty far down, but she could just make out a shape—the car.

Somehow Arni Sturlson had managed to save himself by swerving in time, preventing an unquestionable tragedy, but the SUV had tumbled head-over-heels, down at least twenty metres. It was perched between the jagged rocks below like a shiny metallic bird's nest.

'It's still in one piece,' Gunnar said incredulously, as Ásta ran over with an armful of climbing ropes.

Erik paused on the radio as not one, but two voices sounded out from the vehicle below.

Mahlia clutched Gunnar's arm. A chill ran down her spine. 'There's a child down there!'

'We need an anchor. Help me tie this round that tree,' he said to her, new urgency coating his words as he took the climbing ropes and hurried to a thick tree nearby.

Snow sprayed from its branches the second it was disturbed, coating their shoulders as they secured the line. The wind had died down, thankfully. It was at least a little easier to do everything when the snow and wind weren't lashing at their faces.

Gunnar made quick work of threading the rope from the tree through the rappel rings and attaching them to his waist.

'Get the stretchers ready,' he told her. 'I don't know what I'm bringing up.'

Several other trees along the ledge had been flattened, no doubt by the car. They'd probably slowed its descent somewhat, she thought as Erik took over, installing the rappel back-up, then guiding Gunnar's descent down the steep, rocky cliff.

She held her breath as he moved, watching the top of his helmet, praying no rocks or broken branches would land on him. The bulk of him as he descended, kicking at the rocks as he went in heavy boots, sent snow, ice, leaves and shards of jagged rocks splintering off the vertical surface in his wake. Some bounced off the car below.

Mahlia heard the child scream again, and she winced as she dragged the stretchers from the rescue vehicle.

It was hard to comprehend how anyone could survive such an accident and yet here they were: mother and eleven-year-old daughter, bruised, sore but alive.

'I thought we were going to die down there.' The woman sniffed as Mahlia took the pale little girl's vitals where she lay on a stretcher under a quickly darkening sky.

Kitta Guðmundsson had been driving carefully north towards her mother's house in the next village when the speeding motorcyclist had taken her by surprise on a blind corner. He was vocal in his apologies, although the police weren't letting him off the hook. Mahlia listened as they questioned him and gave him a stern talking-to about speeding.

By the time she'd run her checks on the little girl, and Gunnar and Erik had navigated removing the car efficiently from the crop of trees with the lauded front-mounted winch, a road assistance vehicle had appeared to clear the debris from the road. And by the time all three injured but lucky people had been deposited at the hospital for further check-ups, and the rescue team were back at the hangar base, the darkness had closed in on Reykjavik and Mahlia had only just stopped shaking with adrenaline.

What a day.

'I have to go and check on my cat,' Ásta announced. Then she stopped halfway to her car, wincing to herself. 'I should probably go to the hospital first and see my husband.'

'I'll come and see how he's doing, too,' Erik said. The two of them left in their respective vehicles, leaving her and Gunnar alone. Again.

Before she could announce her plan to stop her growling stomach by pouncing like a snow cat onto the first morsel of food she came across in her pathetically stocked fridge, Gunnar cleared his throat behind her.

'Did you lose your keys again?' She smiled, turning to find him leaning against his car, a beacon of orange in the floodlights.

The sight of his wild, unruly hair and sharp jawline, illuminated by the glow of the floodlight behind her, did funny things to her insides. He dangled a keychain on one finger.

'No,' he said. 'But I forgot to eat all day and I owe you for last night. Do you have any plans for dinner?'

Mahlia could hardly believe it when they pulled up at the famous Blue Lagoon. Milky blue water surrounded the modern wooden structure, turning it into a fairy-tale fortress in the floodlights. Behind them the mountaintops shone white on a rare clear night. People came here to swim in the healing, steaming waters, but Gunnar had brought her to the restaurant.

She'd read that it was one of the most expensive in Iceland, which made her wonder if he still had access to a hidden stash of that dirty money his father had allegedly been stripped of. Surely not... She didn't want to even think these things...or be so attracted to him when she had come here to avoid a man who'd showered so much attention on her she'd suffocated. But how could she not?

The concierge took their coats. She pressed her hands to the front of her wraparound dress and hoped she looked OK in it, with her black boots and sheer tights, as they were guided quickly and politely up two staircases into the show-stopping restaurant.

When he'd dropped her home to change, saying he'd be back for her in one hour, she'd tried on every single item in her wardrobe twice. Trusting a man she'd only just met to take her anywhere was new to her, but there was something about this man that was hard to put a finger on. Normally she'd have made her excuses and gone home to be alone, where no man could twist her thoughts the way Javid had a habit of doing even now! But Gunnar and all his mysteries had her mind spinning and, to be honest, any time that wasn't spent worrying about Javid flying over here to find her was time well spent.

'A friend of mine is doing a guest chef and wine pairing thing—I promised him ages ago I'd come,' Gunnar had told her in the car, by way of explanation.

Now, sitting opposite him at a table with the most impressive view of Iceland she had ever seen, she was struggling to tell herself this was a normal night out. He'd calmed his hair and put on a pale blue shirt that matched his eyes—an expensive one, she noted. The buttons were engraved with something she couldn't read, and the cuffs were turned up, revealing a Rolex watch and more of his big, strong hands than she'd ever seen before. He'd always worn gloves. The sight of them made her instantly picture them on her body...

'I thought we'd go to a restaurant in Reykjavik,' she told him, suddenly self-conscious as a waiter fussed over them, placing a soft cloth napkin in her lap. They'd driven half an hour to get here.

'Is this place OK for you?' he asked her now, pressing his hands together in a steeple as the waiter placed a wine list down in front of him.

Oops, had she offended him?

'It's fine—how's the shark here?'

'It's actually pretty good, with a few potatoes and...'

'I'll be fine with the salmon,' she said hurriedly.

His eyes were glinting in the candlelight now, mischievous and teasing, and the spicy scent of his aftershave with its hint of manly musk was as bewitching at the views. This was so unlike her... To be rendered a teenager again. To be looked at like this—as if she was a woman with worth and merit, and not an inconvenience.

When he'd ordered the wine, the chef came over to greet him. The two men chatted briefly in Icelandic, and she noticed several people at a table further along throwing speculative glances his way. They didn't look at all impressed that he was here, and were clearly still chattering amongst themselves about him when the chef left.

'I've known that guy for years; he's a great chef,' Gunnar told her, as she took an awkward sip of her crisp, cold Sauvignon Blanc, glancing over her glass.

Gunnar noticed her discomfort. He glanced around, catching the people looking. Instantly the expression on his face resembled a storm.

'Those people don't seem to want us here,' she whispered.

'That would be the Johansson reputation at work. I try to ignore it. There's not much else I can do. Do you want to leave?'

Something in his tone tore at her heart. She'd wanted to leave every place Javid had taken her, but now... 'No, I don't want to leave. It's because of the bank and your father, right? I heard some…stuff.'

Gunnar took a swig from his crystal wine glass, forcing a smile to his face that didn't show in his eyes. 'It'd be impossible for you not to hear *stuff*. People think what they want to think about me and they don't always keep it quiet.'

It was almost as if he'd accepted his fate. She pressed her hands to the table. 'But you save lives, literally every day, so how can people hold anything against you?'

'You don't know my people,' he said grimly. 'Stubborn Viking mentality.'

A thin smile crossed his lips as he stared out of the window. The rolling glacier and snow-dusted volcanoes with their slow flowing rivers of lava made her feel as if they were on a movie set, but he didn't seem to notice to it.

The chef came back, bearing plates of the reddest salmon she'd ever seen, with pickled beets and rye bread. She nibbled in silence, feeling the tension mount.

Say something.

'So, you said you once lived in the US? Did you move there after the banks crashed? To get away from it all?'

Gunnar put his fork down. He studied her carefully, as if weighing something up, and she swallowed her salmon, feeling every last morsel slide down her throat under his blue-eyed scrutiny.

'I was already there when it all happened.'

He explained how he'd moved to California two years before the crash. He'd been twenty-two then, and had taken a scholarship at Stanford University's School of Medicine. His mother was half-American, so he'd wanted to live and work there for a while.

'Everyone told me not to come home after it happened—

they said it was a nightmare. So I stayed in California, even after my...' He trailed off.

The expression on his face put her on high alert, despite his jokes. Even after his what?

'I started working for myself...got a life going that was pretty good, actually. You know, I still dream about the burgers at the diner on my block.' He dragged a hand through his hair. 'Then Demus got diagnosed with MS, six and a half years ago, and I knew it was time to come home.'

'Your brother?' she said. Why was her heart galloping like a pony?

He nodded. 'Dad left the country as soon as he was released from jail. Ma was...not in a position to help Demus. He's my older brother, my only sibling. He's pretty independent, you know, and still lives alone, luckily, but I wanted to be here for him. So, yeah, I came back permanently.'

'You must have come back to a totally different world after what happened to your dad,' she said, trying to let it sink in.

Gunnar said nothing, but the look on his face told her everything. His father's betrayal had blasted his world to pieces. No doubt his brother's diagnosis had, too.

More food appeared in front of them—steaming bowls of lobster soup—and they ate in silence again, while her mind churned with questions she shouldn't ask. This attraction to Gunnar was already highly inappropriate. She was still fending off Javid! And she was supposed to be enjoying being alone.

'So, what do you do when you're not saving lives with the search and rescue team?' she ventured anyway. 'Or what don't you do?'

She watched his mouth twitch and hoped he didn't think she was stepping out of line, but he told her how his bouldering and climbing adventures in the US had led him to lead weekend tours in the mountains there. He'd trained as a winchman in more recent years, when he'd returned home to Iceland, and enjoyed search and rescue as much as his time in surgery.

'You live in Reykjavik full time?' she asked.

'I have a couple of places for when I need to escape the city.'

Escape. There was a word she could related to.

'Does that happen a lot?' she asked now, just as the people who'd been gossiping about him glanced in her direction. Two of them were laughing.

She stared them down till they looked away. Gunnar caught her and she flushed—it wasn't her job to defend him, so why did she feel obligated to?

'I just like to be alone,' he told her, scraping back his chair as if trying to distance himself from her suddenly.

Her brain went right to another question. Had he ever been able to have a serious relationship here, with half of the island seemingly against him?

'You say you have a couple of places?' she said instead, and he stuck a fork into lettuce heart, nodded.

Impressive, she thought. From what she knew of him, he really didn't seem to be the kind of man who'd take dirty money accumulated from the misfortune of others. He had clearly done well as a surgeon, separately from his family's former wealth.

'I have a little cabin outside of Reykjavik, about fifteen minutes up north. Or an hour if we're stuck in a blizzard. Sometimes I take my brother,' he said, putting his napkin down on the table. 'We sit up and talk, play music, watch the lights… or the midnight sun.'

Mahlia smiled as the chef delivered a fresh sorbet and a sweet white wine for dessert, picturing the cabin and the midnight sun, and in the winter the northern lights dancing above them in the wilderness. He obviously cared a great deal about his brother if he'd moved away from the States and his life

there, risked everyone looking down on him and his family.
in order to look out for Demus here. He really was a hero.

What was the catch?

There was always a catch; she'd just failed to see it at first
with Javid.

Not that she was here to get all dreamy-eyed over a guy
anyway, she reminded herself, turning her gaze out to the blue
lagoon, steaming below them under the soft orange lights.
Several people were floating, or standing with hot drinks and
glasses of wine in the mist. The stars were the brightest she'd
seen them since arriving here.

It suddenly occurred to her... Was this a date?

The notion sent her cold. The reasons she was here in
Iceland were to get the new e-assist devices into trial mode
somewhere other than New Zealand and learn from the SAR
crew, all while staying well out of Javid's way. Hopefully with
enough time and distance between them he'd finally agree to
sign the damn divorce papers.

She felt her fist clench under her seat as her heartbeat sped
up. If Javid so much as suspected she was on anything resem-
bling a date he would come for her. He'd try and assert his
claim over his property, or what he thought was his property,
like he always did. He would get into her head. She was still
too scared to actually *be* there, where he could physically reach
her with all his powers of persuasion.

An alert on Gunnar's phone drew her eyes from the steaming blue lagoon and her thoughts back to him.

'Looks like we might be in luck tonight,' he said, making
her heart leap even more.

What?

'The northern lights?' He turned the phone to her.

An app was open, showing circles of yellow and swirls of

neon-green. It sent alerts when the northern lights were due to put on a show.

'I know you don't have a bathing suit with you,' he said, motioning to the waiter for the bill. 'But should we rent you one?'

CHAPTER FOUR

MAHLIA FELT GOOSEBUMPS flaring beneath her fluffy white robe as Gunnar ushered her to the edge of the lagoon, his hand featherlight against the small of her back. Her nostrils quivered at the mild scent of sulphur. The stars sparkled above them in infinite constellations and for a brief moment, as she watched him slip off his robe and stride out ahead of her into the warm blue liquid and curling steam, the night sky and everything below it seemed alive with possibility.

She'd never seen anything like this before—never so much as stepped foot into a geothermal pool. Sure, they had them in New Zealand, but she'd always been too busy or, if she was totally honest with herself now, too afraid of Javid criticising her choice of swimwear. The beauty of it all was mesmerising. And Gunnar with his shirt off…

Oh, my. She had not been prepared for this at all.

The steam rose from the pool and cloaked his form with a foggy haze as he turned back to her and beckoned her in. Only his broad shoulders and muscular arms were visible now. He looked protective which, combined with his chosen profession, told her he was someone she could instinctively trust—as long as she didn't get all goo-goo over him.

But, oh, the way his arm had been flung out to stop her at the cliff-edge earlier today…the way he'd caught her on the pond on day one. *Hot.*

Sliding off her robe, she feigned a confidence in her body that she didn't quite feel, glancing up at the restaurant windows, to where they'd just been sitting.

'Don't be scared…it's not deep,' he told her, stepping towards her again.

His eyes lingered on her as she took the ramp down from the cold concrete deck into the warm waters of the lagoon. The temperature was just right—not too hot or cold—and a welcome relief from the frigid winter air.

'Drink?' he asked her now, motioning to the open bar in the middle of the pool. 'I was going to get us a hot chocolate.'

'Sounds perfect,' she said, taking in the couples standing close, arms around each other in the water. None of these people seemed to have noticed Gunnar, and if they had they didn't care.

Mahlia felt herself relax, spreading her arms out along the steaming surface. At the bar, Gunnar pulled himself onto a stool. His body rippled with solid muscle. His shoulders were square, his chest full and broad. His abs were so tight they looked as if they must have been carved from marble…or just honed from years of climbing rocks and boulders and working the winch.

Up close, as he'd taken off his robe back there, she'd seen the fine hair that covered his chest. It tapered to a light blond point, disappearing into the waistband of his shorts in a way that made her question her type. She'd always assumed she liked dark-haired men, like Javid. Now, everything about Javid repulsed her—so much so that she had a new type now. Blond. Gunnar-blond.

What did he think of her? she wondered, before she could tell herself it didn't matter. Javid had always said her hips were the best kind for birthing, but that her legs were too chunky to be feminine.

Screw Javid, she thought crossly. He was interfering in her life even now. This was a new start for her. Being free was imperative. She'd spent seven years bending to Javid's whims and now she was here. With *this* guy…who probably just wanted to get to know and trust his co-worker. Finding people who trusted him was obviously not all that easy for Gunnar.

'Hot chocolate?' He was back now, handing her a cup loaded on the top with whipped cream. Emphasis on 'hot', she groaned to herself, unable to move her eyes from the lines of his glistening shoulder blades.

Stop drooling, she told herself sternly. *You are his co-worker; that's all he sees you as.*

Besides, there was no way any man was taking control of her again, physically or emotionally. No way.

Then there was a squeal. Several squeals.

'Look.' Gunnar pointed upwards, guiding her to the side of the pool so they could put their cups down.

Her gaze shifted skywards as they waded, and she couldn't help the grin that spread from ear to ear. The northern lights!

They started off weak and slow, like musical notes dancing out of sync in the silence. Then they changed their speed, starting a more enthusiastic, fully choreographed dance in vibrant greens, yellows and purples. They flickered across the dark sky like a liquid rainbow, snatching her breath away. It was so breathtakingly beautiful she found she had tears in her eyes. She'd never seen them as clear and bright as this.

'You know,' Gunnar said now, floating on his back beside her, 'when we were kids, growing up, our parents used to tell us the northern lights were monsters.'

'Monsters?'

'It was their way of making sure we went home at night before it got too late. We were so afraid of the monsters in the sky we used to run home before they could get us.'

Mahlia laughed. 'I can't believe you grew up afraid of this!'

'We literally ran away from them.' He laughed too, and his arm pressed against hers as they were swept together in the water. 'I missed them when I was in California, though.'

'You're proud of your country. I can tell.' Her fingers brushed his for just a little too long as her heart thumped behind her rented bathing suit. He was so sexy...all wet and glowing beneath the northern lights. Almost as sexy as he looked in his jumpsuit.

She would remember this night, she thought, and this new, addictive feeling of awe, power and freedom, for as long as she lived.

'I am proud of my country,' he said. 'I never stopped being proud to be Icelandic. Even if I'm not exactly proud to be my father's son.'

Mahlia turned to him. 'What your father did isn't your fault. It shouldn't be a reflection on you.'

She felt him tense beside her. He was quiet for a moment and she sensed there was a lot about her new colleague that she'd never know. He'd taken on a more than he'd bargained for, thanks to his father's actions, but none of that was Gunnar's fault.

Then he turned to her, with a different expression in his eyes. A look of shrewd perception that told her he had questions.

'What really brought you here, Mahlia? You could work on your e-bikes in plenty of rugged terrain back in New Zealand, couldn't you? You could join a search and rescue team there.'

'I like to see new places,' she said, as her stomach did somersaults.

'This seems like a long way to go from home, though, on your own.'

She forced her eyes back to the light show in the sky. He

was trained to be assertive and astute, to notice the finer details. Of course he'd ask. 'I just like to be alone,' she told him tightly, mimicking what he'd said to her earlier.

He huffed a laugh. 'Touché. A fellow loner. I won't ask any more questions. All I know is that people don't move to the middle of nowhere unless there's something they want to get away from.'

She sighed through her nose, biting the inside of her cheek. Despite his questions, his attention on her made her heart dance like the aurora, but no way was she letting on how Javid was such a master manipulator that it had taken five years of her life for her to even realise how he was destroying her soul from within, and another two years to gather the strength to leave him. She felt stupid enough about all that as it was.

'I should go and dry my hair,' she told him, getting to her feet and stumbling instantly. He caught her wrists, drawing her close as he corrected her. 'Sorry…dizzy…' she managed, finding his piercing blue eyes in the steam. She swallowed again. 'I'll see you back outside the changing rooms?'

A woman she recognised from the table of people who'd been staring at them in the restaurant cornered her by the sinks. Mahlia pulled her robe tighter, trying to avoid her eyes, but the woman, who must be in her mid-forties stepped closer, ramming a hairbrush through her hair.

'You're brave,' she told her in the mirror. 'Going out on a date with Gunnar Johansson.'

'That's none of your business,' Mahlia told her curtly, towelling her own hair. It had already sprung back into its corkscrew curls.

The woman rolled her eyes. 'It's everyone's business what his family did to this country.'

'I don't really know the full details, but he seems like a

good man to me,' she insisted, wondering if she should be saying anything at all.

The woman folded her arms. 'A good man?' She sniffed. 'I bet his ex-girlfriends don't think he's a good man. Don't they know what his family did? Watch out—that's all I'm saying.'

Mahlia frowned. 'Do you always attack people you don't know like this?'

The woman rolled her eyes, then sashayed off, leaving Mahlia shaken, gripping the sink.

'None of my business,' Mahlia reminded herself.

But her heart was wedged like a whole lemon in her throat and the woman's words about his ex-girlfriends—plural-stayed with her the whole drive home, as the craggy lava rocks slipped past and the lights came out to dance again ahead of them. It had been such a nice night…how dared someone try and spoil it?

Gunnar hadn't tried anything with her—he'd been nothing but a gentleman. But she *was* too trusting, too naive. Wasn't that what Javid had always said? He was probably right about that.

The feeling of lighter-than-air empowerment she'd felt in that lagoon, floating next to Gunnar, vanished like the northern lights as he pulled up at her door and said, 'I hope you have enough lip salve to last till we meet again.'

He was so good. So nice. Did he really go through women like hotcakes? *Ugh.*

Mahlia didn't want to be in the *slightest* bit affected by Gunnar Johansson. But already she knew she was probably in trouble.

CHAPTER FIVE

GUNNAR WAS EXHAUSTED. So was everyone. The rescue team had hiked the rough terrain for two hours already, scouring each turn and crevasse until their legs ached and their lungs burned.

The spectacular Njardarfal waterfall cascaded with fury up ahead. It tumbled in white blurry curtains down the rocky ledge, slamming into the foaming pool below. Its roar echoed off the crisp mountain air and was probably loosening more than a few snowdrifts.

Hopefully the man and his dog had taken shelter somewhere and weren't hurt, he thought, hunching against the wind. The missing man's partner had been beside himself in Reykjavik when they'd got the call. Leo, a thirty-six-year-old local man, had set out with his husky at six a.m., he'd said, and hadn't come back.

'Coffee?' Mahlia handed him the flask and he took it gratefully, feeling the hot liquid on the back of his parched throat.

She was still as striking as ever, with her coffee-coloured skin against the white faux fur of her hooded jacket, but she also looked tired. Her eyes were black as obsidian, but with less of a sparkle than he'd seen that night two weeks ago when she'd looked all wonderstruck—and wet—under the northern lights. He hadn't seen her since—not to talk to, anyway. Only in passing. He'd missed her, which surprised him.

It was always a kick, seeing people's eyes light up when they saw the aurora, but there was something interesting about this woman. Not just her lilting New Zealand accent or those unbelievably sexy curves in a swimsuit. Her caution and care, her burning ambition to help and change lives, seemingly with every single venture she attached herself to, was impressive.

The way she'd stared those people down in the restaurant had touched him.

It took a lot to move him.

'We need two of you to go east,' Erik said now, stopping just ahead at the crossroads on the little-used hiking trail. 'Most people know not to take this trail till summer, but we should check.'

'Maybe his dog shot off that way and he followed it,' Gunnar said. 'I've seen plenty of snow foxes round these parts.'

'I'll go with Gunnar,' Mahlia said, glancing his way, and he heard himself agreeing.

So she'd volunteered, before he'd suggested it, he realised in surprise. He wasn't used to women wanting to go anywhere with him, what with his family legacy... But she was only a colleague, he reminded himself.

'We'll meet you back here in thirty?'

Mahlia shrugged her backpack straighter and followed him towards the falls, while Erik and Ásta turned north. With a pressing sense of urgency they began their search again, probing the crevices between large boulders as they approached the falls and scanning with their eyes for any sign of life. It wasn't snowing yet, but it was on the way. The sky hung low and grey.

'So, you've had a busy couple of weeks, huh?' she asked him now as they stepped over more rocks, testing the snow as they went.

He nodded. Yesterday he'd spent six hours straight alone with his mother, picking out paint for her kitchen while she swigged from a hip flask, thinking he didn't know she was doing it. Then he'd helped clean her house, because the cleaners had stopped coming months ago and she was always too drunk to do it herself.

He was supposed to be with his brother today, but here he was, and luckily Demus understood. His brother would have been right here with him if it weren't for the fact that his legs were giving out even more every year.

'How's your e-bike project going?' he asked her now, remembering how she'd said she was doing it to help people like Demus.

'Pretty good,' she said, as they neared the falls. 'I had my meeting with the programme analyst. She says the data on most of the trails here is outdated. We're actually going to fly some of the prototypes over and use the new e-assist bikes to help gather new data, as soon as the snow clears. We're gathering volunteer bike riders at the moment, so we'll be trialling the bikes here *and* helping a nationwide data collection project at the same time.'

'That's really...wow...' he said, impressed yet again by her tenacity.

The snow wouldn't clear until June or July, but she was thinking of sticking around till then? Why did that suddenly make him feel equal parts excited and on edge? She definitely had a way of sticking in his brain. He still couldn't shake the idea that she was running away from something in New Zealand—that call she'd ignored in the car that first night had got him thinking. But maybe he was wrong. She liked to be alone, and there was nothing wrong with that. So did he, after everything his father had brought down on his head. Because of that, he was good at being paranoid, too. Too paranoid to mention Idina to Mahlia, at least...

His ex-girlfriend—the only woman he'd ever really loved—

had not come up in a single one of their conversations about his past in California. It was better if she didn't, he supposed. He still couldn't keep all his emotions in check when he started down that path. Mahlia might look her up on the Internet and read about how she'd all but disappeared on him, thanks to the shame he'd brought upon her and the career she'd always wanted in politics.

Idina had kick-boxed her way into his heart on the way out of their class, back when things had been normal, about a year before the financial crash. Well, when things had been *his* version of normal. He hadn't known it at the time, but back in Iceland his father had been flying pop stars out to private yachts in Capri in an effort to acquire assets worth ten times the size of Iceland's economy.

Things had just been getting good with her when the news had broken about his father's arrest. The press had come down on Gunnar hard, reporting how he was out in California 'running from responsibility'. Even though he'd been there two years already. Some of the girls he'd met before Idina had told their 'story' for a quick buck. Idina, with her law degree pending and the political dream she'd had for ever under threat, hadn't been able to run from his life fast enough.

They still talked about him here, too. The women he dated never lasted long. As soon as they asked to meet his family he made his exit. He wouldn't do it to them! Anyone serious about him would only get dragged through the dirt along with him, like Idina had. Or they'd want to start a family with him. No, thanks. Kids…? With a name like his trailing behind them? What kind of life would they have? The more women's hearts he 'broke', the more people believed he was a serial player, so eventually he'd just stopped dating altogether.

Ma was still so broken by it all that she was trying to find the answers in the bottom of a bottle. She needed him…even if she never admitted it. And Demus... He was pretty self-sufficient, living on his own with the help of two carers who came in on alternate days, but there was barely a day that went by when he wasn't helping his older brother out with *something*.

A faint cry from up ahead made him stop in his tracks.

Mahlia grabbed his arm. 'Did you hear that?'

The cries grew louder as they hurried over rocks and boulders towards the roaring falls. The rush of the water almost made it too loud to hear much else.

'Stand back,' he told her, much to her visible annoyance.

He apologised quickly—was he being too protective? He knew he was overly protective of his mother and his brother—people he *cared* about, he realised. How quickly his protective instincts had grown to include Mahlia, even if she didn't seem to like it, he thought wryly, stepping over the crunchy dry snow towards the edge and straining his ears.

'Leo!' he yelled into the roar. 'Are you here?'

'Leo!' Mahlia was further along the ledge already, just behind him.

They yelled his name again. A dog's bark followed, only just audible above the water.

Then an answer. The man yelled out from below, the desperate plea of someone in pain.

'They're down there.'

Mahlia pointed into the falls as he reached her. He followed her stare down the snowy rock surface until his eyes fell on a figure, barely visible aside from a bright blue hat.

'I'll go. I know the way.'

'I'll go with you. He's hurt.'

'No. Wait here. I *know* this path,' he told her, but he could see the resolve in her eyes.

It reminded him of someone. Idina. Back when they'd met in that kick-boxing class. The ice cracked beneath his feet and the dog's barking upped in volume as he stepped down from one boulder to the next on what was a pathway to the bottom of the falls in the summer. Now, though, it was treacherous—even to people who knew the route down, like he did.

Water rushed over rocks as the waterfall grew louder to his right, his footsteps slid and earth and pine needles crunched underfoot as the dog's barking grew ever closer. He went for the rope, in case he had to lower himself down off the path to parts where there really was nowhere to stand. His foot slipped again.

'Damn....'

'Gunnar!' Mahlia's hand went for his arm. With a strength that defied her size she yanked him back and pushed him against the damp stone wall, flattening herself against it next to him, heaving for breaths.

What the...?

'You followed me,' he panted.

'Lucky I did,' she bit back.

But he saw the relief in her eyes, as well as a fierce determination to be seen and heard and acknowledged. It was like looking in a mirror.

'Look, he's just down there.'

They held each other's arms tight as they peered over the ledge together, the spray coating their faces like a thousand snakes spitting in fury. Leo was huddled there—what they could see of him, at least—beneath layers of weatherproof gear, just far enough away from the path to be unable to climb back up.

'I'll go down from here,' he told her, eyeing the terrain for something to tie a line to.

'Use this,' she said, motioning to a thick, ancient tree root protruding from the rocks just below.

He tested it out; it seemed strong enough.

'I'll help pull you back up.'

Mahlia was already on the radio, signalling their location to the others. Within moments Gunnar had lowered himself on the line and reached the grateful Leo, who was huddled beneath a rock shelf, shivering in pain. His foot was badly twisted, obviously broken or dislocated from his fall down into this isolated, windy corner.

'Mahlia, we need you,' he called up to her.

She was already hooked to the line, though, as if she'd done it a thousand times, proving once and for all that she didn't need the protection she seemed to inspire him to provide. It wasn't far—maybe two or three feet—and she was at his side in less than a minute, shrugging out of her backpack, checking Leo's leg.

'My dog…' He was wincing now. 'Katla. I was trying to reach her.'

Gunnar scanned the surroundings. All he could see was water. It was spraying his face and eyes, an ice bath he hadn't asked for. Then, down on the next ledge, he saw a beautiful young white husky, whimpering now instead of barking, probably sensing that her owner was finally getting help.

'I see her!'

'Can you reach her?'

Mahlia had wasted no time getting to work. With great skill and care, and lips visibly bluing from the cold, she was securing Leo's leg, soothing their shaken patient, making sure his pulse was strong, giving him water. All he seemed to care about, though, was his dog.

'I can reach her,' Gunnar said, helping Mahlia tie a tourniquet to Leo's leg so they could hoist him up more comfortably, and then securing another rope to a boulder.

It slipped several times before he caught it, and Mahlia rushed to help again, casting him an apprehensive frown. He told her with just one look that he was going for the dog, and that he'd be fine. He was met with a nod of silent acquiescence before she turned her attention back to sheltering Leo from the wind.

Her pretty face, slick and wet from the spray of the falls, was the last thing Gunnar saw as he lowered himself over the edge. Despite the situation, all he could do when he was out of sight was shake his head and smile. This woman was really something else...

From the looks on their faces, Gunnar could tell Erik and Ásta could hardly believe it when he and Mahlia emerged from the rocky lava field back onto the road, with a limping Leo and a bouncing white husky called Katla. She wasn't the first pet to be named after the island's most mysterious volcano.

'She's a little shaken, but she's not hurt,' Gunnar heard Mahlia telling them about the dog.

Ásta knelt to pet the thick-furred husky, being the animal fan she was, while he and Erik prepped a stretcher for Joe. The rescue truck was already waiting, its doors open wide. The snow had started up again now, and Gunnar watched Mahlia intently as he packed up his lines quickly, listening as she spoke, mesmerised by how capable and engaged she was with everything around her.

He could only thank the heavens he'd been lucky enough to have someone like her join him out there. She was fearless.

Not that he was going to do a damn thing about this unfortunate attraction. What had started out as a dinner with a colleague had turned into something more on his part—a need to know more about her. But with that would come more questions from her; she would want an intro into more of his world, which never did anyone any good. She had too much going for her to be burdened by his reputation.

* * *

At the hospital, he and Mahlia waited anxiously for the results of Leo's scan.

'Have you been a dog-sitter before?' he asked her, gesturing to Katla at her feet.

They hadn't been allowed any further than the waiting room with the young husky, but there was no one else to watch her; Ásta and Erik were already en-route back to their homes, to shower off the cold that had kept them all out there for most of the morning.

He was trying not to watch the clock. He really had to get back to Demus if there was still any hope of them making it to the cabin in the few hours of daylight they had left. He'd promised him barbecued lamb chops and a soak in the hot tub. It always helped Demus relax, took *some* of his pain away. But it didn't seem fair to leave Mahlia alone here…waiting.

Mahlia ran a hand over the dog's rug-like back, and he watched her slender fingers sinking into the white fur.

'My husband would never allow me…us…to get a dog,' she said sadly.

Then she bit down hard on her lip and adjusted herself on the hard plastic seat. Gunnar turned to her. Her face was strained as she stared at the floor, her eyes pinched, her lips pressed together into a frown. There was no wedding ring on her finger.

'Your husband?'

'Technically he's still my husband, but we're separated,' she said tightly, dragging a hand through her curls.

Gunnar felt the muscles in his brow pulling together as he struggled not to ask what had happened. It was none of his business. Instead, he said, 'He wouldn't *allow* you to get a dog? You make it sound like you wanted one and the man just stood in your way.'

'It wasn't practical…not with my lifestyle,' she followed up, too quickly. 'I didn't have the time. I didn't know how to care for a dog properly. I couldn't have given a dog what it needed.'

'OK…'

He nodded, soaking it all in. There was something in her demeanour now, not just in her words, that told him she was repeating what someone else had told her—an opinion that wasn't entirely hers. Maybe she wasn't so fearless about *everything*.

'But aren't you always outdoors on your bikes?' he pressed. 'Dogs love joining in with exercise.'

Mahlia shrugged. 'I couldn't have taken it to the hospital with me, though, could I? When I worked a twelve-hour shift? And Javid wouldn't have taken it out. He hates dogs.'

'Javid…' he repeated softly, pondering the sudden apathy in her voice and studying the soft sheen of her heart-shaped mouth. That was the name he'd seen on her phone that night in the car.

He should shut the hell up and butt out of her business, but intrigue made his tongue loosen. 'How long were you married to Javid?'

She paused a few breaths. 'Seven years. We still *are* married, like I said. Stubborn ass won't sign the divorce papers.'

'I get it. OK…' He stared at his hands in his lap. So, her ex had—still did have—some kind of twisted hold on her. *That* was what she was running away from.

The door was flung open. A broad man in a ski jacket burst through, bringing a flurry of snow in with him. Right away, Katla leapt from the floor. She pounced on him, jumping, barking, dancing, her bushy tail wagging a million miles an hour.

'Leo's partner,' they said in unison, rising to greet him.

The burly man, who introduced himself as Gisli, lowered

his hood, fussing over the husky in relief as he asked the woman at the front desk where Leo was.

'We're waiting to hear if it's a break or a dislocation, but it seems he got off pretty lightly,' Gunnar explained.

'You were the ones who rescued him?

Gunnar nodded curtly as the guy seemed to recognise him. He saw Mahlia's eyes bounce between them. Would Gisli take a step backwards? he wondered. Turn his head to see who'd noticed them interacting? He never knew what to expect, bearing a name like his. Thankfully, this man was different.

Gisli thrust his hand out at him, then drew him into a grateful, manly embrace with the strength of a bear. 'Thank you, thank you, thank you,' he gushed. 'He probably would have died if it wasn't for you, Dr Johansson.'

Gunnar cleared his throat, stepped backwards, brushing the snow off his front as Mahlia bit back a smile.

'Mahlia was with me. She helped patched him up and helped carry him from the waterfall. And the rest of our team...'

'Well, then, I offer you my eternal gratitude too, Mahlia. That man...he's the love of my life...'

Gisli extended to Mahlia the same form of heartfelt appreciation, pulling her into a tight embrace that made her smile. She hugged him back as he sniffed emotionally against her shoulder.

'You have no idea...'

A nurse came to inform them that it was a dislocation and not a break, as they had feared. Leo would now receive treatment to ease the pain and they could visit him soon. They were assured that he'd be back on his feet before long. Although maybe he shouldn't be hiking for a while—and definitely never alone.

'He knows not to go out alone,' Gisli grumbled, ruffling

Katla's ears. 'He thought Katla would protect him, but she's young, you know?'

'The husky *did* need a bit of help too,' Mahlia explained. 'Gunnar went down a few more feet to another ledge to get her. He was quite incredible, considering the force of the water and...'

She trailed off quickly and flushed. Gunnar kept a straight face, even as his heart performed a strange shift that sent his blood to places he'd rather it didn't go in public. Whether she was saying it because she'd seen the way some people treated him, or because she really thought he was 'incredible' shouldn't matter, but it did. His pulse was leaping and falling like a pair of fish on a line.

Gisli gasped dramatically, as if he'd just remembered something. 'We will have you both over for dinner. Soon. When Leo's had some rest. Do you like reindeer?'

He fixed his eyes on Mahlia, who stuttered, 'I... Reindeer? I don't know.'

'We just had one butchered and frozen. I make a very good stew. I insist.'

Gunnar was trying his best not to laugh at the look on her face as Gisli asked for his number, so that he could send them both an invitation, and was led away by the nurse. The nurse told them her assistant would look after the dog till her owner returned, or one of them, and that Katla would be fine.

Gunnar was just telling himself that Gisli would probably never call when Mahlia turned to him from her phone. The look on her face told him she'd had some disappointing news.

'Everything OK?'

She sighed. 'One of the guys who signed up for the e-bike trial has had to pull out. He's had a relapse, and his physician doesn't think it's smart for him to make any commitments. I was planning to go and meet with him now, but...' She looked at him askance. 'I guess I'll have to spend my birthday after-noon doing something else.'

Birthday?

Gunnar released the breath that had somehow got lodged in his windpipe. He'd been about to excuse himself and make for his car, but now... 'It's your birthday?'

She bobbed her head, shrugged.

'Today?' he followed up, incredulous.

She'd accepted this search call-out on her birthday. She could've been in a spa, or on a Golden Circle trip, or any of the other things tourists did in Iceland to have themselves a fairy-tale day.

'Yes, today.'

His mind was racing now. 'Happy birthday. Do you have a back-up plan?'

She laughed. 'In a place where I know next to no one? Sure—let me just gather all my besties.'

He felt his mouth twitch with a hint of a smile. Sarcasm suited her. 'In that case, how would you like to join me for dinner? We can celebrate your birthday and make up for the lost e-bike trial participant at the same time. Sound good?'

Mahlia's mouth flew open for a second, and then she closed it. The surprise on her face made his heart swell with warmth and anticipation, even though involving anyone in his messed-up family life was actually the last thing he should be doing.

A smile lit up her face suddenly. It made him forget every-thing and wonder what it might be like to kiss her.

'OK,' she said softly. 'That sounds like a nice idea...thank you.'

Excitement bubbled in Gunnar's chest, erupting into a goofy grin that he quickly suppressed behind his hand. He'd worry about his dumb decisions later—it was her birthday!

'There's one catch. We have to drive fifteen minutes out of town. And we have to bring my brother.'

'Your brother?' Mahlia grabbed her bag and slung it over one shoulder.

'I promised Demus we'd hang out at the cabin—fire up the grill, maybe take a dunk in the hot tub,' he said, walking her to the door. He opened it for her.

'Hot tub?' she repeated, and he didn't miss her glance at him, or the way she bit her lip thoughtfully.

Hopefully she wasn't thinking he just wanted to get her in a bathing suit again. Then again, she wasn't exactly hard on the eyes, fully dressed or not.

Touching her arm lightly, he noticed for the first time how small she was compared to him; it made him feel even more protective of her.

'What are you grilling?' she asked.

'I promise no reindeer,' he said, yanking on his hat. 'Not that I don't recommend it. It's very high in protein.'

'I wouldn't say no to trying it...'

Of course you wouldn't.

Mahlia stepped with him out into the snow. She pulled up her hood and her curls flew from it, whipping his cheek for just a second. The feeling sent an unexplainable warmth right through him. Then, as he slid into the car beside her, another pang of apprehension struck him.

They made small talk as he drove. From what he knew so far, she was warm and kind and fascinating. He also saw in her bravery and vulnerability—two qualities he admired in a woman. There was a certain captivating mystery to her wholesome aura, too, and he found himself wanting to learn even more. Who wouldn't want to know more?

Trusting her enough to take her with him to meet Demus, though, had surprised him the second he'd suggested it. What the hell was he doing, inviting a woman he barely knew to the cabin to meet his brother? A married woman, no less, with a controlling husband at large? He could only imagine what had driven Mahlia all the way here to Iceland.

Ah, chill out, he told himself. It wasn't as if she wanted to sell a story about his messed-up mother or force him to continue his doomed legacy by popping out his babies…not like the last girl he'd gone out on only three dates with.

This wasn't even a date. And anyway, she was barely out of a marriage.

Mahlia probably wanted nothing from him. And the second she knew more about him, she never would.

CHAPTER SIX

THE DRIVE IN the fluttering snow was breathtakingly beautiful, even as Mahlia's heart thumped with trepidation. What was she doing, accepting this invitation? All she knew was that some long-forgotten part of her had spoken up about it being her birthday almost in the hope that Gunnar would ask her out, and now the recklessness of her actions was already threatening to bite her in the backside. She barely knew him. And if Javid ever found out…

Gah! He has no hold on you now, she reminded herself, focusing in on Demus in the rear-view mirror.

He looked like Gunnar but a few years older. His hair was darker, his chin sharper and his body slimmer, but the resemblance was there. He was chatting to his brother from the back of the wheelchair-adaptable SUV.

Mahlia couldn't understand a word either of them was saying, but the rhythm and cadence of the Icelandic language sounded like music to her ears. It was lilting and lyrical. The gentle, rolling quality of the words in Gunnar's deep baritone reminded her of waves crashing on a shore.

Oh, no. Just as she was relaxing… There was her phone again.

'You OK?' Gunnar glanced at her, frowning, as she clutched at her bag.

She was trying to ignore the perpetual vibration on her

lap. There was no way she was answering. Javid could take a running jump. If she turned it off, though, he would know she was ignoring him; he'd be so angry. He'd never sign the divorce papers if she enraged him. Her stomach knotted the way it had been trained to do at the mere *thought* of any adverse reaction from him.

'I'm great,' she answered chirpily, meeting Demus's liquid blue eyes in the mirror. 'Thank you for inviting me on your boys' night.'

Demus laughed. 'We're happy to have you. You know Gunnar just wants to show you how long he can stand shirtless in the snow while he flips the lamb chops on the grill.'

'I'm not going to get dressed every time I climb out of the hot tub,' Gunnar reasoned.

She felt herself flush as he glanced at her, picturing him with his shirt off again.

'And anyway,' he continued, '*you* can't wait to show Mahlia how terrible you are on the piano.'

'I blame my useless hands,' Demus replied, holding up his fingers.

'They've always been useless,' Gunnar teased, but the love and respect in his eyes for his brother spoke volumes about how he really felt.

She'd already seen how Demus's hands had trembled slightly when he'd tried to open a pack of gum earlier. The look of intense concentration on his face had eventually given way to irritation and pain. Gunnar had reached over and taken the packet from him, deftly opening it before handing it back.

She smiled at the way they teased each other, too—at their easy familiarity and tenderness towards one another, despite their differences. They laughed often in between words. There was a good-natured camaraderie that underscored their shared bloodline. In a way, it kind of made her envious. She'd often

wondered if a sibling in her life would have changed anything…been someone to talk to who might have steered her
away from Javid, noticed she was changing, suffocating, when
so many of her friends hadn't.

She'd hidden it too well.

The snow-capped mountains that ringed the cabin looked like
something off a postcard. The hot tub sat on a deck that looped
around the small two-bedroom structure, and Gunnar had it
steaming and bubbling in no time. The whole of the tiny place
had been adapted for Demus's wheelchair; there were ramps
to every room. It wasn't as flashy as she'd imagined, judging
by the apartment building he lived in in Reykjavik. It was
cosy, and homely, and felt full of love. As if they'd had a lot
of happy times here before…

But the last thing she needed right now was to get emotionally invested in a man—look where that had got her till now.

Hiding out in Iceland, that's where!

Still, Gunnar looked like the picture of Viking masculinity
as he stood at the grill, piling on lamb chops and seasoning
chicken fillets, while she and Demus helped prepare a salad
in the kitchen. She watched him through the kitchen widow,
bent over the flame in the orange glow of a heated lamp.

The ubiquitous knitted cream and brown Icelandic sweater
he'd picked up from the back of the couch and thrown on was
like nothing she'd seen him in so far. It looked almost a little
old and bedraggled. Loved, like the cabin. She wanted to feel
the wool on her face, snuggle into it. He probably gave the
best cuddles…

Demus caught her looking at Gunnar. 'What's going on,
then?' he asked her, rinsing tomatoes and lettuce in a bowl on the
specially low-placed workbench. 'Are you dating my brother?'

There was a certain wariness to his voice that suddenly set her on edge.

'No,' she said, too quickly.

'He hasn't invited anyone here before,' Demus said thoughtfully, his hands shaking around the lettuce leaves. 'Not even Idina. Not that she'd have left California anyway, even before it all went wrong. Too much of a valley girl. You know, I only met the woman once before…this.' He gestured to his fragile body in the wheelchair. 'If I'd known then how badly she was going to treat him… Don't believe everything you read about Gunnar, Mahlia. Or what people around here might tell you.'

He put the bowl of salad down on the workbench a little too hard. Through the window, Gunnar looked up at the sound, his face instantly swallowed by smoke.

Mahlia's heart was in her throat, but she feigned ambivalence. Obviously she'd been thinking about it, wondering if that lady's comments at the Blue Lagoon had been true… about how Gunnar tore through women. This was the first time she'd heard the name Idina. So that was what he'd left behind in California…

'He hasn't told me anything about her… Idina,' she said carefully. 'And why should he? We barely know each other, really.'

'Indeed,' Demus said, but a smile hovered on his lips.

'I form my own opinions anyway,' she followed up. 'I know he's a good man. And I know what it's like to be scrutinised and judged for something you haven't even had the *chance* to do yet.'

She shut her mouth. Demus stared at her a moment longer, as if sizing her up. Even as he nodded, her heart was like a wild bird, just from thinking how Javid had stolen her confidence, made her believe she was incompetent, small, incapable, worthless, *less than*. If either of these men knew how she'd lost herself in his shadow, they'd think she was an idiot. But then, maybe Gunnar had been through something similar, but on a global scale, after his family name had been trodden into the dirt. Maybe Demus had too—as if he wasn't dealing with enough now.

You never knew what a person was hiding behind their tough facade. Idina had clearly been someone special. Someone who'd hurt Gunnar...

'Food's ready!' Gunnar called.

Demus saluted him and Mahlia watched as Demus moved his hands in front of her, flexing and unflexing them before trying and failing to open the bottle he'd just pulled from a cupboard. The juxtaposition between the strength of his arms and the frailty of his fingers was stark—an all too familiar sight to Mahlia. She had seen it before in people with multiple sclerosis.

She took the bottle gently, loosened the cap and handed it back. He unscrewed it and sniffed it, pulling a face that made her laugh. 'Moonshine never gets any better,' he said.

'Then why drink it?'

He rolled his eyes and grinned. 'We're Vikings, baby.'

She laughed, carrying the salad past the piano and a well-worn couch to the table as he balanced the bottle and three mugs on his lap in the wheelchair.

Maybe she should ask Demus if he wanted to take part in the e-assist trial, she thought. Gunnar had said they both enjoyed cycling. She'd wanted to ask Gunnar the second the other guy had pulled out, but something had stopped her. Perhaps a fear of getting closer to him...involving herself in his world?

That wasn't why she was here, she reminded herself firmly, taking a seat at the sturdy wooden table by the roaring fire. Even if she had pretty much forced him to invite her somewhere today.

Maybe she shouldn't have done it.

God, stop beating yourself up, woman, just because Javid's not here to do it for you. It is your birthday. It's not like this is going to be a regular thing.

Demus lit three red candles in the centre of the table as Gunnar walked in with a giant plate of meat, the epitome of swoon-worthy masculinity. Gosh, he was ridiculously good-looking, she thought, swallowing as he caught her eye in the candlelight. How could a man be this gorgeous? This would definitely have to be a one-time thing. She wasn't going to be another of his brief flings. Though she somehow doubted he was as callous as that woman in the changing room had made him out to be, what if he came to have so much of a hold on her that she literally *couldn't* leave him?

OK, so she was getting way ahead of herself, but nope. Never again. Never, ever, ever would she put herself in that position—not for anything. So what if having a family one day was something she still dared to dream about? Maybe she'd get a donor, or adopt—whatever it took to have a child on her own. A man wasn't necessary for that any more. Anyway, right now being single was definitely what she needed…even if the way Gunnar's blue eyes holding hers put her on edge in the most exciting way.

An hour later, with her belly warm and full, she sat back in the hot tub, thrilling at Gunnar's gaze flickering to her cleavage as he offered her a drink.

'What is it this time?' she asked.

'A different kind of moonshine,' Demus answered for him, stretching his arms out in the water.

Gunnar had carried him here carefully, lowering him gently down to a special raised seat, and she'd bitten the inside of her cheek, watching every corded muscle in his broad shoulders straining, dripping with hot water.

'How many kinds are there?'

'The bad kind, and the absolutely intolerable kind,' Gunnar said, toasting her and then Demus with his cup, then discarding it without taking so much as a sip. He was going to have to drive them home after all.

Already she didn't want to leave. The sky was clear now. The stars shifted above them against a velvety sky like brilliant diamonds. Everything seemed more vivid out here. She took a sip of her drink from the thick ceramic mug, eyeing the surrounding mountains, willing the northern lights to come out and dance. This moonshine was so powerful, it almost tasted as if it had been distilled twice—firstly on earth and then again in the pits of hell. The taste was intense, and both brothers laughed at the look on her face.

'It's awful,' she conceded. But she took another sip as her phone vibrated from inside the cabin, wishing she had the courage to just turn it off completely.

'Want me to get that for you?' Gunnar offered.

'No, it's fine, really,' she said hurriedly, ignoring the look of confusion he threw her way—or was that suspicion?

While she wanted to see as much of his bare, muscled torso as possible, she did not need to see Javid's name on her screen.

Instead, she let the moonshine warm her from the inside, feeling it spreading outwards through every crevice of her body like liquid fire. It burned all the way down to her stomach, leaving behind a lingering warmth. She felt alive and invigorated, especially in the spotlight of Gunnar's gaze...but also as if something more dangerous was brewing.

He knew she was running away by coming to Iceland. She'd told him too much earlier, at the hospital, about how Javid had never 'allowed' her to get a dog. The indignation in his eyes—all over his face, in fact—had shaken her. It had been as if he was personally offended that someone could be so controlling…that she'd let anyone dictate what was best for her.

Gunnar was a protector, not a dictator, that much she could tell. But who was Idina to him? What had happened with her in California?

It felt as if they'd sat there for hours. Gunnar would occasionally point out constellations or stars that were especially bright, explaining their stories laced with Icelandic myths and legends.

When he labelled one star her 'birthday star', flashing her that jokey grin that was starting to show itself more and more tonight, her heart leapt and bucked. This was something special she was experiencing now; she was feeling things she hadn't expected to ever feel. For a second she found herself wondering what Gunnar might be like as a father, teaching two little kids to start the hot tub, flip chicken on the grill.

What?

She caught herself. Two kids. That had always been her dream. A boy and girl. But, as she'd already decided, she did *not* need a man for that!

Demus announced that he'd drunk too much and was going for a nap.

'So much for your piano concert,' Gunnar teased, before carrying him inside to the couch by the fire.

Mahlia tried not to look as if she was staring at the hot liquid steaming off his shoulder blades as he strode across the deck. But when he walked back outside several minutes later she found herself eyeing him through the steam, holding her breath. They were alone. And, to her horror, he was holding her phone.

'Seventy-eight missed calls from Javid?' Gunnar handed

the phone to her, almost laughing. 'The guy must really want to talk to you. Maybe he signed your divorce papers?'

'Yeah, right…'

Mahlia clambered out of the hot tub, limbs dripping water onto the deck. Mortified and embarrassed, she snatched the phone from his hand, but her wet fingers slipped before she could grip it. It tumbled past them into the hot, bubbling water.

For a moment she froze, staring as it sank to the bottom. She considered the fact that she was more relieved in this moment than annoyed, actually. Funny, that. But Gunnar was already diving for it. She watched in shock as he emerged with the gadget like King Triton from a well, shaking off a treasure.

'Lucky it's waterproof,' he said, turning it around in his big hands.

She stepped back into the hot tub, meeting him in the middle of the pool. Their fingers brushed as she took the phone from him and glanced at the screen. If only it wasn't waterproof, she thought in dismay. He was right. Seventy-eight missed calls.

Just a few moments on the deck had been enough to ice her blood, and now she couldn't seem to move. It felt just as if Javid was here, yelling at her from behind the phone's screen to call him back. And yet Gunnar's handsome wet face was inches from hers.

Two different worlds.

'I'm not calling him back,' she told the blue of his eyes, before she could think.

'Do you really just never talk to him?' he asked as she finally forced her hand to put the phone down on the side of the tub.

'Not if I can help it.'

'Why don't you just block his number?'

She swallowed, turning back to him, feeling even smaller

now. It was a good enough question. If only she *could* block his number. Ignoring him was a little passive, she knew that, but if she blocked him altogether he would come for her. It would be worse. He'd just be more angry...or he'd do the whole emotional manipulation thing: crying, begging her not to leave him, not to have her attorney take it further.

The whole situation was a mess. To get a default judgement from the court she'd probably have to prove the breakdown of the marriage and his mental cruelty. The thought of recounting it all, hearing herself admit what a weak pushover she'd been all this time, was debilitating.

Gunnar was still waiting for an answer. The warmth of his gaze pressed against her skin like a physical touch before the moonshine loosened her tongue.

'A conversation with Javid always goes one way,' she told him on a sigh. 'Besides, I don't want to be constantly reminded of our failed marriage when I'm trying *so* hard to move on from it.'

Gunnar growled in agreement, the sound drawn from deep within his chest. He towered over her as he reached for her fingers, holding them in his own large, warm hand, sending electricity coursing through her body, lighting up every molecule of her being.

'I know what it's like...trying to move on from something, and feeling like you just...can't.'

His words came out as if he'd wrestled them from the depths of his heart. He was staring into her eyes now, as if she was the only thing that mattered in this moment. The sudden rush of something more powerful than she was ready for consumed her.

'Is that what you had to do with Idina?'

A look of sadness flashed across his features and she kicked herself for mentioning her, but that look just now, and the way he'd gripped her fingers…that was way too intense.

'How do you know about her? Go on—tell me what you've read,' he said, sinking back against the edge of the tub.

'Nothing,' she said, while her world rearranged itself. 'Demus told me there was someone called Idina, in California.'

His jaw shifted as he lowered himself further into the steamy water. 'He did, huh? Well, I guess it's not surprising the love of my life ran for the hills as soon she learned what had happened with my father. Who'd want to be involved with all that?'

Mahlia sank against the side of the tub wall, suddenly too hot. 'She left you?'

'I told you before that I stayed in California after it happened. But she was gone the second the press descended—before Dad was even sentenced. She wanted a career in politics, and she couldn't risk all that being snatched away because of my family's reputation.'

So that's what happened, she thought.

Idina had freaked out, left him, and broken his heart. He'd stayed there and dealt with everything alone. God, poor Gunnar.

Behind him, the faintest trace of green was lighting up the sky above the mountains. 'I've only met you and Demus, but so far I *like* your family,' she told him.

He snorted, sending bubbles her way. 'Demus is the only sane one left besides me.'

'You said your mother worked in television?'

'No, I didn't say that.'

She grimaced. Maybe she'd read that on the Internet.

Busted.

Gunnar frowned. 'She never worked again after the network fired her. And Dad… Well, I don't know how much you've read about him, but he's somewhere in Asia now. I don't know where. Last I heard it was Cambodia.'

'What's he doing there?'

'Your guess is as good as mine.'

Mahlia bit down on her cheek, wishing she'd never asked. What a mess.

'Well, for what it's worth, Gunnar, this is the best birthday I've ever had,' she told him anyway, watching the neon green light behind him start to spread and separate into ethereal strands and swirl amongst the stars. 'Should we run from the monsters yet?'

He followed her eyes to the sky, then moved beside her again, shoulder to shoulder. The tension fizzed between them as the lights started dancing like a private show just for them.

He nudged her gently. 'I think the monsters will let you off, seeing as it's your birthday. Sorry for unloading all that on you.'

'Don't be sorry,' she said, trying to ignore the shiver of anticipation at his touch.

'Is it really the best birthday you've ever had?'

She smiled softly, buoyed by the heat of him and the water, and the lingering buzz of the drinks. 'Two birthdays ago I was locked in a bathroom at a theatre, crying. I'd say this is much better.'

'Why were you crying in a bathroom?' He was visibly appalled.

'Javid always made the plans for my birthday,' she told the sky, aware of Gunnar's every breath beside her.

His closeness both settled her and sent hundreds of fluttering Monarch butterflies on a frenzied path through her stomach.

'I was never allowed to see my friends. He always took me to some opera he wanted us to be seen at. I didn't know how to admit to my friends that he was so controlling; they never knew. I let them think I *wanted* to be at the opera instead of the dinner they'd booked for me.'

Gunnar was silent. The northern lights kept swirling.

'Some of them stopped talking to me after a while,' she told him, wondering why she was still speaking.

'I've lost a few friends myself over the years,' he said. 'But... Mahlia, I'm so sorry you got caught up in a relation-ship like that. I don't blame you for getting out of it.'

'If only I could!' She half laughed. 'I had to tell my solici-tor where I am, so of course Javid knows I'm in Iceland, too. I wake up every day thinking today's the day he'll track me down and demand I come home.'

To her shock, Gunnar reached for her face, turning her at-tention from the sky. Her breath caught as his fingers lingered on her jaw, his gaze intense and full of a fire that kick-started a riot in her belly.

'You don't have to worry about him coming here,' he growled. 'He's not going to get anywhere close to you. I can promise you that. Not while I'm around.'

Mahlia stared into his eyes, too stunned to speak. A spark of hope sprang up within her, rising like an ocean around her pounding heart. For the first time in years she truly believed that she could and would escape Javid's oppressive grip.

Was Gunnar actually going to kiss her?

His hand moved up to gently caress her cheek, sending shiv-ers down her spine. She wanted nothing more than for him to close the gap between them and seal their lips together with the northern lights flickering above them. But just as he leaned closer nerves got the better of her. What was she getting her-self into here? Everything she'd vowed she hadn't come here looking for? She was being so naive. This was how it had all started with Javid! The trust, his warmth, his desire to 'protect' her...

Make that control her.

So why did this feel so good?

Conflicted she pressed her hands to his warm chest, biting back a laugh. 'To think I so wanted to have his babies. I couldn't wait to start a family. He knew it too—knew how much I wanted to be a mother. But he kept putting it off. He'd say, "Not yet. It's not the right time for us, Mahlia." I'm lucky he did. I mean...imagine him being a father. The man's incapable of caring for anyone other than himself.'

She shut her mouth, realising Gunnar had retreated. He'd backed off again, settled at the other side of the tub, and was watching her cautiously. Oh, no. Why on earth had she said all that? She wasn't that drunk...was she?

It was just so overwhelming: him, this magical moment, the newness of it all, finally hearing him speak more openly about his past and getting some of the load off her own chest.

He'd been going to kiss her. Or maybe he hadn't. Had she just misread him completely?

'I'm so sorry, Gunnar. I'm not used to talking about him, or any of this. I don't know what to say,' she admitted, letting out a nervous laugh. 'You must think I'm crazy.'

Gunnar was watching her with an unreadable expression on his face now. 'You don't have to say anything,' he said softly, as she cringed inside. 'But no. I don't think you're crazy. You're special to have come through something like that and survived—do you know that?'

Mahlia could have died! They were colleagues, and she was married—there were so many reasons why he might have backed off. But the way he'd said 'you're special', as though it were an indisputable fact instead of mere words, had only sent her heart into even more of a riot.

* * *

When they emerged from the hot tub a little later she was cold to the bone, even inside by the fire and with her clothes back on. Gunnar went to wake Demus, and she resisted helping him get his brother into the wheelchair. It was something he obviously enjoyed managing on his own.

'What were you two talking about out there?' Demus asked, yawning and pulling his hat over his head.

'Nothing,' Gunnar said, shooting her a look that made the shame of her revelations flare back into her brain.

The heat from the tub had made the moonshine go to her head. Now, on solid ground, she was stone-cold sober. What an idiot she was, spilling her heart and soul when she barely knew him. Her worries seemed so trivial compared to the pain he'd revealed. His girlfriend had put her career prospects above their relationship and left him to cope with a global scandal alone. His brother was in a wheelchair, and his mother...well, who knew how she was managing? And yet here Mahlia was, pretty much admitting she'd messed up her life through her own cowardice and poor judgement in men.

No wonder he'd backed off!

Helplessly she sat on the couch, watching Demus go round in the wheelchair, turning off the lights. The cold had got into her bones. When he saw her shivering, Gunnar handed her the knitted sweater he'd been wearing earlier, and she pulled it on gratefully over her own.

'This is nice,' she said, breathing in the scent of it.

It calmed her. It smelled like him...like this cabin...like woodsmoke, pine and a sweetness she couldn't define.

'It was my great-grandfather's,' Gunnar told her, crouching to put out the fire in the hearth. 'He spent his whole life in a small fishing village off the coast.'

'Up north,' Demus added. 'It's beautiful up there, with the whales all swarming round the boats.'

They explained how their great-grandmother had knitted the sweater by hand, with wool from their Icelandic sheep, to keep her husband warm in Iceland's unforgiving winter months. The images they painted without even trying made her smile. And the fact that he trusted her to wear such a precious heirloom warmed her as much as the wool. He thought she was 'special.'

Then she remembered again how she'd ruined the moment outside and the shame crashed back in.

It didn't leave her for the whole drive back to Reykjavik. She would never, ever stop cringing inside over everything she'd blurted out. As if he needed to take on her problems after everything he'd been through himself!

Which reminded her… She should have asked this question before…

'Demus,' she ventured, turning to him. 'I have a place open on the e-assist trial, so if you'd like to, maybe you can join it?'

She hadn't asked Gunnar if Demus might be interested, fearing it might seem as if she was trying to get involved in his life, when she knew he kept his cards close to his chest about his family, but she'd been invited to come here with the brothers today, hadn't she?'

'I'd love to know more about it,' Demus said enthusiastically. 'Gunnar's told me about what you're doing. Did he tell you how I used to beat him in every bike race?'

'In your dreams!'

The two started up their brotherly banter again, and before she left the car Mahlia promised to be in touch about the trial. Gunnar's gaze lingered over her lips before she closed the passenger door. He was probably thinking how glad he was that he hadn't kissed a crazy person tonight. But he had talked about her venture with his brother before...

Interesting.

This news helped her shame abate a little, even if she was still reeling over how she'd just proved how right Javid had been when he'd told her... What was it? That a woman like her was 'wholly unattractive to most men'.

She shouldn't care what Gunnar thought of her—he wasn't why she'd come here. He was too complicated, and she was not available! Even so, she clean forgot to look at her phone again.

She didn't take the sweater off either.

CHAPTER SEVEN

THE CALL CAME in at four minutes past six a.m. Gunnar was already on his second cup of coffee. Erik gave him the update as he drove to the hangar, and he turned up the heat inside the truck to beat off the draught of icy air at the edges of his scarf. The snow flurry was unrelenting around his windscreen. It had been snowing non-stop for the last two days. Getting anywhere fast this morning would be impossible.

To think just three nights ago, out at the cabin, they'd had clear skies. Clear enough for him to see way more of Mahlia than he'd expected to. He'd seen inside her head—enough to realise exactly how emotionally abused she'd been by her ex. She wasn't something he could fix; he had enough on his plate. She wasn't staying here, and she definitely wasn't fling material. She wasn't like anyone else he'd ever met…

Shaking that near-kiss from his head—again—he focused on the road and on Erik's voice. The blizzard last night had rendered the small village of Hvítaeyri on the Víkurfjall mountainside unreachable, which wasn't unusual at this time of year. But in this case, a twenty-eight-year-old pregnant woman called Helga had just gone into labour. They needed to get her medical attention stat, which meant flying the chopper in as soon as possible.

'You're here—good man.'

Erik greeted him at the hangar, head bent against the howling wind and snow. He was talking on the radio now, Gunnar assumed with someone at the village. Mahlia's car pulled up with a slight screech. He found himself watching her as she exited with a slam of the door and hurried for shelter, huddling into her scarf.

'We've done rescues like this before, but she might be too far into labour by the time we get there for us to get her out,' Ásta was saying to him and their pilot, Sven. 'We really need a midwife, but the only volunteer we know is away...'

'I can deliver the baby if I have to,' Mahlia said.

Gunnar swung around.

'I've done it before.'

She brushed the snow from her hood and met his eyes. A flicker of caution crossed her face—at seeing him, probably—but then she straightened up, folded her arms, all business, and asked Erik for the latest.

He had to admit, whatever she'd gone through with that idiot Javid she was a force of nature. He'd delivered a baby before too—once. All physicians received basic obstetrics training in the US, as part of their clinical rotations. It didn't mean he'd enjoyed it. It had made him dwell on all the things he'd never have, thanks to his messed-up family.

What did Mahlia think, now she knew about how Idina had left him? The press were still relentless in their pursuit of him. There was a story about every woman he was seen with, either printed, blasted all over the Internet, or shot from someone's loud mouth. Hopefully the vultures wouldn't get to her, too. All the more reason to be very careful...

Ásta and Sven began to brief Mahlia on what to expect when they reached the village. They said she might have to be lowered on the winch, with him.

Gunnar focused on her face. She didn't look scared—far from it. If anything, she seemed resolute, determined to help this woman and her baby no matter the cost. A new wave of respect washed over him as she helped them stow the medical gear onto the chopper.

An hour later, the snow had subsided enough for them to take off. Mahlia sat opposite him and didn't meet his eyes.

'How are you doing?' he asked her, over the whir of the blades.

He'd spent the last hour prepping the winch and fielding calls, and she'd been talking with Ásta. He wondered if she'd been avoiding him since that night. Since he'd made it awkward for her...on his territory.

'I'm good,' she said tightly. 'Sorry I haven't been in touch about the trial yet. I'm still trying to line up potential times for Demus to meet Inka, the programme analyst I told you about. She's been away in Spain.'

He nodded, told her it was fine, although he wanted to say she could have been in touch to tell him that. She was definitely avoiding him. He watched her profile as she studied the mountains through the windows, her curls flapping around her hood. Was she still wearing his sweater under that coat?

It was shameful how much he'd wanted to kiss her in the hot tub the other night. He'd taken a vulnerable woman out to the middle of nowhere and made a move. Well, almost made a move. Maybe he would've done if she hadn't mentioned that she wanted a family. That had snapped him back to his senses.

Not only was taking a married colleague to his private retreat the kind of behaviour to get everyone talking more nonsense about him, if they found out about it, but he would never have children. She was too special a person to be fling material, and too vulnerable to involve in all his family drama—she was trying to rebuild her own life! He'd made the right decision, backing off.

They were nearing the village already. Mahlia was applying

the lip salve he'd given her that first night, talking with Erik, making plans, focused and determined to help this woman any way she could.

That was the kind of thing he wanted to be known for too—making a difference to people's lives, not wasting the time of someone who wanted more from him than he could give. There'd been that fashion designer, Frida, a couple of years ago. He'd liked her, and she hadn't been that bothered that he'd never let her meet his mother. Ma had been was causing a stir in the media at the time, showing up drunk for her yoga classes.

Then Frida had started hinting at marriage and having babies. He'd told her that was never going to happen.

The last one had been Ingrid, eight months ago or so—a tourist from Norway. She hadn't known who he was. Then some influencer had tagged her out in a bar with 'the son of Iceland's biggest disgrace', and she'd done what Idina had: hightailed it out of town early, blocked him and never spoken to him again. He'd sworn after her there would be no more women.

It was just that Mahlia's quiet spirit and determination, mixed with her vulnerability, had woken something up inside him—something he'd been holding back for far too long. He'd felt it that night at his cabin with her, boiling up and bursting through every pore. It was as if she had taken a hammer to the walls he'd constructed, and he still wasn't exactly sure what to do with that.

Demus had seen it too.

'You like her! And she seems great,' he'd enthused, when he'd carried him inside to the couch. *'It's all on you now, brother. No need to thank me…just don't mess up your chance.'*

He'd messed it up on purpose. She wanted kids—badly, by the sounds of it, and he did not. And his reputation preceded him. There was no way he'd play any part in Mahlia getting ridiculed or slandered. She'd been through enough.

The engine roared in the snow-filled sky, and soon enough Hvítaeyri came into view. 'You can see how blocked the roads are,' he told them, pointing to the mile-high snowdrifts where the cross-section was in summer.

'I hope we can reach her on foot once we're down there,' Mahlia said as Erik relayed to Sven which house they needed to head for.

Gunnar got to his feet and started strapping on his harness.

'There's no way I can land,' came Sven's voice over the headset. 'You're going to have to go down on the winch, Gunnar.'

'Already on it,' he confirmed.

'Helga's contractions are getting closer together,' Erik followed up.

He'd been talking with whoever was with the woman in labour the whole way here, and it was clear Mahlia was taking mental notes. Gunnar had no doubt she could deliver that baby on her own if she had to. Was there anything she couldn't do? he mused, pulling his line tighter around his middle. How her ex could have tried to repress her in any way made him want to hunt him down in the chopper and throw a live alligator at him from the winch.

'I'm ready for you,' he told her.

Mahlia stood up, meeting his eyes with fierce resolve. He hooked up the winch line to his harness and then secured it around her slim waist, making sure she was safely attached to him. Now they were strapped together, their next movements were vital. She was his responsibility on this wire—it was up to him to ensure she got down there in one piece.

He checked all the connections twice before giving a nod of approval. Mahlia took long, deep breaths as she followed him closer to the chopper door, now open wide onto an abyss of white. Maybe he was attuned to her now, but he was sure he could feel her trepidation radiating outwards, despite her brave face. She was obviously wary of jumping in this weather.

'I'll be with you,' he said against her ear, as her hair sprang free and tickled his cheeks. Her natural, musky, womanly scent had him struggling to resist the urge to take her hands, but he gave her an encouraging pat on the shoulder in front of the others, and she leaned in, eyes on his. 'We can do this,' he said. 'Just keep your eyes on me.'

Ásta and Erik were watching, offering words of encouragement, double-checking that Mahlia's radio was strapped on and the backpack was tight on her back over the harness. The cold wind seemed to howl louder as they edged further towards the door. Below them, villagers had gathered, cheering them on, some dragging sledges loaded with supplies.

Mahlia locked her gaze onto his. 'I'm OK, I trust you,' she told him.

So he stepped with her off the ledge.

Soon, the rotors' thumping, deafening noise was metres above them as they were lowered slowly to the ground, swaying in the wind. He didn't need to feel the cable—he knew from memory it was secure, with or without him holding it. He felt Mahlia's gloved hands wrap tightly around his, watched her look around her in awe as she dangled, suspended with him, her hips pressed to his in the air.

Not kissing her suddenly took every ounce of restraint in his body.

On the ground, Gunnar quickly unhooked Mahlia from his harness. The chopper would circle, but if the snow picked up they'd have to head back without them and return later. It was just him and Mahlia now.

'This way—Helga lives down here,' someone told them,

pointing down a street with snowdrifts so high at the sides they could barely see the buildings.

'Give me the backpack,' he told Mahlia, but she refused.

'It's not heavy,' she told him, beckoning him to follow her as she strode on ahead, with a crowd of people eager to be involved.

'Fine,' he responded to himself, suppressing a smile.

With heavy snowfall covering most of the houses in sight, and a thick blanket of fog rolling off the mountainside, they trudged through several streets. They would have identified which house it was without any help, he thought. The cries of pain coming from inside were impossible to miss.

Mahlia rushed indoors to the woman's side and stood by her bed, shrugging off the backpack. Helga was groaning in pain, a nightdress heaved up around her thighs under a thick blanket.

'Helga,' she said, taking her hand. 'I understand your contractions are coming quickly… I'm a paramedic, and I'm here to help. My name is Mahlia.'

'They're coming so fast, I can't…'

Helga squeezed her blue eyes shut, clutched her bump. Then let out the most agonising wail that ricocheted around the room and might have started an avalanche somewhere outside.

Mahlia quickly took stock of the situation. The sheer curtains were drawn closed over the small window above a dresser loaded with animal ornaments. The only light came from the fireplace in the corner, where flickering red flames threw shadows across the room.

'Gunnar, open the curtains,' she instructed him, pulling off her coat and draping it over an upholstered chair in the corner.

They needed all the light they could get. Although Helga's contractions were coming quickly, she was not yet fully dilated. Still, it was too late to try and transport her anywhere else. She and Gunnar were going to have to deliver this baby themselves.

A gruff, burly, red-faced man appeared holding one hand out. He stopped Gunnar in his tracks halfway to the window. 'Not you. I don't want you near my daughter.'

Mahlia hurried back to them as Helga huffed and puffed on the bed. 'What's the problem?' she asked calmly, throwing her scarf on top of her coat. She assumed this man was Helga's father—someone else who had an issue with Gunnar. She noticed his leathery hands, gnarled with scars.

'I know who you are,' the man said gruffly, still looking threateningly at Gunnar. His cheeks were ruddy, his eyes watery and bloodshot, as if he'd been up all night. 'Your father helped bring my fishing business to its knees, Gunnar Johansson, and we lost *all* our foreign buyers. It took us years to turn a profit again, and we're still not back to how it was before…'

'Gunnar is *not* his father—and now is not the time for this.'

Mahlia's authoritative tone shocked even herself. She caught the surprise and admiration in Gunnar's eyes, just as Helga let out another shriek behind them.

Mahlia raced to the curtains herself, flung them open, then hurried back to the bedside. 'Gunnar, can you find us some warm, dry towels?'

Gunnar, still dripping snow from his boots onto the wooden floor, moved to pass the angry man—only to be stopped again.

'Sir!' Mahlia called out, furious now. 'With all due respect, this man got up at five a.m., drove through a blizzard, and has just lowered himself *and* me on a wire from a helicopter to help your daughter. Are you really going to stand in his way?'

'Daddy!'

Helga's scream of agony stunned the man into silence. He staggered back against the wall, finally letting Gunnar pass.

Mahlia heard a woman in the hallway with him, hopefully
getting them some towels. Her heart was pounding. This was
not what she'd expected when she'd woken up this morning,
but at least Gunnar was here, and had been allowed back in
the room.

Thankfully the antagonistic father kept away as she encouraged poor Helga through another wave of pain. Her bedsheets
were soaked in sweat now. She was shaking from the pain of
her contractions. Gunnar squeezed her hand and kept passing
warm towels, counting between contractions, monitoring her
blood pressure, while Mahlia checked for a crowning head,
reminding her to take deep breaths.

'You can do this, Helga,' she soothed.

'You're almost there,' Gunnar encouraged, handing her the
Entonox mask, which she grabbed and pressed to her mouth
for dear life.

Her face seemed both pale and flushed in the firelight,
and her eyes were tightly closed as she drew breaths through
clenched teeth, then the mask, then her teeth again.

'Almost there,' Mahlia repeated.

Helga writhed in pain. She was panting faster and faster,
her grip tight on Gunnar's hand. When he met Mahlia's eyes
in the firelight a flush of gratitude for his silent strength made
her smile at him and mouth *Thank you*.

His silent strength and approachability were exactly the
things that had kept her talking the other night—more than the
moonshine had. She didn't care what his father had done...but
she did care how it affected him and his family, she realised.
He *wasn't* his father; he was a good man.

As far as you know, a little voice tinkled in her head.

She didn't want any reason to doubt that—not after what
she'd been through with Javid. That was the real reason she
wasn't reading the rest of the stuff about Gunnar on the Inter-

net, the gossip and slander. She didn't want to wonder if any of it might be true.

Learning something she *didn't* like about this man would prove Javid right: that she was a terrible judge of character, too trusting, too naive, unworthy of the career she'd built and the dreams she'd dared to share and put into action. But some of those ideas *were* worthy—like the e-assist bikes. With Demus on the trial she could bring some light to his life while she was here, and to Gunnar's by association. And after she was gone they'd *still* have that.

'He's coming…he's coming!' Helga winced, before emitting the biggest scream yet.

The baby's head was crowning. Mahlia urged Helga on, and so did Gunnar. His hand had turned white in the young woman's grip. Then a little head appeared between Helga's legs, followed by two tiny shoulders.

'He's here!' she told them excitedly, and a within minutes a beautiful baby boy had slipped out into the waiting towel in Mahlia's hands.

'Well done, Helga, you have a son.'

Gunnar checked the baby over—ten toes, ten fingers, a cute button nose. Mahlia watched the way he held him like a precious treasure, so tiny in his massive hands. When he caught her watching he seemed to hurry up. He snipped the cord like a pro, and she handed the warm bundle to a sobbing, relieved Helga.

'He's beautiful and healthy,' she told her.

'He's Magnús.' Helga sniffed, beaming through her tears. 'Oh, Magnús, you look just like your daddy. He's on his way to meet you, I promise. He's just stuck in the snow.'

Hearing the name, and the reason why Helga's partner wasn't there, made tears spring unexpectedly into Mahlia's own eyes. She was exhausted, but outside the snow was coming down thick and fast again. The helicopter wouldn't be able to land...maybe not for hours. Days?

She started picking up the towels, wondering how they were supposed to get out of here without going back up on the winch, just as Helga's father broke away and stuck his hand out to Gunnar.

'Sorry about what I said before,' he told him, somewhat reluctantly. 'I shouldn't have judged you without knowing you. We couldn't have done this without you.'

Mahlia fought to hide the smug look on her face as Gunnar accepted his apology. Then he threw her a slightly sheepish, pleased grin that made her heart soar like an eagle in her chest.

The two of them walked in silence in the snow to a tiny café bar. It was more like a shed, and almost empty. Snowdrifts blocked the windows, but the place was fire-lit and welcoming, and only three doors down from Helga in case she needed them while they waited for news from the team.

Gunnar placed two cups of coffee down on a rickety old table and took the seat opposite her. She excused herself to use the bathroom, and on her return, before she could take her seat again, he scraped his chair back loudly. Before she knew what was what, he'd swept her up against him into a giant embrace.

'Thank you,' he said into her hair.

His arms wrapped around her and his warmth seeped through his clothes into hers, into her skin.

'What for?' she asked him, wiping at her eyes against his shoulder.

It had been a long time since a man had swept her up into a hug—one so solid and protective and sincere. She breathed into it, committing the tender moment to memory. It was like wearing his sweater, but better.

'For what you did in there. And for saying what you said to Helga's father. You didn't have to.'

'Yes, I did.'

She let her arms fall around his shoulders for a moment, relishing the bulk of his muscular frame against her small one and his words. He really did think she was special. They were pretty special as a team too. And there was no point denying the way her heart had almost escaped through her mouth onto his lips when she'd been harnessed to him on the winch earlier. There was something between them, but was it a good idea to explore it or not? She needed to know what had happened the other night to make him pull back. Suddenly there were lots of things she needed to know, for her own peace of mind.

Releasing herself, she slid back into her seat. 'The other night, in the hot tub, I thought you were going to kiss me,' she said, with a nervous laugh.

Gunnar's mouth became a thin line as he averted his eyes. 'That wasn't why I invited you out there, Mahlia.'

She sat back, blinking. 'I didn't think it was.'

'Well, you're married. People talk. We shouldn't...'

His eyes darted around the room now, as if he was suddenly worried someone might have seen their embrace. No one was looking. It was only them and the barman here, and he was out at the back.

'But you did,' she pressed. 'You did almost kiss me, despite all that.'

His mouth twitched. 'Maybe I chickened out. For numerous reasons.'

'It sounds like you were counting a lot of reasons *not* to kiss me, Gunnar.'

'Did you want me to, then?' he tested.

She shut her mouth as her pulse quickened. Already she had no clue where she was getting the courage to say all this to him. He went through women like hotcakes, apparently. But maybe part of her wanted to be one of them. Maybe she wanted something hot, fast, delicious, to remind her that she could be desirable. She'd been far too scared to do much at all with Javid, in the end, stuck in her shell. No way was she ever going to be that person again.

'Did I want you to kiss me?' she mused aloud, stirring her coffee with a shiny teaspoon. 'I did and I didn't. I was confused Javid was bugging me, and you and Demus were being so nice. And...'

'Moonshine,' they said at the same time.

She dragged a hand through her hair, realising it was tangled from their windy descent on the winch. 'I just wanted to know more about you, Gunnar. From you.'

'Well, now you know,' he replied stoically, stroking a hand across his chin and letting out a sigh. 'That guy has a right to be upset with my family. My father ruined so many people's lives.'

She tutted at him. 'He didn't do it on his own. And *you* had nothing to do with it.'

He sipped his coffee, frowning. 'Not directly, I guess, no.'

'So why are you letting yourself think that somehow you're the bad guy?'

'It's what *everyone* thinks.'

'Not everyone,' she told him sternly. 'Your brother adores you. I like what you guys have together. I'm jealous, actually.'

He curled his fingers into his palms. 'You don't have any siblings?'

'Nope. Mum and Dad always seemed pretty happy with just me. Mind you, they weren't around a whole lot. Mum was a scientist—a botanist. She spent all her time in the lab until she retired. Dad used to joke how she would've rather married him in a white lab coat instead of a dress, and honeymooned in the greenhouse if he'd let her.'

Gunnar smiled a shadow of a smile. It boosted her to keep talking.

'Dad's an art historian. He started lecturing at the local university when I was a kid. So they were probably too busy to have any more children.'

He looked at her thoughtfully, and she found herself considering for the first time how maybe she'd been seeking attention from Javid, and done her best to always please him, because she hadn't had much attention from her parents growing up. While they'd loved her, they certainly hadn't seemed too pleased when she'd been hanging around in the school holidays, taking up space and time. And in later years, following her aunt's death, depression had gripped her grieving mother so hard it had forced up a wall between them all.

'But you want children of your own?' he said slowly.

Mahlia blinked. What was he getting at? He knew the answer to that, didn't he? Something told her he wasn't one to forget. Somehow it felt like a test.

'I did... I do. I know I have a few trust issues, after what's happened. And I also know my age could be a factor... But there are ways. I've already thought about how I might do it,' she admitted in a rush.

She needed to feel needed. Always had done. Kids would give her a new purpose, as much as her career was giving her one now. She'd never doubted it.

Gunnar was nodding quietly. She caught his eyes and he looked away quickly.

'How did you meet Javid?' he asked.

'We reached for the same loaf of bread at the bakery,' she told him over her coffee cup. 'It was the last one. I let him have it.'

Of course she'd let him have it. And he'd taken it, too.

'He asked me out and that was it, really. I know now we had nothing in common.'

'So why did you like him initially?'

Mahlia stared at him. Somehow she was thinking about his sweater, still folded up on her bed in her apartment. It had felt so comfortable on her, in a way nothing of Javid's ever had. Maybe that was why she hadn't given it back yet, she thought, guiltily.

'I don't know. He was...different.'

Different meaning he'd seemed like a dependable choice compared to all the losers she'd seemed to meet online, she thought. He'd arranged their dates and hadn't ever cancelled.

'Why did you like Idina?' she asked.

Gunnar was silent for a moment, as if pondering the question. 'She was tough. She was really into sports. She encouraged me to pursue my goals. She was...like me, I guess. We had a best friend type of vibe. Best friends with benefits. We just *liked* each other.'

And that's the difference, Mahlia thought to herself, feeling envy seep like poison through her pores. That was why Gunnar had loved Idina and been so hurt by her abandonment.

She was here in Iceland trying to distance herself as much as possible from Javid. They'd never been friends, she and Javid. She'd never really even *liked* him. She had settled for the first man who'd shown an ounce of commitment, then turned herself into his puppet.

Gunnar's radio sprang into life. It was as they'd feared. There was no way out for a least a few hours. A team was still working on clearing the road back to Reykjavik and it was too dangerous to bring the chopper back in.

'What do people do in tiny mountain villages when there's a blizzard raging outside?' she asked him, staring at the relentless snowflakes, just as the barman came over and told them the coffee was on the house. He'd heard what they'd done for Helga.

Gunnar looked surprised. He always seemed surprised when someone was nice to him.

The two men exchanged a few words in Icelandic, before he turned to her: 'Looks like we have an invitation.'

'To what?' she asked.

'You want to see what Icelanders do when there's a blizzard raging outside?'

CHAPTER EIGHT

THE SMALL ONE-LEVEL house was half hidden by snowdrifts, like most of the homes in the village. Mahlia followed Gunnar up the pathway, which had clearly been dug out by hand.

He stopped by the door for a minute, casting her a look. 'I don't usually do this, but the guy in the café said they're expecting us.'

'Who?' she asked, intrigued.

'The villagers.'

Sinister giant icicles glistened ominously from the low roof above the windows, threatening to fall and pierce whatever they struck, and she felt his apprehension. He was probably thinking there'd be at least someone in there who wouldn't want him around, but he was doing this for her.

She touched his hand through his glove. 'We don't have to...'

Too late. The door was flung open.

Lively Icelandic voices assaulted her ears as a beaming, red-faced woman in her sixties ushered them inside. It was toasty warm.

'A party?' Mahlia looked up at Gunnar in surprise.

'People in small villages take it in turns to host nights like this—especially when the weather's bad,' he told her, unzipping his coat, holding his hand out for hers, still looking around warily. 'Which is most of the time. Everyone brings a dish. Everyone can play.'

'Play what?' she asked, just as a piano sprang to life.

A tall, striking middle-aged man in a vivid red and blue sweater was playing something jovial she didn't recognise, but it reminded her of Christmas parties back when she'd actually gone out with her friends. At least five more people instantly gathered around it and started singing. Everyone had a glass of something—probably alcohol. From what she'd learned so far about Icelanders, they loved to drink.

'Gunnar, this is so nice!'

The scent of cinnamon and nutmeg filled the air. Evergreen branches were strung up by the windows, illuminated by twinkling lights and candles. There must be about twenty-five people here. Not one of them was looking at Gunnar the way Helga's father had. In fact they came over one by one, introduced themselves, thanked them for being here. She felt like a minor celebrity.

'Help yourself to food,' their hostess said warmly, taking their coats and directing Gunnar to leave their bags in an adjacent room. 'Ólafur told me you delivered Helga's son today. You're our guests tonight—we're really grateful you could make it.'

Mahlia hadn't realised how hungry she was until she was standing at a large buffet table. Her stomach growled as she took in the array of food. Smoked salmon sandwiches, glazed ham, giant meatballs, pickled herring, intricate pastries and gingerbread cookies shaped like stars and hearts. *Delicious.*

Gunnar popped a tiny sandwich into his mouth whole, just as Helga's father emerged from what she assumed was the bathroom and spotted him.

'Here he is!' he exclaimed, lunging forward like a hulking barrel and aiming for a one-armed hug.

Gunnar accepted it awkwardly.

'How is Helga? How's the baby?' Mahlia asked him.

'They're wonderful…just wonderful,' he proclaimed, re-leasing Gunnar. 'Sleeping now.'

'That's great.' She smiled around her cookie, which was the best cookie she'd ever tasted.

'Everybody, this is Gunnar Johansson! All is forgiven—right, my friend?' He paused, screwing up his nose. 'Well, you. Not your father. If Ingólfur Johansson was here I'd…'

'Not now, Sigurður,' their hostess said, throwing them both an apologetic look.

She led the man away, to the piano. Gunnar looked aston-ished, to say the least. Helga's father was clearly about five drinks in already.

'Drink?' Gunnar asked her, pouring himself one from a decanter on the table.

She shook her head. There was no way she was ever drink-ing around Gunnar again; the effects of this homemade Ice-landic stuff were unpredictable, to say the least.

This group of Icelanders turned out to be incredibly tal-ented. Gunnar was right—everyone seemed to be able to play an instrument. There were guitars, a flute, a violin, even a tambourine.

It had been years since Mahlia had played the guitar. Javid had laughed at her the last time she'd picked hers up…told her not to give up her day job.

She sipped on mint tea and sneaked glances at Gunnar when he wasn't looking. He seemed to be relaxing, chatting to people with ease. She couldn't help wondering what he'd been think-ing earlier, when he'd held that baby. There had been a look on his face then that she hadn't been able to read. Maybe he wanted a family someday, she thought idly, not for the first time. He'd be a good dad, someone like him, a leader…

Why are you even thinking about this?

She rolled her eyes, just as her phone chimed in her pocket. Pulling it out in surprise she stared at it. There hadn't been a signal till now. Her heart lurched. Javid.

Are you ever going to talk to me again? I'm worried about you. Are you OK? How can you just ignore me like this, Mahlia? It's so heartless!

She ground her teeth, scowling at the screen. Ever since she'd ignored him on her birthday she'd kept it up. It was the longest she'd gone without pandering to his needs in seven years. She'd felt pretty powerful at first…at times had even forgotten about him!

'What's happened?' Gunnar asked.

He was standing in front of her now, frowning.

'Nothing.' She shoved the phone away, feeling stupid. Of course he probably thought she was silly for not just blocking his number altogether.

'I've got a signal too,' he said, holding up his phone. 'My mother's in trouble again.'

He didn't sound pleased.

'What?'

'Nothing you need to get in involved in,' he grunted.

She watched his brow crease harder. The shadow of stubble on his cheeks and chin gave him more of a Viking aura than ever.

A woman took the piano stool behind him; everyone started singing.

'I don't think we'll be getting out of here any time soon, though. Not tonight, anyway. We've been offered two rooms at the guesthouse.'

'OK…' she said, wondering what was up with his mother.

He'd been pretty vague about her so far. It was none of her business, of course, and she simmered in silence, berating herself for wanting to know anyway. He was already taking up far too much of her headspace. First Javid, now him.

Scrolling through her emails quickly, for anything she might have missed today, she spotted a message from Inka. She was back from Spain and keen to get the trial moving—and, yes, of *course* she'd like Demus Johansson to be involved.

'She calls him "high-profile",' she told Gunnar. 'Is that a good thing or a bad thing?'

'What do you think?' he replied, folding his arms, propping up the wall. 'He'll do your trial, but he probably won't want to do any press around the bikes.'

Mahlia chewed on her lip, focused on the tapestries on the wall behind him. It hadn't really crossed her mind that Demus would be wary of the media, but she knew Gunnar was right; she'd seen the way it had treated the family when she'd briefly looked up Gunnar on the Internet.

Gunnar looked as if he was somewhere else in his head. Thinking about his mother, maybe? What was going on?

A huge cheer erupted as the pianist finished her song. 'Anyone else? Our special guests, maybe?'

Everyone turned to look at them in anticipation. Gunnar shook his head, still lost in his thoughts. Mahlia felt rude, not getting involved, standing over here with Gunnar, reading messages, while everyone was being so hospitable. Should she play? It had been years…and Javid had said she was bad at it…

Oh, stuff Javid.

Before she could chicken out, she strode to the piano, picked up a guitar from its stand and dropped to the stool. She ran her fingers over the strings, feeling the familiar vibrations of the instrument against her skin. Her mind raced, trying to remember the chords of a song she'd used to play in high school.

How did it go?

Oh, yes.

Mahlia began to strum, and each chord swept her further into the music. It was like visiting a house she hadn't seen in years, remembering every nook and corner.

The crowd soon recognised the song. Helga's father started singing along in his thick, deep baritone. Others followed, and Mahlia couldn't keep the smile from her face as Gunnar took his place beside her on the piano stool.

To her total shock, he started accompanying her on the keys. Their harmonies cascaded through the room, his fingers flying like a master musician. She watched him in awe, picking at the guitar strings beside him. Wow. He was so talented!

All around them hands were clapping, voices joined in harmony. She hadn't felt this sense of togetherness in a room in years...maybe not ever. As they hit the final notes the cheers and applause turned deafening, and she realised she was shaking with adrenaline. She turned to Gunnar. His bad mood had dissipated somewhere between the piano keys. She met his huge smile face-on, and before she could stop herself her body reacted to the moment.

She leaned forward over the guitar and kissed him on the cheek. 'You were so good,' she whispered, laughing with the shock of her own actions.

'*Me?* You were...'

For a moment Gunnar looked just as he had that night in the hot tub. She held her breath. His gaze moved over her face, lingering on her lips till his smile faded. The intensity of his eyes burned into her.

But in a beat, he was on his feet. She watched in horror as the stool scraped out from under her and Gunnar snatched someone's phone from their hands.

'No photos,' he barked, sending the crowd silent.

He apologised straight away, keeping his voice calm enough, but he was visibly annoyed. 'Please, guys, no photos. That's all I ask.'

Mahlia felt sick, and angry. But mostly sick. The girl apologised profusely, and Gunnar told her it was fine, but the moment was ruined. She hadn't even seen anyone taking photos!

'Why is it such a big deal if they take a photo?' she asked, her tone rising as he guided her towards the hallway. His hand was only resting lightly against the small of her back now, but his intent was clearly to leave. To urge her out of a moment she'd been enjoying.

'Gunnar, don't be so…domineering!'

'We should go,' he said, gathering up their coats.

He fetched their bags while her mind spun.

'I don't want to go,' she said, glowering at him.

This was all too familiar; she couldn't even count on a thousand people's fingers how many times Javid had forced her to leave somewhere she'd been having a good time.

'*You* go. I'm staying here.'

Her words hung heavy between them, daring him to challenge her. Inside her chest her heart beat a frantic tempo, faster than whoever was now on the guitar. Every nerve-ending bristled as she waited for his response. She watched his face change, his eyes narrow, the faintest twitch of his lips.

'I'm sorry,' he said after a moment, swiping up his stuff. 'You stay as long as you want. The guesthouse is just up the street.' He turned his back on her, making for the door. 'I'll see you tomorrow, Mahlia. Have fun.'

Wait… What?

She watched in disbelief as he left.

Staring at the door, she half expected him to open it again and demand she leave with him, but it stayed closed.

Really?

He hadn't argued or pushed or tried to make her do something she didn't want to—he'd just apologised and agreed with her.

Warmth flooded through her body—so much so she found herself laughing behind her hand as she turned back to the party. They were all dancing now, pulling her in as if they were old friends, telling her how great she was on the guitar. Gunnar's reaction to the phone camera was clean forgotten. Javid was forgotten.

She joined in with the dancing, let her hair flow down around her shoulders, felt her hips loosen and her worries fall away. She forgot the blizzard outside...forgot everything. In this one moment she felt more powerful than she'd ever felt before.

Gunnar balled his fists at his sides, pacing the tiny room. There was only just enough space in here for the bed and a rather old, shabby-looking couch that had seen better days. He'd be sleeping on it as soon as Mahlia got back.

There'd been some mix-up. The guy who'd let him in had rushed off somewhere afterwards but Gunnar had only been able to find one unlocked room in the place. Now there was no one around to ask for another.

He stopped at the window to look for her through the falling snow for what must have been the hundredth time. He'd locked the door downstairs against the snow and wind, so he'd have to let her in when she returned, but she'd been gone for three hours. The message he'd sent her about the room-sharing situation was still unread. Maybe he should go and check she was OK.

No.

She'd made it more than clear she didn't need him there. These gatherings went on all night sometimes, especially in weather like this, and he was still kicking himself for reacting that way to the girl and her phone... No wonder Mahlia was annoyed. He'd tried to get her to leave! He'd probably reminded her of her awful ex.

Gunnar sank to the bed, pressed his palms over his eyes and yawned. It turned into a growl. God knew that idiot Javid was controlling enough; the last thing Mahlia needed was for *him* to start acting so... What was it she'd called him? *Domineering*. It was just that the thought of a photo like that getting out...of them in a situation like that... She didn't know the storm it would cause for her, being linked to him. He was flirting with danger enough, being seen with her anywhere that wasn't work-related, and now this.

A buzz came from his phone. He grabbed for it, expecting it to be her. It was Demus. Quickly, he answered. 'It's the middle of the night...are you all right, bud?'

'Ma finally passed out in her bed. I just got back to my place. I figured you'd still be at that party.'

Gunnar walked to the window again, telling him he was alone for the moment. 'I'm so sorry you had to deal with all that by yourself. Was your carer OK to stay with you while you rescued Ma? Did she help you run the bath for her?'

He watched for any sign of Mahlia through the howling wind and snow, biting the inside of his cheek as Demus filled him in on the latest. Ma had got herself so drunk that she'd locked herself out of her house. Failing to reach him, she had called Demus. Demus and whichever one of his carers had been there with him at the time had then had to undertake the hellish mission to go out in the snow with the spare key and locate her in the backyard, where she probably would have frozen to death if she hadn't been so loaded on vodka.

'Any news on when you'll be back yet?' Demus asked.

'Tomorrow. They're clearing the road as we speak.'

Demus sighed, his voice tight. 'We need to do something about Ma, Gunnar. It's getting out of control...it can't go on like this.'

'I know,' he said gruffly. Just hearing his brother so weary made him angry; he wasn't supposed to be dealing with any of this. 'Maybe it's time for rehab.'

'She won't go—you know that. She wants to be home in case Dad comes back.'

He gritted his teeth. God, every time they talked about this he fought a tidal wave of shame and anger and loathing for his father that felt so toxic he wanted to vomit.

His eyes fell to a figure beneath the window, huddled against the snow. *Mahlia.*

'Demus, I'll call you tomorrow. Get some rest.'

He met her at the door, before she could press the buzzer— there was still no one else here to let her in.

She almost stumbled into him in surprise. 'Gunnar. How come you're still awake?'

He ushered her inside, shutting the door against the snow.

Mahlia studied his face and her eyes darkened. 'What's wrong? You're still worried about your mother?'

He almost laughed. He'd been expecting her to be angry with him, but instead she was asking about his mother. She seemed to sense his internal stress, as if she was peering into his very soul.

'Gunnar?'

He scraped his hands through his hair, so as not to touch her. 'Can you forgive me for acting like I did back there? I should *never* have tried to make you leave. I had no right.'

Snowflakes glistened in her hair as she smiled. 'I had the best time,' she said, eyes shining. 'You have no idea. And you didn't make me do anything.'

He frowned. 'I tried, though. Then I just...left you there.'

She laughed. 'Exactly—it was perfect!'

Maybe it was the conversation with Demus, or maybe it was his own shame over his reaction earlier, but he was just so happy to see her face, free from any anger and resentment, that it was all he could do not to draw her into him and never let her go.

Instead he led her up the stairs, told her about the mix-up with the rooms, said that he'd take the couch. She eyed him cautiously as she took off her coat and pulled off her shoes, and he forced a smile into his voice, pulling off his sweater, hoping he was hiding his inner turmoil.

'If this is a little awkward I can…'

'What? Sleep in the hall? Take the bed,' she told him.

He stopped halfway through unbuttoning his shirt. 'No way.'

Mahlia's gaze fell to his chest. Then she tore it away. 'I'm smaller than you. The couch is fine for me. I'm so tired, I could probably sleep in the bathtub.'

He grunted, pulling off his shoes, watching the way she looked at his feet in his socks, then averted her eyes again.

'We'll leave sleeping in bathtubs to my mother,' he said, before he could think.

She dropped to the couch as he pulled some spare blankets from a cupboard. 'What happened? Talk to me.'

'I don't want to talk about it,' he said. Why drag her into it? She didn't need to be involved. 'Everything's good.'

'It's not good,' she insisted.

'It's *good*,' he repeated.

She was biting back a smile now. 'You know, you were really *good* on that piano. I wish you could've stayed longer.'

He crawled under the down quilt on the bed, trying not to watch as she shrugged out of her sweater and huddled under the blankets on the couch. This was torture, just as he'd known it would be.

Suppressing a groan, he told her she was pretty incredible on the guitar too, leaving out the word *sexy*, even though she'd looked sexy as hell playing that thing.

'It's probably not a good idea for us to do anything like that again, Mahlia,' he said instead, willing his heart to stop crashing through his ribs. 'If you knew what kind of reputation me and my family have…just being seen with me could…'

She clicked her tongue. 'Oh, so *that's* why you didn't want a photo! Gunnar, your family legacy doesn't have to end with what your dad did. And I'm a big girl. I can look after my—'

A creak from the couch made her close her mouth. Before Mahlia could even stand up, a shuddering splitting sound tore through the room, and the couch broke clean in half. She sat there swallowed by cushions, on the broken frame, stunned, mouth agape. Gunnar stared in horror, too shocked to move.

'Oh, my…'

He couldn't help it. He started to laugh—a huge belly laugh that shook him and pushed every negative thought he'd been thinking straight from his head. It was just too funny.

Her face was mask of disbelief as she surveyed the wreckage around her, mortified. 'How did that even happen?'

'It looks ancient,' he told her.

He slipped off the bed and helped her to her bare feet. She was shorter without shoes. Her toenails were painted a deep green, he noted, running his eyes back up to hers. Carefully he reached for a piece of stuffing in her hair.

'How do you always do this?' he murmured as she froze in his gaze.

'Break ancient couches?' Her voice was a whisper now; neither of them were laughing.

'No. Make me want to kiss you.' He stepped closer, reached

for her face, tracing her soft, full lips with his thumb. She closed her eyes and swallowed. 'I've been telling myself not to.'

Mahlia's hand came up over his, holding him in place. 'But what if I want you to?'

Every inch of Gunnar's body was alive with desire; it was highly probable he'd never wanted anyone more than he wanted her in this moment. Mahlia's whole face had glazed over with a longing he'd never seen, and in that second it was inevitable.

She went for him, pulling him in, kissing him passionately, till their tongues were tangling and exploring and they were falling back onto the bed, not caring if that broke, too.

Neither of them could pull away for what felt like an eternity. The electricity between them was palpable, heating up the room, sheening their skin. Mahlia's shirt and bra were on the floor by his clothes…her caramel skin and dark curls were on the pillow beneath him… It all felt like a dream in the dim light. The way her lips and hands felt on his mouth, on his body…

Gunnar finally pulled away, looking down at her, his face inches from hers. Her heart was racing like a motor against his chest. Taking a deep breath, he forced himself to roll away, slamming his head back against the pillow. 'If I keep going, I won't be able to stop.'

'I don't want you to stop,' she said.

The need in her voice was agonising and it tore at his soul. She reached out and touched his face gently, before leaning in to kiss him again, this time more slowly and tenderly than before, as if she was pouring her heart into him. How was it possible to want her even more? All of her…

'No, Mahlia.'

He forced his feet to the floor and went into the bathroom, determined to shake it off. If he made love to her now, he'd get hooked—and then ruin her life, probably. This had already gone too far.

He kicked off his briefs, turned on the shower, standing there till the water scalded his skin. What the hell was wrong with him? He'd only hurt her... And worse, selfishly, he'd be the one left missing what might have been when she disappeared.

You said you'd never do this to yourself again!

'It's just one night,' came a voice from behind him.

He spun around. Mahlia was stepping out of her black cotton panties. They were already damp—he'd felt them, felt *her*, enough to know that if they didn't do this now it would torture them both. But he would *not* do this—to either of them.

'I'm not good for you,' he groaned as she walked towards him slowly.

He stood under the water, paralysed by the full sight of her, sculpted arms, shapely legs, hips, breasts, curves...the most beautiful creature he'd ever seen. Oh, God, why did she have to be so perfect?

'Mahlia, I'm warning you.'

'I'm not asking you to be good,' she told him, stepping into the cubicle, pressing herself up against him, sucking softly on his shoulder. Her soft skin glistened under the spray as he moaned, feeling every last ounce of resolve wash down the plughole. He surrendered, let her take control of him. What else could he do?

She wanted it, she wanted to feel powerful, and he'd never been so turned on by anyone. When she got down on her knees under the pouring water he ran his hands through her hair, watching the water running over the curve of her shoulders, and blanked everything else from his mind.

CHAPTER NINE

'THAT WAS SO much better than I ever expected,' Mahlia found herself saying in disbelief. 'I never thought I'd be so emotional about this...sorry.'

Standing in the wind, she ran a hand across her eyes and her jaw in disbelief as Demus sped over the line on the trial circuit, faster than he'd done it the first time.

Gunnar boomed, 'Yes!' thumping the sky with his fist, and Inka clapped her hands together in delight, along with the other participants all waiting their turn.

'That's even faster than I did it,' Inka squealed, high-fiving Mahlia from her wheelchair beside her. 'Thirty-two miles per hour.' She looked between her and Gunnar in disbelief. 'On this terrain that's pretty much...'

'A miracle?' Gunnar said, finishing Inka's words.

Inka made her way over to greet Demus with a huge grin on her face, no doubt to check the gadget on the bike was functioning correctly. It fed data to an app on her phone— something else Mahlia had been working with a developer to perfect.

'I never I thought I'd see it. Maybe this means we can finally ride together again, out there.'

Gunnar waved a hand out to the mountains beyond the covered trial circuit. His blue eyes were flooded with such pure, childlike joy she couldn't help a laugh bubbling up.

He wrapped his arms around her waist suddenly and pulled her close, pressing a searing kiss to her forehead that seemed to burn with an intensity of its own. Instantly she was shot like a bullet in reverse, back to the first night they'd made love. Seven amazing, unforgettable nights ago. They'd spent most nights together since, but that first time…

When they'd finished making love in the shower, and on the bed, the clock had read six a.m., and neither of them had slept at all. That had been the first time in a long time she'd felt in control like that, she thought, swallowing the lump that built up in her throat every time she recalled the intensity of their lovemaking.

'I'm not good for you.'

The way he'd said it, like a warning, hadn't stopped her. If anything, it had spurred her on. Every whisper of a touch on her skin, every growl against her mouth with the snow flying around outside…it had all driven her deeper into his eyes and his arms and made her burn to feel him deeper inside her.

He released her now, seeming to remember they weren't alone. She buzzed from his heat, even in the freezing weather.

In that moment, after dancing all night at that party, her confidence had shot through the snow-topped roof. *Now or never*, the voice in her head had encouraged, the second she'd stepped into that bathroom and seen him in all his glory, standing like a Viking with the water cascading off his broad shoulders, over his firm abs.

Eventually Javid had appalled her so much that sex with him had come to feel like a performance, a duty—something to get over with as fast as possible, then wash off. Now she knew sex could be so vastly different, it was near impossible not to want it to happen again and again with Gunnar. He touched her in a way that sent her mind spinning away from her and left her body tingling from her fingertips to her toes.

Addictive, she thought, as Demus took off on the track again. Yes, they'd meant to stop after one delicious night, but the sex had been so amazing they'd just continued. Why talk about where it was going, or when it would inevitably have to end? Why not just live in the moment and enjoy it?

Gunnar hadn't been able to resist her either. In the kitchen of his penthouse apartment, on the rug on the floor of her rental, in the bathroom at the hangar before the others had arrived for a rescue mission last night. No one had any idea.

'This is so great for him,' Gunnar enthused, releasing her. 'Do you know what you've done here, Mahlia? It's life-changing.'

'I've hardly done it alone—but, yes, that was my intention.'

Her heart soared with pride at the thrill of his admiring words—she'd never had anything but negative remarks about her bikes from Javid, and now here she was, watching a successful trial in Iceland, next to Gunnar, who loved what she'd achieved. It was as if she was living in a dream.

Gunnar reached out and softly caressed the skin under her hair for a minute. A bolt of desire went straight to her groin.

'I want to pick you up...take you to that bike shed over there...' he growled against her ear, and she grinned against his cheek.

Then, seeing Inka heading back to them, he pulled away as if she was firing darts from her wheelchair, and put enough space for at least three people between them.

Mahlia bristled, catching her breath. He'd been doing that a lot in public these last few days—reaching for her, making her the centre of their own little universe, then dropping her like a hot potato.

She rubbed her hands together against the cold, focused on what Inka was saying as behind them Demus, his biceps strong from using the chair, transferred himself with ease from the e-bike back to his wheelchair. No, there was no way Javid's low opinions of her worth or sexuality would infiltrate this experience. Gunnar wasn't holding back behind closed doors. Whatever his issues were, even if they stemmed from what his ex had done to him, they were not about her.

But it didn't stop him from keeping her in the dark about some things. Like what was going on with his mother. He still hadn't said what was wrong; it was as if he didn't trust her.

He'd gone to see his mother and Demus at various points all week and hadn't told her anything. She was telling herself she didn't care, that having his body next to hers, having him worship her all night was enough, that it wasn't her business to know everything about him. It wasn't as if they were married!

She still had the tiny issue of getting divorced from Javid to deal with. A formal separation wasn't enough, and a divorce was not something she should be hanging around for, waiting for *him* to decide when he'd sign the papers.

Gunnar excused himself to answer a call without looking at her, and she watched the way his face changed as he spoke. He was worried about something else now. She could literally feel his mood doing a one-eighty.

'What's the matter?' she asked when he returned.

Sure enough, he told her it was nothing for her to worry about—as usual. 'I have to go with Demus now. Are you OK getting back to Reykjavik after the trial?'

She looked around her at the four other participants, chatting amongst themselves, waiting to test out the bike. They only had one prototype here, thanks to some mix-up with the order. The rest would be flown out next week. She'd be at least another couple of hours.

'Where do you have to go? To your mother again?'

His lips tightened as he looked to the floor, and she knew she was right.

'Why won't you tell me anything about what's going on? Maybe I can help.'

'You can't help, Mahlia. And the less you know the better, so you'd do best to stay away,' he almost snapped back.

'*Don't* tell me what's best for me, Gunnar.'

She watched him deflate; he knew he'd struck a nerve. *Good.*

'Just let me know you can get back to Reykjavik on your own,' he said, more gently.

Mahlia's heart thumped in her chest. She straightened, forced the annoyance from her face and voice as best she could, even as she simmered. Now her good mood was ruined too.

'Inka and her carer can take me back.'

'Before you head out, can we get a quick team photo?' Inka said now, coming up to them.

Demus agreed good-naturedly, letting his eyes linger on Inka's profile. Inka noticed and smiled behind her hair. Aha! Was that a spark Mahlia sensed between them? Demus and Inka? How cute!

Gunnar just looked agitated. 'What will the photo be used for?' he asked, checking his phone again.

Inka smiled. 'The Wilderness Association's blog.'

'No social media?'

She told him no, not that she was aware of. Demus rolled his eyes, wheeling over to the others for a line-up, muttering something about Gunnar's extreme paranoia.

Mahlia noticed how Gunnar kept his distance from her even more obviously once the cameras were out, and something inside her shifted irrevocably. Even if she wanted to be linked to him, she couldn't trust that he wouldn't always go out of his way not to link himself to her. He was so ashamed of his family he didn't want her associated with any of it—as if she could care less about *them*! When she was with him she thought she was invincible.

Knowing he was troubled by so many things out of her control made her sadder than it should have. All she cared about was him…all she wanted was his strong arms around her. Which, in essence, should have made her want to run a mile already.

So confusing.

He said his goodbyes, and she watched helplessly as he and Demus's carer loaded his brother into the SUV and drove away.

Mahlia did her best to match Inka's enthusiasm for the rest of the participants. So far all the data looked promising when it came to opening an official e-bike wilderness trail in this area. They'd extend the test circuits to other parks as soon as the snow cleared. Of course she was thrilled it was going so well, but the truth was…

Ugh—where was Gunnar going? Where was he now?

His secrecy was affecting her and overshadowing everything she'd worked for. It was getting more frustrating every time he tried to hide what they were doing, every time he tried to hide what he was doing from her. And it wasn't her place to show it! She wasn't bound to him, and nor was he to her.

So much for being in control of a fling, she thought in despair. She'd stupidly thought it would be a simple hook-up… something to pass the time and boost her confidence…toughen her up so she could give Javid the ultimatum she knew she needed to give him—sign the papers or she'd take it to court. But now Gunnar had her heart in a vicelike grip and she was helpless to break out of it.

This was how it had begun before—how she'd wound up losing herself, she thought. She'd had to keep secrets from Javid. About her needs and her hopes and her friends, her longing for children, to be a mother, to be needed. So much of the last seven years had been about her trying to hide her truth, her*self*...

It was all a lie, pretending she was in control of a casual romance here. Already she was letting someone else overwhelm her emotions.

Not smart, Mahlia. It's been one week, and you're already giddy like a fawn over him. This is going to blow up in your face, one way or another. He is not right for you!

Maybe it was time she ended all this and remembered why she was really here...

The rescue vehicle rumbled down the dirt track like a thunderstorm, its tyres cutting through the melting ice, sending plumes of water high into the air. Huge puddles collided with the windows like angry tsunamis, threatening to swallow them up as Erik drove on.

'Read me those co-ordinates,' Erik said from the driver's seat, his eyes on the difficult road.

Gunnar complied. 'We're almost at the point they were headed for—they can't be far.'

The Portuguese hikers, a young husband and wife, had gone out of range since making a distress call, and were now somewhere outside the north-eastern corner of Niflheim Valley. A low fog hung over the mountains, which hadn't been the case when the hikers had set out.

Beside him in the back seat, Mahlia was huddled into her hood, her eyes glazed over in thought. She'd been quiet all morning. He had the distinct impression she was annoyed with him and it was obvious why: he'd clammed up on her, as he had a tendency to do when anyone got too close to his business—but what else was he supposed to do?

Just because they were sleeping together, it didn't mean he was about to drag her headfirst from his bed into the Johansson family circus. Besides, this couldn't go anywhere—not really. Not when she held hopes of starting a family of her own—it would only mean more innocent people to pull down with him.

The image of Ma crying into her dressing gown sleeve wouldn't leave his head. He and Demus had had to sit her down the other day, prise the bottle out of her hands and tell her that if she didn't get professional help and support they wouldn't be available to help her out any more. It broke his heart to think about it, but maybe it would force her to take some damn action.

That photographer had sprung up from nowhere when they were on their way out of her house, too, asking when his father was coming home—as if anyone knew! It happened from time to time. Who could tell when another roach would crawl from the woodwork and plaster another hyped-up story about Ma, or Demus, or one of his 'flings' all over the Internet? This was *exactly* why he and Demus always made their visits to Ma alone.

'Over there!' Mahlia's voice caught him off guard.

'I see it!'

Erik sped up. The car jolted over the deep ruts in the road and her fingers wrapped tighter around her seatbelt, gripping it for dear life, while Gunnar strained his eyes to see what or who they'd spotted.

A lone figure in the distance was scrambling towards them over the snowdrifts. A male, he thought. The husband, whose name was Rodrigo, in a scarlet jacket, flailing his arms in desperation.

Erik veered closer. Mahlia was already out of her seatbelt, poised to open the door. He followed as she burst from the vehicle, snatching up the emergency bag, and he stayed close on her tail as the icy wind whipped through her hair and forced her hood back. He almost yelled at her to let him go first, but knew she'd only ignore him.

Meeting the man halfway, he took in the grizzled beard and haggard face. 'Rodrigo?'

He stumbled as they reached him and collapsed onto the ground. His clothes were soaked through, no doubt from his attempts at wading through the snowbanks to reach help.

'Please...' he begged, his eyes wide with fear.

Mahlia wrapped her own blue scarf around his neck and supported him while he tried to tell them what had happened. Rodrigo's wife Heloísa was back some way, he said. She'd fallen just after she'd started saying she felt sick, and clutching her chest in pain. Panicked, they'd wandered the wrong way back to the path and become lost.

'Don't try and speak any more...just show us where you left her,' Gunnar told him, putting a hand to Mahlia's elbow as the others caught up with a stretcher and blankets.

Words failed Rodrigo as he convulsed with cold and exhaustion. Soon he was bundled up, and they left him with Erik and Ásta, walking on the way he'd pointed.

Gunnar pulled out his GPS. They ventured deeper into the Niflheim Valley in silence. The snow was coming down through the fog now, thick and treacherous. Icy winds tore at their clothes. But Mahlia trudged on as if he wasn't even there, her face a picture of determination.

He caught her up. 'I know you're mad at me,' he shouted over the wind.

She pursed her lips, but didn't look at him.

'Mahlia,' he persisted. 'You've barely said two words to me for two days!'

'We're not talking about this now.'

'Look, I didn't mean to shut you out,' he continued earnestly as she forged ahead. 'That's the last thing I want to do. There are just...things you don't understand.'

'I'll tell you what I *do* understand,' she said, stopping short in front of him.

Her eyes were gleaming with an unnerving coldness he wasn't used to. It threw him off guard.

'What we've been doing...we shouldn't have been doing,' she said. 'It was a stupid mistake. You're not good for me, Gunnar. You were totally right about that. And I'm still married.'

It was all he could do not to laugh. 'What are you doing about that, by the way? Have you spoken to him yet? Did you tell him you'll drag his backside through the courts if he doesn't sign the papers?'

She huffed air through her nostrils, gritted her teeth, and he knew the answer. She'd avoided every call he'd seen come in from the guy since they'd met.

'You don't want to talk to him at all? In case he gets an actual hold on you again? In case he makes you go running back to him? Is that it?'

'Give me some credit, Gunnar. I'm not ever going back to him.'

She said it with her brows furrowed and her eyes averted, and he balled his fists. He'd avoided butting in on this topic so far, but now he couldn't hold it in. Her being married was no excuse to end whatever it was they'd kept on doing since that night in Hvítaeyri. She hadn't exactly been acting like someone's wife in *his* bedroom for the last week.

'Then why don't you just have the lawyers do their thing and block his number? Get him out of your life for good?'

'Stop trying to...'

'Trying to *what*, Mahlia?'

'Control what I do!' she spat. 'It's none of your business. We're done, Gunnar.'

He held his hands in the air, forcing his mouth to stay shut as anger pulsed between them.

Done. OK.

This was his fault; he'd kept his business private for her own good, kept them a secret, made sure the whole thing with them existed on *his* terms. That had pushed her buttons, and he could feel the invisible shackles her ex still had her in stretching all the way here from New Zealand. If he ever met this Javid idiot he'd have a real problem not rearranging his face. She might not want to go back to him, but if she didn't cut ties soon...

Not that he should do anything at all—not when he was no more right for her than Javid. She should find someone who wanted the same things she did, he reminded himself. A family!

He spotted something over her shoulder now: a figure in the distance, slumped on the ground, half hidden under some kind of makeshift canopy.

Mahlia followed his gaze. 'Heloísa!'

She sped ahead of him, trudging through the thick, knee-high drifts to reach her. They both dropped down at her side beneath the waterproof sheet. It was propped up with branches, barely functional against the wind and snow. Gunnar took in her face, pale and waxen, as Mahlia pulled a bottle from the bag.

'Heloísa, can you hear us?'

The blonde woman's eyes were closed tightly against the cold. Gunnar feared the worst as he radioed Erik and told him where to drive. But then, with a groan, her eyelids fluttered open.

Thank you, God.

They propped her up against them under a blanket and she

mumbled incoherently. Mahlia urged her to sip some warm water from her canteen.

'Erik's on the way,' he told Mahlia, leaning in closer, registering the woman's shortness of breath, the redness in and around her eyes. This wasn't hypothermia. This was something he recognised.

'What is it?' Mahlia demanded, her voice low.

'Check her blood pressure,' he said, as Erik's voice sounded out again on the radio.

The snowbanks they'd climbed across were pretty high, but they'd do their best to get the vehicle through. Heloísa's pulse was weak and erratic, her blood pressure dangerously low.

'I think it could be her kidneys,' he said, dread seeping deeper into his pores.

'How do you know?' Mahlia took off her coat and wrapped it tightly around the woman's shoulders, holding her against herself.

'Experience,' he said, immediately shrugging his own jacket off and wrapping it around Mahlia. She almost refused it, but then clearly thought better of it, wrapping half of it around their survivor while he checked Heloísa. Both her legs and ankles were puffy and swollen—a sure sign that he was right.

'Oh…' Mahlia said, pursing her lips again. 'Sometimes I forget what you actually do for a living when you're not doing this.'

The wind howled like a pack of wolves as he radioed Erik again, shaking the canvas shelter with such force he thought it might rip apart. Sliding one arm around Heloísa and the other around Mahlia, he turned his back to the opening, taking the full brunt of the wind, praying Erik wasn't getting the wheels stuck in the drifts.

Mahlia leaned further into him, soothing Heloísa, who was conscious but fading fast. 'Help is coming…stay with us,' she told her. 'Your husband is fine. He's on his way to the hospital already.' Mahlia offered her more warm water, monitoring her pulse, doing her best to keep her calm.

Gunnar breathed in her damp, snowy hair and all the words he wished he could say to her built up like an army in his head while the radio stayed eerily quiet. So she was calling it off, declaring it all a mistake. He should fight for her, tell her this past week had meant more than anything had meant to him in a long, long time… And maybe he would, if he didn't keep remembering the look that had swept over her face when she'd told him she'd do anything to start a family.

Mahlia was the kind of woman he hadn't even known he needed. But he couldn't give her what *she* needed or wanted. Definitely *not* kids.

'Gunnar!'

He swung around at Erik's voice. The SAR truck's tyres were crunching on the gravel, spinning in the snow. Another vehicle had sped Rodrigo to safety, and they'd come back for them. But they didn't have long before they risked getting stuck again.

He stood, telling Mahlia to stay sheltered. Already her lips were as pale as Elioze's.

'Did you call for the chopper? Could you reach Sven?' Erik shouted.

'We might not have enough time to drive her out,' Mahlia called. 'Gunnar thinks it could be acute kidney failure. I have to say he could be right.'

'We need to get her to the hospital fast,' Gunnar confirmed, meeting her eyes. All the anger he'd seen there earlier had dissipated. They were a team. For now. 'Over land won't be fast enough.'

'Sven's on his way,' Erik told them.

Sure enough, in less than two minutes the powerful beat of

the rotors filled the air, deafening them, and then the winch was being lowered precariously from the hovering chopper. With a drumming heart he worked with Mahlia and Erik to attach first Heloísa, then himself and Mahlia, so they could leave their remote perch and be lifted up into the safety of the chopper.

The snow and wind had eased enough for them to fly. Hopefully they'd done enough to get Heloísa to the medical care she needed, he thought, helping Mahlia attach a drip.

But knowing things were over with her as fast as they'd started was still hitting him repeatedly, like a ton of bricks to his brain. It didn't feel right. But what could he do? It was just the way it had to be.

Gunnar felt as if he had his heart in his throat the whole way to Reykjavik.

CHAPTER TEN

'YOU'RE GOING TO be fine, Heloísa,' Mahlia said, touching a hand to the woman's arm around the tubes.

Heloísa smiled warmly. She looked exhausted, but her cheeks had more colour in them than they'd had a couple of hours ago, when they'd rushed her through the hospital doors. The intensive care unit was busier than she'd ever seen it, but the staff had wasted no time with tests and dialysis and now she was resting in a private room.

'I'm so grateful that you and Dr Johansson found me. One of the nurses said he's famous? She said that most people get the man all wrong. What did she mean?'

Mahlia bit down on her lip. Of course a tourist from Portugal probably knew nothing about Gunnar's past. And he would like it to stay that way, she thought.

They weren't exactly in a great place, the two of them, seeing as she'd pushed him so far away from her. she might as well have shoved him off a cliff without a harness. But her heart still beat wildly, just at seeing him through the glass. He was waiting for her outside, talking on the phone.

'His family's a little messed up, that's all. It has nothing to do with him.'

'Are you…you know…together?' Heloísa asked curiously.

It was all she could do to stop her chin wobbling as she

shook her head, but Heloísa had closed her eyes anyway, exhaustion taking over.

Mahlia left her to rest and closed the door softly behind her.

'I think if you hadn't seen the signs that something was wrong with her kidneys it would have been a different story,' she said, noting the tell-tale crease between Gunnar's eyebrows.

He shoved his phone back in his pocket quickly as she approached. She wouldn't even ask what was up, she decided. It would only annoy her more when he refused to tell her, and his secrecy wasn't her problem any more.

'Gisli,' he said quietly, motioning her to follow him down the corridor.

'Sorry?'

'That was him—messaging about tonight.'

Mahlia cursed under her breath. She'd clean forgotten they'd agreed to go for dinner at Gisli and Leo's place. The sweet couple wanted to thank them both for rescuing Leo and Katla, and they'd agreed on tonight when she'd still been deep in her infatuation bubble. They'd messaged them together, from Gunnar's bed—somewhere she would never be again, she reminded herself as tingles of desire sprang up on her skin regardless.

She already felt bad for accusing him of trying to control her. She'd panicked under his scrutiny, embarrassed that he'd called her out on the whole Javid thing. Gunnar was right: she *was* too much of a coward to face her ex, in case he doled out more emotional blackmail and made her hate herself all over again for giving in and allowing him more time with the divorce papers.

But there were so many reasons why freedom, time and having a clear mind were better for her right now than being Gunnar's secret fling. So many reasons why she'd ended it. It was just difficult to remember them all when she was next to him, and he was being so… *Gunnar*.

'I can always cancel,' he offered, holding the door open.

She stepped outside ahead of him. The sky was clear, littered with stars now. Sighing, she crossed her arms around herself and turned to him, wishing she wasn't so magnetically drawn to him that it was an act of physical restraint between her mind and her limbs not to reach for him and tell him she'd changed her mind.

'Maybe that would be best,' she forced herself to say.

Her heart fluttered in her chest as she looked up at him, thinking how her conflicting interests were probably written all over her face.

'It *would* be best,' he agreed, his steel-blue eyes holding hers like anchors. 'But Gisli said they've got the huskies out now. The sled will be waiting for us in an hour.'

Mahlia felt her eyes grow wide. For a second she couldn't speak.

Huskies?

'Doctors! I'm so happy you could make it!' Gisli, in his puffy blue ski jacket, was a ball of warm, welcoming energy as they exited Gunnar's car in the gravel car park. He lunged at them with hugs and air kisses before ushering them beyond the gate to the edge of a nature trail.

Mahlia couldn't help but gasp and laugh in awe.

Eight wide-eyed huskies barked and pawed at the snow with enthusiasm as they approached the red-and-blue-painted wooden sled. The seats were draped with sheepskin blankets that almost swallowed her in their soft white fluffiness as she sat down, taking another from Gisli to put over her lap.

'It's big enough to share,' he said, and grinned as Gunnar was made to squish in close beside her.

Before she could argue he'd tucked the blanket around them both and handed them a hip flask of moonshine each. She tucked hers away as soon as he wasn't looking. It wouldn't do to be rude, but she was *not* drinking that stuff.

'We could have taken the car, but this is more fun, no?' He winked at them, taking a seat at the front. He told them to enjoy the ride. It would be at least an hour and a half.

In seconds, they were speeding away down the small winding road and up the trail into the mountains. Mahlia couldn't help the silly grin that spread across her face as the sled jostled and shook and the pine trees whipped by in a blur of green against the snowy banks. The night sky above was an inky black canvas, lit up with stars, giving just enough light for Gisli and the dogs to navigate the way. Her heart was racing in excitement; she had never done *anything* like this.

'Gisli and Leo run a husky sled retreat,' Gunnar explained in her ear, sending tingles straight through her veins.

She realised he'd been staring at her, probably thinking she was grinning like an idiot.

'Usually this is reserved for tourists.'

'Well, I guess I am a tourist,' she said, tucking her hair back self-consciously just as the sled flew over a rock and almost sent them flying.

Her hand flew to Gunnar's knee impulsively and he pressed a firm hand over hers, under the blanket. Before she could even think, she was holding his hand. Neither of them let go.

The dogs wound expertly across frozen lakes and rivers, past chunky-legged Icelandic horses and through snow-covered pine forests. She pretended to sip from her flask in silence, until Gisli stopped the dogs in the middle of an open meadow. She didn't have to ask why. The northern lights were dancing joyously above them in greens, pinks and purples, as if an artist had spilt an entire paint box across the sky. The only sound was the dogs' panting and the whoosh of wind in the branches as they watched the impossible beauty of this moving picture amongst the stars.

Amazing!

When she turned to Gunnar in awe, sucking in the icy, crisp air, perfumed with pine, the aurora shone back at her from his eyes. It sent a flood of something so pure and magical through her bloodstream she almost felt as if she was floating. This moment was perfection.

'You know, apart from when I saw you playing that guitar, I don't think you've ever looked as radiant as you do now,' he told her, his grip on her hand tightening.

His voice was anguished, and full of longing, and Mahlia held her breath, feeling her stomach twist into knots as she watched the emotions play across his face. He wanted to kiss her. And she wanted nothing more than to kiss him, too. Every fibre of her body was telling her to make the move as desire coiled deep inside her, but no… Logic *must* prevail. If she acted on her impulses now, when would she stop?

'Stop…' she whispered, closing her eyes and letting go of his hand. 'I told you…'

'I know, I know,' he growled from somewhere deep in his throat.

And her heart thrummed in pain as she felt him ball his fist at his side against her thigh.

The dinner plates were already on the table when Leo welcomed them all inside to the warmth. She was pleased to see he was walking just fine after his accident.

Every inch of the cosy lodge seemed to have been delicately crafted in a classic Swedish style, from the exposed logs on the walls to the plush sheepskin rugs. In one corner an enormous fireplace roared, its heat inviting Mahlia closer as she looked around—everywhere but at Gunnar. That almost-kiss in the sled was still playing on her mind, but she hadn't caved. She could be proud of herself for that, at least.

Katla padded up to give them a good sniff, wagging her tail, and Gunnar got down on his haunches to pet her. Damn him for looking so handsome and sexy stroking a dog…was there anything that *didn't* make him look good?

Mahlia gave him a wide berth as she walked around him to where Leo was stirring something in a cast iron cauldron on the open fire. 'It smells so good,' she told him, taking a lungful of the delicious aroma.

'Reindeer stew, like Gisli promised.' He smiled. 'We always cook it like this for our guests. Take a seat!'

Mahlia's phone pinged just as she was about to sit at the table. She didn't miss Gunnar's eyes on her as she pulled it out. He probably thought it was Javid, and so did she for a moment.

'It's Inka,' she announced, scanning the message. 'The rest of the prototypes have arrived. She's just signed for them, before she goes out to meet Demus in Reykjavik.'

'Demus?' Gunnar cocked an eyebrow.

Mahlia couldn't help smiling as he peered over her shoulder at the message. 'I think she's trying to tell us she's going on a date with your brother. You know, I could tell they had chemistry the other day! I think that's so great—good for them.'

Gunnar just nodded thoughtfully. She could see he was stewing more than the reindeer. 'He kept that one a secret,' he said after a moment, scratching his chin and pulling out his phone as if a confirmation from Demus might pop up, telling him about his date.

'He's not the only one who's good at keeping secrets,' she quipped, before she could stop herself.

He scowled darkly as he took a seat opposite her at the table. Thankfully any planned retort was shut down as Leo and Gisli placed steaming bowls of stew in front of them and launched into a conversation about the nice Australian tourists who'd left them some biscuits called Tim Tams after their five-star husky sledding holiday with them.

She liked this couple a lot, thought Mahlia as they ate and talked, and the dogs barked occasionally outside. If they were picking up on any tension between her and Gunnar they weren't saying so.

But she'd have to talk to him eventually, she thought, feeling hot at the idea. They hadn't exactly had closure...

Sometime later, over a dessert of hot apple strudel, which Mahlia had to admit was just as good as the reindeer stew, Gisli asked if she'd consider sending some of her prototypes to them, for their guests. She'd told them about the venture over dinner, and he'd said he'd heard about it. Everyone knew everyone here, after all.

'We need to test them properly first,' she told him. 'But you can look at some when we're certain the design is ready.'

'I think some of our less mobile guests would enjoy that,' he said thoughtfully. 'They like riding the sled, so why not taking the trails independently too? It would open up a lot more opportunities for us and them. You know, it's great to see your brother getting involved, too, Dr Johansson. He's really quite the ambassador already.'

Mahlia felt her breath catch as Gunnar put his fork down. She hadn't mentioned Demus at all. Then Gisli pulled his phone out, showing them the team photo that had been taken for the website that day. It had somehow made it onto social media anyway—one of the other participants on the trial must have reposted it.

She waited nervously for Gunnar's reaction, but he met her eyes as if grounding himself and sat back in his seat, drumming his fingers on the table. Maybe he was starting to realise it wasn't such a big deal, she thought hopefully. The Johanssons were out and about, living their 'normal' lives just like everyone else. The world hadn't ended, had it?

Eventually, Gisli got to his feet. She thought he was going to offer to drive them back, and went to find her jacket, yawning behind her hand.

But he said, 'Are you guys ready to see your room?'

Mahlia's stomach dropped. Gunnar looked at her in surprise. They were expected to stay over? She was totally unprepared for this, but they were so far off the grid at this tourist resort she probably should have expected it.

'Everything you might need is in there. And on a night like this,' Gisli continued, leading them to the door, 'I think you'll *really* appreciate the ceiling.'

CHAPTER ELEVEN

BEHIND THE LODGE, in the centre of the camp, connected by a series of wooden walkways that criss-crossed the premises like a lattice, were a series of stunning, sleek, modern tepees that took Mahlia's breath away. Each one seemed to be equipped with its own layer of glass panels on top, held firmly in place by steel frames and bolted to the ground.

Gisli unzipped one, beckoning them inside, and she pressed a hand to her mouth in shock. The glass ceiling acted as a viewing panel above them, perfect for stargazers and for watching the northern lights from the bed. The huge, comfy-looking king-sized bed was complete with even more sheep-skin blankets. A small wood-burning fire was already blazing behind a glass door.

'This is incredible!' Mahlia exclaimed.

Gunnar looked embarrassed, at best.

'The others are already booked, for guests who'll arrive early tomorrow, but I figured you wouldn't mind sharing this one.'

Gisli winked at her and she felt her cheeks flame. So the couple had clearly picked up on *something* between them, de-spite their recent rift. Was it that obvious?

'This will be fine. More than fine—thank you,' she said quickly, dropping to the bed.

Gisli bade them goodnight and zipped up the canvas door

behind him. The silence was overwhelming, but the northern lights had come out to play again. She'd focus on that, she thought, while Gunnar slept on the... On the what? There was no couch here—just the rugs on the floor.

'Sorry about this. I didn't even think...' he started, walking around the bed, inspecting the wooden dresser, the ornate lamp, the tiny attached bathroom.

'It's not your fault,' she said, taking off her shoes, watching the way his muscled frame cast long, slender shadows across the bed in the firelight. 'This *is* incredible. Look at the lights. I could get never get tired of those monsters coming at me.'

Gunnar huffed a small laugh, shrugged off his boots and climbed onto the bed beside her, thumping an overly soft pillow into shape before putting his head on it. Her heart went wild at his proximity, but she kept to her side, her pillow, and focused her eyes on the blackness of the sky, studded with stars and decorated with dancing green swirls.

'I'm not like him, you know,' Gunnar said suddenly, through the silence. 'Your ex. I would *never* try and control you...not intentionally.'

'I know. I'm sorry I said that to you earlier,' she said, and sighed.

He sniffed, fixing his own eyes on the ceiling. 'And as for my secrets... I didn't want you getting involved in what's going on with my mother, but I shouldn't have shut you out completely. That wasn't fair.'

Her body tensed. She continued to watch the lights move through the glass roof. They weren't a couple any more—if they ever had been to begin with. She should just accept his apology and move on, take this as closure. But she wanted to know what was causing this pain to radiate from his every pore. So she asked him what was going on *really*.

His voice was so sorrowful as he answered that she found

her eyes straining against tears, and her chest felt so tight she thought she might burst. Finally, as if unplugging a valve that had been bursting to be free, Gunnar told her exactly how lost and sick his mother really was—mind, body and soul. How he and Demus had tried to get her help for years, but she'd kept on refusing, waiting for her husband to come back for her. He told her how it had torn him up, wanting to protect her but only creating more problems for himself and Demus as he did so—as if that was *his* fault.

She told him that it wasn't, and confided in him about her own struggles. How her mother's depression had spiralled several years ago, after her sister had died—Mahlia's auntie Jazz—and how not even her father had been able to bring her out of it. They'd started recommending that Mahlia not visit them on weekends like she'd used to, which had only pushed her even further into the grip of Javid's toxic control.

Then Gunnar opened up about the reporters who liked to follow them and hang around his mother's house, waiting for something juicy to boost their click rates.

'I didn't want this to end up with everyone talking about *you*,' he said. 'I don't think I could handle someone else just...'

'Leaving you because of your family? I know.'

She reached for his hand despite herself, feeling closer to him than ever after what he'd just confided. As if she'd ever leave him because of anything someone else had done.

But it was more than that with her—it was the fear of someone leaving her, if she ever decided to trust a man enough to let one in again. The fear of losing herself.

'Look, Demus is fine, isn't he?' she continued. 'No one thinks anything's wrong with him being involved with the bikes or Inka. And I'm not like your ex, either. You are the man I...' She tailed off, surprised and slightly embarrassed by what she'd been about to say. 'You've come to be really important to me.'

Composing herself, she sat up, hugging her knees.

'Gunnar, it's just… I came here to be *me* for once. Not to—'

'I know. And I don't want to stand in your way.'

She let out a long sigh that turned into a groan, pressing her palms to her eyes. 'The funny thing is, I've never felt more *me* than I do in the moments when I'm with you. And that's a little scary. I have a whole bunch of what-ifs going round in my head. What if Javid doesn't let me go…?'

He sat up, matching her stance, arms around his knees. 'You're in control of that outcome, Mahlia. Only you.'

She swallowed tightly, wanting to be honest. 'But there's more…about you…going round and round and round. *What if he likes me? What if he doesn't? What if I fall in love and then…?*'

'What if he doesn't want kids?' Gunnar finished, making her turn to him.

'Kids?'

'You said you wanted them someday. I don't, by the way. I don't want any children—ever.'

Mahlia swallowed, wishing her heart hadn't just raced like a freight train to her frontal lobe, screeching a warning at her. 'You don't?' she managed, trying to hide her disappointment.

'It wouldn't be fair…' He sighed. 'All things considered.'

All things considered?

She frowned at him. 'Because you're ashamed of your name, you mean? Your name is something any child should grow up to be proud of, Gunnar.'

'Maybe *you* think so,' he muttered.

'A lot of people think so. Why else would we be here? Look at where we are now because of you. You help people, Gunnar. I don't think I've met anyone more impressive, actually. Well, maybe your brother. He's pretty cool...'

He cut her off with a soft groan. His warm hand swept across the curve of her face, cupping her chin gently before he pressed his lips to hers, testing her.

Mahlia looped her arms around him. Resistance to his kisses was futile. She knew she should resist... She needed things in the future that he couldn't give her...unless...unless just having him, and *this*, was enough?

It felt like enough right now.

Laying her down again gently against the sheepskin, Gunnar traced his hands along her body, exploring the contours of her neck and shoulders, kissing her with a concentrated intensity and a connection to her soul that threw all their previous encounters into shadow.

'I'll stop if you want me to,' he said, hovering over her on his forearms.

And the hunger in his eyes told her how hard he would find that. As hard as she would.

The aurora played above them, giving him an emerald halo, and she knew it was pointless even trying to deny herself or him—even if this wasn't something that could ever last.

'No, don't stop,' she whispered, and pulled him back to her lips.

She surrendered completely into a passionate kiss, shuddering as his fingertips ran lightly over her collarbone, before travelling softly down the line of her spine, feeling their way across every vertebra, making her skin prickle in pleasure.

How did he do this to her?

Tingles took over her flesh as he caressed her curves, and when he moved even lower, lingering over the swell of her hips and the smooth planes of her thighs, she arched into him with a ragged sigh, opening herself further to him. Whatever he wanted to do, she'd reciprocate. She was undeniably his in this moment...beyond the point of no return. His lips trailed blissfully behind his fingertips as they travelled, exploring every inch of her body as she trembled.

'Gunnar...' she moaned, wiping at her eyes, clutching fistfuls of his hair.

So this was what it was like to be completely overwhelmed by a million sensations... The heat of their desire grew like a wildfire, consuming them both in its intensity until they were making love—real love, she realised, as they moved as one in a hot jumble of blankets. This was like nothing else she had ever experienced. In this moment, nothing else mattered but them.

When the night had passed in a blur of lovemaking, and the faint morning sun was peering through the glass roof, Mahlia awoke to find Gunnar gone. A faint shuffling sound outside had her pulling on a robe and opening the canvas door.

'Good morning.'

She blinked as Gunnar held out a hand, and she stepped from the tepee, hardly believing her eyes. Pancakes, poached eggs and bacon, freshly baked pastries and a pot of tea with honey were waiting on a little terrace table under a giant heat lamp. He pulled out a chair for her, poured her tea, and she marvelled at how good he looked, considering they'd barely slept.

The mountains glistened with snow beyond the pine trees as they ate, touching feet under the table, and the sound of the dogs fussing around the guesthouse was strangely calming.

'Gisli will drive us back when we're ready,' he said.

'I don't want to go back. Can we just stay here for ever?' she pleaded, noticing how the napkins were embroidered with little husky dogs. She felt as if she was in a dream. 'Last night was amazing...'

'Thank you for listening,' he said, taking her hand across the table. 'I haven't spoken to anyone like that for—well, *ever*.'

'Your mother's going to be OK,' she told him, swallowing back a flock of butterflies. 'So is Demus, and so are you.'

'I hope you're right,' he said, running a thumb across her knuckles. 'I made the call this morning. We're taking her to the Five Lakes Rehabilitation Centre on Saturday. Whether she wants to go or not.'

Mahlia told him that she'd be there; she'd go with him if he wanted. He didn't reply, which set her on edge a moment, before she realised he'd opened up more to her than he ever had before last night, and that was a pretty big deal for him—especially as she was still married, not available, and wholly unsuitable, really, if he didn't want children...

Oh, my God, stop, Mahlia! Just be happy for him!

She had helped him realise he didn't have to go through everything alone—that he could involve people in his life without fearing they'd run a mile if things got shaky.

Maybe he'd meet someone else after she'd gone home to New Zealand, she thought suddenly, as he talked about the rehabilitation centre's facilities and poured her more tea. He would meet someone who belonged here, not halfway across the world. Someone who didn't want to bring children into a relationship.

Ugh. Why were her stupid thoughts ruining the moment again? Could she not just enjoy this little fantasy of being treated well and appreciated while it lasted?

Gunnar stood and pulled her to her feet, kissing her softly, but with so much heart she wanted to drag him right back to bed. In fact she might have done so, if her phone hadn't started to ring with the dreaded ringtone she'd reserved for Javid.

She pulled away gently, resting her head on his shoulder with a sigh.

'That's him, isn't it?' Gunnar said into her neck, and she nodded.

He took her shoulders now, making her look at him. 'Answer it,' he said.

She sucked in a breath, searching his blue eyes. 'And say what? That I spent the night in a tepee at a husky retreat, having crazy sex with my winchman under the northern lights?'

'Sure—why not? And put him on speakerphone.'

She snorted with horror. 'Gunnar! No!'

Frustration glimmered in his eyes. 'The longer you don't answer, the longer you're going to torture yourself, wondering what he wants.'

'I know what he wants. He wants to remind me how good we were together. How there's no one for me except him.'

'So tell him he's wrong.'

'I will. I just...'

He stepped back from her, starting to gather up the cups and plates, and she cursed herself under her breath. He was biting back his words in case she accused him of trying to control her actions again. They'd just gone round in a circle... Stupid.

Stupid.

Ramming her hands through her hair, she reached for her phone, let her finger hover over the answer button. She should just pick up. Gunnar was right—this was insane!

Pick up, Mahlia! Tell Javid you've had enough. Tell him if he doesn't sign the papers by the end of the day, you'll have a court summons on his doorstep by next week.

That was what she should do. That was what she'd imagined saying to him so many times. Yet her finger still wouldn't swipe. Just seeing his name sent waves of dread so intense through her body she needed to sit down. If she answered, he'd steal back the power she'd regained. He'd make everything she'd done here, away from him, smaller, less important. He'd make it all about him and leave her feeling worse, like he always did.

No one understood what it was like, living every moment in fear of losing yourself, having your autonomy pulled out from underneath you and stomped on. It wasn't something you could just wish away and make disappear. Seven years... Seven years had a lasting effect—like a ripple through everything she did. And now she was an incorrigible coward on top.

But it was almost as if Javid knew...as if he'd *sensed* what she was doing and was hellbent on ruining her high. She could almost picture him storming into the tepee, berating her, telling her she looked ridiculous, that no man would put up with her for long, that she'd do better just coming home to him. Either that or he'd cry again. Beg again.

The phone rang and rang until she flicked it onto silent mode. Still, it rang.

Coward, the voice in her head accused, when eventually he gave up.

Turning around with a sigh of relief, she realised Gunnar was standing in the doorway, watching her.

'We should go,' he said gruffly, grabbing up his jacket.

CHAPTER TWELVE

GUNNAR WATCHED DEMUS take another corner on the trail up ahead, the sunshine blazing off the pristine e-bike as he and three more trial participants zoomed at full speed. The snow was finally clearing, with fewer storms per day, so for the last few days, with only one SAR call-out to deal with, they'd been here every afternoon, and Mahlia was in her element.

Everyone wanted a piece of her and her ideas, it seemed. From the press to the Wilderness Association, to the CEO of the Icelandic Disability Alliance. Gunnar had kept his distance from the cameras. But with her, for the first time in his life, he wasn't the first person people looked at when they walked into a room.

'Demus looks so happy,' Mahlia said now, as Inka steered up to their side, grinning broadly. 'And I'm sure you have something to do with that smile on his face,' she teased her friend.

Inka grinned behind her blonde hair. He noticed the way both women shot him a querying look, but he pretended not to see. The jury was still out on what to make of this blossoming relationship, and he was trying not to let his fierce protection of Demus cloud his views. Maybe he was also a little jealous…

'These prototypes are incredible, Mahlia,' Inka said. 'We had another company asking when they can buy them this morning.'

'I need to work on securing a manufacturer in Europe,'

Mahlia told her thoughtfully, and Gunnar listened as they discussed the bikes, his eyes never leaving his brother.

Demus did look happy. Deliriously happy. To be riding the bike, to be in control, to be dating a great woman who understood his struggles. He deserved it, Gunnar thought. He couldn't picture himself like that—being comfortable, carefree, happy, without the gnawing feeling that it was all about to fall apart for one reason or another. These calls from Mahlia's ex weren't helping...

Still, despite his head and his heart telling him it was a bad idea to take this further, to involve her in his life, she'd wriggled into his heart enough for him to break down a few walls in front of her. Enough for her to forget she'd tried to end things and now had offered to come with him and Demus to his mother's house this afternoon. Enough for him to go along with it all.

He'd almost refused to let her come, point-blank, several times, but it *had* felt good opening up to someone...to feel that maybe he didn't have to do everything alone.

Even if she wanted a life he couldn't give her.

Even if she was still bound to her ex, and on the verge of going back to New Zealand.

Even if she might realise at any minute that being caught on camera with him in any precarious situation would get her a very different kind of publicity from that surrounding these e-bikes.

Who was he to deny her something she wanted to do for him? She'd been repressed enough, and he was not about to come off as a control freak.

'Are you worried about this afternoon?' Mahlia whispered now, touching his shoulder.

She must have seen the look on his face. Instinctively he whipped his head around to look for cameras, but all the photographers had taken their shots of the bikes already and were long gone. He willed himself to relax...not to step away from her.

'A little,' he confessed, surprising himself by admitting his emotions.

Ma didn't know yet, but they were about to ruin her day. The Five Lakes Rehabilitation Centre was expecting them.

Pulling up around the corner from the house, Gunnar found his hands gripping the steering wheel till his knuckles were white.

'Where are they?' Demus asked from the back seat, checking his phone. 'They were meant to...'

'I think this is them,' Mahlia said, one hand on the door.

Sure enough, a van was pulling up behind them—away from the house, as he'd instructed, so Ma couldn't anticipate their arrival and try to run away.

Two male staff members from Five Lakes exited the vehicle in their off-white uniforms and jackets and, to his surprise, Mahlia got out to meet them with him, helping him get Demus's wheelchair unloaded in record time.

Just having her here, he realised, was giving him strength and courage. Not that he was calm—not by a long shot! His heart was pounding a million miles an hour as they followed the staff up the driveway and rang the bell. Next door, the curtains twitched, and Demus waved at their elderly female neighbour. Mrs Sigurðsson loathed them all. Mahlia too offered a wave, at which the old woman scowled and drew the curtains across roughly.

'Who is it?' came his mother's voice from behind the shiny black door.

Gunnar swallowed the golf ball in his throat, glancing behind them for any lurking opportunist photographers.

'Mrs Johansson, we're here to help you,' one of the staff said in Icelandic as the door opened slowly.

Ma peered out, her red, bloated face and bloodshot eyes telling them all she'd been on the bottle today already—probably since the minute she'd woken up.

There was a crash of glass shattering on the floor before Ma tried to slam the door shut again, crying, *'No!'*

Demus wheeled his chair into the doorway, forcing it to stay open.

'Ma, you have to go with them,' Gunnar said kindly but firmly, his boots crunching on the broken glass as Mahlia stepped inside with him.

Ma stumbled up the stairs, unsteady on her feet, 'I should... I should pack then.' He and Mahlia ran after her, would she really pack, or would she try to escape through a window?. 'I'll pack an overnight bag,' she slurred, and his heart ached as it became clear his mother was deeply uncomfortable, even in her intoxication, and obviously in denial.

Mahlia was strong. 'It's going to be OK,' she said gently to his mother.

'Well, where are we going, exactly?'

'Trust us, Ma,' he soothed, struggling not to let his voice crack.

'Well, how long will I be gone for? I can't be gone too long, you know that.'

Gunnar told her where she was going, and said they weren't sure how long for yet. 'It's for your own good, Ma. I'm sorry. It's the best thing to do to keep you safe.'

'Everyone just wants you to get better,' Mahlia said now.

Gunnar knew she didn't need to know Icelandic to see that his mother was stuttering every excuse she could think of now, as to why she didn't need to go for longer than one night.

'And who are *you*?' Ma asked, pulling up short in front of Mahlia.

'She's with Gunnar, Ma. Don't make a scene, please,' Demus said coolly.

The Five Lakes staff soon had her out through the door, explaining gently and calmly again where they were taking her, saying that everything was arranged.

'I packed her a bag a few days ago,' Demus told them. 'I had my carer leave it on top of the wardrobe in her bedroom.'

'I'll get it.' Mahlia was already hurrying up the stairs.

Dread pooled in Gunnar's stomach as he followed after her. *Oh, God, no.* He could only imagine the state of it up there...

'Which one is her room?' she asked, stopping on the landing. The open doorway to the left and the revealing stench of stale alcohol sent her forward. She stepped over a pile of clothes and stopped short in the dank, dark room, pressing a hand to her mouth at the sight.

The room was a mess, the bed unmade, the walls streaked with spilt red wine and candle wax. Clothes, empty bottles and takeaway containers were strewn haphazardly across the floor. The musty smell of years of alcohol consumption lingered in the air, as if it had soaked into the very fabric of the house he and Demus had used to play in. This place held so many happy memories, but now, in this sad, sorrowful room, every single one of them felt like a lie.

Mahlia took a few steps further in, and he saw her mouth turning down in dismay as she took in the curtains, drawn tight over sash windows that hadn't been opened in months. A small bedside table was cluttered with bottles and glasses, and the ashtray overflowing on top of it made him wince. Ma clearly smoked in bed every day. It was worse than he'd thought. She'd done her best to hide the extent of her troubles when she'd known people were coming, but alone, she was…broken.

A wooden wardrobe stood in one corner, its doors wide open, revealing more discarded clothes inside. Mahlia reached up high, locating Ma's bag.

'Is this it?'

She turned to him with it. Then, taking one look at his face, she dropped it immediately and crossed to him, wrapping her arms tight around his middle.

Gunnar realised he'd been watching her taking it all in through clouded eyes, his fists clenched in his hair as he stood in the doorway. Only now, in her arms, did he blink the tears free. Shame and embarrassment burned his cheeks as he wiped them away quickly. He itched to pull away from her, to create as much distance as possible before she did it first—because surely she would leave him after this? How could she not? But at the same time he never wanted her to let go.

She held him till Demus called out from downstairs. 'Did you guys find it?'

'Coming!' Mahlia called back. 'This must be so hard for you,' she whispered, caressing his cheek. Her face was contorted in sympathy. 'Are you OK?'

'I'm just sorry you have to see this,' he croaked, picking up the bag with shaking hands.

He couldn't even look her in the eye right now. Instead he muttered another apology for having exposed her to this, the full extent of the chaos-tinged mess that was his reality, and thought that this was yet another reminder of why bringing children into his world would be a very bad idea.

They followed the van under an ever-darkening sky, and behind the wheel Gunnar tried not to imagine how terrified Ma must be, strapped in there with the staff.

'She's going to be fine…you've done the right thing,' Mahlia assured him softly.

He glanced over at her in the passenger seat. She'd been so understanding and supportive throughout this whole ordeal. She'd never know what that meant to him. But *was* he doing the right thing with Ma? With her?

His chest felt like a lead weight.

She seemed to sense his consternation and gave his hand a reassuring squeeze. Gunnar took a deep breath, steeling himself for the rehab clinic: the doctors, nurses and social workers who would all swarm around Ma soon enough. They'd figure out the best way to help her get better—he had to believe that. But what if it was too late? What if none of them—none of this—was able to make a difference?

A motorbike appeared ahead, its headlights swerving erratically. Mahlia gasped and gripped the door. 'He has a camera!'

She whipped her head around as the bike fell in behind them, then sped up again. There were two people on it: a rider in leathers, wearing a black helmet, his face obscured by its tinted visor, and a smaller figure on the back in a full-face cover, holding a huge camera.

Gunnar's heart sank as he hit the gas harder, clenched the wheel tighter.

'They know where this road goes,' Demus said from the back. 'They must have followed us from Reykjavik. How did they even know…?'

'Everyone will know now. Cover your face,' Gunnar told Mahlia, his eyes on the road.

His heart was racing…his tongue felt thick. There was nowhere to pull over and the motorbike kept pace, weaving between them and the van. Whoever was behind the camera kept snapping, even when Mahlia—who hadn't covered her face at all—rolled the window down and yelled at them.

'Get out of here! This is none of your business!'

Demus chuckled into his hands, like he always did when he was overwhelmed by drama.

Gunnar closed the window on her, trying to keep his seething anger in check. 'Ignore them,' he instructed, feeling his jaw harden as she glowered through the windshield at the bike.

He was hopeful they'd be gone for good by the time Mahlia helped him escort Ma up the snow-lined steps to the grey, mansion-like facility of the rehabilitation centre, which fringed the National Park. But just as they reached the veranda he saw it: the glimmer of a lens peeking from the trees at the perimeter, just beyond the security wall.

No sooner had he swung around to confront whoever was there than the branches rustled and the stealth photographer disappeared. In seconds the roar of the motorbike's engine told him they were getting away.

Ma was still making a scene in his arms. There was nothing Gunnar could do but let them go.

CHAPTER THIRTEEN

MAHLIA CURLED HER legs up on the couch, watching Gunnar's fingers flying over the piano keys. The snow swirled in tiny flakes outside—nothing like the blizzards she had grown accustomed to. She could read him well by now, and could tell when he was bottling things up. Right now he was taking his frustration over those photos out on the poor piano, with a million thoughts creasing his brow, and she knew he felt guilty over the press furore.

They'd been here three nights already. Gunnar had suggested it, of course. No one knew where the cabin was, as opposed to their homes in Reykjavik, and when Demus had last called he'd said there were still photographers and camera crews outside their apartments, as well as at the gates of Five Lakes.

It was a bigger deal than she'd anticipated, admittedly, the fact that the once-loved TV news anchor and renowned alcoholic Kaðlín Johansson was finally being admitted to rehab. And she understood now why Gunnar had been so wary of the media all this time—how they could pull the rug out from under someone before they could even blink.

'Get the guitar,' Gunnar said to her now, swivelling on the piano stool, but Mahlia shook her head.

'I don't want to play,' she told him, failing to keep the frustration from her voice.

Javid was calling off the hook again in her pocket—so much so that she'd almost answered earlier. She was ready now, she realised. She'd been ready to have it out with him for days. Something about being here for Gunnar, knowing he valued her the way she'd always wanted to be valued, instead of owned and ordered around, had given her the courage to kick Javid out of her life once and for all.

But the signal here was bad. It would take three times as long to talk to him here, with the line cutting out every three seconds.

'Gunnar, we need to get back to the city.'

'You're free to go,' he said abruptly.

Of course, he would say that.

'I'll have someone fetch you and drive you back in an unmarked car.'

'I don't want to go without you,' she told him quietly.

Her mind was spinning. Part of her knew she *should* go without him. Javid aside, the longer she bound herself to Gunnar, the harder it would be to tear herself away for good and go after the life she wanted—two kids and all, however she might have to get them! But then again… She couldn't imagine a future without Gunnar in it any more. Maybe it wouldn't be so bad…just the two of them. It wasn't as if she didn't have enough to keep her busy!

'I shouldn't have put you in this situation,' he said, clutching her waist, making those butterflies start up again in her belly.

'I chose to come with you, and…' She sighed into the top of his head. He was wearing the sweater she'd kept up till now. 'Gunnar, all that matters is that your mother receives the help she needs to get better.'

Her words fell on deaf ears. 'As soon as you get back there will be someone waiting for you, Mahlia. They'll all want a piece of you now.'

'Maybe so...' She sank back to the couch again with a sigh, looking at the article about them still face-up on his iPad. The TV was on, on mute—something about a volcano making noises somewhere—but she couldn't focus on anything.

Gunnar went back to playing the piano despondently. Her phone buzzed. Javid again. He must know exactly where in Iceland she was now and who she was with, thanks to the news. Oh, God, what if he came for her? She just had to get back now, to Reykjavik. Have that one-to-one talk with him on the phone in private...get it over with. She'd do it tonight.

'Gunnar,' she said, 'maybe you should call me that car. I'm going back to Reykjavik.'

She went and packed her bag to the sound of his piano-playing, noting when he stopped to pace the room, hearing his feet padding across the floor. The sheets were still strewn halfway down the bed, messed up from their lovemaking. Why had she kept on sleeping with him? Because their connection was so strong it was practically impossible to deny herself, and being with him like that felt like plugging into a life source.

Maybe it's enough. Him and me, together.

'Don't forget this,' Gunnar said, handing her her phone the second she stepped back into the room with her bag. 'I called for a car.'

'OK.'

She was about to thank him, and reach up for a kiss, but he walked away from her, shoulders hunched as he leaned against the kitchen counter, studying her.

Instincts primed, she slid her phone into her pocket, crossed her arms. 'Gunnar...?'

He narrowed his blue eyes at her, then looked to the floor, making her heart skid. Something was wrong.

'Gunnar, please don't worry about me going back. I'll be fine.'

'I can't keep doing this,' he said. 'And I don't know how you can either.'

Her stomach dropped. 'Doing what?'

'Mahlia, we both know this is going to end eventually. We've said it all before. It's not just about the press…' He gestured around the cabin, at the iPad and the TV. 'I can't give you what you want. I'm just casting more and more shadows over you and your future.'

Oh, God. So he was doing it. Really ending it for good. Her knees felt weak. She'd felt it coming in the silences between their conversations; in the way he'd been looking at her all day.

'But what if you're enough for me and having children doesn't matter?' she tried, suddenly panicked. Her heart was racing now and her voice felt small, choked.

'You'd only come to resent me,' he said gravely, studying her face.

Mahlia felt frozen to the spot, as if her world was getting colder by the second.

'You want kids, and we both know that *does* matter to you. But that's not what I want, Mahlia. I'm not lying to myself about that, and you shouldn't lie to yourself about what you want either.'

Rage bubbled up within her. 'Don't tell me what to do or what I think or need.' She couldn't help it now. The tears were bristling in her eyes and her palms felt clammy.

He stepped closer, pressing a long kiss to her forehead that felt so final it broke her heart.

'I'm doing this to save you.'

'What?'

OK, that was totally not necessary.

She shoved at his chest—hard. 'I don't need you to *save* me from anything, Gunnar. I just want *you*. And if you don't trust that that's enough for me, then you're right—this should end.'

He closed his eyes, drew his lips together for a moment, and she felt her heart shatter.

'It's not that I don't trust you. I just know you, Mahlia.'

'No, you don't. Don't think you know me. If you knew me, you'd know I can make up my own damn mind about what I need in my life!'

Gunnar sank to the couch, buried his face in his hands, shaking his head. When her car pulled up he didn't get up and walk outside with her. He simply tossed a heavy log onto the fire and refused to look at her.

Gunnar woke the next morning with a headache. The bed was empty beside him, as expected. He checked his phone, seeing zero missed calls from Mahlia. As if she would have called him after what he'd done. But he'd done the right thing. He had already caused her enough trouble. He wouldn't keep stringing her along selfishly, telling himself he was enough for her.

OK, so there had been moments when he'd felt his resolve weaken—she'd been resilient enough over this whole media debacle with his mother to assure him that maybe she'd stick around if things got tough, so she wasn't another Idina. But no… His being with her was still selfish. She was kidding herself, and him, if she thought she could sacrifice having children for him!

Slinging the sheets back, he went to hit the shower, trying to drown the relentless thwack of pain to his brain whenever he thought about her—and also about what he'd seen on her overturned phone the second he'd picked it up last night.

In the living room, he flicked on the TV just as Demus called.

'Can you believe those scientists took the mayor out there?' Demus sounded worried.

'Where?' Gunnar yawned, sloshing some coffee into a chipped mug.

'To the village...the one in the news, right in the lava's path!'

'There's no lava yet. Nothing's happened,' Inka told him in the background.

So, they were together now? Something like envy rattled him.

'That volcano has been dormant for decades,' he heard her say.

'But it's rumbling, Inks. I don't trust it,' Demus said.

Gunnar slugged his coffee. He was only half listening. That text message was still burning all other thoughts from his brain.

As he'd handed her phone back to her last night, before he'd called for a car to take her back to the city, he'd had to force his brain to wrap itself around the fact that Javid was the reason she'd wanted to leave, really. Her ex's message had been right there in his hands, on her phone, along with a photo of his smug face.

He couldn't unsee it now.

Mahlia, I'm in Reykjavik. Ready when you are.

When and why the hell she'd agreed to let her ex come all the way here from New Zealand, who knew? He'd been too angry at the thought of her finally succumbing to her ex's pleas for her attention to even question her about it. She'd had every chance to admit that she was putting herself in his line of fire in person, but she hadn't said a word.

He seethed as his mind reeled.

It didn't matter now. They were over.

Don't think any more about it, or her, he told himself,

grappling for any bricks he could find to put up a wall in his mind before the pain rushed back in. *She's leaving for New Zealand soon anyway. You always knew you had a time limit! She was always going to leave. You can't give her what she needs.*

'Oh, man… What the…?' Demus was still on the line. 'Gunnar?'

'If it's just a little rumble it's probably not a big deal…'

'Not the volcano. Gunnar, it's Dad.'

Gunnar flicked to the channel his brother was watching. His heart raced like a runaway train as he stared at the screen, his mind swirling. It was his father, standing outside the Five Lakes Rehabilitation Centre. The man was almost unrecognisable in sunglasses, a hat, and a thick winter coat flapping around his too-thin frame.

'I can't believe it,' Gunnar muttered, as at least seven microphones were shoved in his father's pale, drawn face.

'He looks…different…' Demus said softly, as if afraid to break the spell.

No one spoke for a few moments, listening to him address the flock of reporters who'd never stopped swarming around the front entrance to Five Lakes. They had an even juicier story now.

He'd seen his wife on the news, he said. He'd been shocked into action at the look on her face as they'd admitted her. He said his heart had been shattered, hearing her say she'd been waiting for him all this time, afraid to go anywhere too far in case he came home for her. He apologised, called himself a coward. He said he'd let himself, his country, and worst of all his family down.

Inka broke the spell in the end. 'Well?' she said in the background. 'Are you going to go and see him, or not?'

Gunnar's heart jumped into his throat.

* * *

Mahlia stared at the phone screen, watching the morning news replay in a stupor. The water she was sitting by in the shadow of the cathedral fell clean away. First the shock of Javid descending on her in Reykjavik without warning, and now this!

Simmering as she studied the man on the screen, she could hardly believe it. So *this* small, sheepish-looking, skinny man was Gunnar's once lauded and powerful father, who'd helped bring this country to its knees. Back from Cambodia, or wherever he'd been hiding.

Gunnar looked less than impressed, standing there at the Five Lakes rehab centre with him and Demus, the photographers all snapping around them like piranhas. But at least he'd gone there. She couldn't help being impressed with him for that, despite their argument.

Should she call him? No…of course she shouldn't. He'd broken things off, even after she'd told him that being just the two of them would be enough for her!

Not that there wasn't still some niggling doubt in her mind about that. She sighed. Maybe he did know her better than she thought. Maybe he *was* right to try and 'save' her from another huge mistake, putting another man before her own needs.

At least she'd drawn enough strength from Gunnar to have it out with Javid once and for all, in person. Which was not what she'd been expecting to do at all when she'd come back to the city.

Mahlia, I'm in Reykjavik. Ready when you are.

She'd almost thrown her phone away, seeing that he'd flown here and was 'ready' for her. What the hell did that even *mean*? When the message had come in she'd been packing her bags at the cabin, so she hadn't seen it till she was already on the way to Reykjavik, but pure fury and fire—no doubt a result of Gunnar's bombshell too—had propelled her to Javid's hotel.

The universe had clearly told her to grow a pair, to knock on his door and tell him to his face, in a way he understood, that she was sick of this, that there was no way in heaven or hell they would ever get back together…that she'd met some-one else.

She'd left out the part about Gunnar breaking things off. In that moment she'd clean forgotten. Looking at Javid, she'd known without question that her heart was and probably al-ways would be Gunnar's!

She sighed at the sky. OK, so she'd been living in a bit of a fantasy, thinking they could actually make things work—and not just because of the whole children issue. She had a life to live elsewhere! Not that she could fathom going back to New Zealand, really, when there was so much going on here. She'd built something here for herself, regardless of Gunnar.

A few people were looking her way from the other side of the pond. Raising her hand, she half expected a scowl or a scathing remark, but the group of teenagers just waved back and smiled awkwardly, as if they'd seen a celebrity. Gunnar was so paranoid it had rubbed off on her!

After walking home, she hid behind the wall outside her apartment for a moment, till the man with the camera looked the other way. Then she darted to the door, jiggled the key in the lock, praying she wouldn't be snapped, and hated herself for caring at all.

It was only Gunnar who cared. And Javid, now.

Javid's own jealousy and ego had sent him to the airport. He'd known all along she was in Iceland, but he'd only flown here after seeing her photo with Gunnar. Typical. He didn't even know who Gunnar was.

The sight of his jet-lagged face last night, first furious and scathing, and then begging, crying and pleading, trying to block her from leaving his hotel room, had just made her angry instead of wanting to cower under a table. He'd dropped to the floor broken, a mess, but he'd agreed to sign the papers— finally. She'd almost wanted to feel sorry for him. But all she'd been thinking about was how he wasn't a part of her life any more. And neither was Gunnar.

Some hours later, Mahlia was between emails with her solicitor when a shriek from outside caught her ears. Suddenly several people were yelling, gathering outside, and Mahlia's heart almost bottomed out when she craned her neck on the balcony to look at the mountain range.

The volcano, far in the distance, which just last week had been largely inconspicuous, disguised as a harmless mountain, was now spitting fire. A thick cloud of steam and smoke rose faster than she could contemplate, threatening to blot out the sun.

The sky was turning darker and darker, and Mahlia felt a chill run through her as she took the stairs two at a time down to the street, glancing around. People were starting to evacuate, loading cars with whatever they could carry, running inside their homes to grab what they'd need. Dogs barked and children whimpered in confusion while she just stared at the mountains, realising there were probably people out there, *up* there...

The volcano was erupting, spewing molten lava and ash high into the air like a firework display. It was surreal.

Already her phone was ringing off the hook.

CHAPTER FOURTEEN

ERIK, ÁSTA AND Gunnar were in a huddle when she swerved into the hangar and hurried from her car.

'You're here.' Ásta pulled her into a quick one-armed hug.

She was panicked, which put Mahlia even more on edge, but she straightened up—not least because Gunnar was staring at her. He looked tired.

'Thanks for coming,' Gunnar said gruffly, and her heart panged just at seeing his narrowed eyes, the way he shoved his hands harder into his pockets.

Erik and Gunnar had already gathered intel. The eruption had sent a slow flow of lava spilling down the south-eastern side of the volcano, and the mayor of Reykjavik was in danger of getting trapped at the research base he was visiting with the scientists. They were still up there, in an area that would soon become inaccessible or swallowed by lava.

Mahlia's heart raced as she looked from Erik to Gunnar, then back again. Behind them more volunteers were loading vehicles with supplies, organising themselves into groups to head there by land and in helicopters.

'What about the villagers?' she asked as they headed towards Sven, who was hauling several boxes of water and supplies into the chopper.

'Some of them have already evacuated,' Gunnar said, hauling up another crate.

'Yeah, and some of them think their prayers will keep them safe,' Erik followed up.

Gunnar didn't touch her or talk to her as they boarded the chopper.

As they flew closer to the danger zone, the air felt thick and hot. The winds were picking up ash and debris all around them, visibility was decreasing rapidly, and every minute brought them closer to potential disaster...

What if they couldn't reach them in time?

It didn't bear thinking about.

Gunnar started working with the winch equipment and Mahlia's heart rose to her throat. She took his arm suddenly, leaning in over the roar of the blades. Hair whipped furiously around their faces as he partially opened the door and peeked out, sending ash inside to swirl between them. His gaze lowered to her fingers. She was clutching his arm tighter by the second.

'You wouldn't go down unless it was totally one hundred percent safe, would you?' she said, trying and probably failing to keep the emotion from her face.

He stared at her. 'Nothing about this is safe.'

She rolled her eyes. 'I know, but...'

'Nothing's going to happen to me. Or you. OK?'

His eyes drilled into her and she fumbled for words—professional words...words that might befit the current unprecedented situation—but he got in first.

'Why didn't you tell me Javid was here?' he said, stepping into a fire-retardant suit, yanking the zip up roughly.

She sat back, stunned. How did he know Javid was here?

'I saw it on your phone,' he said to her, reaching for the harness, tightening the belt around his waist. 'Before you left. You didn't tell me he was in the country. Did you think I'd try and stop you seeing him. Was that it?'

Mahlia gaped, feeling Ásta's eyes on her as she looked over a map of the area. Was that why he'd broken it off so fast? He could have told her...so she could have explained.

'I didn't know he was coming till I'd already left. He saw us in those photos and he flew here. But, yes, I went to see him. I told him what I had to, and he's signing the papers.'

Gunnar looked shocked. 'Well...good.'

'Anyway, you didn't tell me your father was here!' she continued, raising her voice above the roaring blades. 'You really don't trust me at all, do you? You don't trust me with your family, and you don't trust me to make my own mind up about my own future!'

He shook his head. 'You want what I can't give you.'

'I only want *you*!'

She almost crumpled into him, but his eyes held hers now, and she swallowed a sob. This was pointless! He did know her, and he knew a part of her did still want a family, to be a mother. She always would...even if she willingly sacrificed the chance for him.

'At least I thought I did. I don't know, Gunnar.'

He said nothing, and she bit her tongue as he yanked on thick rubber boots.

'I didn't know my father was coming back,' he said eventually, 'not till this morning. That was news to me, too.'

She stared at him, grappling for words as the sequence of events started slotting into place. 'But you went to see him and the world didn't fall apart, did it? And you're here now, risking your life for others all over again, because your past isn't what's important.'

His jaw shifted this way and that as he held her eyes. Her legs were shaking with adrenaline. She could see his thoughts churning, something weakening, but then he seemed to brush it off, as if he didn't want to think about it. He tugged at the straps of the harness, then dragged his hands through his hair. She forced her mouth shut, cursing herself. She wanted to say the future was more important...the *only* thing that mattered. But his silence said it all.

She should book a flight home as soon as this mission was over, she thought defeatedly. Reassess, deal with the divorce with a clear head—not distract herself with someone she couldn't have.

'The research centre is there.'

Erik stuck his arm out to point between them, and she sucked a breath in, followed his finger. They were approaching the side of the volcano now, and the tiny research centre where the mayor and the scientists were trapped looked like nothing more than a series of shacks from up here. The spilling lava had already curled around the buildings, blocking the path for a rescue by land.

Despite the imminent danger, the sight was breathtaking. How could something so beautiful be so deadly?

Whenever the smoke cleared the molten lava glowed a brilliant orange-red against the deep hues of the ever-darkening ash-laden sky. Bright sparks flew off like fireflies as it spilled and spread like red treacle. It looked almost alive, with its own powerful energy, creating poker-like new paths for itself as it seeped and bubbled forward. Some trees had been charred black by fire, and whole sections of land had been swallowed up by molten rock already.

'How many people are down there?' she asked, sudden dread pooling in her stomach at just how close the lava was trickling to the research centre.

'They just confirmed five,' Erik said, his voice gruff with worry. 'I'll drop a cable once you get them out. The mayor is asthmatic, and with this smoke... We're the closest team already—the only chance they have right now.'

'I'll bring him up first,' Gunnar said. 'Mahlia, get ready.'

For a second too long she held his gaze, searching for a hint of the man who'd made love to her so passionately. He looked almost pained as he pulled his eyes away, and she swallowed back the urge to tell him to be careful. He was already pulling away, trying to push her out of his life. She should keep a shred of dignity and accept it. This trip had never been about *him* anyway. At least, it had never been *supposed* to be…

Ásta shook her shoulder gently, urging her away from the door. Gunnar co-ordinated with Sven from the cockpit, checked the winch line with Erik, then shoved oxygen masks into his pack as they hovered closer. Below, Mahlia could just make out arms waving from a skylight in the observatory at the research centre, and her heart leapt as she grabbed up her backpack, ready to go with Gunnar.

'Stay here,' he commanded her.

She felt a jolt to her heart as Gunnar shoved the door further open, pulling his oxygen mask on tightly. The wind buffeted through her hair and dust and ash filled her lungs as he met her eyes one last time. In a heartbeat the clouds consumed him, and then he was gone.

The smoke was so thick it was more like a wall, but Gunnar kept going, forging through the ash towards the research centre. His lungs burned against his ribs and his heart pumped in his ears as he tried to breathe and stay calm. The steel shack that was the research centre was only metres away from where he'd landed, but the air around him was hot and toxic, and he could feel the intensity of the heat even from this distance, singeing his cheeks around the oxygen mask.

Above him, the chopper wove through a barrage of ash and debris, and he pictured Mahlia, gripping the doorframe, watching out for his return.

He'd pushed her away again… Why did he keep on doing that? Demus had got all up in his head on the phone, on his way to the hangar, telling him to keep Mahlia safe, that she was the best thing ever to have happened to him.

He *knew* that, he thought, glancing up as another chopper hovered into sight, then another, and another. Some were full of photographers and news correspondents. He couldn't escape them even on the side of a damn volcano.

The main door to the research centre was blocked by a massive lava rock boulder. He shouted to the guys they'd seen in the observatory. There was no way he could get into their line of vision, and the other door was blocked already by more huge black boulders. Heaving against their weight, he started to try and move it, picturing the much-loved mayor in there, feeling more ashamed than ever of how he'd treated Mahlia before he'd ordered her not to come down with him.

His old demons had come out in force, convincing him she was going to leave him like Idina had, and he'd made every excuse under the sun to himself as to why he was wrong for her—including the whole children thing. Was that really what he wanted? To be alone in life?

'Stop focusing on problems that don't even exist or your whole life is going to pass you by. Look at me and Inks. If we can make it work, then you can!' his brother had urged.

Demus saw through him and all his excuses, of course. He didn't deserve a brother like him, Gunnar thought, urging the boulder to move, cursing when it still didn't budge. And he probably didn't deserve Mahlia either, the way he'd just spoken to her. He'd messed up. She hadn't even seen that Javid was in Iceland when she'd asked him for a car back to Reykjavik from the cabin! And she'd finally given the guy his marching orders in person, all by herself. That must've taken courage, considering how the guy had had her in an emotional stranglehold for the last seven years—and he, as her trusted colleague, winchman and lover, had just broken things off with her.

Damn, this boulder was not giving an inch!

He almost turned around in defeat, but suddenly Mahlia was behind him, running through the swirling ash straight towards him. His stomach did a somersault as he watched her jump over a pile of glowing rocks. The smell of sulphur filled his nose and for a second he saw the strangest image in his mind: a little version of Mahlia, stubborn, determined, needing him despite trying her best to prove she didn't, him sweeping her up in his arms... A daughter?

The smoke must be getting to his head.

'Mahlia, you can't be here.'

Her mouth twisted with exasperation as she pulled out a rope. 'I made them let me come. I'll stay away from you after this, if that's what you want,' she said through her mask. 'We need to move fast, Gunnar.'

Her knuckles went white as she tightened the rope around the boulder, and together they heaved and tugged until the way was clear. Gunnar yanked at the heavy steel door, revealing their way in with an ominous creak.

'It's so dark...' Panting, Mahlia grabbed the back of his suit by the belt as they entered the pitch-black corridor.

'The generator's out,' he said, pulling out a flashlight and putting a hand out to steady her.

The air was filled with the echo of distant shouts for help as they felt their way around the walls towards the sound of the cries. She stumbled against a trolley full of glass vials and he caught her, holding the flashlight under his chin for a second, an inch from her eyes.

'I'm sorry I overreacted about Javid flying to Reykjavik,' he said.

Mahlia turned away from him, edging along the wall. 'You did overreact, yes.'

'But that doesn't change anything, Mahlia. You deserve a better future now he's out of your life. You shouldn't have to sacrifice your dreams for me...'

'Great—so now there's another man telling me what's best for me,' she huffed over her shoulder, stumbling again and righting herself. 'I'm flying back to New Zealand soon anyway.'

He could have kicked himself. 'Really? You've booked a flight already?'

She sighed. 'Not yet, but there's legal stuff to sort out there...and I probably won't be back. Not for a while at least.'

'Mahlia—'

His words were cut off. A huge rumble from overhead made Mahlia gasp, and they staggered into each other. He dropped the flashlight.

'What was that?' she asked, wide-eyed, just as the cries sounded out again.

This time they were close enough to gauge where they were coming from. Together they hurried the rest of the way, till the noise brought them to another giant steel door. Gunnar's radio squawked.

'Gunnar, this is Erik. We've got a problem. All entrances are blocked by lava so you'll need to get the mayor and the others out through the roof. It's too dangerous for you to go back the way you went in.'

Mahlia turned pale, but Gunnar steeled himself. He spoke into the radio for confirmation and then pushed at the door. It was stuck.

'It's probably locked now the power's out,' he said, banging on the door.

Sure enough, a man who sounded very panicked confirmed

they could no longer open it. There were five people in there, including the mayor, who was probably the person they could hear coughing hoarsely.

'Time to get creative,' said Gunnar, his eyes darting around in search of a plan.

Urging Mahlia back a safe distance, he grabbed a metal pipe off a nearby wall. The stench of burning rock wafting down the corridor made his nostrils burn and his stomach lurch.

'Can you do this?' she asked him from the opposite wall, removing her mask, then coughing with the ash.

His heart swelled at the look on her face—the same one he'd seen in the chopper. She was trying not to appear fazed by the situation, but her voice was trembling with fear and uncertainty, and it made him want to pull her into him, ask her to stay, not to take that flight. *Ever.*

Maybe she was right in what she'd said before. His father had come back, Ma was getting help, and despite everyone knowing about all the ugly skeletons in his closet, the world hadn't ended. He was making the past into a bigger deal than it had to be. And because of that he was destroying his own future!

Gunnar steeled himself, gripped the pipe hard and slammed it with all his strength repeatedly into the bar across the door. Over and over. On the fourth or fifth blow the lock shattered into pieces and the door swung open.

They pushed at it with one hard shove, and his eyes took in the facility, full of strange machinery, and the researchers, who flocked towards them in relief. The mayor, whom Gunnar recognised instantly, dropped to his knees on the floor when he saw them, holding his chest.

Gunnar passed out oxygen masks as Mahlia helped the mayor up, sitting him on a chair. 'We need to get everyone out of here *now*,' she said, eyeing the glass dome of the observatory above them nervously. It was so high.

'The power outage has left the dome closed,' one of the scientists told them. 'I don't know how else we can get out!'

Gunnar met Mahlia's eyes, saw the look of despair she shot him. *No.* They would *not* be stuck in here, waiting for a river to molten lava to snake in and swallow them—not if he could help it.

Casting his eyes around, he saw his answer—the ventilation system.

'See the ventilation system up there?' he said, racing for the ladder against the wall. 'That was obviously installed before the dome. Maybe we can climb up into the shafts.'

'Maybe?' someone said doubtfully.

Gunnar ignored him.

'How do we get up there?' the mayor managed to ask.

Gunnar pushed the ladder against a shelving unit and shone the flashlight up, squinting against the thick smoke as one of the scientists produced a map of the system.

Shoving items from the desk to the floor, Mahlia spread it out on the table. 'We *can* climb up into the shafts,' she said. 'The map shows there's a way out to the left, if we head through the ventilation system.'

The mayor had started coughing and spluttering so hard he could barely breathe. He tumbled from the chair, gasping for breath. Mahlia raced over to help him put his mask back on, throwing Gunnar a look that said *Hurry!*

Gunnar took the ladder three rungs at a time. It barely reached the vent they'd all have to fit through, but he was ready. Opening out the rope ladder he'd just yanked from his backpack, he made quick work of fastening it to the bottom of the vent. Soon it swung the whole way to the ground.

'Use the metal ladder to get onto the rope one. I'll pull you all up,' he called down.

Mahlia tried to make the mayor go first, but to Gunnar's dismay he refused.

'*They* should go first,' he insisted, gesturing to the team.

The scientists didn't argue with him.

'Hurry—one by one…climb up to me,' he instructed, as the first one took to the ladder.

Eyeing the space around him, he prayed it would hold them all and that there was a way out. He was crouching in the entrance to a long ventilation shaft. The end of the shaft had been made slightly wider—evidence that at some point this space *had* been planned as an escape route? He only hoped no one had sealed up the other end…

From the corridor below, an ominous groaning sound told him the building was far from stable now. One side of it— the side they'd entered from—was likely already engulfed in the lava.

'Gunnar, we're right above you. Can you see a way out?'

Erik's grave voice over the radio made his heart buck wildly as the first of the researchers reached him. His supposition was correct—he just knew it, he thought, straining his arms to pull the man up.

'Go! Go as far down the shaft as you can,' he told him as the second scientist almost fell from the ladder.

Mahlia ran to steady it.

Soon, the mayor and Mahlia were the only ones left in the lab below.

'Mahlia, I need you up here first,' he told her.

She wasted no time obeying him, for once, and when she was safely at his side he scrambled past her, climbing back down. The mayor was so weak that Gunnar had to carry him over his shoulder up the rope ladder, and Mahlia helped him pull the heavy, panting man into the shaft, where he tumbled into a heap against them, apologising.

'I know who you are,' he told Gunnar, breathing raggedly against Mahlia's shoulder.

He clutched Gunnar's collar in his fist for a second, hauling him closer, as if for inspection, and for a beat Gunnar wondered if the man might just shove him backwards from the shaft, down to the ground, and let the lava take him.

To his shock, the mayor mumbled, 'Thank you, Gunnar Johansson. Even if we die in here, you will die a hero for your bravery.'

'We are not going to die in here, sir,' Gunnar told him firmly, prising his hand away from his suit, praying that was true as he pulled out a compass.

'The map said that way,' Mahlia told him, without even looking at it.

She was right.

'Let's go,' he told her, ushering her along the shaft, taking the left turn, making sure the mayor was between them. The shaft was just big enough to be used as a crawl space, but the air was thick, more acrid than ever. Everyone was coughing now, despite their masks. The heat of lava burning through the walls and floors spurred them further forward, until finally a sliver of light appeared ahead.

Thank God!

His radio buzzed. Erik was asking where they were. His heart was like a drum as he explained as best he could. The building was now on weak foundations. They had to make it all the way outside before it was engulfed—only who knew how much time they had left?

Fumbling onwards on all-fours, he reached for the metal grate. With a strangled cry and a prayer, he pulled at one side of the thick iron bars, coughing against the smoke. Mahlia came up beside him and pulled on the bars with every ounce of strength she had, but his heart sank like a rock in his chest as they tugged and tugged together to no avail.

The grate just wouldn't move. They were stuck.

CHAPTER FIFTEEN

MAHLIA'S BODY WAS fighting to empty her stomach. She knew the shaft's exit was embedded into the side of the volcano. The heat scorched her skin, and the smell of burning rock was overwhelming now. It had already taken every bit of strength she possessed to help the struggling mayor through the shaft without injury, and now this...

She heaved at the grate again with Gunnar, watching the veins in his neck strain against the impossible task. She could see the ominous orange glow of lava snaking less than twenty metres away from them. With her hands burning, and the mayor of Reykjavik floundering behind her, she threw Gunnar a helpless look. The chopper was hovering noisily above, but they were on the brink of being devoured.

Was *this* how she was going to die? Next to Gunnar, at odds with Gunnar, having never even said the words *I love you*?

She did love him, she thought wryly as the smoke tickled her already bone-dry throat. More than anything. For all the good it had done her. Why the hell had she told him she was definitely flying home to New Zealand, with no plans to return any time soon? OK, so she'd decided to do that in a snap decision, but she knew she'd only be running away again. Hurting him before he could hurt her more.

Now she knew what love—real love—felt like. It had never felt possible till Gunnar came along. She would probably never get over him, but at least going forward she'd have more confidence in the fact that she could love and be loved without suffocating or losing herself.

'Gunnar...' she started helplessly, blinking through the tears in her eyes she slumped backwards against the wall.

The second she hit it, she reeled back in pain.

Gunnar reached for her. 'What is it?'

Something hard was digging into her thigh. Gasping in relief, she yanked out the metal pipe Gunnar had used earlier, to bash down the door. He'd thrown it to the ground before grabbing the ladder, but she'd shoved it into the backpack, just in case.

Gunnar's eyes widened.

'Can you get us out with this?' she asked.

Behind him the team of researchers watched nervously, holding their hands over their masks. The mayor had his eyes closed, praying in Icelandic between coughs and sucks on his inhaler. At least he had one with him.

'I won't have the strength on my own, we'll all have to help,' Gunnar told her quietly, and she nodded, pressing a palm to his cheek without thinking.

He'd lifted every single one of these men single-handedly from the rope ladder up into the shaft, and then carried the mayor! Quickly, she ordered everyone to get behind them and take a part of the pipe, creating one long tool that hopefully, they could power enough between them.

Together they hammered at the rusty iron bars till her joints felt like jelly, hearing the men stagger and gasp, watching as the chopper's blades spun against the ashen sky outside. The bars creaked and groaned under the weight, but didn't move. Erik was still urging them to hurry over the radio. He'd sent down the winch line already.

'It's giving way…' Gunnar panted eventually, as one of the hinges came apart.

She grinned ridiculously at the faint glimmer of hope.

'One more time, Mahlia, everyone!,' he encouraged, gripping the other end of the pipe.

She gathered every last bit of energy left in her exhausted body, and with everything she had rammed at the grate with him, again and again, until miraculously it sprang from both hinges, sending both her and Gunnar and two of the men behind them tumbling out onto the rocks. For a second she lay there, stunned and panting across his chest, his ash-streaked face less than an inch from her lips.

'That was close,' he said dryly, blinking.

Adrenaline made her laugh. His blue eyes smiled back into hers and she almost forgot they were at odds, almost kissed him in relief. But he hoisted her up to her feet, nodded towards the molten rock spewing from the volcano's crater, and darted back for the mayor.

The other men staggered out from the shaft one by one, shaking themselves down. She ushered them away from the approaching lava flow towards the waiting winch line as the heat burned her cheeks and Gunnar scooped the mayor into his arms. The man was fading fast, but still he insisted the research team go first.

'*You* go first,' Gunnar told Mahlia quietly when he reached her.

Above them, Ásta was waving urgently from the chopper's open door.

'No, Gunnar…'

Panic almost stole her voice. Metres from where they stood, blazing hot red rocks rolled ominously closer, like living predators, making one of the researchers cry out in fear. It was almost too hot to think, but she couldn't leave him—not now. They were in this together.

'Mahlia, you need to go,' he urged, putting the mayor down carefully on the blackened ground. 'I need you up there. I'll send them up to you one by one. OK?'

She reluctantly agreed, but she was far from OK as he helped her with the harness, then signalled to Ásta and Erik.

'Gunnar, I...' she started, grappling for words even as the volcano spewed another shower of lava behind him. 'I'm not going anywhere.' She was suddenly desperate to retract her words. 'I mean, I don't have to leave, Gunnar. Not if you feel the same way I do. I wasn't expecting you. I didn't ask for any of this. But I've spent the last seven years feeling like I can't speak my truth, so I'm saying it now, out loud, even if it's scarier than this!' She gestured around them at the blazing landscape. 'I love you, I want you, and I won't let you push me away—children or no children. We can work something out.'

He studied her eyes, clicking the last strap of the harness into place, and for a moment it was just the two of them.

'You *are* good for me,' she continued as the blades whirled the ash around her. 'I don't care about anything else and I'll prove it to you, even if it takes for ever.'

Pain flashed across his face for a second as he glanced upwards, and her heart lurched in response. 'Save yourself, Mahlia,' was all he said.

She didn't have time to vocalise anything else before a giant roar tore their eyes from each other. The research centre was collapsing behind them. It seemed as if the entire island was shaking with the force, and every breath she took was smoke and sulphur.

He tugged on the line with urgency. The wind whipped her face and tore at her hair as she strained to keep her eyes on him in the chaos, but soon all she could see was ash as she was hauled away from him up into the sky.

Gunnar watched her go, clenching his jaw as she disappeared into the dirty sky, hopping back from the rolling debris, urging the men up to a higher platform of dangerously wobbly rocks. He couldn't believe he'd just frozen—but what was he meant to say in response to that? All of her heart on display, on the line, for *him*. He'd shut down cold, even as she'd dangled right in front of him, in a situation like this.

God…he was such an idiot!

His head reeled as he waited for the line to reappear. He wanted to trust her more than anything. She truly thought that they could be more together than he was alone, a lonely one-man island, drifting through life in a sea of people who didn't even see him. Not the way she did. Maybe Mahlia really didn't care if any future children carried his name; maybe all she wanted was for *both* of them to stop putting up all these walls right now. She'd let hers come down, but him… He'd been hiding away where no one could stamp down on his heart for so long it was second nature for him to keep on believing his own excuses and creating new ones.

All he'd wanted to say to her just now was *I love you*, or *I need you too*, but he'd squished it down hard under his stupid pride and fear. He was so afraid of losing her the way he'd lost Idina that he was losing her anyway.

The winch line was back, swinging his way.

He shouted above the roar of the blades for the research team to get into the harness one by one. He'd have to stay on the ground; there was no point taking them up and down each time by himself. The air above him was too thick—he'd choke before he got them all into the chopper. They scrambled towards him, fear evident in their eyes—especially the mayor's. But the man still insisted the scientists all go before him.

'Mr Mayor, I don't think that's wise. Mahlia and the team are waiting up there to help you!'

'Everyone's going to need help after this,' he told him, banging on his chest and sucking on his inhaler again.

Gunnar frowned, but determination took control of his tired limbs as he sent the men up towards Mahlia, working more quickly than he'd ever worked before. He muttered words of encouragement the whole time, even as his brain churned, hoping he wasn't showing a shred of the panic and doubt that were threatening to choke him more than the smoke.

The lava was creeping closer still... In minutes it would be licking at his heels like an eager pet if he didn't get up into that chopper.

The other helicopters were swirling above—news reporters, probably. Everyone wanted to see them get the mayor away from this disaster zone. Tears ran down the other men's faces as they expressed their wobbly gratitude, all of which he brushed away.

They weren't out of danger yet—not completely. But as soon as they were he would tell Mahlia he wanted her to stay, he decided. For ever. The thought of letting her down and seeing her walk away was crippling. He was a better man with her here, in every single way. He could even be a father, he realised, if she was with him. He'd been telling himself he didn't want children of his own, but that had been his fear talking too. They could do anything together.

Suddenly, he wanted nothing more than to see her walking down an aisle towards him, carrying his babies, cooking up a storm next to him at the cabin with their kids running around them... What the hell would he do if he couldn't have all that now?

'Gunnar, send him up!' Erik was ready for the mayor.

Gunnar clicked the last strap of the harness into place and for a moment it was just the two of them. The mayor nearly crushed his hand with a tight grip that defied his current state of health.

'I owe you my life, Dr Johansson,' he said gravely as the wind whipped his grey hair into a puffball. 'Don't think I'll forget this.'

Gunnar nodded as the winch line lifted the other man off the ground. The lava stream was almost too close for comfort now. He skipped along the rocks, away from it, waiting for the line to come back down. But just as he spotted it through the ash a giant rumble sent him to the ground. His radio went flying.

A shower of rocks had loosened and were rolling towards him, sending up so much soot and ash he couldn't see a thing. Holding his arms above his head for protection, he fumbled for the radio, straining his eyes against zero visibility. The winch line was nowhere in sight. He pushed himself off the ground and staggered forward, blindly feeling for it in all directions. The heat of the lava radiated behind him, almost unbearable.

He knew he had minutes at most before he was consumed by molten rock, and it was Mahlia's face he saw in his mind's eye as he prayed for a miracle.

The mayor was wheezing—everyone was now—but no one could speak, knowing Gunnar was still down there.

'Do you see him?' Mahlia asked Erik, doing her best to appear as if she wasn't completely breaking down on the inside. Her clothes were black, her face was thick with filthy dirt, and her heart was screaming out to Gunnar to tug on the rope and tell them he was OK.

'His radio's out,' Erik replied, trying him again.

Mahlia swallowed back a desperate sob. This was inconceivable. Gunnar was still down there, obviously unable to find the line in all the chaos and smoke. The mayor was coughing and retching in the thick air and Sven was still circling over the spot where they'd pulled the team up. But it was almost too hot to breathe now; her lungs felt ragged.

'We have to wait,' Mahlia begged, seeing Ásta and Erik throwing looks at each other. They didn't think... Surely, they didn't think he was already dead? 'We can't leave him down there. Let me go back down there.'

Ásta caught her arm, then gripped her hand. 'No, Mahlia.'

She was shaking. 'But we can't just leave him. He might be... He's *waiting* for us.'

A pause.

'Gunnar would want us to get out of here,' Erik said gravely, still watching the line. 'We have all these people who need attention and we're running low on fuel.'

Beneath them, the research centre had now been swallowed whole, and the river of lava glimmered ominously where they'd just been standing. Mahlia could barely think straight.

'There are other teams on the mountain...everyone will be looking for him,' Ásta told her reassuringly, but Mahlia knew what she was really thinking.

Gunnar was already gone.

It was all she could do not to scream. Had she really lost him for ever? Oh, God... Oh, God, how would she cope? And how was she going to break it to Demus?

The hangar was hive of activity when they landed. Sirens wailed in the distance, while several ambulances and other rescue trucks were parked on the concrete in the floodlights, already attending to the injured people who'd made it off the mountain. News reporters were swarming all around them, asking about the mayor, asking about Gunnar, but Mahlia just trembled against Ásta's shoulder as they let the paramedics take over their stunned researchers.

Ásta drew her close. 'It's going to be OK.'

Nothing is ever going to be OK again, she felt like saying.

It felt as if the bottom had just fallen out of her world—as if the life had been sucked right out of her. She'd finally told him exactly how she felt, finally stopped cowering behind her own fears. Whether her feelings were reciprocated or not, at least she'd told him... And now she'd never see his face again.

Tears welled up in her eyes as she tried to process it all. She'd taken a risk, told him exactly what she wanted, despite her fear that he wouldn't feel the same way, wouldn't respond in kind, but it hadn't been enough. Nothing would bring him back.

Then came a voice.

'Mahlia...'

Mahlia's head snapped up. Gunnar was standing in front of her, blackened and weary, a look of pure relief on his face.

For a second, she blinked in disbelief. He was alive!

'Gunnar!'

Ásta released her and started crying into her hands, but Mahlia ran for him, barely believing her eyes as Gunnar caught her mid-stride. She sobbed into his chest. The news reporters were clamouring around them now, but for once he didn't seem to care; he kept his focus solely on her, not letting her go for a single second.

'I'm so sorry,' he told her, speaking into her hair. 'All I wanted the second I sent you up there was to tell you that I love you, too. I want everything you want, and I want us to make this work.'

'I thought I'd lost you,' she said, her voice coming out strangled.

'One of the news choppers threw me a line,' he told her

wryly, pressing his hands to her face, scrunching up her hair, kissing her. 'Who'd have thought it? Mahlia, I wasn't ever going to give up on us. I fell in love with you a long time ago. I just didn't know what to do with my feelings, or if I could give you what you needed…what I need too. You know…' He paused. 'I never thought children were for me, but then I met you and everything started to change…'

Mahlia almost laughed. 'What I need most is for you to love me, and to let me love *you*, and let that be enough for us both.'

'And it will be. For now.'

Gunnar's eyes shone with so much love and hope she almost burst.

'I can really see myself as a dad. In fact, I can see myself doing a lot of things with you I never thought I'd get to experience. But life is short, and we need to grab every opportunity we can to make the most of it.'

'Life is *too* short,' she whispered.

Mahlia couldn't even speak any more. Instead, she kissed him back, as the circle of press and onlookers grew wider and his arms around her grew tighter.

He was still holding her tightly in his arms when the mayor was wheeled over to them in a chair, seemingly determined to address the press while in the same shot as Gunnar.

Mahlia moved to step away, frantically wiping the tears from her face, but Gunnar held on to her hand, pulled her closer to his side, and made sure to kiss the top of her head tenderly in front of the cameras. Whatever parts of her that hadn't already been singed in the day's heat melted.

The mayor cleared his throat and stood, pressing a hand to Gunnar's shoulder as he did his best to recount in his own words how they'd helped them all to escape from the research centre before it collapsed.

'Tonight, I stand here very much alive, in awe of these brave men and women who risk their own lives to save the people of Iceland. I want to thank you and your team, Dr Johansson, on live television, so that all of Iceland knows how much I personally applaud and appreciate your courage and dedication. You've done your country proud tonight. We will never forget this moment.'

The mayor went on to praise Mahlia. Covered in dust, and still drawing breath through his inhaler, he concluded his speech by proclaiming that from this day forward they would be known as heroes throughout the country.

Mahlia almost laughed as excitement and happiness bubbled through her, and when the audience erupted into a standing ovation her chest swelled with joy. Gunnar looked quite shellshocked, standing in stoic silence beside her, but he never let go of her fingers. She knew he was showing all of Iceland that they were together, trusting that she wouldn't run from the consequences—not that they could be anything but positive after this.

The applause and cheering almost caused her eardrums to burst as the mayor was wheeled away towards a waiting ambulance, and people Mahlia had never even seen before moved in to embrace her and thank her.

She caught Gunnar's eyes as the cameras clicked away, capturing every second. He held her hand through every question she went on to answer, about who she was, how she was the founder of the e-bike company that had recently thrown Demus Johansson back into the spotlight, and how, yes, she was also Gunnar's girlfriend.

'She's more than that,' he said then, facing the cameras. 'She's the love of my life.'

And as he kissed her again, despite the chaos, Mahlia had the most delicious, all-consuming feeling that everything was going to be just fine for her and Gunnar. More than fine...

EPILOGUE

One year later

MAHLIA STOOD ATOP a cliff overlooking the North Atlantic, her heart racing with anticipation. The sun was setting on the horizon, casting its rosy hue across the rocky shoreline and painting Gunnar's handsome face golden. He had taken her to the most romantic location in Iceland, and she could sense he was distracted and twitchy as he took her hand in his and led them slowly down onto the secluded beach, where several people were riding horses across the sparkling black sand.

Gunnar smiled down at her and then dropped to one knee.

Wait... What?

Mahlia gasped, almost dropping down onto her own knees in front of him. She'd been right. He was planning to propose.

'Gunnar...'

He pulled a small velvet box from his pocket, opened it up, and she could barely see the exquisite antique diamond ring through the tears in her eyes.

'Mahlia, you know I love you with all my heart. This past year has been the best year of my life, and I'm in awe of everything you are, everything you do. Will you marry me?'

He was looking at her with so much admiration Mahlia couldn't believe it. She was stunned into silence for a moment before she managed to say a thing.

'Gunnar, yes. I will absolutely marry you!'

Tears streamed down her face as she pulled him to her in the last remaining streaks of glistening sunlight. How a person could love someone more than she loved him was hard to imagine, she thought, as he slid the ring onto her finger.

With Iceland now her adopted home, language lessons taking up three nights a week and her e-bike company flourishing, she was beyond thankful for how far they had come together over the past year…how much they had done.

Gunnar was a changed man. Ever since they'd given in to their feelings for each other and committed to starting again, together, he had been not just the partner she'd always dreamed of, he had thrown himself into everything the community asked of him, and was using his notoriety to create a whole new legacy—with her.

'Demus will kill me for not getting your acceptance on camera,' he said to her now, as she wiped at her eyes and kissed him.

'We don't have to share everything we do with the world,' she told him, smiling, studying the stunning ring in astonishment.

She was lucky to be spending these precious moments with him this week. He'd been in hospital for what felt like days on end already, with his kidney patients—not that they didn't try to make the most of every second of their spare time together.

'Besides, I'm sure he and Inka are waiting with some cocktails and canapés or something somewhere—am I right?'

'You are correct.' Gunnar grinned. 'But would you mind if we go and see my mother first?' he asked. 'She deserves to be the first to know.'

Mahlia drew his hands into hers and squeezed them tight as three women on horses trotted past and held up their hands at them, smiling in recognition.

Kaðlín Johansson was doing so much better now, almost a whole year sober, and Mahlia was humbled to have been invited into her world since her release from rehab. After Gunnar's father had left again, for Greece, the family had at last put most of their struggles behind them, and she and Gunnar spent every Sunday with his mother, Demus and Inka, at her newly renovated home. The bond she'd rekindled with her sons had got her thinking a lot about her own family, and she was excited to be flying her parents over again soon—the first time they'd met Gunnar had been magical.

'I know we have a lot to plan, but I was thinking Demus should drive an adapted vehicle to bring us to the church,' Gunnar said now, walking with her along the sand, the wind whipping up his shaggy hair beside her.

She nodded, smiling to herself. So he'd been thinking about this for a while, then. The idea didn't surprise her; he was now as much involved in her venture as Demus. In fact, he and Gunnar had applied for government grants to develop pioneering solutions for sustainable living across the country. Their team was building solar-powered charging stations across rural villages, as well as helping to develop innovative ways to harvest energy from glaciers and other natural forces to provide clean power sources.

They were becoming known across Iceland for their eco-initiatives, as much as Gunnar's life-changing surgeries, and between his new ventures and her e-bike events there wasn't a party in Reykjavik they weren't invited to.

Not that they attended them all.

It was nice relaxing at the cabin, just the two of them. And one day soon they'd be three, she thought with a misty smile, touching a hand to her belly.

She'd fallen pregnant a month ago. It had been a little nerve-racking, telling Gunnar, just in case he had any lingering reservations, but he'd lifted her up and spun her around in the kitchen and seemed as excited as a child who'd just been told he'd be getting a new puppy.

He'd reassured her once again that he was definitely ready to be a father, and that he couldn't wait to make the announcement—although just to their families for now. She'd been so relieved she'd actually cried down the phone to her mother, and again in front of his.

They *would* be the best parents. She knew it. She could feel it. Their children would be loved by everyone—not just them.

And now, she thought in excitement, staring at the orange sun sinking into the sea, they had a wedding to plan, too. And *this* marriage was going to last for ever.

* * * * *

ER DOC'S
LAS VEGAS REUNION

DENISE N. WHEATLEY

MILLS & BOON

To my mother, Donna, who is the reason for it all.

PROLOGUE

EVA'S CELL PHONE vibrated through her black satin clutch. She quickly pulled it out, expecting to see her fiancé's name flash across the screen. But it was Amanda, her friend and fellow ER doctor at the Black Willow Medical Clinic, calling for the third time.

"Hey," Eva whispered into the phone. "I can't talk now. I'm about to—"

"Let me guess. Attend yet another elaborate campaign event with your devastatingly handsome, soon-to-be senator fiancé?"

"No, not tonight. Kyle and I are actually having a quiet dinner at the Chateau Eilean."

"Ooh, the hottest new restaurant in all of Iowa? Fancy. Just the two of you?"

"Yes, can you believe it? No campaign manager and no entourage. Which is nice considering we haven't had a date night in months."

Eva stopped in front of a gold antique mirror inside the chateau's lobby and smoothed her long loose waves, then tightened the belt on her red wrap dress. She didn't know whether it was the triweekly spin classes or wedding planning stress that had whittled her size 8 frame down to a 6. Either way, her charmeuse trumpet bridal gown had to be taken in a few extra inches after the last fitting.

"I wish tonight could be all about rekindling the romance that's taken a back seat to our busy schedules," Eva continued.

"But I've got to use this rare time alone with Kyle to finalize plans for the big day." She paused, wincing at the death stare on the hostess's face. "Listen, I've gotta go. Phones aren't allowed in here and I'm pushing it. I'll call you later."

She glanced at her watch, realizing she was fifteen minutes late.

Good. Let Kyle wait on me for once...

A Little Leaguer had shown up to the clinic at the last minute with a hamate hook fracture that Eva had to cast before heading to dinner, which set her back. But while she worked hard to stick to her schedule and be on time whenever possible, it was Kyle who always ran late these days thanks to his unpredictable campaign activities.

"Hello," Eva said to the hostess, whose scowl quickly transformed into an artificially sweetened smile. "My name is Eva Gordon. I'm meeting Kyle Benson for dinner. The reservation should be in his name."

"Yes, Dr. Gordon. Right this way."

The haughty, model-thin greeter led Eva through the elaborate Victorian-style dining room to a table near the window. It was empty. No Kyle.

Late. Per usual.

A server approached the moment she sat down.

"Good evening, Dr. Gordon. May I offer you a beverage while you wait for Mr. Benson? A glass of wine, perhaps?"

"A glass of cabernet sauvignon would be perfect. Thank you."

She checked her phone. It was almost seven twenty. Their reservation was at seven. Kyle hadn't called, nor had he texted.

Eva sent him a message asking what time he'd be there, then glanced around the beautiful eatery. Crystal chandeliers hung from the vaulted ceiling. Intricate carvings outlined the cream wooden walls, which were adorned with vintage oil paintings. Blue silk chairs matched the curtains hanging from arched bay windows.

The chateau was buzzing with the who's who of Black Willow. Bankers, attorneys and politicians hobnobbed over charcuterie boards, steaks, seafood and pasta. Eva's mouth watered at the sight. She hadn't eaten since breakfast.

Just as she checked the phone once again, a commotion erupted near the entrance.

Eva watched as Kyle came strolling through the restaurant, stopping at practically every table on the way to theirs.

The handsome six-foot-three former soccer player turned political pundit was hard to miss. His movie-star smile could light up a night sky. His almond-shaped brown eyes danced when he spoke on his plans to change the world. His warm demeanor made people feel as though they were all that mattered.

The chateau's manager rushed over and shook Kyle's hand. "It's great to see you here tonight, Mr. Benson. So, what do you think? Is this the best night of the week to come out and rub elbows with Black Willow's elite or what?"

"It certainly is. I've already got my eye on several potential donors."

Eva dug her fingernails into the linen tablecloth.

So that's why we're here. To network. Not spend a quiet evening alone.

"Good luck with that," the manager told Kyle. "If there's anything I can do for you, please do not hesitate to let me know."

"Will do, Douglas. Thank you."

Kyle glanced over at Eva, grinning and waving as if he were about to deliver a victory speech.

"Hey, babe," he breathed, finally reaching their table. "Sorry I'm late."

She arched her neck for a kiss, despite being slightly irritated. Kyle's lips barely grazed her cheek before he greeted a group of men seated nearby, then searched for the server.

Let it go. Don't start the night off on a sour note.

"I was going to order appetizers," Eva said, "but couldn't decide on what to get. Everything looks so good."

"Well, I'm glad you didn't. I can't stay long. I've got to get back to the office soon. Things are really heating up."

"Wait, what about dinner?"

"Can't do it. I've only got about thirty minutes to spare, if that. Just enough time to have a quick drink."

Eva tossed her menu to the side. "What's so important that you're skipping out on what I thought was a special date night for just the two of us?"

"A meeting with my campaign manager. Stan added a last-minute speech to my calendar that I need to prepare for. It's happening first thing tomorrow morning down at the mayor's office. This is a big deal for me, Eva. And great exposure. Several media outlets will be there. I've got to be ready."

She opened her mouth to speak but was interrupted when the server approached with her wine. While Kyle ordered a whiskey sour, Eva pulled out a stack of floral design photos.

"Since you have to leave so soon, can we at least look through the arrangements that Louise pulled together for the wedding?" She slid a picture in front of him. "I love this one. The etched crystal vase is gorgeous. And the various shades of pink peonies with eucalyptus added throughout is just perfection. But I also love the idea of keeping things traditional and going with roses. Or maybe even calla lilies. What do you think?"

Kyle remained silent, too busy typing away on his phone to respond.

"*Excuse* me," Eva said stiffly. "Could I at least get my allotted thirty minutes to finalize these plans before you have to leave? We're going to end up with a flowerless ceremony if we don't make a decision and place the order—"

He held up a finger. "One second. I need to approve a couple of key points that Stan thinks I should add to my speech."

Eva dropped the stack of photos and gulped down several sips of wine. Shards of anger sliced at her chest while her heartbeat pounded inside her eardrums. She was *this close* to suggesting they nix the wedding ceremony altogether and exchange vows at the courthouse once the election was finally over.

Kyle didn't set his phone aside until the server brought over his drink. He took a long swallow, then rubbed his hands together.

"You know, I think I might go off script a little bit during my speech. Throw in a couple of bullet points on my education initiatives. I could cover how parents should be receiving school curricula, and suggest that fundraisers be held throughout the year in support of various scholarship programs. What do you think?"

Eva slowly exhaled. "I think those are both good ideas, Kyle. But can we just take a few minutes to look over the floral arrangements and choose the ones we want—"

His cell phone buzzed. He grabbed it, then began typing away once again.

"Kyle!" Eva said, louder than she'd intended.

He jumped in his seat. Several patrons turned and stared.

Kyle glanced at the nearby tables, smiling sheepishly before throwing Eva a look. "Will you please keep your voice down?"

"Sorry. I just wish you would tear yourself away from that phone and listen to me for once. Your *fiancée.* I understand that you've got work to do, but so do I. I left the clinic early tonight to be here with you. You're already cutting our evening short. The least you could do is help me with all this planning. I've done most of it on my own. A little input would be nice."

He dropped his head in his hand. The server approached and asked if they were ready to order. Kyle shooed him away.

Eva sat there silently, waiting for him to apologize and look through the floral designs.

"I can't do this," he muttered instead.

She reached over and caressed his arm. "Come on, Kyle. Of course you can do this. I've narrowed the choices down to four. All you have to do is pick one. As for your speech, you'll knock it out of the park, just like you always do."

"I'm not talking about flower arrangements, Eva," he snapped, pulling away from her. "Or my speech. I'm talking about us. I can't do *us* anymore."

She stared across the table through wide eyes, certain she'd misheard him.

"I—I'm sorry," Kyle continued, his voice barely a whisper. "But this is…this is too much. There's no way I can run a successful campaign, win the election *and* marry you. So I think we should call off the wedding."

Everything around Eva blurred, except for his sullen expression. She sat silently, waiting for him to recant the statement. But he didn't. He just continued sipping his drink while avoiding her stunned gaze.

"Hold on," she uttered, her voice trembling with shock. "Let me get this straight. You're telling me that you want to cancel our wedding because of an election that you're already on track to win?"

"Can you lower your voice? People are looking at us."

"*Kyle*, you just ended our relationship, and you're worried about who's looking at us? Oh, but wait. Why am I surprised? You've always been overly obsessed with your image. That's all that matters to you. To hell with reality. As long as you're keeping up appearances, you're good."

"Okay," he said, pushing away from the table. "I'm going to end this conversation now before things get ugly."

"Oh, trust me. Things can't get any uglier than they already are. Thank you, Kyle."

"Thank me? For what?"

"For wasting the last five years of my life!" she snapped before jumping up and storming out of the restaurant.

Anger coursed through Eva's chest as she ran to her car. But underneath it was the pain and confusion of knowing such a huge part of her life was over, and that for the first time ever, she had no clue what her future would hold.

Eva paced back and forth across the dark hardwood floor of her chic two-bedroom loft. She stopped at her desk, plopped down in the chair and logged in to her online journal. While waiting for it to open, an ad popped up.

"Weird," she mumbled, double-checking to make sure her pop-up blocker was on. It was.

The words *Are You Looking for a Change?* flashed across the screen in bold red letters.

"Hell, yeah, I'm looking for a change."

Eva clicked on the ad and leaned in closer, her eyes squinting as she read the details.

Hello! Do you work in the medical field? If so, are you interested in making a change? If the answer is yes, then we have an exciting opportunity for you! Las Vegas's Fremont General Hospital is looking to fill temporary positions in our neonatal, radiation, intensive care and emergency room departments.

"A temp job in the ER?" she murmured, double-clicking the emergency room button. It opened a new screen.

Fremont General Hospital's state-of-the-art ER is an intense, fast-paced environment, where the responsibility is as great as the reward. We are searching for an experienced emergency room doctor with in-depth knowledge of current medical treatments and procedures. Keen attention to detail along with excellent analytical and communication skills are a must. If you thrive on fascinating, fulfilling experiences, and possess the ability to think and act quickly, then click the link below to apply!

Eva's fingertips hovered over the keyboard. She thought about the moment Kyle spoke the words *I can't do us anymore.* Imagined all the scrutiny she'd be under once their small, gossipy town got word that their wedding, which had been dubbed "the event of the decade", had been canceled. The struggle to mend her broken heart, along with the humiliation, would be unbearable.

She'd always done the right thing. Followed in her father's footsteps by becoming a top doctor in her field and withstanding the pressure to be the best, just as he had. Abided by her mother's fervent desire for her to marry well by getting together with Kyle soon after he'd been crowned Black Willow's most eligible bachelor, then accepting his proposal. That had all worked for Eva, at least for a while.

When she and Kyle had met at a charity event five years ago, Eva felt as though he could be the man for her. His charm, his charisma, the way he seemingly adored her...it didn't take long for Eva to fall in love. But as Kyle's political career began to blossom, their relationship withered. His focus was solely on work as each new achievement grabbed his attention, making him crave more of the professional spotlight and less of time spent with her. Eva had thought his proposal would bring about a fresh start for them both. When nothing changed, she wondered whether Kyle really wanted the marriage, or simply the look of having a successful ER doctor on his arm.

Playing it safe to appease others had gotten her nowhere. Now it was Eva's turn to do things her way.

"Here goes nothing," she said grimly before clicking the link and filling out the application.

CHAPTER ONE

Month one

"HERE WE ARE, Dr. Gordon."

Eva's heart dropped to the soles of her feet. She stared out the Tesla's back-seat window, eyeing Fremont General Hospital's sleek reflective glass and white cement exterior.

The crowded driveway was bustling with activity. Cars and emergency vehicles maneuvered their way around a beautiful garden filled with exotic succulents. A steady stream of guests, patients and hospital workers flowed in and out of the automatic glass doors. It was a far cry from the simpler inner workings of her clinic back home.

Eva, you're not in Black Willow anymore...

The driver's phone dinged, indicating another pickup request. He turned in his seat and cleared his throat. "Best of luck to you, Doctor."

"Oh, umm...sorry. I should let you be on your way. Thank you."

Her calf muscles trembled as she stepped out of the car. Eva's first day on the job, in a big new city no less, had sent her entire nervous system into a buzzing frenzy.

What in the world have I gotten myself into?

The last two weeks had been a whirlwind. Despite spontaneously applying for Fremont General's temporary ER position, Eva had struggled to recover from her breakup. She'd avoided all social functions and buried herself in work, while constantly refreshing her email inbox in hopes of hearing from Fremont's hospital administrator.

It took five days to find out that her application had been accepted and she'd landed the job. Since then, she'd had to console her supervisor, who was completely distraught upon hearing that Eva was taking a leave of absence, hire a house sitter, bid adieu to her family and friends, then jet off to Las Vegas, all without telling her ex-fiancé that she was leaving.

"And now, here I am," she whispered to herself. "Here we go."

Eva took a deep breath and walked inside the hospital's bright, airy lobby. Beams of light shone through the woven timber ceilings, highlighting vivid floral murals covering the walls. Plush leather chairs lined the vast waiting area. The space felt more like a lavish hotel than a hospital.

I could get used to this, she thought, making her way to the reception desk.

"Good morning," the receptionist said. "May I help you?"

"Yes, my name is Dr. Eva Gordon. I'm scheduled to meet Nurse Brandi Bennett here at the front desk. She works in the emergency room—"

"Dr. Gordon?" a petite, curly-haired blonde with rosy cheeks and a warm smile asked as she bounced toward Eva. "Hello there. I'm Nurse Bennett. But please, call me Brandi."

Eva shook her extended hand. "Hello, Brandi. It's nice to meet you. And finally put a face to the emails. Thanks again for all the advice you shared before my move here. It made things so much easier."

"You're welcome. I was happy to help. Trust me, I know what it's like to leave your small town behind on a whim and move to a big city. I'm here by way of Clemmington, California, which is only a few hours away. Your commute from Black Willow, Iowa, was a much longer one."

"It was," Eva replied, glancing around the lobby. "I just hope I can adjust quickly."

"I'm sure you will. This is going to be an amazing experience. It certainly has been for me. Are you ready to take a tour of the facility?"

The knots in Eva's stomach slowly unraveled, transforming into sprouts of excitement. "Yes, I'm ready."

"Great. We'll start on the top floor, where the coronary and intensive care units are located, then work our way down. I'll save the emergency room for last. Follow me."

As the women headed toward the elevator, Brandi turned to Eva. "So, what was it about the temporary position here at Fremont General that pulled you away from home, if I may ask?"

"It's a long story. But for now, let's just say that a change of scenery was much needed."

"So, that's it in a nutshell," Brandi said. "A rather large nutshell, but you get the gist."

"I do," Eva told her. "It's a lot to take in. This is such a beautiful hospital. I'm sure I'll get lost more times than I can count. Hopefully it won't take long to learn my way around." She glanced up ahead. "And now, saving the best for last?"

"Yes, the emergency room. We're almost there. The cafeteria is on the way. Would you like to stop in and grab a cup of coffee?"

"That would be wonderful. I can't believe I've lasted this long without my daily caffeine fix."

Eva followed Brandi inside the sunny dining hall. They passed an array of food stations, from sushi and hot dog stands to pasta and salad bars. Right before they approached the Drip & Sip Coffee Stop, a familiar figure appeared near the delicatessen.

"*Wait*, is that…?" Eva began, thinking she might have just spotted Idris Elba.

No, it couldn't be. There aren't any cameras around filming a movie. So why would he be here wearing a lab coat?

"Is that who?" Brandi asked, glancing around the area.

Eva hesitated, not wanting to admit that she'd mistaken a doctor for a movie star. "Oh, it's nothing. So what do you recommend?"

"My go-to is the iced shaken espresso with a shot of oat milk and a dash of stevia. It keeps me on my toes throughout the day."

"Sounds like that's exactly what I need."

"Awesome. I'll grab a couple."

While Brandi placed their order, Eva's eyes drifted toward the exit. The Idris Elba look-alike was walking out. Despite his back being to her, Eva couldn't help but feel as though she knew him. The way his tall, lean build broke into a swaggering gait, his short wavy hair tapered down the back of his neck, and his large hands gestured emphatically all rang familiar bells.

"Here you go," Brandi said, handing Eva a cup. "I hope you like it."

"I'm sure I will." She took a long sip, closing her eyes as the rich, smoky java settled into her taste buds. "Mmm, this is delicious. Great choice."

"Awesome. Ready to head to the ER?"

"Absolutely."

A burst of exhilaration shot through Eva's veins as her nude pumps clicked along the speckled white tile.

Finally, a look at my new digs for the next three months...

The pair exited the cafeteria and made a left turn.

"Oh, hold on," Brandi said, staring down the other end of the hallway. "Dr. Malone!" she called out.

Eva followed her gaze. It fell on the Idris doppelgänger. His head was buried in a file. A husky, bald-headed man he was speaking with nudged him, then pointed at Brandi. He looked up, peering down the corridor.

"Do you have a minute?" Brandi asked. "I'd like for you to meet someone."

As the men walked toward them, Eva's entire body went numb.

"No..." she whispered. "It can't be..."

"I'm sorry?" Brandy asked her.

"That's—that's Dr. *who*?"

"Dr. Malone. Dr. Clark Malone, to be exact. He's one of our emergency room physicians, so you two will be working very closely together."

Eva's knees gave way. She leaned against the wall, her racing heart palpitating inside her throat as she struggled to grasp Brandi's words.

Clark Malone...

He and Eva shared a tumultuous past that she'd buried deep in the corners of her mind. Up until now. Because as he approached, a whirlwind of memories came racing to the forefront, the first being that he was no longer a handsome yet wiry young medical student. Clark had matured into a full-blown, broad-shouldered, extremely fine-looking man.

They'd met during their first year of medical school. Despite the undeniable chemistry between them, Eva and Clark had formed a tight platonic bond. Together they'd helped each other adjust to a new city, an extremely challenging course load and a rigorous schedule. While free time was sparse, they'd sneak off on occasion to Cedar Rapids, Iowa's Black Sheep Social Club for live jazz music, or Pub 217 for veggie black bean burgers. The friendship they'd built was solid, inimitable even. But all that had changed one night during their third year.

Hours of intense studying for a genetics exam, mixed with a few beers and joke-telling challenges, had turned an evening cramming session into a fiery romp between the sheets.

While Clark had hoped that the moment would lead to much more, Eva had regretfully explained to him that she was laser-focused on her studies and couldn't continue anything that might jeopardize her medical goals.

She didn't, however, completely reject him. Eva had told Clark that while they couldn't be together back then, she was open to something more once they'd settled into their new jobs after graduation. In the meantime, they'd tried to remain friends, but things just weren't the same. They'd slowly drifted apart, then lost touch after graduation, with her staying in the Midwest while he'd jetted off to the West Coast.

Losing Clark as a friend had hurt her deeply. But Eva's aspirations had taken precedence over her emotions—she'd worked too hard to risk getting distracted. But she'd thought about him many times over the years—particularly that one steamy night they'd shared. While it had been amazing, Eva couldn't help but regret how it led to the demise of their friendship. She'd contemplated contacting Clark on numerous occasions but had always talked herself out of it. After the emotional rollercoaster ride they'd endured, she didn't think he would want to hear from her. Since he'd never reached out to her, either, Eva had figured he'd moved on and decided to do the same.

Now here he was, standing before her at Fremont General Hospital of all places.

What were the odds?

Eva pushed herself away from the wall and straightened her fitted black blazer. Their eyes met. She raised her hand, waving feebly.

The bright, welcoming smile on Clark's handsome face fell instantly as his jaws clenched. His rich brown complexion turned a pale shade of gray. His eyes narrowed, as if he couldn't believe what he was seeing. The reaction caused a hurt so deep that it left Eva wishing she could teleport herself straight back to Black Willow.

"Dr. Malone," Brandi began. "I'd like for you to meet—"

"Dr. Eva Gordon," Clark interjected coolly.

"Hello, Dr. Malone," she practically choked through quivering lips.

Brandi's head swiveled from side to side. "Wait, you two know each other?"

"We do," Eva murmured, her gaze fixated on Clark's pulsating temples. It was a trait she remembered him exhibiting whenever a stressful situation presented itself. "Dr. Malone and I attended Cedar Rapids Medical School together."

Clark squared his shoulders, folding his hands in front of him while staring at her.

His defense mechanism whenever he's guarding his feelings, Eva thought, surprised at how easy it was to read him after all these years.

"I…um…" Clark paused, his forehead creasing with confusion. "I'm surprised to see you here at Fremont General, Dr. Gordon. What brings you to Las Vegas?"

"Actually," Brandi chimed in, "Dr. Gordon has accepted a temporary assignment here in the ER for the next three months. So you two will be working very closely with each other, which should be an easy transition since you attended medical school together."

"Wait, you accepted *what*?" Clark barked right before his colleague stepped in and extended a hand.

"Dr. Gordon, welcome aboard. It's great to have you here."

"Oh!" Brandi uttered. "My apologies. I was so surprised to find out that Dr. Gordon and Dr. Malone know each other that I've forgotten my manners. Dr. Gordon, this is Leo Graham, our esteemed director of emergency medicine. Any questions or concerns you have, he's your go-to guy."

"It's nice to meet you, Director Graham."

"Likewise. And please, call me Leo."

Clark glanced down at his watch, then nudged Leo's shoulder. "We need to get back to your office. I've got some files to review with you, and several patients to check on. Dr. Gordon, welcome to Fremont General. I guess I'll be seeing you around."

"Great meeting you, Dr. Gor—" Leo began right before Clark grabbed his arm and dragged him in the opposite direction.

"We'll catch up with you two inside the ER!" Brandi called out to their backs. She turned to Eva. "Don't mind them. Things can get pretty hectic around here, so I'm sure they're just in a hurry. Are you ready to wrap up the tour?"

"Sure," Eva muttered, remorse burning her eyes as she watched Clark swiftly stride off.

He can't stand to even be in my presence. This isn't going to work. I shouldn't have come here.

"Wait," Eva continued hurriedly. "Before we finish the tour, I need to stop by the ladies' room. Is there one close by?"

"There is. It's straight ahead and to your right. Once you're done, why don't you meet me inside the emergency room? It'll be little farther down the hall on your left. Just follow the signs. You can't miss it."

"Thanks. I'll be right there."

Beads of perspiration popped up along Eva's hairline as she tore down the corridor. She dumped her coffee inside a trash receptacle, her stomach churning at the thought of ingesting anything.

This cannot be happening. This cannot be happening!

Just when she reached the restroom, a group of mothers with screaming toddlers in tow bolted inside. Eva continued down the hallway, her head spinning in search of a quiet nook.

Three empty phone booths appeared up ahead. Eva slipped inside the first one, pulled her cell phone from her purse and said, "Call Amanda Reinhart!" into the microphone.

Amanda picked up on the first ring. "Hey! How's it going out there in sunny Sin Cit—"

"*Amanda*! You will never, and I do mean *never*, guess who works at Fremont General."

"Wait, slow down. I can't understand you. I'll never guess *what*?"

"Who. Works. At. Fremont. General!"

"Who?"

"*Clark*. As in Clark Malone!"

Eva closed her eyes, sliding down the cool oakwood wall before plopping down onto a worn burgundy stool.

The other end of the phone went silent.

"Amanda? Are you still there?"

"I—I'm here. I just… I don't even know what to say, except *wow*. You and Clark, together again? You two didn't exactly leave medical school on the best of terms. So to be reunited with him after all these years, under these circumstances no less, is—"

"Wild as hell," Eva interjected.

"Exactly. And you all were such great friends. Until you slept together. You know, I never did understand why you didn't give him a chance after that. Especially considering how good the sex was, according to you."

"Amanda, please. You know why I didn't give him a chance back then. I was focused on graduating top of our class and landing my first-choice residency. I didn't have the time or the emotional bandwidth for a serious relationship."

"More like you were working to live up to your father's legacy and appease your high-society mother—"

"Which is perfectly understandable considering everything they sacrificed for me, isn't it?" Eva interrupted. "Especially my mom. This is a generational thing. She watched her parents struggle for years, saving until they were in their mid-fifties to purchase their first house. Then my mother worked two jobs to help my father get through medical school. She didn't want to see me go through those same tribulations."

"Is that why she's always been so intent on you being with Kyle, too?"

"That is absolutely why. My mother loves that he comes from a good family and has done well for himself. She's old-school. She wants me to be well taken care of, despite me being able to take care of myself."

"And I understand all that, Eva. But this is *your* life. When are you going to start living it on your terms? You've proven to your parents that they did a wonderful job raising you. You are their wildest dream come true considering you've become such a successful doctor, just like your father. That's why everyone here at the clinic was so distraught when they found out you'd accepted this temporary assignment! Now, what about your dreams? Which I know include finding love again. I've always said that when it comes to Clark—"

"I know, I know," Eva interjected. "You've always said that I may have very well passed up the love of my life." A muscle pulled inside her chest at the sound of those words. "Right now, that's the last thing I need to hear. Can we please just focus on the issue at hand?"

"Sorry, my friend. I'm just being honest. But wait, what exactly is the issue at hand? You and Clark reuniting could be a good thing. Maybe this is the universe's way of bringing you two back together."

"Look, I just got dumped by my fiancé. The main reason I came to Las Vegas was to escape all the reminders of my heartbreak and heal in peace. I don't want to get caught up in another situation where I could get hurt again. Plus Clark seems to hate me. When we ran into each other just now, he couldn't wait to get away." Eva groaned loudly, slumping down deeper into the stool. "This was a mistake. I should come back home."

"You should do no such thing. Give this awesome opportunity a chance, Eva. And don't worry about Clark. He was probably just as shocked to see you as you were to see him. You two will find your footing, and hopefully even rekindle your old friendship. Trust me. There is more to this serendipitous reunion than you may think."

"I don't know about all that, but thanks for the advice." Eva sighed, glancing at the time. "I'd better go. The nurse who's giving me a tour of the hospital probably thinks I got lost."

"Keep your head up, Dr. Gordon. And believe that everything is working in your favor."

"It doesn't feel that way, but okay. I'll let you know how things go."

Eva disconnected the call and stared at the wall, forcing down the lump of despair creeping up her throat. She stood on wobbly legs, making her way to the ER while praying she wouldn't run into Clark again. Once there, Brandi handed her a lab coat.

"Here you go, Dr. Gordon. You never know. We may have to step in and lend a hand during the middle of the tour. So it's best to be prepared."

"From the looks of things," Eva replied, jumping back as paramedics flew past her with a stretcher in tow, "that seems very likely."

The waiting area was filled with weary-looking patients, sitting among worried friends and relatives. A security guard waved his hands in the air while struggling to organize a large group of people swarming the reception desk.

"Follow me," Brandi said. She led Eva down a long corridor while pointing from side to side. "These are our areas of care. From the resuscitation and trauma units to the operating rooms and observation areas, this is where you'll be spending the majority of your time."

Eva slowly pivoted, taking it all in. "Wow. This is so much different from what I'm used to."

"Let's head to the back. I'll show you where the library and prayer room are located. And don't worry. You'll adjust to this place in no time. I'm sure Dr. Malone will be more than happy to take you under his wing."

I highly doubt that... Eva mused, smiling through her apprehension while still rethinking her decision to come to Las Vegas.

CHAPTER TWO

"UM... CLARK?" LEO ASKED, rushing to catch up with him. "What was *that* all about?"

"Nothing I wanna talk about."

Clark could barely see through the blur of disbelief clouding his vision. Thoughts of Eva filled his head. She was the woman he'd once called his best friend. Whom he'd accidentally fallen in love with. Who'd then proceeded to break his heart.

And who is now going to be my colleague for the next three months. What the hell?

He stormed inside Leo's office and grabbed a stack of patient files off the cluttered desk.

"Where is Mr. Johnson's chart?" he barked.

"The triage nurse has it. Dude, what is wrong with you?"

Clark ignored the question as memories of med school flashed through his mind. Memories he'd struggled to forget, of all the times he and Eva had sat on the beige-carpeted floor of her studio apartment, venting about classroom woes and family drama, or past heartbreaks and future dreams. Through it all, their bond had intensified. So had Clark's feelings. But he'd resisted the urge to act on them during their first couple of years, afraid of ruining the friendship.

Their third year, however, he broke, no longer able to restrain his emotions. That sensual evening they'd spent together had been electrifying, filling Clark with hope. He was convinced they'd finally take things to the next level and had broached the subject of dating exclusively.

But Eva's head was in a different space. Clinicals, passing the boards and landing the perfect residency were her primary focus, leaving no room for a relationship. Her decision to remain friends pained Clark. For him, reverting back to the way things were, as though nothing had happened, had been impossible. He'd been down that road once before and already knew how the story would end—just as it had with his high school sweetheart, Jessica Hardwick.

Clark and Jessica had dated throughout their teenage years. After the pair graduated from Chicago's St. Pierius High School, he'd looked forward to maintaining a long-distance relationship as she went off to college in Georgia and he'd headed to Michigan.

But Jessica had other plans. She wanted to be single while exploring her new life in Atlanta. Clark had objected, insisting that their relationship was too solid to just throw away. Jessica, however, disagreed.

"Come on, let's live a little," she'd said. "See who else may be out there for us. We'll always be the best of friends. And if we're meant to be, trust me, the universe will bring us back together."

Clark had no choice but to let her go. Just as he'd suspected, once the pair went their separate ways, the connection had crumbled. Jessica's calls, texts and emails slowly subsided, while his went unanswered. The visits she'd promised never happened. After pledging a sorority and joining the student body government, that was it. Jessica cut him off completely and moved on.

The experience had left Clark feeling extremely cautious. He spent the rest of his college years casually dating, refusing to allow himself to get hurt again. Whenever a woman attempted to get serious or mentioned settling down, he'd walked away, determined to safeguard his emotions.

Then along came Eva. The only one who was able to shatter his shield of protection. It was as if he had no control over his own feelings. The power she'd had over him was frightening, but equally exhilarating. For the first time in a long time, Clark dropped his guard and let her in, even sharing what he'd gone through with Jessica. Despite knowing Eva was focused more on her goals than a relationship, that night they'd slept together had prompted him to put his heart on the line, only to be hurt once again. Since then, Clark's heart had remained firmly under lock and key. And he had no plans to release it.

Beep!

The hospital's blaring intercom jolted him out of his thoughts.

Pull yourself together...

"I'll be back," Clark told Leo. He charged out of the office and into the ER, approaching the triage nurse. "Is Mr. Johnson still here, or has he been transferred to the ICU?"

"He's still here. We're waiting for a bed to become available in intensive care. But don't worry, he's stable. Nurse Collins is in with him now."

"Good. I'll go check on him."

Footsteps pounded behind Clark as he headed to the trauma unit.

"Hey!" Leo called out. "Wait up. There's something I want to ask you."

Clark threw his hand in the air. "Please don't start with the line of questioning. It's already been a long day and I'm running on fumes. We've treated four heart attacks, three strokes, a couple of near-fatal car accident victims and an overdose. All before noon."

"Well, they don't call Las Vegas the city that never sleeps for nothing. The action doesn't cease. Neither do the injuries and illnesses. But wait." Leo stopped Clark in the middle of the hallway. "Are you running on fumes because of work? Or because you were out late last night with Veronica?"

Clark opened Mr. Johnson's chart, focusing on the myocardial infarction victim's vitals rather than his friend's curious stare. "Didn't I just tell you not to start with the questions?"

"You did. But I figured you were referring to Eva. Not Veronica. So come on. Spill it. I already know things must've gone well considering she made it all the way to a fifth date. That's a record for you, isn't it?"

Clark ignored him.

"Okay, just answer this question. Do you think Veronica is the one? Because judging by what you've told me, she sounds phenomenal."

"She is phenomenal. But here's a better question. Am I even *looking* for the one?"

Leo's dark green eyes rolled into the back of his shiny bald head. "If you're not, you should be."

Clark fell silent.

"Oh, no." Leo sighed.

"Oh, no, what?"

"You've got that look on your face."

"What look?"

"That little scowl you get every time one of your flings has fizzled out. You and Veronica are over, aren't you?"

"I wouldn't say we're over," Clark rebutted, "because that would imply we were actually in a relationship to begin with. Veronica and I agreed to keep things casual from the start, which we did. Now we're both ready to move on."

Leo crossed his arms over his potbelly. "You're both ready? Or *you're* ready?

"You know," he continued without giving Clark a chance to respond, "for such a smart, cool, good-looking guy, you're a lost cause. Why were you ready to move on, exactly? Wait, let me guess. I bet you pulled the whole *I'm a busy physician* spiel. Claimed you work long hours and don't have much free time."

"That's exactly what I did. Because it's true. And guess what? Veronica, who is a smart, beautiful, in-demand entertainment attorney, understood completely. She doesn't have much free time on her hands, either. So there were no hard feelings. We do enjoy each other's company, though. If we ever wanna get together again, the door is open."

"Most men would kill to date a woman like Veronica. Yet here you are, ending things yet again. What is the problem?"

"There is no problem," Clark replied matter-of-factly while approving Mr. Johnson's prescriptions for amlodipine, metoprolol and atorvastatin. "Because I only date women who are looking for something casual. Fun. Nothing too serious. Thus far, that's working out just fine for me."

"I disagree, man. Having the right woman in your life— *one* woman—would only make you better."

"Why is it always the single ones dishing out the most advice?"

Leo snorted loudly. "Hold on now. Let's not forget, I wasn't always single. I'm speaking from experience. I learned my lesson the hard way. It wasn't until my ex-wife left me that I realized how wonderful it is to have a great partner by your side."

"Point taken. Now let's end this conversation. I've got patients to see."

Clark continued down the hallway and stepped inside Mr. Johnson's room. Nurse Collins was hovering over the side of the bed. She looked up and held a finger in the air.

"Hey, Doc," she whispered. "I just need a few more minutes. I'm inserting Mr. Johnson's catheter. Once I check his vitals and change his IV, I'll go over his chart with you."

Clark gave her a thumbs-up before quietly slipping out.

"Nowhere to run to now, is there?" Leo taunted, his thin

lips spreading into a Cheshire cat grin. "I think it's time that we get to the bottom of your commitment issues."

Clark brushed past him and posted up at a mobile workstation. Just as he opened Mr. Johnson's health record, his cell phone pinged. A notification appeared from one of his various dating app accounts.

You have a new private message!

Leo peered over his shoulder, staring at the screen. "You're already back on a dating app trying to meet someone new, aren't you?"

"Mind your business, Director Graham."

"That's hard to do when you make it so obvious. I recognized the sound of that ping. It's an alert from Two of Hearts."

"How do you even know that?"

"Because I'm a platinum member myself."

"Of course you are." Clark handed him the phone. "Now that the cat's out the bag, check out Kelsie's profile. She's a dancer at the Bellagio hotel. According to her message, she's interested in becoming a doctor and wants to pick my brain."

Leo stared at the screen, shaking his head while swiping through the photos. "She's gorgeous. But judging by the looks of her expensive shopping sprees and fancy nights out on the town, Kelsie isn't interested in becoming a doctor. She's interested in *landing* one."

"Hater," Clark quipped, snatching the phone back and replying to the message.

I'd love to get together with you and discuss my work as a physician. Are you free for drinks tonight?

Kelsie responded within seconds.

Hold, please. Let me check my schedule...kidding! Yes, I'm free. My rehearsal ends at eight p.m. How about we meet at the Bellagio's Baccarat Bar and Lounge at eight thirty?

That sounds good. I'll see you there. Looking forward to it.

Leo placed his hand on Clark's shoulder. "As a friend, I'm advising you to stop with all the serial dating and take some time to figure out what you're so afraid of. Truth be told, I already know what it is. You just need to admit it to yourself."

"Admit *what*?"

"That the stunning doctor we just ran into, who you are refusing to talk about, is the reason you're such a commitment-phobe."

Clark's mouth went dry. He racked his brain for a snappy response but came up empty.

"Dr. Eva Gordon," Leo pressed. "Also known as the one that got away. You may not realize this, but you talk about her all the time. I won't even get into how you stalk her social media."

"Oh, so now I'm a commitment-phobe *and* an online stalker?"

"I'm just calling it like I see it. Don't think I haven't noticed you scrolling through her Instagram from time to time. Isn't that how you found out she'd gotten engaged?"

The reminder made Clark's heart ache. He pulled up Mr. Johnson's chest X-rays and focused on his coronary calcium scan results, avoiding Leo's inquisitive gaze.

"Dr. Malone, please report to the ER reception desk. Dr. Malone to the ER reception desk."

"Ahh, saved by the bell," Leo said drily, following closely behind Clark as he trekked toward the front of the emergency room. "But don't think this conversation is over just because you've been called to the principal's office. Because it isn't."

Clark ignored his well-meaning yet irritating friend and entered the lobby. When he caught a glimpse of the front desk, he stopped abruptly.

"Wait!" he whispered, grabbing Leo's arm and pulling him back.

Leo yelped loudly after almost tumbling into the wall. "What is the problem now?"

"Eva and Brandi are at reception."

"*Okay.* They're probably the ones who called for you. Why don't you go find out what they want?"

Clark didn't budge as the tremors in his feet shot straight to his gut.

"Ugh, how do I say this?" Leo sighed, staring up at the ceiling. "I know the subject of Eva is off-limits. But come on, she's going to be working here for the next three months. Avoiding her will be impossible. You need to resolve these issues that you have, *quickly.* Maybe even try to reestablish the friendship. Better yet, rekindle the relation—"

"All right," Clark interrupted. "Don't get ahead of yourself. Come on. Let's get this over with."

His limbs transformed into cement as he dragged himself through the waiting area.

Deep breaths, Clark thought, only managing to pull thin streams of air through his constricted lungs. The closer he got to Eva, the faster his pulse raced.

"Las Vegas," Leo muttered. "Also known as the city of second chances. Gotta love it…"

Brandi gave the men a thumbs-up as they approached. "Dr. Gordon and I just finished our tour of the hospital. I was hoping the two of you could give her a more in-depth look at the ER, maybe discuss some of the things that she can expect to encounter while working here at Fremont General."

All eyes turned to Clark. He was silent, still stunned by the fact that Eva was in his presence. While he just stood there, blinking rapidly in search of something valuable to contribute, Leo stepped forward.

"Well, one thing I can tell you is that here in Las Vegas, there isn't much you *won't* see inside the ER."

"Now that is a fact," Brandi added.

Clark looked on as the threesome bantered back and forth, hating himself for freezing up. But the idea of Eva being thrust back into his life so suddenly, so unexpectedly, had thrown him off his game. Rather than join the conversation, he remained motionless, quietly taking it all in.

Eva had somehow managed to become even more beautiful than she'd been years ago. Her toned, curvy figure proved she hadn't missed many gym days. Those wide-set eyes, with their dazzling hazel specks, could put the coldest soul in a trance. And those lush lips, the top one puckering slightly over the bottom, ignited memories of them wrapped around his—

"So, Dr. Gordon," Leo said, his booming voice disrupting Clark's lustful thoughts. "Where were you working before coming to Fremont General?"

"A small medical clinic in Black Willow, Iowa."

"Huh, interesting. And you left Black Willow behind for *Las Vegas* of all places?"

Eva hesitated, her eyes shifting as she pulled a stray brunette curl behind her ear. "Yes, that's right."

"But what about your fian—?"

"You know," Clark interjected, grabbing Leo's arm, "what I think Leo's trying to say is that Las Vegas is quite a switch-up from such a small community. Nothing you can't adjust to, I'm sure, Dr. Gordon. Have you uh…have you found a place to stay yet?"

"I have. I'm staying at the Cascade Tower. It's not too far from here."

"I'm familiar with that complex. It's really nice. I lived there for a while when I first moved to Vegas—"

The conversation was interrupted when a team of paramedics came rushing through the door. As the group turned toward the entrance, Leo leaned toward Clark, whispering, "There's trouble in small-town paradise between Eva and the fiancé. Mark my words."

"We'll talk about it later."

Clark's attention was solely focused on the distressed patient being wheeled in on a stretcher.

"It hurts," the man yelled, writhing against the mattress. "It *hurts*!"

Clark jumped into action, charging toward the EMTs. Brandi and Eva followed closely behind.

The patient's entire face was charred, and patches of hair had been burned off his scalp. His navy blue T-shirt was tattered, and the white jeans barely hanging from his blackened legs were scorched. The skin on his arms, torso, chest and neck was covered in burn wounds that oozed blood from the raw inner layers.

"Talk to me," Clark said, leading the group toward the trauma area. "What happened to our patient?"

"We've got a severe burn victim," a paramedic panted. "Second or third degree judging by the leaking fluid and black center encased within majority of the wounds. There's deep partial thickness. We tried to dress the wounds before leaving the scene, but the patient wouldn't allow it. So we covered him in sterile burn sheets instead. We've been monitoring his airway and it doesn't appear compromised, so we don't believe intubation will be necessary. All other vitals are stable. We also established an IV to help with the pain management—"

"Pain management?" the patient shrieked as they wheeled him inside room 7. "Every inch of my body is stinging like hell!"

"What is your name, sir?" Clark asked, quickly washing his hands, then slipping into personal protective equipment.

He glanced over at Eva and Brandi. They were both pulling on surgical masks and gloves.

Just as I remember, he thought of Eva. *Always ready to jump in and help however she could...*

"Sir, what is your name?" Clark repeated after getting no answer the first time.

"Fr-Frank. Frank Rojas."

"Nice to meet you, Mr. Rojas. My name is Dr. Malone. My colleagues and I are going to take good care of you, okay? Now, can you tell us how this happened?"

"I—I don't wanna talk about it. Just fix me up so I can get the hell out of here."

Mr. Rojas emitted an excruciating howl. Paramedics positioned the stretcher next to the hospital bed, and on the count of three, transferred him while disconnecting the EMS monitor.

Medical team members swarmed about the room. But Clark's eyes were focused on only one—Eva. She had teamed up with Brandi and Rian, the surgical technician, to gather sterile saline mist and moist gauze.

"We should we set up an IV for fluids to prevent dehydration and organ failure," Eva said.

Even in a totally new environment, she's still a boss...

Clark gave her a reassuring nod. Business first. Despite their rocky past, he wanted her to feel at ease now that she was a part of his hospital's staff. "Good idea, Dr. Gordon." He grabbed a pair of scissors and began cutting away at Mr. Rojas's clothing while speaking to the paramedics. "Do you all have the details on how this happened?"

"According to the patient's friends, he was sitting in the back seat of a car setting off fireworks."

"I-I'm sorry. He was doing *what*?"

"Setting off fireworks inside a car."

"Ahh!" the patient screamed. "Don't remind me."

"Mr. Rojas, how is your eyesight?" Clark asked, grabbing

an ophthalmoscope from the custom procedure tray. "Are you able to see clearly?"

"I guess," he rasped. "It's blurry. So blurry..."

Clark switched on the instrument's light, adjusted the diopter dial and peered into the patient's eyes through the viewing window.

Mr. Rojas screamed out in pain. "What is that? It's excruciating! I can see, *dammit*. I can see!"

"I'm sorry, sir. I just need to check for any damage to your eyes."

Eva approached, picking up an otoscope and checking the patient's ears. "Do you detect any injuries thus far?"

"Not as many as I'd expect considering the circumstances. There's a bit of bleeding in the right eye. But no ruptures, burns or abrasions. No retinal detachments, either. How are his ears looking?"

"There's some redness and minor blistering. I'm not noticing severe burns or fluid buildup."

"Good. That's nothing a little ofloxacin otic solution can't fix." Clark set the ophthalmoscope on the procedure tray, his hand brushing against Eva's as she returned her instrument. They both quickly pulled away, glancing at each other apologetically. But he couldn't ignore the tingle shooting up his arm.

Stay focused...

"Mr. Rojas," he said, "further testing will need to be done on your vision and hearing. But the fact that they're both still intact after what you've been through means you're one lucky man."

The patient moaned, giving Clark a feeble thumbs-up.

Brandi began administering the IV just as Rian brought over the solution and gauze. Together, Clark and Eva began treating Mr. Rojas's burns.

Eva shifted from wound to wound, cleaning and wrapping while comforting the patient. Her seamless movements sent a jolt of electricity up Clark's side. He was reminded of moments they'd shared during medical school, adjusting to being out of the classroom and on the ward together. The invaluable time during clinical rotations and studying for the Step Two CK exams had created an inexplicable bond between them. Which is what ultimately led to that night...

You're doing it again... Focus!

"Dr. Malone," Eva said, "take a look at the index finger on the patient's right hand. There's a significant amount of burnt tissue."

Clark studied the dark, stiff mass. "Looks like eschar, a result of the circumferential skin burns. If we don't take care of that now, the accumulation of extracellular and extravascular fluid will cause the tissue to lose its viability."

"I'm thinking we should perform an—"

"Emergency escharotomy," the pair said in unison.

"Great minds," Brandi told them. "I bet you two were a force to be reckoned with during your med school days. I can tell by the way you work together so effortlessly."

Eva nodded and Clark followed suit, not quite knowing how else to respond. He kept his eyes on Mr. Rojas's injury, palpating the finger and wrist, then pointing to an area that was severely scarred.

"Feels like there's some extreme stiffness running all the way across the wound. But his pulse is strong. Rian? Can you gather the tools needed for an escharotomy?"

"You got it."

Eva positioned Mr. Rojas's arm at a ninety-degree angle with the palm facing upwards. She cleaned the wound with chlorhexidine solution and swathed the area with sterile surgical drapes. "Lidocaine, please?"

Rian handed her the local anesthesia, which she quickly applied to the unburnt skin. While waiting for the numbing effect to take hold, Eva continued treating the remaining burns on Mr. Rojas's body alongside Brandi.

It was difficult for Clark to take his eyes off her. The thought of Eva being there for the next three months thrashed through his mind. Moments ago, he was being badgered by Leo over their lingering issues. Then next thing he knew, *boom!* She was working right next to him in the ER. Life could be funny.

And painful. So don't forget the past and keep your head on straight. This is just business...

Clark used a surgical marker to designate the area where he'd initiate the incision, then placed a scalpel near the top of the wound. "I'm going to begin the incision here, cutting one centimeter longitudinally into the healthy subcutaneous tissue so that the finger can swell without constricting the underlying blood vessels."

"Which will hopefully avoid amputation," Eva murmured.

"Exactly." Clark skillfully carried the incision through the deep partial thickness of the skin, watching as the dead tissue separated. The subcutaneous layer of fat, located just beneath the skin, immediately split, indicating the pressure had been relieved.

"Excellent job, Doctor," Eva said, nodding her head. "That hardened tissue should soften up in no time."

Clark sucked in a deep breath of air, his chest swelling from the compliment. Considering Eva graduated top of their class, he didn't take the statement lightly.

"Thank you, Dr. Gordon." He ran his finger along the incision in search of constricted areas. There were none. "The blood appears to be flowing properly, which will allow for adequate ventilation. Can you please hand me the—"

"Of course," Eva interjected, grabbing a bundle of sterilized impregnated gauze soaked in bacitracin.

"See, that's what I'm talking about," Brandi said. "You two

make a great team. Dr. Gordon, looks to me like I was right. You'll adjust to Fremont General's ER just fine."

"Let's hope so."

Clark could feel Eva's eyes on him. *Deflect*, he thought, quickly dressing the wound, then turning to Brandi. "We need to arrange for Mr. Rojas to be transferred to the burn unit."

"Leo said he would reach out and let them know we have a patient coming their way."

"Great. Rian, can you follow up and find out if a room is ready? As long as Mr. Rojas's vitals remain stable, he can be moved there."

"I'm on it."

"I love the teamwork around here," Eva said. "As hectic as things are, everyone does their part to make sure it all flows smoothly."

"That's the beauty of Fremont General," Clark said. "There's a camaraderie that you won't find in too many other hospitals. I've been told that by several of the temporary employees who've come and gone. Plus, you'll never get bored. I'm assuming this is a far cry from your typical day in a Black Willow ER."

"*Far cry* would be an understatement. The last patient I saw before moving here was a Little Leaguer who'd fractured his elbow during practice. And he was one of only four patients I treated that day."

"Well, the experience you'll get here will be incredible," Brandi chimed in. "That Black Willow ER will be even more of a breeze once your temp assignment is up and you return home."

Hearing Brandi speak of Eva leaving sent a wave of sadness mixed with regret and disappointment through Clark. The flurry of emotions triggered another reminder to keep his distance and focus on instating a platonic working relationship with Eva.

He turned toward the monitor, focusing on Mr. Rojas's vitals rather than his own baffling reaction. The patient was stable. He'd been calm for the past fifteen minutes, indicating the pain medication had finally set in. Clark examined his body from head to toe. Each of his burns had been treated and wrapped securely.

"Good work, everyone," Clark said briskly. "Dr. Gordon, thank you for diving right in and lending us your expertise. You were great."

"Thanks. That's what I'm here for."

Brandi tapped Eva's shoulder. "Doctor, the hospital administrator just paged me. You're twenty minutes late for your meeting."

"Oh!" Eva glanced at her watch. "I was so caught up in the moment that I forgot all about it." She turned to Clark. "It… um…it was good seeing you again, Dr. Malone. I'm looking forward to us working together."

"Same here. This was pretty nostalgic. Brought back some fond memories." He paused, reflecting on the not-so-fond memories her presence had brought on as well. The thought darkened his expression.

Eva removed her mask, revealing a bright smile. She stared at Clark, as if waiting for him to say more. Instead, he abruptly turned to Rian.

"Did you speak with Leo?"

"I did. The burn unit is prepared to receive Mr. Rojas whenever he's ready. Should I put in a call to patient transportation?"

"Yes, please. Thank you."

"Ready to head over to the administrator's office?" Brandi asked Eva, whose eyes were still on Clark. Her smile had faded and eyes dimmed. He figured she'd sensed his shift in demeanor. But he couldn't help himself. It was an honest reaction to their tumultuous past. He had to protect himself.

"Yes," she uttered quietly, slowly backing away. "I'm ready."

"Hey," Brandi said, "why don't we all get together for drinks after work? It would be a nice way to end this chaotic day. *And* an official welcome to Las Vegas gathering for you, Dr. Gordon. I'll invite Leo, and we can hit one of our favorite wind-down spots, the Oasis. How does that sound?"

"Sounds good to me," Eva said, her tone tinged with apprehension as she focused on Clark. "But what about you, Dr. Malone? Would you be comfortable with that?"

He hesitated.

It's just drinks. Can't hurt. As long as your head stays on straight and you keep your distance.

"Yes, I'm fine with that. My shift ends at six. See you shortly thereafter?"

"See you then."

Clark watched as the pair walked out of the room. His eyes gravitated toward Eva's swaying hips and shapely legs. The stirring below his belt quickly turned him back around.

"Reel it in…" he muttered, already feeling himself starting to unravel.

In that moment, Clark made a promise to himself to remain professional, but keep his guard up. Because when it came to Eva, being vulnerable would lead him right back where he was all those years ago—hurt and filled with regret.

CHAPTER THREE

EVA PULLED IN front of the Oasis and handed her keys to the valet. She felt like the new kid at school, walking into the homecoming dance alone, as nervous energy surged through her veins.

This is a bad idea. I should've stayed back at the apartment and finished unpacking.

A tsunami of emotions swirled through her head. She still hadn't fully processed the surprise reunion with Clark. The reaction seemed mutual, with him appearing just as stunned. At times, Eva sensed that he was very wary of her. Looking back, she wished she would've clarified where she stood before their steamy night together and made sure they were on the same page. Because then perhaps Clark would not have walked away afterward so hurt, to the point that it had cost them their friendship.

But once the burn victim arrived in the ER, she and Clark had fallen right back in sync with each other. It was as if they hadn't skipped a beat since their days of joint clinicals. The chemistry between them was still evident, and as far as Eva could tell, so was the attraction.

When she was leaving the ER, however, things took a strange turn. Clark suddenly turned cold. Eva was shocked he'd even agreed to drinks.

Just keep things light tonight. You're here to work. Not struggle to get back into Clark's good graces.

Eva entered the rustic bar, immediately realizing she'd over-dressed. Her violet silk blouse and black pencil skirt stuck out in a sea of tank tops, denim shorts and flip-flops.

"Over here, Dr. Gordon!"

She spun around and waved at Brandi, who was tucked away in a corner booth near the DJ's station. Leo was sitting across from her, bopping his head to the beat of a nineties dance track. Clark was nowhere in sight.

Maybe he decided not to come after all.

Eva made her way over to the other side of the lounge, struggling not to stumble as her patent stilettos sank into the grooves of the cracked hardwood floor.

"Hey," Leo said. "Glad you could make it."

"Thank you for inviting me." She took a seat next to Brandi. "I really needed this after the day we had."

Brandi slid a plate of nachos in front of her. "Tell us about it. The Oasis has become somewhat of a savior. We've spent so many evenings here in this very booth, recouping and vent-ing over—"

"Rounds of vodka martinis," someone said.

Clark.

A slight flutter flowed through Eva's chest as he approached with drinks in hand. He appeared slightly overdressed as well, albeit extremely handsome, in his pale blue button-down shirt, slim-fitting navy slacks and Italian loafers.

Clark set the cocktails on the table, then handed one to Eva.

"An old-fashioned for you, assuming it's still your favorite."

His lips formed a slight smile, revealing the deep dimple in his left cheek. The flutter in Eva's chest morphed into full-blown palpitations.

"You remembered. And yes, old-fashioneds are still my fa-vorite. Thank you."

Clark slid into the seat directly across from her. "Of course

I remembered. That was your drink of choice all throughout med school."

Leo snorted, his gaze bouncing back and forth between the pair. "So, Dr. Gordon. We didn't get a chance to talk much back at the hospital. I know you're here in Vegas by way of Iowa. How did that happen?"

The question stiffened Eva's spine. She sat straight up, debating exactly how much she should share.

"Please, call me Eva. And um… I was just looking for a change of scenery. And pace, obviously. Things can get a little slow in a small-town ER. I figured coming to Vegas would offer up an invaluable experience that I could take back to my colleagues."

"Yep," Leo replied. "This could very well be the experience of a lifetime for you."

Eva noticed Clark throw him a sharp look. Leo slumped down in his seat, avoiding Clark's glare while burying his face in his drink.

"Here's what I'd like to know," Brandi said. "How many patients have you treated in Black Willow who've let off fireworks inside a car?"

"Not one. I must say, that was a shocker."

"Only in Vegas," Clark said with a smile that quickly faded when Leo chimed in again.

"So, hold on, Eva. Is that the *only* reason you left Black Willow? To gain experience?"

What is with this guy?

"Yes," she replied firmly. "It is."

"Well, whatever the reason," Brandi interjected as if sensing the strain, "we're just happy to have you here."

The DJ turned down the music and hopped on the mic.

"Hello, hello, hello, my party people!" he shouted.

Eva relaxed against the back of the booth, grateful for the interruption.

"Welcome to Benny B.'s Bodacious Cocktail Hour. I hope you're enjoying the half-priced drinks and bottomless baskets of buffalo wings. In between all the sips and nibbles, be sure to hit the dance floor and groove to the beat of these old-school throwbacks."

Boom!

Eva jumped in her seat when a loud bass drum blasted through the speakers.

"Let's *go!*" Benny B. yelled.

Montell Jordan's "This Is How We Do It" began to play. The crowd rushed toward the middle of the lounge.

"Leo!" Brandi squealed. "This is our song. Come on. Let's dance!"

The words were barely out of her mouth before he hopped up, grabbed her hand and led her to the dance floor.

Eva watched them shimmy away, tapping her fingernails against the table as nauseating jitters kicked in. She wasn't ready to be alone with Clark. The thought of him pulling her into an impromptu interrogation about their complicated past was worrying to say the least.

She glanced at him. He was staring into his glass, his soft, full lips curled around the rim. The sight sparked memories of his mouth pressed against her neck, her breasts, her stomach, her...

What are you doing? Stop it!

"So, how are your parents doing?" Eva asked, hoping to extinguish the heat rising inside her. "Are they still sending you those amazing care packages like they used to back when we were in medical school?"

"Ha! I wish. They're both doing well. My father retired from his principal position at Wellington High School last year. But he hasn't been able to talk my mother into leaving her job at the Archway Art Center. She's teaching collage therapy to teens and senior citizens and loves what she's doing. I told him to just let her be. She'll retire when she's ready. What about Dr. and Mrs. Gordon? How have they been?"

"They're doing well. My dad is still running his practice, and my mom is heavily involved in her charity work and Black Willow's social scene."

"Nice. Glad to hear it." Clark pointed at her drink. "How's your old-fashioned? You've barely touched it."

"It's good. Strong, but good. They don't make them quite like this back home."

"Speaking of home, how is life there? Better yet, how's life in general? Since we…you know, lost touch."

The cool distance in his low tone tightened her throat.

Don't get too deep. Keep it simple.

"Life is pretty good. Not as exciting as Las Vegas, I would imagine. But I've got my family there, and a great group of friends. Remember Amanda Reinhart?"

"I do. Wasn't she on the ward with us during most of our rotations?"

"She was. Well, after graduation, she ended up moving to Black Willow and works at the clinic with me now."

"Uh-oh. The two of you, together again? Nothing but trouble. I sometimes wonder how that woman ever graduated considering how hard she used to party."

"Yeah, well, her days of partying are long gone. Amanda is married with two daughters now."

"Really? Wow. I didn't think settling down was in the cards for her." Clark hesitated, twirling the stem of his glass between his fingertips. "What about you? You didn't date much during med school. Did that change after graduation?"

Eva's jaws clenched at the mention of dating and med school in the same sentence. Would talk of their failed friendship be next?

"It did change. I had a couple of serious relationships.

But…" She shrugged, downing a gulp of whiskey. "Wasn't meant to be, I guess."

Clark's forehead creased with confusion. "Wait, but I thought you were engaged…" His voice trailed off.

"I'm sorry," Eva said, leaning into the table. "You thought I was what?"

"Never mind. I don't know what I thought. Anyway, isn't it something how one or two decisions can change the course of your entire life?"

Eva studied Clark's expression. There was a confidence in his steely gaze that she'd never seen before. A strength to his posture that oozed self-assuredness. She was taken aback by his newfound swagger, yet more intrigued by this unfamiliar version of him than she was comfortable with.

Do not let this man pull you into a conversation you're not ready to have.

"What about you?" she asked, avoiding the question with a turn of the tables. "I imagine dating is difficult considering how frenzied life as a big-city ER physician must be."

"Not really. Time management is key. Work-life balance is important to me, so when I'm at Fremont General, I give it my all. Then when I'm away from the hospital, my personal life gets my undivided attention. I always make room for both. You may not be able to relate to that concept, though."

Ouch.

The jab left Eva at a loss for words. She sat silently, debating whether to let it go or snap back.

"You're doing that thing you do," Clark said.

"What thing?"

"Biting the inside of your cheek. You used to do that whenever you were deep in thought. Or faced with a question you didn't want to answer. Speaking of which, you didn't answer my question."

Eva pressed her palms against the bench's hardwood surface, still failing to respond.

"Hey, relax," Clark said, running his fingertips across the top of her hand. "This isn't a cross-examination. It's just two old friends, catching up."

Confusion bubbled inside Eva's brain as his actions swung like a pendulum. One minute he was running hot, seemingly still attracted to her. Then he'd make a cool, pointed remark about their past. The turmoil left her wondering whether she belonged there in Vegas.

Of course you do. If for nothing else, maybe just to try to rekindle our friendship.

Eva held her glass to her lips, allowing the spicy bourbon to linger on her tongue before responding. "To answer your question, yes. I do understand the importance of creating a good work-life balance. Have I always maintained a healthy one? No, I haven't. But I've gotten much better at it over the years."

"*Humph.* Well, I'm sure there's some lucky man back in Black Willow who appreciates that."

It sounded more like a statement than an inquiry. Either way, Eva avoided the comment by slipping an ice cube inside her mouth.

"All right, y'all," the DJ crooned into the mic. "Time to switch things up for a minute. I know you're gonna remember this classic. If you're here with that special someone, then you'd better hit the dance floor right now, because this one's for you."

Shania Twain's "You're Still the One" came streaming through the speakers. On impulse, Eva reached out and grabbed Clark's arm. "Remember this? It was my go-to karaoke song!"

"I sure do. I probably still have the videos from every performance. You know I recorded all of them." He took her hand in his. "Come on. Let's dance."

Clark didn't wait for her to respond. Not that it was a question. It was a command that she gladly followed.

He led her toward the middle of the lounge. On the way there, Brandi and Leo breezed past them.

"We need a break!" Brandi said, swiping her frizzy bangs away from her damp forehead. "*And* a drink."

"You two hitting the dance floor?" Leo asked Clark.

"Yeah, man. This was Eva's theme song back in the day."

"This song? 'You're Still the One'? Seems to me like it could be the theme song for both of you. Especially now that you're—"

Clark gripped Leo's shoulder, promptly shutting him up. "Why don't you go take a load off? Have another vodka martini." He turned to Eva. "Shall we?"

"Yes," she replied, side-eyeing Leo as he walked away. "Is he always in frat boy mode?"

"Not always. He's a good guy. Just gets a little overenthusiastic from time to time. But he means well."

Clark found an empty corner on the packed dance floor and wrapped his arms around Eva's waist. She tentatively leaned into him, clasping her hands against the back of his neck while trying not to inhale the scent of his cedarwood cologne.

Their bodies swayed to the rhythm of the music. When he pulled Eva closer, her nipples stiffened against his chest. The sensation sent a back-arching quiver straight through her.

"Are you okay?" Clark murmured, his lips lightly caressing her earlobe.

"Mm-hmm," was all she could muster. Anything more and she might've climaxed right there on the dance floor.

Being nestled in his embrace felt intoxicating. She realized uncomfortably it was a thrill she hadn't felt with Kyle in quite a long time, if ever. Their heads swiveled simultaneously, bringing their lips together for just a brief moment. Eva attempted to pull away and apologize. But she couldn't move an inch within his tight grip.

Clark's firm hands glided down the sides of her body, each finger savoring every curve before they rested on her hips.

Keep this up and you might have to come home with me, the potent old-fashioned was beckoning her to say.

A startling buzz vibrated against Eva's thigh. She stepped back while Clark reached inside his pocket.

"Sorry," he muttered. "Somebody's texting me."

The heightened sense of arousal rising inside Eva deflated suddenly. The backlash of emotion sent her thoughts reeling toward Kyle again, guiltily wondering how she'd gotten sucked back into Clark's charms so quickly when she was supposed to be heartbroken over her ex-fiancé.

She waited while Clark grabbed the phone and opened the message. Her eyes roamed toward the screen. Despite the tinted protector, she could still read the text. It had been forwarded from the Two of Hearts dating app.

Hello, handsome. My rehearsal ended early. I'm heading to the bar now. Can't wait to meet you. See you soon. Kelsie XO

Clark looked up at Eva. She quickly turned away, hoping he hadn't noticed her snooping.

"Sorry to cut the evening short," he said curtly, "but I have to get going. I've got another engagement."

"No worries," she told him, almost choking on the lie. She'd allowed herself to get caught up in the moment, and just like that, some woman named Kelsie had brought her right back to reality. "I should probably get going, too. I've still got some unpacking to do."

Eva's shoulders slumped at the thought of going back to the corporate apartment, alone no less, with its cold hospitality furniture and pretentious neighbors. A chill swept over her when she and Clark headed back to the table. He didn't appear nearly as disappointed as she felt while he was saying his goodbyes, which were accompanied by smiles and embraces. The thought of him happily leaving her to go and see another woman sent an inexplicable stab of jealousy straight through her gut.

Don't go, Eva wanted to tell him just as Shania sang out about how far they'd come.

Before she knew it, Clark was out the door.

"Another round, Eva?" Brandi asked.

"I'd better pass. It's been a long day, and I'm still feeling a little jet-lagged. I should probably go since I have to be back at the hospital early in the morning. But thank you for inviting me."

"We'll have to do it again soon," Leo said, smiling slyly. "I'm glad you're here, Eva. I think your presence is going to have a great impact on Fremont General. In more ways than one."

The spark in his eyes ignited Eva's curiosity. She waited for him to elaborate. He didn't, instead turning to Brandi. "Another round for you, my friend?"

"Yes, please!"

Eva watched the pair nudge each other playfully. Suddenly, she began to feel like a third wheel. "I'll see you two tomorrow. Enjoy the rest of your evening."

"See you tomorrow, Eva!"

The moment Eva stepped outside, she was hit with a hard reminder.

You came here to work and mend your broken heart, not get entangled in a new situation.

But the chemistry between her and Clark was just as palpable now as it had been back in the day. Eva couldn't help but wonder whether Amanda was right, and this really was fate. Had the universe brought her to Las Vegas to reconnect with Clark?

The man who couldn't wait to leave and meet up with another woman?

That thought was all Eva needed to reel her emotions back in and push any romantic ideas of Clark out of her head. When a valet driver pulled her car to the curb, Eva handed him a tip, then collapsed into the seat, completely spent.

And just think. It's only day one...

CHAPTER FOUR

CLARK MADE HIS way through the Bellagio's casino. After taking a left turn past the Lily Bar and Lounge, the Baccarat Bar appeared up ahead. Clark's heart raced with anticipation. He was never this discombobulated before a first date. But tonight felt different. He couldn't seem to pull it together.

What in the hell is wrong with you?

A fresh sheet of sweat drenched his forehead.

Wiping it away, he thought, *You know exactly what's wrong. Dr. Eva Gordon.*

Clark still hadn't fully recovered from the moment he'd laid eyes on her outside the hospital cafeteria. While he had managed to perform alongside Eva inside the ER, seeing her at the Oasis had left him completely rattled. Especially after the seductive dance they'd shared. He couldn't lie to himself—it had felt far too good having her in his arms again. All those old feelings came rushing back, both physical and emotional.

I should've just canceled this date, Clark thought with a wince, his breathing quickening as he entered the bar area. *And stayed at the Oasis with—no!*

He gripped his forehead, attempting to pull the notion from his mind. Clark couldn't allow himself to forget what Eva had put him through. She'd left him high and dry back in the day, knowing how much he cared for her. Eva's goal of graduating top of their class and winning her father's approval were always her main priorities. Their friendship, and the possibility of there being something more between them, had seemed like an afterthought to her. That had hurt him beyond measure. Clark refused to open up to her again now and allow history to repeat itself. Not to mention Eva was on the rebound and probably didn't want to jump back into anything anyway.

You're thinking with your heart and not with your head. No backsliding. Stay focused. More importantly, keep your feelings in check...

Clark sucked in a puff of air, hoping the oxygen would shake his uneasiness. His roving eyes scanned a row of bright blue velvet barstools surrounding the circular gold bar. They landed on a woman sitting near the middle. Her long, toned legs were flung over the side of the stool. Her slender hand was wrapped around a martini glass filled with what appeared to be a lemon drop. She flung her wavy jet-black hair over her shoulder and turned to him, smiling sexily as soon as their gazes connected.

This was the moment Clark had hoped would calm him. Seeing Kelsie sitting before him, not only matching her photos but looking even better in person, should've been reassuring. But instead of being overcome with excitement, he was hit with an anticlimactic feeling of disinterest.

She stood, pulling her shimmery cream tank dress down her thighs while sauntering toward him. The dress clung to her overflowing surgically enhanced breasts, tiny waist and curvy hips. Almost every man in the vicinity turned in her direction. Even a few of the women's heads swiveled. But Clark's vision was blurred by thoughts of Eva's body pressed against his as they swayed back and forth on the dance floor.

"Hello, Dr. Malone," Kelsie purred. She slid her hands along his chest, then rested them on his biceps. "It is so nice to meet you. And finally lay eyes on all this handsome, broad-shouldered glory."

"Nice to meet you, too," he croaked before clearing his throat. "Please, call me Clark."

"Okay, *Clark*."

She grabbed him by the hand and led him to an empty barstool. "I took the liberty of ordering you a lemon drop martini. They're my fave. Hopefully they're yours, too."

He hated lemon drops but didn't have the heart to tell her. "That's fine, thanks. I hope I didn't leave you waiting for too long."

"Not at all. I just hung out with a couple of the other dancers to pass the time. I actually saw you walking through the casino, so I dismissed them before you got to the bar. I didn't want the competition hanging around, if you know what I mean!"

Kelsie threw her head back and unleashed a cackle so loud that several patrons turned and stared.

Shifting in his seat, Clark emitted a forced chuckle. "So, which show do you perform in here?" he quickly asked in hopes of distracting her.

She took a long gulp of her drink. "Whew! Maybe I shouldn't have ordered this fourth martini. Sorry, did you say something?"

Fourth?

"Yes. I asked which show you're a part of."

"Oh! Yeah, so I dance in the Mayfair Supper Club show. It is so good, Doc. The best in town, really. Our choreographers have worked with Janet Jackson, Nicole Scherzinger, *Dancing with the Stars*… You should come see it tomorrow night! But all eyes on *me*. None of the other girls. You got it?"

"Er… I'll need to check my calendar first."

He lurched when Kelsie's hand slid up his knee and settled near his groin.

"So, Dr. Matlock," she murmured, "enough about me. Let's

talk about you. Remember how I was telling you that I'm interested in becoming a doctor?"

"I do," Clark muttered, scooting back in his chair. "And it's Malone, actually."

"Ma—*who*?"

"Malone. My last name is Malone. Not Matlock."

"Oh! My apologies, Doc. Anyway, inquiring minds wanna know what a day in the life of a physician is like."

"My days can be pretty hectic. I wake up at about five o'clock in the morning to make sure I get a workout in, then—"

He stopped when Kelsie squeezed his biceps approvingly. "Mm-hmm. And it shows…"

Normally, the touch from a beautiful woman would've sent quivers straight below his belt. Tonight, he felt nothing. Clark wanted to blame it on the alcohol he'd consumed at the Oasis. But deep down he knew the real culprit.

"Hey!" Kelsie squealed, waving her hand in the air. "Are you listening to me?"

"I—Sorry, could you please repeat that?"

"I was saying that I get it. You work out, and you're probably busy at the hospital all day. Since I'm considering entering into the medical field and I have a certain lifestyle to maintain, what type of salary could I expect to make as an ER doctor?"

In other words, what does your paycheck look like?

Clark turned away from Kelsie's curious stare and signaled the bartender. "A glass of sparkling water, please?"

"Is there something wrong with your martini?" she asked.

"No, it's fine," he lied, considering he hadn't even tasted it. "I actually went out for drinks with a few of my coworkers right before coming here, so I'm good for now."

"Aww, you're no fun!"

When his phone buzzed, Clark snatched it from his pocket, thankful for the interruption. It was a text from Leo.

What's up? How's the date going? We need to discuss whatever's going on between you and Eva. She left the Oasis shortly after you. Seemed pretty down once you were gone.

"Who is that texting us?" Kelsie joked, leaning over Clark's shoulder and peering at his cell.

He quickly slipped it back inside his pocket. "Just my director of emergency medicine checking in." He paused, suddenly overcome by the urge to cut the night short. Hearing the details of Eva being disappointed after he'd left the bar was way more interesting than a shallow date that wasn't going anywhere.

"Why am I getting the feeling that you're not really into me?" Kelsie asked.

Taking a long sip of water, Clark racked his brain for the right words. "It's not you. I've just had a long day and need to get some patient files over to my coworker. That's one thing I didn't share about being an ER doctor. Our work is never done."

"Humph, interesting…"

She slumped down in her stool and drained her glass. Clark wanted to apologize. He knew he hadn't been good company. But he couldn't get his head in the game because it was clouded with thoughts of Eva.

Kelsie raised her glass in the bartender's direction. He nodded and immediately began prepping another lemon drop martini.

"You seemed so enthusiastic when we were exchanging messages. But now that you're here, you're just, like…*blah*. Is it that you're more outgoing on an app than in person? Takes you a minute to open up to people?" she asked.

Clark shrugged despite knowing that wasn't the answer. "You know, that could be the case."

His cell buzzed with another text from Leo.

Dude, are you okay? At least let me know you're good and your date hasn't kidnapped you!

"Could you please excuse me while I respond to this text? It's another message from my coworker."

"Go right ahead." She waved him off and pivoted in her chair, focusing on the casino floor.

Clark typed.

Not good. Kelsie and I aren't connecting on any level.

A woman that gorgeous and you're having trouble connecting? Sounds to me like your mind is elsewhere. And by elsewhere, I mean stuck on Eva.

Clark tucked the phone away and turned his attention back to Kelsie, who was busy chatting up a buff man sitting next to her wearing a cowboy hat and sleeveless plaid shirt.

"Sure, let's do it!" she said to him before hopping out of her stool. "But I'd better warn you. I'm a blackjack master." Before walking off, she threw Clark a tight side-eye. "I'm gonna go hit the casino floor for a bit. Can I meet you back here in fifteen minutes or so?"

"Or," the cowboy chimed in while tipping his hat, "your friend can join us if he'd like."

"Thanks for the invitation, but I think I'll pass. Actually, I need to get going. I've got some work to do."

"Suit yourself," the cowboy said before taking Kelsie's hand and leading her away from the bar. She turned and pointed in Clark's direction.

"Don't forget to pick up the tab before you leave!" she tossed over her shoulder.

Just as Clark opened his mouth to reply, the bartender slid the bill in front of him. It was close to three hundred dollars.

"Excuse me, but I think you've given me the wrong check."

"No, that's the right one. Kelsie and her girls had a few rounds before you got here. She told me that her date would cover it. That's you, right? The doctor, not the cowboy?"

Clark tossed his credit card down onto the silver tray without dignifying the question with a response. The minute he signed the check, he jetted out of the casino.

"You should've just stayed put at the Oasis," he told himself before calling Leo.

CHAPTER FIVE

EVA WAVED AT a group of intensive care nurses on the way to the hospital's cafeteria. She hadn't slept well and needed an iced shaken espresso before stepping foot inside the ER.

Thoughts of Clark being out with another woman left her tossing and turning all night. She wondered whether he'd reminisced on those sensual moments they'd shared on the dance floor like she had. The way her fingers caressed the back of his neck. His hands, gripping her hips as his mouth grazed her ear. Their lips touching ever so slightly...

A warm sensation rushed through Eva as she turned the corner. She fanned her flushed face before entering the cafeteria and eyeing the long line of patrons crowding the Drip & Sip Coffee Stop. Her stomach dropped to her knees at the thought of running into Clark, who she'd heard stopped by the station for green tea every morning.

Relief hit after Eva scanned the group of customers and didn't see him. She wasn't ready to face Clark just yet. At least not until she'd downed her first cup of coffee.

"Hey!" someone chirped behind her.

Eva jumped, startled by the high-pitched voice.

"Ooh, sorry," Brandi said. "Did I scare you?"

"You did. But it's not you, it's me. I didn't get much sleep last night so I'm probably a little on edge. Nothing a little caffeine won't fix. Or make worse. I don't know. Either way, I need it."

"Sounds like you and I are in the same boat. Except my excuse is that I stayed out *way* past my bedtime. Leo and I were having too good a time to cut the night short. But you left the Oasis so early. Did you stop off somewhere else before going home?"

"No." Eva crossed her arms over her chest. "I guess I'm still adjusting to being in a new place. In a new city. Working at a new hospital. You know…"

Brandi's eyes narrowed as her lips formed a slight smirk. "Yeah, I think I do know."

She's onto me…

"So, you and Clark seemed to have had a good time last night."

Eva moved up in the line while twirling a button on her lab coat, thinking of a way to deflect considering she knew the exact direction Brandi was steering the conversation. "I think we all did. Like you said, the Oasis is a great place to kick back and unwind. And the drinks were incredible."

The gleam in her gaze told Eva that her response was not convincing.

"It would be nice if the four of us could turn drinks at the Oasis into a weekly thing," Brandi suggested. "My friends don't understand what I go through working in that ER. Decompressing over cocktails with you three would be fantastic because you all get it."

"That we do. Weekly drinks sounds like a good idea to me."

Eva's nonchalant tone totally contradicted the flutters inside her chest. While she appreciated the idea of a group outing, all she could focus on was getting to spend time with Clark outside the ER.

Just as the pair approached the counter, Brandi's phone buzzed.

"Clark wants to know if I can pick up a green tea for him. Hot today, not iced. He's in the middle of a sign-out with Dr.

Abrams and doesn't want to disrupt the exchange of patient information. Oh, in case you didn't know, Clark can barely function without his morning dose of green tea."

"So I've heard. By the way, our morning fixes are on me today."

"Thanks, Eva!"

On the way to the ER, Brandi turned to Eva. "Hey, can I ask you a question? And please stop me if I'm being intrusive."

"Of course. Ask away."

"What's the deal between you and Clark? Leo and I both picked up on the chemistry between you two, and it was giving more than just former classmates vibes. And again, feel free to tell me to mind my business if you don't want to answer that."

"No, you're fine," Eva replied while contemplating how much she should share. The soft expression on Brandi's face convinced her to come clean. "It makes sense that you two picked up on something, because Clark and I were really good friends during medical school. Then one night that friendship crossed over into something more. *Way* more. Afterward, Clark wanted to pursue a relationship while I thought it'd be best to remain friends and focus on our studies."

"Oh, wow. Were you able to maintain the friendship after that?"

"Unfortunately, no. We ended up drifting apart, then lost touch after graduation. So seeing him here in the ER was pretty shocking."

Brandi slowly nodded while taking a sip of her drink. "Interesting. That explains a lot."

"What do you mean?"

"Clark is somewhat of a serial dater. I've always wondered why he hadn't settled down considering he's such a catch. When I asked Leo about it, he reckoned he's still hung up on someone he'd gone to medical school with. Someone he'd loved deeply. *The one that got away*, as Leo always calls her, who'd turned Clark into a commitment-phobe. Sounds to me like that someone is you."

The sound of rattling ice filled the air. Eva glanced down, realizing it was her trembling hand shaking. Hearing that Clark may still have feelings for her sent her entire body into a fit of flurries.

But the sensation quickly fizzled once Eva realized that Leo must've been mistaken. Clark had been cool and distant toward her for the most part. And after the way he'd run off to meet up with another woman, she was sure that whatever feelings he may have had for her at one point were now long gone.

When they reached the ER, the doors swung open and Dr. Abrams came flying out. "Have a great day, ladies!" he huffed over his shoulder. "I'm late for my son's science fair presentation. Dr. Gordon, Dr. Malone will catch you up on the patient handoffs."

"Okay, thanks!"

Eva entered the emergency room, her eyes darting around the lobby in search of Clark.

Breathe, she thought, realizing she'd been holding a ball of air inside her chest. Just as she released an exhale, Clark appeared near the triage nurses' station. As if sensing Eva's presence, he glanced at her. His stern expression softened. He held a stack of patient files in the air and signaled her over.

"Clark probably wants to get started on the workups with you," Brandi said. "While you do that, I'll assess my patients and get their rooms stocked with supplies. Check in with you in a few?"

"Sounds good. Thank you."

As Eva headed toward the nurses' station, hot tea spilled over onto her hand. She'd been squeezing Clark's cup so tightly that liquid poured from the spout.

"Dammit," she hissed through clenched teeth.

Clark rushed over with tissues in hand, taking the cup, then gently patting down her fingers. The gesture brought back memories of how caring he'd always been. Had that been Kyle, he probably wouldn't have even looked up from whatever he was doing, let alone asked if she were okay.

What were you thinking when you let Clark go?

"Ooh," he uttered, "this cup is hot. Are you okay? Do you need me to grab some ice? Or antibacterial ointment?"

"No, no, I'm okay. That's actually your tea. I hope I didn't spill too much of it."

"I'm sure it's fine. Why don't I catch you up on these medical charts before we make our rounds, start the workups, then check patients' test results?"

"Let's do it."

The pair headed down the corridor toward the trauma unit. Clark stopped at a mobile workstation and opened the chart at the top of his pile. "Bradley Turner was admitted last night after suffering a hemorrhagic stroke."

"Was it a subarachnoid or intracerebral hemorrhage?"

"Intracerebral. He was bleeding inside the brain."

Clark leaned into Eva, pointing at the notes section. "He suffered an ischemic stroke two years ago, which was pretty mild. Since then, he's sporadically taken his blood pressure medication and hasn't been keeping his diabetes under control. His labs show that he suffers from high cholesterol, which has gone untreated. We'll need to put together an ongoing treatment plan for him. For the time being, he's on losartan, furosemide, rosuvastatin and rapid-acting insulin. We'll see how his body reacts to those meds and make adjustments if necessary."

Focus on the chart. Not Clark's lips...

"Have his kidneys been affected?" she asked.

He flipped to the second page, his hand accidentally brushing against Eva's breasts in the process. She gasped slightly, not from the shock of it, but the shivers shooting through her chest. He continued obliviously as if not noticing a thing.

"According to his chart, they were. As of last night the patient's kidneys were functioning at forty-five percent. So we'll keep an eye on them."

"We should warn him that if he doesn't get his blood pressure, sugar levels and cholesterol under control, that function will continue to decrease. Let him know he'd be facing end-stage kidney failure and wind up on dialysis."

"Absolutely. We'll go over all of that with him. As for the rest of the patients…"

Clark shuffled through the remaining charts, briefing Eva on each of them as they moved farther along the unit. There was a new mother who'd given birth prematurely at almost seven months, a teen who'd overdosed on a mix of fentanyl and alcohol, and a pedestrian who'd been hit by a car and endured a concussion, shattered pelvis and dislocated shoulder.

"Those are the sickest patients we're dealing with right now," he continued. "Dr. Abrams has everyone else stabilized, so we'll check on those three first, then work our way through the rest of the rooms. Let's start with our stroke victim, Mr. Turner. I'll grab his most recent lab results."

Eva followed Clark to the nearest workstation. While he entered the patient number into the computer system, she felt the sudden urge to ask about his evening.

Don't do it. You are at work. Keep it professional. Plus, you're gonna be mad if he tells you it was great. So just leave it alone.

"How was the rest of your evening?" she blurted out.

The minute the words flew from her mouth, Eva wished she could reach into the air and snatch them back. But it was too late. Her stomach clenched as she anticipated his response.

Shrugging nonchalantly, Clark kept his eyes on the computer screen. "It was okay."

She waited for him to elaborate. Instead, he remained silent while pounding his index finger against the mouse.

Let it go. He obviously doesn't want to talk about it.

"Just okay?" Eva pressed, once again defying her inner voice. "I thought it would've gone better than that considering the way you rushed out of the Oasis..."

Her voice trailed off. She wanted to kick herself for saying too much.

"Put it this way," Clark replied drily. "I probably would've been much better off staying at the Oasis." His wide, inquisitive eyes scanned Eva's face. "What about you? How was the rest of your night?"

Miserable and sleepless, she wanted to admit.

But Clark didn't need to know how alone she'd felt, tossing and turning restlessly while wondering about his date.

"It was fine. I left shortly after you did. I was pretty exhausted."

"Hmm...okay." He turned his attention back to Mr. Turner's labs. The twitch in his lips told Eva that he wanted to say more but was holding back. His resistance left her longing for the days when they were close friends, able to share everything.

You have no one to blame for that but yourself.

"Okay," Clark said, grabbing a printout. "I've got Mr. Turner's lab results. Let's go check on him, then start the rest of our rounds. After that, we'll review the remaining patients' labs."

Clark moved from room to room with ease, treating each patient with kindness as he provided updates and care plans. Memories of making rounds together during medical school came flooding back to Eva, making it difficult to focus on the tasks at hand. Clark was just as charming now as he'd been back then. But his aura of complete confidence was new to her and only added to his charisma. Patients and their families alike grew enamored the moment he walked through the door. While it was a trait that most doctors didn't possess, he'd mastered it.

Eva prided herself on handling patients with great care. But after watching Clark, she realized there was room for improvement within her own process. His method of slowly reviewing charts and medication details, along with extensive conversations on wellness strategies post–hospital stays, were tactics that she'd definitely take with her when she left.

By the time the pair checked in with each patient on the floor, it was lunchtime. Eva expected to part ways with Clark and meet back up afterward. When he suggested they grab something together from the cafeteria, she was pleasantly surprised.

"Deb's Delicatessen has a really good turkey and Swiss on rye, and a delicious grilled chicken wrap, great avocado toast. But if you already have lunch plans, I understand. I just—I figured we could, you know, talk about the morning and go over plans for the afternoon, and—"

Placing a hand on his arm, Eva put a halt to Clark's rambling. "I don't have plans. Lunch with you sounds good."

His tense biceps relaxed against her palm. The reaction eased Eva's own angst slightly, making the idea of sharing a meal with him even more enticing.

But then fragments of anxiety crept through her mind as they headed to the cafeteria. How would the conversation go? Clark did say they'd be discussing work, but Eva suspected talk would drift to more personal matters, which, in their case, could be dangerous.

Just relax. You'll be fine...

She noticed a little bounce in his stride while strolling down the hallway. It became clear that Clark was Fremont General's resident celebrity. Practically everyone they passed, from doctors and nurses to transporters and custodians, greeted him with enthusiastic salutations and hearty waves.

"You are quite the superstar around here, aren't you?" Eva teased, his endearing response pulling at her heartstrings as she realized just how much of his growth she'd missed out on over the years.

"Nah, I wouldn't say that. But I will admit to being one of the friendlier doctors on staff."

Just as she looked down to adjust the clip on her ID badge, a stretcher came rushing toward them. Clark grabbed Eva by the waist and pulled her to the side. His hand lingered there well after the commotion had passed them by.

"You all right?" he asked.

"I'm fine," she breathed. "Thanks for pulling me out of the way. I almost ended up on top of that patient!"

He chuckled, guiding her back down the hallway. Eva's skin tingled underneath his touch as his hand slid down her hip. Overcome by a warm sense of comfort, she sensed their med school dynamic gradually beginning to resurface. His hot and cold vibes were tapering off, as was his wariness toward her. Eva wondered what had sparked the change in his behavior. Whatever the reason, she was grateful for it.

The twosome entered the cafeteria and made a beeline for the delicatessen. After Clark ordered their meals, they settled into a quiet booth tucked away in a corner.

"Thanks for treating me to lunch," she said. "You didn't have to do that."

"Don't mention it. I'm sure I owe you for something you did for me back in the day."

Slowly unwrapping her sandwich, Eva glanced up at Clark. "What's going on with you?"

"What do you mean?"

"Why are you being so nice to me?"

Leaning back in his seat, Clark crossed his arms over his chest in feigned shock. "When was I *not* nice to you?"

"Ha! We can start with the moment you laid eyes on me my first day here, then go down the list."

"Well, can you blame me? Never in my wildest dreams

did I imagine reuniting with you of all people. *Here.* On my home turf. In all honesty, I'm still in shock over the idea of us working together." He paused, fiddling with the lid on his iced green tea.

"I could sense that. This was a shock to us both. But… you know, reconnecting with you has been good. Awkward at times. But good."

"I agree." Wrinkles creased Clark's forehead. "I owe you an apology. I did have a couple of moments last night when I wasn't exactly kind."

"A couple," Eva quipped, before quickly adding, "Blame it on the alcohol?"

"As much as I'd love to blame it on the alcohol, I won't. Charge it to my bruised ego. I shouldn't have been so aloof, drilling you about our past then leaving abruptly on your first night in town. That's not something a friend would do."

"Oh, so we're friends again?"

"We're getting there…" Clark murmured through a sexy half smile.

"Well, I appreciate you saying that and accept your apology. Listen, why don't we start over from scratch? I know we can't erase the past, but we can agree to a clean slate while I'm working here. Not only would that be good for us, but it would be good for the patients and staff as well. How does that sound?"

"Like a plan."

"Good." Eva bit into her sandwich, attempting to take a cute, tiny bite as Clark eyed her across the table. The move proved to be an epic fail when a chunk of turkey fell to the floor and a glob of mayo hung from her lip.

"Oh, no," Eva choked out, scrambling for a napkin. Within seconds, Clark had grabbed one and pressed it against her mouth.

"I guess some things never change, huh," she murmured.

"I guess they don't. Because look at me. Still looking out for you."

From the corner of her eye, Eva noticed Leo standing in line at the All-American Surf & Turf food stall. She hoped that he wouldn't interrupt her and Clark's conversation now that they were finally getting somewhere.

Clark followed her gaze, then grabbed his phone. After sending a text, he turned his attention back to his wrap. "So now that we've wiped the slate clean," he said, "let's start from the beginning. Have a *real* catch-up. What's life been like for you since med school?"

"Interesting, to say the least. And busy. I spend a lot of time at the clinic, and I'm involved in several charitable organizations. I, um—I was also…"

Just tell him.

"I'd been seeing someone for several years. We got engaged last year, but things didn't work out. So here I am. In Las Vegas."

Eva braced herself, expecting some sort of joke about how she was the one who'd probably ruined her engagement, or had run away when things got tough between her and Kyle. Surprisingly, Clark reacted with a look of sympathy.

"I'm sorry to hear that. And, since we're sharing, I have a confession to make."

He hesitated while watching the cafeteria's exit. Clark nodded slightly. Eva looked toward the door, watching as Leo waved, then walked out.

"Am I dreaming?" she asked. "Or did Leo actually pass up an opportunity to come over and socialize with us?"

"No, you're not dreaming. But in reality, it's because I just sent a text letting him know that we're in the middle of an important conversation."

"So in other words, just get your food and leave?"

"Exactly," Clark replied before the pair burst out laughing.

"But look, back to what I was saying. Since we're opening up to each other, I have to tell you that I've kind of been keeping up with you over the years."

"Seriously? I thought you'd forgotten all about me after med school. It seemed as if you couldn't wait to get away from me."

"I couldn't. But not for the reasons you may have thought. I was still pretty hurt after the way things ended between us, hence me accepting a position across the country. But *forget* about you? I could never do that. We were too close for me just to push you out of my mind completely. As a matter of fact, I kept up with you through some of our classmates. And good ole social media, of course. That's how I knew you'd gotten engaged."

The confession almost knocked Eva out of her chair. "Wait, so you've known about that all this time?"

"I did. What I *didn't* know was that you and your fiancé had recently broken up. Hence my shock when I saw you here at the hospital, then found out you'd accepted a temp position in the ER."

A rumble stirred inside Eva's chest. After all this time, Clark still thought about her. Maybe Amanda was right. Maybe there was more to their serendipitous reunion than she'd thought.

Or more likely he just wants to rekindle your friendship. Don't go digging for something that's not there...

"What are you doing after work?" he asked.

"Unpacking. Why?"

"Why don't you put those boxes on hold and let me take you out? Show you around Las Vegas. Introduce you to the city the right way."

Eva's head tilted, her lips pulling into a smile. "Well, it wouldn't take much convincing for me to pass on the unpacking. So yes, I'd like that."

"Cool. Why don't we wrap up lunch and get back to the ER?

We'll continue this conversation later tonight, outside of the hospital. I feel like we haven't even scratched the surface yet."

"We haven't. Because while you were all up in my business, I didn't get a chance to dig into yours. I can't wait to hear all about what you've been up since we lost touch."

"Uh-oh," Clark muttered, pushing away from the table. "And on that note, let's go."

As the pair headed out of the cafeteria, Eva felt lighter on her feet. Whether it was the fact that she and Clark had cleared the air or made plans for later, she was happy to have him back in her life.

CHAPTER SIX

"I DON'T APPRECIATE the way you dismissed me this afternoon," Leo barked when Clark entered his office.

"Look, don't start. I'm coming in here to apologize. Eva and I were having a crucial conversation, and I didn't want you coming over and disrupting it."

"Crucial?" Leo repeated, pointing at the chair across from him. "Ooh, have a seat. Do tell."

Clark plopped down and propped his elbows against the edge of the desk. "Long story short, Eva and I called a truce."

"Which one of you initiated that?"

"She did."

Snorting loudly, Leo rocked back in his chair. "And what made you agree to that? Your disastrous date from last night? Were you reminded of how good a woman Eva is? And forced to realize that it's time to get over the past and give her another—"

"Are you done?" Clark interrupted. "Because if so, I can inform you that I'm taking Eva out tonight."

"Yes!" Leo shouted, pumping his fist in the air. "That's what I'm talking about, man! Get your girl back. Stop playing the field and settle down with the only woman you've ever loved."

"Hey, can you please calm down and lower your voice? You're getting ahead of yourself here. Tonight is not a date."

"Oh, really? What is it then?"

"Two people casually reconnecting. Eva is new in town, so I'm gonna show her around. That's all."

"Yeah, okay, *that's all*," Leo rebutted, plunking back down in his chair. "I predict that you two will be back together before her temp assignment is over."

"*Back* together? When were we ever together in the first place?"

"You know what I mean. So, tell me, when are you gonna start deleting all those dating apps?"

As soon as the question escaped Leo's mouth, Clark's phone pinged with an alert from Two of Hearts.

"Do not say a word," he warned.

Leo responded with a throaty chuckle. "This is just too good. I wonder if that's Kelsie, wanting to talk about last night. Or maybe it's a new woman, reaching out to say hello. Why don't you pull out your phone and find out?"

Clark stood, waving him off. "I'm ignoring you. Anyway, my shift is over. It's time to head home and get ready for tonight."

"For your *date*?"

"For my *outing*. Have a nice evening, Director Graham."

On the way out the door, the hospital's intercom buzzed.

"Medical alert. Code Blue. First floor. Emergency Room."

Clark's phone buzzed with a text from Eva.

Code 99! Trauma victim with severe snakebites heading into the ER. Get here STAT!

"I've gotta go!" Clark told Leo before charging out of the office.

Clark shot through the ER and headed straight to the trauma unit.

"Which room?" he called out to the triage nurse.

"Ten!"

Clark caught a glimpse of a man wearing a Tarzan costume

and a woman dressed as Jane hovering near the doorway. He brushed past them and hurried inside, diving right into the chaotic scene.

Paramedics had already transferred the patient from a stretcher onto the bed and disconnected the EMS monitor. Eva and Brandi were busy removing his bejeweled purple cape. Once they cut open his spandex bodysuit, several fang marks appeared on his neck, forearms, stomach and thighs. The wounds were red and swollen. Blood oozed from the puncture sites, while a few of them had already begun to blister.

"Rian?" Eva called out. "Where is that antivenin?"

"Timothy went to grab it from the medication room! We keep it stored there inside the refrigerator."

Clark washed his hands, threw on protective equipment and approached the bed. "Talk to me. What happened to our patient?"

"His name is Dexter," Eva said, "also known as the Poisonous Rattlesnake Tamer. According to his assistant, Dexter was bitten by at least three of the rattlesnakes he owns while practicing for their upcoming show."

"Did he specify which species?"

"A speckled rattlesnake, a sidewinder and a western diamondback."

"All pit vipers," Clark said. "Rian, does Timothy know that we need the polyvalent crotalid antivenin to neutralize the toxic effects of all three venoms?"

"He should, but I'll go check just to make sure," Rian responded before running out the door.

Clark bent down to get a better look at the wounds. "When did this attack occur?"

"Within the past hour," Brandi replied.

"Good. We're still within the first three hours of envenoming. That'll greatly increase our rate of success."

"Ahh..." Dexter moaned. His breathing appeared labored as his body began to convulse.

"Nurse Bennett," Eva said. "Cover his body with ice packs while I treat the wounds with glyceryl trinitrate ointment and pressure immobilization bandages. Dexter, this treatment is going to slow the spread of the venom until the antivenin starts working its magic, okay?"

"Oh—okay, but I… I'm so numb," he cried out. "And *hot*. I can't feel my legs." He pressed his thin, cracked lips together. "*Ew*... And my mouth tastes like rubber!"

"Those are all normal side effects after suffering a venomous snakebite," Clark told him just as Rian and Timothy returned. "Stay calm. We've got the antivenin here now, and it's a good one. The fragments of protein in it will work quickly to penetrate the tissue and offset the venom toxins. While I start the intravenous infusion, Dr. Gordon will continue treating your wounds while Nurse Bennett cools you down. Trust me, you're in good hands."

"I'm dizzy," Dexter moaned. "So dizzy. I can't see a thing. And I—I think I'm about to faint…"

"It's okay," Brandi said reassuringly while placing the ice packs against his chest. "These will help with the disorientation."

Eva moved toward one of the wounds on Dexter's thigh, brushing against Clark's body in the process. Her touch induced a sense of calm. Having her by his side filled a void that he hadn't realized was there.

Leaning into her, he asked, "What was Dexter's temperature last time you checked?"

"One hundred and three degrees. I gave him ibuprofen hoping it would reduce the fever along with any inflammation."

"Good. Rian, how is that antivenin IV setup coming along?"

"The line and bag are ready." He rolled the procedure tray toward Clark. "Which size needle would you like to use?"

"The sixteen gauge. Even though it's on the larger end of the spectrum, in a critical case like this, that size is necessary in order to get the antivenin flowing through the bloodstream as quickly as possible."

Clark wrapped a tourniquet around Dexter's right forearm, searched for a large, straight vein, then cleaned the area with an antiseptic swab. Once it was dry, he held the needle at a twenty-degree angle and inserted it, watching as a flashback of blood entered the flash chamber. After lowering the needle, he slid off the IV catheter.

"Do you need me to jump in over there?" Eva asked.

Clark tilted his head, watching as her fingers applied ointment meticulously over Dexter's bite marks. "No, I've got this covered. You're doing a great job treating those wounds."

"Thanks. I'm almost done. Has the infusion begun administering?"

"It has. The duration of this session will last for sixty minutes. Afterward, Dexter will need to remain under close observation for at least two hours. Do we have a dose of epinephrine close by?"

"Yes, it's on the procedure tray," Brandi responded.

"Do we have that in case of an allergic reaction to the antivenin?" Eva asked.

Clark nodded. "That's exactly right. In some cases, the antivenin can cause the patient's system to release a burst of chemicals that floods their bodies, which can lead to anaphylactic shock."

"So we should be on the lookout for a drop in blood pressure," Eva said while bandaging up the last bite mark. "Or swelling in the airway tissue that'll cause wheezing and shortness of breath, and of course loss of consciousness."

"You got it."

There was never a time when Eva wasn't impressive in a medical setting. But through the years they'd spent apart, she had blossomed into a remarkable physician. Clark was amazed by her ability to adapt to a hectic new environment in such a short amount of time.

"The patient's blood pressure is stable at one twenty-eight over eighty-seven," Eva said while studying the monitor.

"I see." Clark eyed the oximetry monitor clutching Dexter's right middle finger. "But his pulse is rising rapidly."

"Should we administer an adenosine injection or a diuretic?"

"Not yet. Let's allow the antivenin to go into effect. Once it does, his heart rate should decrease."

Brandi swooped in and held a straw to Dexter's lips. He drank the entire cup of ice water within seconds.

"Am I gonna live?" he rasped. "I've got a show scheduled for tomorrow. And there are several new moves the performers and I need to perfect. Where's Chuck? And Angel? And my snakes? *Where the hell are my snakes?*"

"Calm down, Dexter," Eva said, gently placing her hand on his arm. "Chuck and Angel are waiting for you in the lobby. Dr. Malone and I will check on them shortly and provide them with an update on your condition. Now, to answer your questions, yes, you're going to live. As for your snakes, I'm not sure where they are at this time, but I'm guessing your assistant may know. Once I find out I'll pass that information on to you. But in the meantime, I need for you to stay calm and allow the antivenin to take effect. Can you do that for me?"

"I'll try. Just make sure no one confiscated my snakes."

As Brandi took Dexter's temperature, Eva stepped back, joining Clark over by the mask and glove station.

He gave her a thumbs-up and a wink. "Great job, Doc. You're a pro at this. *All* of this. Have you ever considered doubling as a therapist? Because I love the way you just handled the patient."

With a shake of her head, she nudged his shoulder. "Absolutely not. I can barely manage the pace of this ER. After today, I might need therapy myself. Because seriously, I have never seen anything like this."

"In a city like Las Vegas, nothing surprises me anymore. This place is the capital of street performers. And everyone on the Strip is hustling to outdo the next act. Dexter isn't my first snake-taming bite victim, either. I've treated a few."

"Were you able to save them all?"

"I was, thankfully. We keep that antivenin fully stocked at all times. What these performers fail to realize is that their wild costars are not their friends. Especially venomous snakes. Those slithery creatures see tamers as nothing more than their next meal. Dexter's reptiles pumped that venom into his system for the sole purpose of paralyzing his body in preparation for digestion."

"That is chilling to say the least. I don't care how competitive it is out there. There's no way in hell I'm messing with those poisonous serpents."

"I hear that," Clark said before approaching Brandi. "What's his temperature now?"

"One hundred and one degrees. So it's going down."

"Good. Can you keep an eye on him while Eva and I go and talk to his partners?"

"Of course."

When Clark and Eva arrived in the waiting area, he overheard Chuck talking to Angel.

"Those snakes *love* Dexter," he sputtered as sweat trickled down his temples. "That much I know is true."

"But if they love him so much," Angel squeaked, "then why would they attack him?"

"Excuse us," Clark said, introducing himself and Eva.

"Doctors!" Chuck bellowed. "How is our boss? Is he alive? Is he gonna be okay?"

"He is alive," Clark said reassuringly, "and he's going to

be okay. We're treating him with a very effective polyvalent crotalid antivenin. It's working to neutralize the toxic effects of all three venoms in Dexter's system."

"Will he be discharged tonight?"

"No, not tonight. Considering the various venoms in his system, we'd like to observe him overnight. We'll have a better idea of when he'll be released in the morning."

"Well, when can we see him?" Angel asked.

"As soon as he's stable," Clark said. "Dr. Gordon and I will keep you posted on his condition."

Bowing in unison, Chuck and Angel lowered their heads. "We thank you, Doctors, for the glorious work that you've done," he proclaimed.

"You're very welcome," Clark replied before leading Eva back to the trauma unit. On the way there, she let off a deep yawn.

"Tired?" he asked, praying she wouldn't say yes and cancel their plans. While his focus had been on Dexter inside that operating room, the thought of spending an evening alone with Eva had lingered in the forefront of his mind. He couldn't wait to see her outside of the ER, wearing something way sexier than a pair of scrubs as they got caught up during their night out.

"I'm a little tired. I was heading out the door when Dexter was rushed into the ER. That was completely unexpected."

"It certainly was. Are you still up for our outing tonight, then maybe settling in somewhere quiet for dinner and drinks?"

Please say yes, Clark thought, his jaw tightening while awaiting her response.

"I don't know if I've got enough energy to explore the city after what we just went through."

The lump of anticipation pounding inside his chest fell to his feet.

"But I love the idea of a quiet dinner," Eva continued. "I'll tell you what. Why don't you come to my place later for wine and takeout? Nothing too fancy. Maybe Mexican? Or sushi?"

"Sushi would be perfect," Clark told her, his spirits immediately lifting.

"Great." She glanced at her watch. "Why don't we check back in with Dexter, complete patient handoffs, then go home to freshen up. Does eight o'clock work for you?"

"Most definitely."

"Okay then. Let's wrap up this day so we can get our night started."

CHAPTER SEVEN

"So how's working in a big city ER been compared to our cozy little clinic?" Amanda asked.

Eva clicked her tongue while digging around inside her makeup bag. "Let's see. It's been chaotic. Unpredictable. Shocking. Challenging. But more importantly, invaluable."

The friends were thirty minutes into a video chat as Eva prepared for her get-together with Clark, which Amanda kept insisting was a date.

"Oh," she continued, "and let's not forget extreme. You know what we're used to seeing in Black Willow. Patients with broken bones or shortness of breath. The occasional heart attack here and there. But in Las Vegas? I'm seeing a constant flow of patients suffering from drunken car accidents, stabbings, gunshot wounds, traumatic brain injuries…sometimes I feel like I'm struggling just to keep up."

"Well, considering where you are, I wouldn't expect much else. At least you've got Clark there for support. Speaking of which, how's it been working side by side with him again?"

"Good, actually. He's always very helpful and encouraging inside the ER. Outside of work, however, has been a different story. At least it was when I first got to town. He was pretty standoffish, more matter-of-fact than warm. Nothing like the guy we used to know. Med school Clark was kind and charming. Always buzzing with positive energy. But since I've been here, he's shown another side of himself. I honestly think he's still harboring some resentment toward me."

"I guess that's understandable. You did break the man's heart, Eva."

"I did," she admitted while applying a coat of mascara. "Anyway, Clark was much friendlier and more receptive toward me today. I'm hoping that means we're moving into a better place. And we'll stay there."

"Did he say anything about his date last night?"

"Nope, not really. When I asked about the rest of his evening, he was very dry. Didn't say much at all."

"So in other words, it was a bust." Amanda pulled the phone closer to her face, smirking mischievously into the camera. "Now back to you. Are you nervous about tonight?"

"*No*, I am not nervous. Why would I be?"

"Because you're about to spend some alone time with the infamous Clark Malone! The man you should probably be married to by now. That's a pretty big deal. Plus, you seem a bit anxious. I can see your hands trembling all the way from Iowa. Breathe, friend, *breathe*."

Eva rolled her eyes until they strained while holding up two tubes of lip gloss. "Which of these shades do you like best? Sheer pink or orangey red?"

"Orangey red. It's sexier. It'll set off the vibes you're trying to give tonight."

"And what vibes are those, exactly?"

"The kind that scream you wanna take this thing between you and Clark outside of the ER and into the bedroom."

"Um…need I remind you that I'm still getting over being dumped by Kyle—"

"*Kyle?*" Amanda interrupted scathingly. "You mean the man who I warned you wasn't right for you? Who was never good enough for you?"

Swiping the orangey-red gloss across her lips, Eva uttered,

"Look, don't make me hang up on you." It was all she could come up with considering Amanda was absolutely right. "And stop making this out to be more than what it is. I already told you that Clark is out here playing the field. He's not interested in starting up anything serious with me."

"Lies."

"No, *facts*. At best, he may want to rekindle our friendship. But that's it. He knows I'm only in Vegas for a few months. I highly doubt he'd want to be with someone who practically lives across the country. Not to mention Clark would probably never trust me with his heart again."

Responding with a frustrated groan, Amanda pressed her fingertips against her temples. "Eva, you and Clark are adults now. It sounds to me like he's trying to move forward and explore what could come of this situation. If that's the case, I hope you'll open yourself up to the idea."

Eva hopped up and assessed herself in the mirror, smoothing her black halter dress over her hips. "I'm ignoring you. Now, are you sure this outfit looks okay?"

"It looks perfect. *You* look perfect. The soft beach waves cascading over your shoulders, the subtle makeup with a pop of color on the lips. It's all working for you, girl. So, tell me again, what's on this evening's agenda?"

"Nothing too fancy. Since Clark and I were too tired to go out and explore the city, I invited him over for wine and sushi."

"Humph. Sounds like a pretty intimate evening to me."

"It's just two people unwinding and catching up over a meal, Amanda."

A series of bells chimed from Eva's phone.

Clark had texted.

On my way. Stopping off to pick something up first. See you soon...

She jumped when Amanda tapped loudly on the screen. "What's with the huge grin plastered across your face? Was that a message from your man?"

"It was a message from *Clark*, letting me know he's on his way."

"Okay, well, before you go, I'd just like to say that I am so glad you two have finally buried the hatchet and started anew. You're working well together, and now I'm hoping you'll start playing well together, too."

"And on that note, I'm hanging up. Have a nice evening, Dr. Reinhart."

"Call me as soon as you can! I wanna hear all about the sexy little romp that's about to take—"

Eva disconnected the chat. The nerves churning inside her stomach wouldn't allow for jokes, let alone thoughts of sleeping with Clark.

She busied herself around the apartment until her phone pinged, alerting her that a guest was in the lobby. After allowing Clark entry, Eva took one last look in the mirror, then waited by the door. Her beating heart thumped inside her eardrums.

Deep breath in, deep breath out...

The elevator dinged. She peered through the peephole, squeezing the door handle for dear life.

Tonight is going to be a good night. Just keep it light. Casual. Friendly.

Eva jolted when Clark knocked. "Hi!" she exclaimed much louder than intended after flinging open the door.

"Hey," he murmured through an amused grin.

She stepped aside and let him in, anxious for a glass of wine.

Seductive notes of bergamot and sandalwood followed Clark inside. By the looks of his freshly cut hair and perfectly trimmed goatee, he'd just left the barbershop. He appeared cool on the surface. But there was a buzz of energy in his steps, as if there was no place he'd rather be than there with her.

"This place is really nice," he said, scanning the apartment.

"Thanks. I've spent the majority of my free time trying to make it feel like home."

He strolled through the living room, pausing at the framed photos of her family and friends lining the fireplace mantel. "I see several familiar faces here. Aren't some of these the same photographs you had at your apartment during med school?"

"They are. Good memory."

"Those days are hard to forget."

A swirl of tension rushed through Eva's chest. She wondered if there was an underlying meaning behind his statement, as if he wanted more of what they'd once shared.

He leaned forward, crossing his arms while studying a black-and-white photo of Eva and Amanda. His biceps flexed through the sleeves of his cream cashmere sweater. Her eyes wandered down to his slim-cut gray slacks. The bulge in front sent her mind wandering down paths that were far from friendly.

Do not go there...

"What is that in your hand?" Eva asked, pointing at the bakery box in his hand.

"A little sweet treat for after dinner. And you won't believe what it is."

She followed Clark into the kitchen, slightly turned on by the way he'd made himself at home. He set the package on the white marble countertop and lifted the lid.

"Smell that?" he asked. "Can you guess what it is yet?"

The scent of vanilla and coconut drifted from the box.

"You didn't."

"Oh, but I did."

She peered down at the Louisiana crunch cake, touched that he remembered her obsession with Entenmann's version back when they were in school. Giving his arm a squeeze, Eva said, "Your memory really is impeccable, you know that? I mean, is there *anything* that you've forgotten?"

"When it comes to you? Not really, no."

The words lingered in the air as the pair fell silent. Clark took a step closer, his hand brushing against hers when he reached for a glass. "May I?"

She slid a bottle of sauvignon blanc toward him. "Yes, please. Thank you."

While he poured the wine Eva plated the sushi, fighting to steady her shaky hands.

"Ooh, you ordered from Kaiseki Yuzu?" Clark asked. "Good choice."

"Brandi told me about it. You should've seen the look on her face when I told her we were hanging out tonight."

"If it was anything like the one on Leo's when I told him, I already know."

A wavering chuckle slipped through Eva's lips. "Those two...always insinuating something that isn't even there. You may as well throw Amanda into the mix, too. She's just as bad, if not worse."

"Really? I'm curious to know what she had to say about this unexpected reunion."

"You know Amanda. She's into the whole cosmic alignment, synchronicity, spiritual woo-woo thing. So..."

"So she thinks fate brought us back together?"

"Exactly."

Clark handed her a glass of wine. "What do you think?"

Eva took a long sip before responding. "I think it's always nice to reconnect with an old friend..."

His penetrating stare sent a rush of heat through her body. Eva turned away, leaning into the counter while sliding sashimi onto a plate.

"What else do we have here?" Clark asked, peering into one of the takeout containers. "I see a little bit of everything."

"I think I ordered the entire menu. We've got tofu, black edamame, mixed tempura, grilled eel, nigiri…"

"Mmm, sounds delish…" He hesitated when his phone pinged. "Excuse me one sec."

Don't look, Eva told herself.

But her eyes defied her as they wandered toward the screen. A double heart logo appeared next to a text box. It was the same logo she'd seen when his date texted him at the Oasis.

Eva cringed against the pull in her chest. She took a long sip of wine, hoping it would wash down the jealousy burning her throat.

A look of irritation crossed his face. He shoved the cell back in his pocket without opening the message.

"Shall we?" he asked, carrying their plates to the dining room table.

"Yes, please." She grabbed their glasses and smiled, that twinge dissipating as she followed him.

"I'm so glad we're doing this," Clark said. "I needed it. *We* needed it. A nice, chill night after a super hectic day inside the ER."

"I concur. Working in Fremont General's emergency room is more than a notion."

"It is. But you've adjusted to it extremely well."

"Thank you," Eva said through a soft smile. "Having you there with me has been a huge help. I'm still getting used to it, though. I'm sure I'll settle in eventually."

"In my opinion, you already have. You were a highly skilled leader when you arrived. Now you continue to show that leadership with every patient you treat.

"And the same goes for you. You've really grown as a physician, Clark. And you have certainly become a great doctor."

"Thanks, E. I take that as a high compliment, coming from

you." He paused, his eyes roaming her body. "Did I mention how good you look tonight?"

"Okay, *that* came out of nowhere," Eva retorted, taken aback by his flattery as she hid her flaming cheeks behind a napkin. "But no, you didn't."

"Well, you do."

"Thank you."

"You're welcome."

The fire in his stare sent her scrambling for a new subject. "So, tell me, how's life been since you left the Midwest for the West Coast?"

"It's been good. For starters, I love the weather. Growing up in Chicago, then going to Michigan for college and Iowa for med school, meant icy-cold winters filled with a ton of snow. Then I move out here, and we're talking balmy days, pleasant nights, barely any rain. It is heaven. And don't even get me started on the scenery. The mountains, the palm trees… it's unreal."

"What about the women? Have you noticed any distinct differences there?"

"Uh-oh," Clark murmured after sliding an edamame pod between his lips. "Why do I have a feeling you're about to grill me about my personal life?"

"Because I am."

"Ha! So, it's only fair that I turn the heat up on you too then, right?"

Eva shrugged, swallowing a slice of salmon. "Of course. But if we're going there, then let me ask you this. Why are you still single?"

"Ooh, now you're pulling out the heavy artillery! I'm gonna need more wine for this." After taking a long sip, he said, "Seriously though, the answer to that question is simple. I haven't been able to settle down with the one."

Brandi's words about being Clark's "one that got away" sprang to Eva's mind.

She'd brushed it off before, but excitement stirred as she wondered whether there was some truth to those words after all.

"Not to mention I've just been focusing on work since moving out here," he continued. "You know how hectic this job is. And these days, since my professional life is such a priority, I keep the whole dating thing casual. That way I can remain at the top of my game with no distractions. It's a win-win situation if you ask me."

Eva held her breath, waiting for him to make a snarky comment about how she could probably relate to his mentality. Surprisingly, he didn't.

There was something cold about his statement, empty even, that made her wonder if this was how he'd felt back in the day when she had prioritized her studies over him and their friendship—especially after their steamy night together.

But what really struck Eva yet again was how much he'd changed. Clark had never been one to push love away. He'd always thrived on relationships and creating meaningful bonds. A hint of sadness hit as she couldn't help feeling somewhat responsible for his attitude now.

"What about you?" he asked, refilling their glasses. "What went down between you and your ex, if I may ask?"

The question stiffened her back. It was only right that she answer him considering how open he'd been with her. "Where do I even start?"

"Wherever you're most comfortable."

"Well, just to give you a little background info, Kyle and I met at a charity event and dated for five years."

"Five years? That's a long time."

"Yeah, it is. Funny how we invested so much time into something that ended so abruptly. But anyway, he proposed a

little over a year ago, and the moment I said yes, both of our
mothers immediately started planning the wedding. I admit
I got wrapped up in the whirlwind of it all, too, and before
I knew it, our nuptials became the talk of Black Willow. We
were both under a lot of pressure. And stress. Not to mention
drama. Kyle is running for state senator, and he's in the middle of a heated campaign. The wedding planning got to be too
much for him, so he broke things off."

"Just like that?"

"Just like that."

"*Wow*. I'm sorry you had to go through that," Clark said,
reaching across the table and clutching her hand. "It couldn't
have been easy, especially if you were in love."

His comment should have been a statement. But it sounded
more like a question.

Eva held her fist to her chin. "You know, it's interesting
you should say that. Because after the breakup, I was forced
to reassess the relationship and face whether or not Kyle and I
were ever *really* in love. Was what we had real? Or did the relationship simply look good on paper? Does that make sense?"

"That makes perfect sense. Just because two people *should*
be good together doesn't mean they actually are. A promi-
nent doctor and a potential senator sound like a great pairing, right?"

"Exactly. But were we really? I don't think so. Because
underneath it all, I've come to realize there wasn't ever any
real passion between Kyle and me. Were we content? Yes.
Happy? I thought so. Maybe I'd mistaken comfort for happiness. I'd convinced myself that the respect we'd garnered
from the Black Willow community was enough to sustain us.
And admittedly, I'd gotten caught up in being the quintessen-
tial power couple. That made up for the fact that there was no
spark. No thrill. And actually, no real affection between us,
not like there had been between—"

You and me, she almost let slip.

"So basically," Clark said after a pause, "you two were more like colleagues than lovers."

"Pretty much."

After popping the last piece of hosomaki in his mouth, Clark picked up their plates and stood. "Well, good riddance to him. No matter what you and I may have been through in the past, I've always known that you're an amazing woman, Eva. You deserve more than a partner who only looks good on paper. You deserve it all."

"Thank you for saying that, Clark."

She followed him into the kitchen, almost stumbling over the plethora of emotions stirring through her limbs. The moment was reminiscent of the evening they'd slept together all those years ago. Just like tonight, the combination of alcohol, good conversation and undeniable attraction had gone straight to her head. Eva could feel the promise she'd made to herself to keep things professional draining from her body.

"How about we finish off this bottle of wine over on the couch?" she suggested.

"You must've been reading my mind. I'd love to stretch out. Give these sore muscles a rest. Are you ready for a slice of this cake?"

"Absolutely." She pulled a couple of dessert plates down and handed Clark a knife. Instead of cutting two pieces, he cut one and fed a sliver to her.

"Mmm, this is delicious."

"I knew you'd love it. Melts right in your mouth, doesn't it?"

"It does."

He fed her another piece. This time, his fingers lingered on her lips. Eva moved closer, their bodies inches apart. Clark tilted her chin and searched her eyes, looking for a hint of permission. She nodded, leaning in as their lips parted. His tongue slipped between hers, swirling softly, then retreating, then going back for more.

Eva felt him harden against her thigh. Spreading her knees apart, he grabbed her by the hips and lifted her onto the island. Their mouths melted into each other's as he thrust his pelvis between her legs. She moaned, falling back while his teeth pulled at her neckline. They nibbled her breasts and teased her taut nipples. His fingertips clawed at her panties while she ripped open his zipper. Before she could wrap her hands around him, Clark dropped to his knees and buried his face between her thighs.

Eva's entire body stiffened, then trembled as her hips moved to the rhythm of his tongue, then his fingers, then his tongue once again. She shivered, emitting a scream almost loud enough to awaken the entire block.

"Looks like you found that spark you've been missing," he grunted in her ear. "Because you just exploded inside my mouth."

Before she could respond, Clark lifted her off the island and carried her into the bedroom. Their clothes were off within seconds. Eva wrapped her legs around his waist as his hands explored every inch of her body, from the edge of her earlobes to the soles of her feet.

Despite only being together that one time way back when, Clark's insatiable touch still felt familiar. His scent, a mix of fresh perspiration and musky cologne, still awakened her senses. And his tongue, assertive and commanding, still made her quiver.

But this was more than just a physical connection. Clark's body evoked deep emotional memories from their past. The long talks and shared secrets that formed a bond she'd thought was unbreakable. Once it dissolved, Eva assumed it was gone forever. Yet here they were, reconnecting in the most intimate way. It was as thrilling as it was scary. Because considering her vulnerable state and their tumultuous history, she feared this dangerous territory could lead to irreparable pain.

In this moment, however, as Clark bit into her neck, Eva swallowed the regret she felt for ever letting him go. The signs of him being the type of man she'd always wanted were all there. Still. And when he plunged deep inside her, she questioned whether she could let him go again once her time in Vegas was up. That's if he'd even want her to stay...

CHAPTER EIGHT

CLARK AWAKENED TO the blaring chirp of an alarm. His eyes shot open and darted around the room. After a few moments, he realized that he was still at Eva's, inside her bedroom.

Surreal...

His head gradually rose from the pillow. She was resting comfortably on his chest, her wavy hair cascading down the side of her face. Even in a deep sleep, she still managed to look beautiful.

Clark reached over and tapped the snooze button on her phone. It was only 5:45 a.m. Another fifteen minutes of sleep wouldn't hurt. They weren't due back at the hospital until eight.

What in the hell are you doing? You don't ever spend the night at women's apartments. Get up and go home!

But this wasn't just any woman. This was Eva Gordon. For her, he could make an exception. At least this one time...

She stirred slightly, her supple lips forming a soft smile. Although her eyes were still closed, her hand managed to find his erection. Clark groaned, watching as her head skimmed his chest, his stomach, then disappeared underneath the sheet.

Eva took him inside her mouth, her jaws tightening as she devoured his entire shaft.

Every muscle in his body tensed. He gripped the side of the bed, thinking *Don't you dare...* when the tip slid past the back of her throat. *Hold it. Hold it!*

"I can't do this," Clark muttered, unable to control the tremors in his legs as he struggled to hold back his orgasm. "I'm not ready yet…"

Despite his body throbbing to release, he threw off the sheet and pulled Eva up by the shoulders. She fell on top of him, hungrily covering his mouth with hers while straddling him with ease. His moans vibrated against her tongue as she arched her back and guided him inside. Their bodies thrust in unison, grinding to the beat of their own familiar rhythm.

Within minutes, they climaxed together. Eva collapsed onto Clark's chest, heaving as he stared up at the ceiling in utter disbelief.

"Well," he panted, "*that* was completely unexpected."

"Yes, it was. Both last night and this morning."

"True. How in the hell did we just go from zero to a hundred like that? I mean, one minute we were having a little dessert, and then the next minute…"

"We were on top of the kitchen island," Eva murmured, grazing his forearm with her fingertips. "I have no idea. But in all honesty? I loved every minute of it."

"So did I."

Silence fell over the pair. But Clark's emotions were far from settled. His feelings for Eva had never left. Over the years, he'd managed to bury them. Last night, however, he'd realized not only had they resurfaced, but they'd come back with a vengeance.

Pull back. Don't forget that Eva is on the rebound and on borrowed time. Three months from now she'll be back in Black Willow, repairing the life she abandoned. Don't set yourself up for failure again.

The reminder was all Clark needed to hit the internal reset button. He rolled over, grabbed his cell and slid toward the edge of the bed.

"I was thinking I could put on a pot of coffee," Eva said. "Scramble some eggs, toast a couple of bagels—"

"I actually need to get going," he interrupted. "I have a few errands to run before work."

The lie was out of his mouth before he knew it. But he'd had to come up with something to release the fear tightening his chest. If Clark left fast enough, he wouldn't have to hear Eva tell him that this was just a onetime thing, and they shouldn't mix business with pleasure. It was his way of getting in front of the situation before it imploded in his face.

"Hey," Eva said, grabbing his hand. "Before you go, are we going to, um...talk about all this?"

"'This' meaning...?" Clark probed, quickly hopping into his gray boxer briefs.

Anxiety simmered in his gut, igniting memories of that night they'd spent together during med school. The elation he'd felt, thinking he and Eva would finally be together. It was indescribable. So was the devastation he'd felt after she'd rejected him.

"'This' meaning us," Eva continued, sitting straight up. "What happened between you and me last night. And this morning."

Don't bite. Keep the ball in her court. See where she takes it.

"It was amazing," Clark told her while pulling on his pants. "Did you enjoy yourself?"

"Of course. Which begs the question, where do we go from here?"

"Where do you want to go from here?"

She turned toward the window, staring out at the palm leaves blowing in the wind. "That's a pretty complicated question," Eva said before pulling off the sheet and revealing her toned, naked body.

Thoughts of lying beside her, being inside her while kissing those soft lips and lush breasts, caused Clark to harden against his zipper. He looked away, resisting the urge to throw her back down onto the bed and indulge in a third round of lovemaking.

Eva stood, slipping on a cream satin robe, then pulling her hair into a low bun. "I know that you're casually dating or whatever. I'm fresh off a breakup and only in Las Vegas for a short while…"

Here we go. This is the part where she tells me this was fun, but that we should consider it a one and done.

"But honestly?" she continued, sauntering over and running her hands along his shoulder blades. "I still have feelings for you, Clark."

Wait…what?

She stood on her tippy-toes, teasing his lips with her tongue.

"So what are you saying?" he asked in between kisses.

"What I'm saying is I want to continue whatever this is we've started. I don't know exactly what that means, or what it'll look like. But what I do know is I want to explore the idea of us being together, in some capacity."

Clark didn't quite know how to respond. So he remained silent, opting to keep his lips glued to hers until he could think things through.

Being with Eva felt good. And right. It was what he'd always wanted. But the pain she'd caused in the past ran deep. He'd managed to heal and was in a good place. Putting his heart on the line once more at the risk of being hurt again did not seem like a good idea. Clark knew he may never recover from losing her a second time.

"Well?" Eva asked, her hands gently cradling the sides of his face. "What do you think?"

He glanced down, mesmerized by her hopeful gaze.

"I'm in," he blurted out.

What are you doing?

"You are?" she exclaimed.

At least protect yourself by putting some stipulations on it!

"I am. But I think we need to lay some ground rules."

Eva's arms fell by her sides.

"Ground rules? What do you mean?"

"What I mean is, you've got a lot going on, and so do I. If we want to establish an intimate relationship, then I think we should keep things casual. No expectations, and no catching feelings. Most importantly, our hooking up cannot interfere with work."

Judging by the dimming spark in her eyes, Eva wasn't too keen on the idea. Clark hoped he hadn't turned her off. But for him, there was no room for error. While both she and his high school sweetheart had broken his heart, it was the relationship with Eva that he mourned the most. Eva was special. A best friend, classmate and confidante that he'd truly grown to love. Their demise had left a gaping hole in his heart that had never been filled. This time around he had to put his needs first. Back in the day she'd held all the power. It was his turn now to reconnect on a deeper level while holding back on the emotions. Because when it came down to it, Clark still didn't trust that Eva would keep his heart intact.

"So you and I will continue to see each other with no strings attached," Eva responded slowly. "Is that what you want?"

"That's exactly what I want. You do your thing, I'll do mine, and we'll come together whenever we want. *Literally.* We wouldn't be exclusive, so if we choose to hang out with other people, we can. And I also think we should keep this between us. I don't want our situation-ship to interfere with work and draw unwanted attention from our colleagues."

"Oh, please. You know you're gonna tell Leo. He's your best friend."

Glancing down at his phone, Clark chuckled then showed her the screen. "I've already got two missed calls and three texts from him this morning. Trust me, he's already making assumptions. But anyway, back to us. What do you think of my proposition?"

"What I'm thinking is," she whispered, leading him back toward the bed, "I'm in."

"Good," he moaned, pulling off her robe on the way there.

CHAPTER NINE

EVA STROLLED THROUGH the door of Fremont General's physician's lounge, unable to turn down the grin on her face.

"Good morning, everyone!" she crooned to several doctors she'd never seen before. They nodded, mumbling an inaudible greeting before turning back to their conversations.

Calm down. Everyone here isn't matching your energy.

Every cell in her body was buzzing. It was a feeling she hadn't experienced in a long time, if ever. Gone were the pangs of anxiety plaguing her mind whenever she'd arrive at the hospital, anticipating what the day would bring. They'd been replaced by a sense of calm mingled with excitement. Apparently, hooking up with Clark had been exactly what she'd needed to settle into a new city.

That's what Eva's mind said. But her heart was thumping to the tune of a different emotion. She'd been caught off guard when Clark suggested they keep things casual. As presumptuous as it may have been, Eva thought he'd be all in and want way more. She could feel herself slipping in that direction, too.

But the idea alone sparked a sharp reminder of what she'd just gone through with Kyle. The pain of giving five years of her life to a man who didn't deserve her love and loyalty was something she didn't want to relive. So maybe it was a good thing that Clark only wanted a fling. A casual affair would force Eva to keep her emotions in check while adding some spice to her three-month stint in Las Vegas.

Regardless of the box Clark had squeezed their relationship into, she felt good about the reunion. Eva would enjoy it for what it was, rack up all the knowledge she could working inside Fremont General's ER, then return to Black Willow with the hope that they'd remain friends.

Pressure filled Eva's head at the thought of going back home. While she hadn't been in Las Vegas long, the city had already grown on her. Especially after last night. Would leaving really be that easy?

The good news is you don't have to worry about it right now. So don't.

Eva poured herself a cup of coffee and exited the lounge, running into Brandi as she rounded the corner.

"Good morning, Eva!"

"Good morning, Brandi. How are you?"

"Exhausted. I stayed here pretty late last night so I could keep an eye on our snakebite victim. I knew he was in good hands with Dr. Abrams, but I just couldn't leave his side. I mean, all those bites from three different snakes? I'd never seen anything like it."

"How is Dexter doing?"

"Really well. He was released early this morning. But Dr. Abrams told him to come back to the ER if he experiences any excessive pain, swelling or shortness of breath."

"Good. I hope he abides by that. What treatment plan did the doctor send him home with?"

Brandi extended her right hand, ticking off her fingers as she spoke. "Prescriptions for ibuprofen, ampicillin, a topical antiseptic and glyceryl trinitrate ointment. I spoke with Dexter's assistants, who stayed in the waiting area all night, and they're going to manage his care at home. Seems like he'll be in good hands. On a side note, the work that you and Clark did to keep Dexter alive was outstanding. Dr. Abrams was amazed that he wasn't in much worse shape."

"Thank you. You did a tremendous job as well. That was actually my first time treating a snakebite victim, so I can't take too much credit. Clark did most of the heavy lifting."

"I love your humility, Eva, but I'd say it was fifty-fifty. Speaking of Clark…"

Here we go.

"Did you two have a good time last night?"

"We did. Clark and I had originally made plans to go out and explore the city. But after treating Dexter, we were both exhausted. So he came to my place for dinner and drinks."

The mere mention of their evening prompted a burst of flashbacks. Clark's fingers, caressing her lips as he fed her cake. His tongue, massaging her nipples. Their bodies, shuddering together while he—

"Eva?"

"Oh, I'm sorry. What were you saying?"

The smirk on Brandi's face told Eva everything she needed to know. The nurse knew she had Clark on the brain.

While Eva had grown quite fond of Brandi and was dying to discuss her evening, she didn't want to break her promise to Clark.

"I was saying that I'm glad you're creating a life outside of the hospital," Brandi continued. "Making friends in a city like Las Vegas can be hard. And even though you'll only be here for three months, it's nice that you've already developed a little friendship circle."

"Thanks. So am I. Having you, Clark and Leo around has really helped me settle in and feel welcome."

Loud voices boomed through the air as the ER doors swung open. Snapping into work mode, Eva said, "Sounds like the emergency room is packed with patients."

"Surprisingly, it's not. A good number of patients were transferred to different units last night and early this morning. But who knows what the day will bring. Dr. Abrams has already done the handoff with Clark, so he'll bring you up to speed on everyone's current conditions."

"Oh, Clark is already here?"

"Yes. He arrived about forty-five minutes ago."

Eva's stomach flipped as they entered the emergency room.

"The situation definitely had its challenges," she heard behind her. "But thank goodness the patient pulled through."

Peeking over her shoulder, Eva saw Clark standing near the front desk speaking to a pretty young medical assistant.

"Yes, thanks to *you*, Dr. Malone," the woman purred, pulling her fingers through a fake blond ponytail. "All that venom rushing through your poor patient's bloodstream? He could have died!"

"He could've. But luckily, he didn't. I'm just grateful I had such a great team working with me. Dr. Gordon in particular. Speaking of which," he said after noticing Eva.

Hearing him mention her name almost sent Eva's feet levitating off the speckled tile floor. She waved, watching as he excused himself, then sauntered over. There was a glint in Clark's stare that held their little secret. The corners of his lips curled slightly, as if suppressing a smile.

"Good morning, Dr. Gordon. Nurse Bennett."

"Good morning, Doc," Brandi chirped. "Are you done with the handoff?"

"I am." His gaze shifted from her to Eva. That grin he'd been fighting to detain came bursting through, his gleaming white teeth lighting up the entire waiting area. "And I'm ready to get Dr. Gordon all caught up on our roster of patients."

Silence fell over the group. Eva knew it was her turn to respond. But she'd fallen into some sort of trance, staring at Clark's handsome face as if they were the only two people there. The charts he shuffled in his hands evoked thoughts of his fingers gripping her back. His lips, as he spoke, were just immersed in between her thighs a few hours ago. That tongue was—

"Dr. Gordon?" Brandi said. *"Dr. Gordon!"*

Eva's neck whipped in her direction. "Um... I...yes? Were you saying something?"

"I was asking if you need anything before I go restock the patients' rooms with extra linens."

Gently nudging her shoulder, Clark asked, "What's going on with you, Dr. Gordon? Long night?"

She swallowed the snicker climbing her throat. "I actually slept very well last night. Thank you."

"That wasn't my question."

Will you stop that? Eva's wide-eyed expression screamed.

Ignoring Clark's satisfied smirk, she turned to Brandi. "I think I'm all set. Go ahead and take care of the rooms while I review the patient charts with Dr. Malone. I'll check back in with you afterward."

"Okay..." Brandi slowly nodded while backing away, her arched eyebrows furrowing into her crinkled forehead.

"Somebody knows what we did last night..." Clark whispered in Eva's ear.

"Clark!" she protested. "Would you please cut it out? Weren't you the one who was so insistent on us keeping this little...*whatever* it is we're doing, away from work?"

"I was. And I have yet to break that rule. So what are you even talking about?"

"Oh, okay. Now you wanna play innocent—"

Eva stopped when the sound of pounding footsteps approached from behind.

"Hey!" Leo called out, barreling toward them. "Just the people I need to see. Brandi, get back over here. I'm in a bind. And I need you. All three of you."

"What's going on?" Clark asked.

"Rita is hosting a huge charity gala for Yvonne's House. It's just over three weeks from now, and you all have to be there."

"Wait, who's Rita?" Eva asked.

"Leo's ex-wife," Clark told her.

"Oh…" she breathed, surprised to hear that Leo had been married. "And, please forgive me for not knowing, but what exactly is Yvonne's House?"

"A nonprofit organization that advocates for the homeless here in Las Vegas," Brandi replied. "Rita is the head of the board."

Leo, who was now sweating profusely, threw his hands on top of his shiny head and pivoted in frustration. "I was dumb enough to tell her that I'd attend the event. I mean, of course I wanna support the cause and all, so when she asked, I couldn't just say no."

"Understood," Clark said. "You're definitely doing the right thing by going. But am I missing something here? Why don't you want to go anymore?"

"Better yet," Brandi chimed in, "why do you need for us to go, too? I'm all for supporting the organization as well, but it sounds like there's more to this than just purchasing a ticket."

"There is," Leo panted. "First of all, Clark, to answer your question, the reason why I don't wanna go anymore is because I just found out Rita is seeing someone, and she's bringing him as her date! Secondly, to answer *your* question, Brandi, I need you all there for moral support. I am *not* ready to see my ex-wife on the arm of another man."

"Wait a minute," Clark interjected. "According to you, there was no love lost after the divorce and you've never wanted Rita back."

"There wasn't. And I don't."

"So why would you care if she brings another man to the gala?"

"Look, just because I don't want to *be* with Rita doesn't

mean I wanna see her with somebody else!" Leo turned on his heels and muttered to Brandi, "Which brings me to my next question..."

"Why do I get the feeling you're about to say something outrageous?"

"Because I am. Bran," he began, crouching as though he was going down on one knee before thinking twice and standing back up. "Would you please, *please* attend the event as my date?"

"As your *what*?"

"As my date! I mean, not my *real* date. Just like a fake date. Because there is no way in hell I'm stepping foot inside of Château Le Jardin's banquet hall alone."

An awkward silence fell over the group. All eyes were on Brandi as she dropped her head into her hand. "Let me get this straight. You want me to pretend that I'm your date, and act like we're a...a real couple?"

"Exactly."

Giving her a reassuring pat on the arm, Eva said, "Come on, Brandi. I think it's a cute idea. Plus, you and Leo always have a great time together. Just pretend like it's a night out at the Oasis rather than a fake dating scenario. Clark and I will be right there with you, won't we, Clark?"

"We absolutely will. I'm all in."

"See?" Eva told Brandi. "It'll be fun. Not to mention you'd be doing your good friend a huge favor."

Leo pointed his praying hands in Eva's direction. "Thank you for your vote of confidence, Eva."

"Don't mention it. I'm team Leo, all the way."

While Eva had meant every word she'd said, it was the thrill of spending an evening out with Clark that swayed her the most. Feeling his gaze on her, she glanced over, grinning when he mouthed the words, *You're the best*.

"So?" Leo asked Brandi. "What do you think?"

She threw her head back and stared up at the ceiling. "What's the dress code?"

"Black tie. Does that question mean you're actually considering it?"

"Maybe..."

As Leo's expression brightened with hope, Eva turned to Brandi. "You know what that means? We'll have to go dress shopping. I didn't pack any formal attire. That would be fun, wouldn't it?"

"It would."

"Pretty please," Leo crooned, his feet now shuffling from side to side.

"All right, fine," Brandi sighed. "I'll go. But you're gonna owe me for this one, buddy. *Big* time."

He grabbed her by the waist and swung her around. "Anything you want, I'll do it. Anything!"

"The first thing you can do is calm down!"

As they continued bantering back and forth, Clark sidled up next to Eva.

"Well, it looks like we've got our first formal outing here in Las Vegas on the books."

"Looks like we do."

"What kind of dress are you thinking of wearing?"

"I don't know. What kind of dress would you like to see me in?"

"Something sexy, for sure."

Exaggerated throat-clearing interrupted the conversation. Eva and Clark swiveled, realizing that Leo and Brandi were watching them.

"What is this I'm seeing here?" Leo asked. "You two are up to something, aren't you? What's going on?"

"Nothing!" they declared in unison.

"A-actually," Eva stammered, "we were just talking about the charity event."

"Yeah, and...discussing what Eva is planning to wear."

"Why would you be concerned with what she's planning to—"

"Leo," Brandi interrupted, "why don't you walk with me while I head back to the patients' rooms? You can check on them and make sure they don't need anything or have any issues."

Before he could respond, she pulled him away while giving Eva a sly wink.

"I think we'd better tone it down at work," Eva warned Clark.

"We should. But considering all the things you did to my body last night and this morning, that's gonna be hard."

"For the sake of our jobs, try harder," she said as they started down the hallway.

"Yes, Doctor."

Just as Eva reached for his stack of patient charts, Clark grabbed her by the waist and pulled her inside a supply closet.

"Hey!" she gasped. "What are you doing?" Not that she cared. For once in her life, Eva was less concerned with work and more into the moment with Clark.

He responded by pressing his lips against hers.

"You're not even trying," Eva murmured in between deep, lingering kisses.

Clark thrust his groin against her thigh. "Not at all."

"You almost popped open a button on my lab coat."

"That's not all I'm trying to pop open. I need to see you again. Outside of here."

"And you will. But in the meantime, we'd better get back to work before both of us get fired."

"You're right," he huffed, readjusting his pants before opening the door. "After you."

Eva peeked down the hallway, making sure the coast was clear while wishing she'd brought a change of underwear. When Clark grabbed her backside on the way out, she moaned, now eager to get that hookup on the calendar sooner rather than later.

CHAPTER TEN

EVA CLIMBED THE stairs to Clark's condo, excited for the night ahead. They'd had a wonderful morning and afternoon exploring Las Vegas, from a visit to the Mob Museum and Hoover Dam Bypass to the Mandalay Bay Shark Reef and fried chicken burgers at CRAFTkitchen. In between destinations Clark had acted as her personal tour guide, showing her the various sights along the way.

After going home to shower and change, they were now heading to Restaurant Guy Savoy at Caesars Palace for fine French cuisine. Eva had already checked out the menu and couldn't decide on which decadent meal to indulge in. The Dungeness crab and Kusshi oysters, Wagyu filet and smoked potatoes, Muscovy duck breast and smoked duck sausage all looked delectable. She'd settled on allowing Clark to choose.

Eva had volunteered to get behind the wheel for their night out since he'd been driving all day. She rang the bell and headed back to her rented silver Audi Q3. Instead of coming downstairs, he buzzed the door.

"Now why wouldn't you just meet me outside?" she muttered.

Eva ran back up and grabbed the handle before the main door locked, then knocked on his condo door. Her fist pushed it open.

"Clark?" she called out.

There was no answer.

Confusion hit as Eva stuck her head inside. The lights were turned down so low that she could barely see. Once her eyes adjusted to the darkness, she noticed soft candlelight flickering throughout the living room.

She stepped inside. Vases filled with red roses were propped in each corner. A bottle of wine was chilling inside a bucket on top of the kitchen's quartz countertop. But Clark was nowhere in sight.

"What is all this?" Eva murmured right before a warm body pressed against her backside.

"What took you so long to get here?" Clark whispered, wrapping her up in his arms.

"One of my neighbors stopped me on the way out and asked a ton of questions about how to treat his recurring dyshidrosis eczema."

"Interesting. Were you able to help him?"

"I was. I recommended a trip to the dermatologist, oral and topical steroids, and drainage for the larger, more painful blisters." She spun around within his grasp. "Um…what is going on here?"

"Did I mention how beautiful you look?" Clark asked, ignoring her question. "And are you hungry?"

Eva straightened the hem on her one-shoulder satin minidress. "You didn't, but thank you. And, yes. I'm starving. Are we still going out to dinner, or—" She hesitated, inhaling the delicious aroma floating through the air. "Wait, are you cooking?"

"I am. We've had a long day. I figured that a nice, intimate meal at my place would be better than fighting our way through all the tourists on the Strip. Wouldn't you agree?"

Slowly nodding, Eva took another look around the condo. "I would. So, wait, was all this prearranged?"

"Somewhat. It was a bit last-minute, but I think I pulled it off. Do you like it?"

"I love it."

Taking her hand in his, Clark led Eva to the dining area. "Good. And don't worry. I promise I'll take you to Guy Savoy's another time. Tonight, I just want you all to myself."

"Well, you got me," she told him, her body heating up in anticipation.

Clark's oval glass table was adorned with tall tapered candles, blue porcelain dinnerware and crystal wineglasses.

"Have a seat," he said, pulling out a chair. "I'll be right back."

Eva sat gingerly, taking it all in. Everything was so thoughtful. And romantic. And far beyond what anyone would do for a casual hookup buddy. The sight left her feeling both excited and hopeful.

Within seconds, Clark returned with a bottle of pinot noir in one hand and a large melamine bowl filled with Italian chopped salad in the other.

"Can I help with anything?" she asked, scooting away from the table.

"Absolutely not. I've got this. You just relax."

Eva observed his confident prowl as he left the room, his gym-honed body looking magnificent from the back. This time, he came back carrying a basket filled with garlic bread and a large dish containing something unknown.

"Mmm, that smells good. What is it?"

"Smoked salmon over linguini with tomato cream sauce."

"It looks delicious."

"I hope it will be."

After pouring the wine and preparing their plates, Clark took a seat and raised his glass. "A toast. To the great work you're doing at Fremont General, us continuing to enjoy each other's company, and exploring whatever the future may hold."

"Cheers."

He ran his fingertips across the top of her hand, sending

sensations straight up her thighs. Slowly lowering her glass, Eva squirmed in her chair, wondering how she was going to get through dinner.

"So, what do you think?" Clark asked before biting into a piece of garlic bread.

"It's amazing. The salmon is practically melting inside my mouth."

His right eyebrow shot up. "Hmm. Glad to hear it. I'm looking forward to *you* melting inside my mouth later."

A forkful of pasta slithered down Eva's throat. She downed a gulp of wine, praying she wouldn't choke to death. If Clark didn't stop with the sexy innuendos, she'd probably expire on the spot.

"Question," she began in an attempt to steer the conversation in a more wholesome direction. "What do you think is going on between Leo and Brandi? It seems to me that they're into each other."

"Well, I can't speak for Brandi, but I definitely think Leo is into her. And while he can be a bit goofy at times, Leo's a good guy. So, who knows. Maybe he has a chance."

"They'd definitely make an interesting couple. With her sass and his quirk? The fun times and joke-telling would be never-ending."

"Sort of like us back in the day."

Eva looked up from the spool of linguini entwining her fork. His statement came off as lighthearted, joyful even. But the intensity behind Clark's penetrating stare told a different story—one that highlighted both the good and bad plotlines woven throughout their relationship.

"Speaking of our past…" he continued.

Uh-oh. Here we go again…

"Working alongside you has brought back so many memories of our time together during our residency. Do you have a favorite moment that we experienced during one of our rotations?"

"Oh, I love that question." Eva's eyes narrowed as her head tilted toward the ceiling. "It had to have been that time you and I were assigned to the ER, and a woman came in with her husband, thinking she had a stomach tumor. Remember that?"

"I do. She came in doubled over from severe back pain, had gained a lot of weight really quickly, and had been urinating frequently."

"Exactly. Poor thing. She was convinced she had ovarian cancer then found out she was three months pregnant."

"*After* being told she couldn't conceive." A glow of happiness surrounding Clark's smile. "Yeah, that moment was beautiful. I remember her husband crying because they'd just begun the adoption process. He was so happy that they'd be welcoming two children into the family instead of one."

"Stories like that make our work well worth it. What about you? What's one of your favorite moments from our med school days?"

"Well, other than the obvious," he quipped with a wink, "I'd say it was the time we were in the emergency room, and an older woman was rushed in who'd suffered a stroke. She was babysitting at the time, and it was her three-year-old grandson who'd called 911 after she'd stopped responding to him during a game of go fish."

"Yes! I remember that patient. Had it not been for that bright, quick-thinking little boy, she wouldn't have survived."

They were suddenly interrupted by the ping of Clark's phone. The moment he grabbed it, Eva felt a pinch of envy pull at her chest.

No strings attached, remember? Whoever's messaging him is none of your business...

"Ha!" He chuckled after glancing at the screen.

"What's so funny?"

"That's Leo texting me. He said that while I'm out here living my best life with you, he's busy losing all his money to some of his poker buddies."

"*Ouch*. So, wait, you told Leo about us?"

"Not in detail. But Leo's a sharp guy. He could sense that something is going on."

"And that's *your* fault. You were being way too obvious at the hospital. But now that the cat is somewhat out the bag, tell me. What does Leo think of us?"

Clark set his fork down and rubbed his hands together. "Put it this way. He has an interesting take on you and me."

"What do you mean?"

"Well, he knows some things about our past, and what brought you here to Las Vegas. I think he's hoping that more will come of us than what we've got planned. I don't think Leo understands our need to keep things casual."

You mean your need to keep things casual?

The words lingered on the tip of Eva's tongue. But she swallowed them down right along with a mouthful of lettuce. "Did you remind him that I'm only here for three months? And that you've got a certain…*lifestyle* that seems to suit you better than settling down with one woman—"

Clark broke into a fit of coughs.

"Are you all right?"

He responded with a heave so deep that Eva sprang from her chair and pounded his back. Once the coughing fit subsided, she ran into the kitchen and grabbed a bottle of water. As he gulped it down, she massaged his chest and back simultaneously.

"Thanks," he wheezed. "I don't know what just happened."

"I thought I was gonna have to take *you* to the ER."

"Please. If something goes wrong and a doctor of your caliber is in the house, I wouldn't need to step foot inside a hospital."

"Aww, you're just saying that because this massage feels so good."

"That it does," Clark responded, sliding his hand underneath her dress.

She leaned into him, closing her eyes as his fingers climbed higher. They touched the edge of her black lace thong, then slipped past the seam and skimmed her core.

Gasping slightly, Eva tightened her grip on his back.

"Why are you so wet?" he whispered.

"Because I've been sitting across from you for almost an hour."

"Mmm," he moaned, removing his hand and slowly licking his fingers. "Are you ready for dessert?"

"Most definitely. What are we having?"

"Tiramisu."

Eva tossed her head back and laughed. "Are you going off script? Because that's not where I thought this conversation was going."

"Oh, it isn't?" He stood, his wrinkled expression feigning confusion. "What did you think I was gonna say?"

"Use your imagination," she retorted, helping him carry the dishes into the kitchen.

As he stood over the dishwasher, she noticed the bulge inside his pants.

"I've got an idea," she said.

"Let's hear it."

"Why don't we hold off on dessert so you can give me a tour of your condo? Starting with the bedroom?"

Clark shot straight up and slammed the dishwasher door shut. "Good idea. That tiramisu isn't going anywhere."

Eva fell back against Clark's black leather sleigh bed. He tore at her dress as she ripped off his shirt. Her mouth roamed his chest, bit at his neck, savored remnants of fruity wine on his lips. Their tongues danced while their hands caressed every inch of each other. She reached between his legs, desperate to feel him inside her.

Clark pushed her hand away, a wicked chuckle tickling her ear. "Not yet," he grunted. Holding her wrists behind her back, he ran his tongue along the edge of her lobes, down her throat and along her collarbone. She arched her back, beating her fists against the sheets as grazed her skin with his teeth. Nipped at her inner thighs. Then devoured her toes, one by one, then all at once.

Eva grabbed Clark by the shoulders, urging him to come back up and satisfy her fully. But he refused, enjoying the tease. Relishing the control he had over her—the power to decide how close she'd come to climaxing. *When* she would climax. How hard her body would quiver once he finally allowed it.

She writhed about as Clark climbed halfway up the bed, his face getting lost between her thighs. The slightest touch of his tongue sent her shivering, but not fully. The tip of his finger tickling her opening ever so slightly, causing a scream to erupt from her throat.

Eva clawed at his back, attempting to inflict just enough pain so that he'd have mercy on her. He didn't. Instead, he crawled up toward the headboard and straddled her face, his knees on either side of her head.

"Open wide."

The pleasure that his command induced almost caused her to weep. Where was this confident, take-charge man back in the day? And why had it taken Eva so long to discover how much she enjoyed being dominated in bed?

Because you'd been with a man who barely enjoyed sex...

Clark reached down and placed a hand on her jaw. "Did you hear what I said? Open wide!"

Eva did as she was told. Clark emitted a guttural moan, still carefully holding her face while she tightened her jaws around him. Determined to maintain some semblance of control, she suppressed a gag as he slid down the back of her throat.

He began to pulsate inside her mouth. His thrusts grew stronger, faster. Just when she thought he was about to explode, he pulled out and finally plunged deep inside her.

Their bodies thrust to the exact same rhythm, never once falling out of sync.

When Clark finally allowed her to come, every nerve in her body shook with ecstasy.

Eva rolled over onto his chest, struggling to catch her breath. Tonight had been exactly what she'd needed. There was no negative talk of their past. Or the challenges they'd faced inside the ER. Or life after her temp assignment ended. The evening had simply been about joy. Keeping things light. Relishing each other's company. And pleasing each other with no strings attached.

But the problem was that Eva still had such strong emotions about their situation. So strong that she knew she should've taken longer to consider the conditions of Clark's ground rules before agreeing to his terms.

CHAPTER ELEVEN

Month two

THE YVONNE'S HOUSE charity gala was in full swing. The organization's planning committee had created a magical atmosphere inside Château Le Jardin's elegant gold and cream La Parisienne ballroom. Soft lights illuminating from crystal chandeliers glowed against elevated floral arrangements. Red carpet lined the entryway, where a professional photographer snapped photos of guests as they entered the event. Beautifully dressed guests wearing an array of evening gowns and custom-fitted tuxedos filled every table.

As far as Clark was concerned, Eva was the most stunning woman there. When she'd stepped into her building's lobby, he'd almost fainted at the sight of her dressed in a strapless floor-length emerald gown. Its slit ended someone near her upper right thigh. The sweetheart neckline revealed the perfect hint of cleavage. Her hair, which had been pulled back into an elegant chignon, put her shimmery makeup, pavé drop earrings and slender neck on full display.

Clark could barely keep his hands off her. As the gala's jazz band performed their rendition of Bill Withers's "Just the Two of Us," he held Eva close while they swayed to the music.

"Did I mention how handsome you look tonight?" she asked.

"I can't remember. Because I've been too busy telling you

how gorgeous you look. I owe Brandi big-time for convincing you to buy this dress."

"I thought it was a bit much with the high slit and low cleavage. However, if you like it, I love it."

"It's perfect. *You're* perfect."

"You are too sweet," she murmured. "Thank you."

Running his fingertip along her chin, he asked, "So what did Amanda say when you told her about us? I can only imagine how shocked she was to hear we're back on."

"You know, I've been so busy that I haven't had a chance to tell her yet."

"Really? I'm surprised. I expected you to call her the minute I left your place that first morning."

"By the time you actually walked out the door, I only had thirty minutes left to get to work, remember?"

"Well," Clark said slowly, "I'm sure your parents must've been surprised to hear we've reconnected. They were so skeptical of me back in the day, thinking I'd distract you from your studies and ruin your chances of becoming a hugely successful doctor. What did they have to say about us *both* being successful doctors now?"

Rolling her eyes, she uttered, "When it comes to my parents, I've kept the details of this entire Las Vegas situation under wraps. They didn't want me to accept the assignment in the first place. Honestly, I think they were hoping I'd stay in Black Willow and try to work things out with Kyle."

Clark's body stiffened. The response stung, leaving him feeling as though they were back in medical school and he still wasn't good enough for her. It served as a timely reminder that he didn't have Kyle's high-society Black Willow background that would elevate Eva even further in her parents' eyes. Their desire to see her marry into hometown royalty left him feeling even more determined to protect his heart and keep their fling temporary.

"Hey!" Leo called out while bouncing toward them. "You two enjoying yourselves?"

"We are," Eva said. "This venue is gorgeous, the filet mignon was delicious, and the band is fantastic. They're loads better than the one I'd hired to play at my wedding!"

Clark's grasp on Eva's back loosened at yet another reference to her ex-fiancé.

"So how are things going between you, Rita and Brandi?" she asked Leo.

"Great. Even better than I expected. After Rita saw me walk in here with someone else, she hasn't taken her eyes off me. She's barely even paying attention to that guy she's with. Wilbur, or whatever his name is."

"William," Clark interjected.

"Whatever. The point is my plan worked. So, thanks again for coming, and a *huge* thank-you for convincing Brandi to be my fake date."

"Of course," Eva said. "We'll always have your back. What are you thinking now? Is there a chance that you and Rita might get back together?"

"*Hell*, no! That's not what this is about."

"It isn't?"

Leo shook his head so vigorously that his jowls shook. "Absolutely not. This is about knowing that I could get her back if I wanted to."

"You're ridiculous, man," Clark said before turning to Eva. "I'm gonna head to the bar and grab another drink. Can I get you anything?"

"No, I'm fine. Thanks. I see Brandi standing on the red carpet and she's waving me over. She must want to snap some pictures. Can I catch back up with you a little later?"

"Of course."

Clark stood rigidly as she planted a quick kiss on his cheek, then rushed off.

"You good, man?" Leo asked, his head swiveling from Clark to Eva, then back to Clark.

"I'm fine," he muttered, ignoring the unease twisting through his gut while walking to the bar. After ordering two Manhattans, he and Leo settled in at a high-top table.

"I have something to admit," Leo said.

"What's that?"

"I think I'm into Brandi. I mean, *really* into her."

"Yeah, I already knew that."

"Huh? How could you? *I* didn't know that until tonight!"

"Oh, please. All that laughing and joking you two do at the hospital? It reeks of a *strong* attraction. And don't get me started on our nights out at the Oasis. But here's my question. What are you gonna do about it?"

"That I don't know," Leo declared while staring across the room at her. "I should be asking you for some advice. Because you and Eva wasted no time in getting together, in spite of your complicated past. What's your secret?"

"You don't wanna take any advice from me. Trust me, I don't have this whole dating thing figured out, either."

"What do you mean? You two seem to be doing great."

Clark responded with a tight side-eye before taking a long sip of his drink.

"Uh-oh. What the hell? You mean to tell me there's trouble in paradise already?"

"Let's just say that Eva's parents are really rooting for her to get back together with her ex-fiancé. And I'm concerned that their influence might override whatever this is we've got going on."

Leo rebutted, "Why do you care? Per *your* ground rules, you two are just keeping things casual, right? Then once Eva's temp assignment is over, you'll go your way and she'll go hers."

Clark's gaze drifted toward her, his groin stirring as she struck a seductive pose alongside Brandi. "Yep, that was the plan."

"*Was?* Humph. Judging by the scowl on your face, the plan isn't working out too well for you. Could it be that you actually want more with the woman you're clearly still madly in love with?"

Clark remained silent.

"See, I *knew* you weren't gonna be able to contain your feelings. And the thing is, you shouldn't! Eva is a good woman, Clark. Just be honest and tell her where you stand. What have you got to lose?"

"What have I got to lose? How about my pride. My emotions. My heart. Basically, *everything.* I've already put myself out there and gotten badly burned by her once. I'm not doing it again."

"Look, all that happened years ago. You two kicked things off on a clean slate this time round, remember? Both of you deserve a second shot at this. Like I keep saying, you have got to open yourself up to love, man."

Clark downed his drink, then waved Leo off. "I've never been enough for Eva. I wasn't back when we first got together, and I'm not now."

"How do you know that?"

"Because she hasn't told the people she's closest to that we're involved. Her parents don't even know that we're working together. They still seem to be hung up on her ex, too."

Leo cocked his head to the side. "I'm sorry to break this to you, but that's usually how it goes when there are no strings attached, my friend. You wanted this to be a casual hookup, so that's exactly what Eva's giving you. Now that you want more, you need to tell her."

"*Tuh.* The only thing I need to do is get my head back in the game and stick to the ground rules that I laid down when Eva and I started this."

"Meaning going back to your casual dating ways?"

"Exactly."

CHAPTER TWELVE

"LET'S GET THE patient inside room 8," Clark shouted. "*Stat!* Where is Dr. Gordon?"

"Right here," she said, rushing toward the group of paramedics. "What's the situation with our patient?"

"She fell from a balcony located thirty feet above a large saltwater aquarium at the No Man's Land Amusement Park and landed inside the tank. She may be suffering from alcohol poisoning along with a slew of other injuries. According to the park's staff, the patient appeared intoxicated and was behaving erratically before falling in."

Brandi ran over and handed the doctors protective equipment. Urgency palpitated through the room as nurses and medical assistants poured inside.

"Make sure she's lying in the supine position with her head turned to the side!" Eva called out when paramedics transferred the patient onto the bed and disconnected her from the EMS monitors. "We don't want her choking on vomit, water or debris. Is she conscious?"

"Yes, but barely," one of the paramedics responded. "Her pulse is faint and her blood pressure is low."

Once Eva and Brandi cut the patient out of her wet clothing, they reattached the precordial leads to the chest stickers and clipped a pulse oximeter onto her fingertip.

While eyeing the monitor, Clark said, "Her blood pressure is ninety-four over sixty-two. We need to get that up immediately."

"Should we administer a dose of epinephrine?" Eva asked.

"That's exactly what I was thinking. Timothy?"

"I'm on it," the medical assistant replied before charging out of the room.

"Do we know how long the patient was underwater?" Clark asked.

"Anywhere between ten to fifteen minutes before the park staff pulled her out," Rian replied. "She was conscious before the fall but unresponsive once she was removed from the water. A park staff member performed CPR until the paramedics arrived."

Waves of adrenaline coursed through Eva's veins. She'd never treated an intoxicated, barely conscious near-drowning victim who was suffering from numerous injuries.

Stay calm. Clark is right by your side. You've got this.

Noticing the patient's cold, blue-tinged skin, Eva turned to Brandi and Rian. "We need to cover her in forced air-warming blankets to prevent hypothermia and administer warming IV fluids to avoid further heat loss and dehydration from the potential alcohol poisoning."

"Yes, Dr. Gordon."

Clark approached with an ophthalmoscope in hand. After switching on the instrument's light, he adjusted the diopter dial and peered into the patient's eyes through the viewing window.

"The patient's pupils are equal, but sluggish. There's movement in her limbs, which is good. We'll know more about her condition once we're able to perform neurological and neurophysiological examinations."

"I suggest we implement spinal precautions as well," Eva said, "just in case there's a cord injury that has yet to be detected. Do we know our patient's name?"

"Yes, Melissa Sullivan."

"Ms. Sullivan?" Eva said, leaning toward the bed. "I'm Dr. Gordon. You're in good hands here at Fremont General Hospital. The medical team and I are going to do everything we can to get you well, okay?"

She nodded, wheezing feebly. When a slight cough progressed into a gag, Eva quickly unstrapped the oxygen mask and turned the patient's head far to the left.

"I need an emesis basin!"

Rian grabbed the kidney-shaped container and positioned it underneath the patient's chin just as a combination of aspirated water, red algae and crushed coral poured from her mouth.

"Nurse Bennett," Clark said, "let's switch out that oxygen mask for a high-flow nasal cannula so that the patient's mouth will remain uncovered."

"Yes, Doctor."

Unwrapping the stethoscope from around her neck, Eva pressed the diaphragm against the patient's chest and listened to her lungs. The loud, low-pitched crackling indicated that fluid was present in the lungs.

"I'm detecting acute pulmonary edema. We need to perform chest X-rays and confirm that as soon as possible."

"We've got the mobile CT scanner here," Clark responded. "We'll get some images once the patient is stable. What is her blood pressure reading now?"

"It's dropped to ninety-one over sixty. We need that epinephrine. *Stat.*"

"I've got it right here!" Timothy panted, rushing over and handing the pen to Clark.

He pulled the safety release from the auto-injector and held it firmly against the patient's outer right thigh.

"Wait," Eva said. "You're not administering the normal dose of one milligram, are you?"

"Absolutely not. Since the patient still has a pulse, that high a dosage could cause malignant hypertension and lead to cardiac arrest. So I'm administering a half of a milligram instead."

"Good. Just making sure."

The pair shared a brief glance, Eva beaming behind her mask when Clark tossed her an appreciative wink. She watched as he inserted the needle into the patient's leg, waited for it to click, then gave her a thumbs-up to confirm that the injection had begun.

"I'm holding the auto-injector in place for five seconds," Clark said, "to ensure that the epinephrine fully activates. Nurse Bennett, how is Ms. Sullivan's oxygen level looking?"

"Still low at sixty-seven percent."

"Is the humidified delivery set at one hundred percent with a flow rate of sixty liters per minute?"

"Yes, it is."

"Okay. Let's keep it there. A combination of the epinephrine and accelerated output should increase her oxygen level."

"And hopefully avoid a prolonged state of hypoxemia," Eva added. "We need to take every precaution that'll help prevent cardiac arrest."

Clark nodded, then pointed toward the mobile computed tomography scanner. "Rian, can you bring over the scanner? We need to perform that trauma CT and check for any initial neurologic or pulmonary injuries."

"You got it."

Despite the dire condition of the patient, Eva was overcome by a sense of ease. It was a level of comfort that she hadn't experienced since her and Clark's days of working together during medical school. Although she'd arrived at Fremont General second-guessing her decision to take on the assignment, his support and guidance had enabled Eva to find her footing and adapt quickly. His presence alone made her feel as though she could conquer anything. And while the city's patient cases had been both complicated and challenging, thanks to Clark, she'd risen to every occasion.

"Preparing to infuse the patient with iodine," he said, "then begin the scan—"

Beep! Beep! Beep!

Eva's eyes shot up toward the monitor. The patient's blood pressure had dropped to eighty-three over forty-one. When she began convulsing uncontrollably while gasping for air, Eva tore off the warming blankets.

"The patient has gone into cardiac arrest! Get the defibrillator. *Stat!*"

Eva exposed her bare chest and immediately began performing CPR while Brandi positioned the defibrillator next to the bed. Grabbing the pads, Clark quickly removed the paper backing and pressed one below the patient's right-side clavicle and the other underneath her left armpit.

"Good job on the CPR, Dr. Gordon," he said while tapping the machine's energy selection button. "Keep that up while the defibrillator analyzes the patient's heart rhythm."

Clark set the biphasic energy level to two hundred joules and hit the charge button. It blinked red, indicating it was fully charged.

"Stand clear, everybody!"

Once the team had stepped away from the bed, he pressed the machine's *shock* button. The first shock was delivered. As the patient's shoulders shook slightly, Eva went right back in and began performing CPR.

"Come on…come on…" she whispered, sweat trickling down her forehead.

Two minutes passed. Eva paused while the team observed the monitor, assessing the patient's heart rhythm. The line tracing was primarily flat with waves that occasionally spiked and dipped. When the new pulse reading flashed on the screen, it came in at thirty-two.

"That heart rate is still too low," Clark stated. "Preparing to deliver another shock. Stand clear, everyone!"

A second dose of electric current shock was administered. Eva proceeded with another round of CPR.

"Please, *please*," she begged, willing the patient to respond.

After another two minutes, Eva stopped the compressions once again. The team held their breath, hoping for a positive response.

"Ough!"

The patient emitted a hearty cough just as her eyes flew open.

"Yes!" Eva panted.

The machine beeped, a new set of vitals flashing on the screen.

"The patient's blood pressure and pulse rate are stabilizing," Clark announced. "Let's keep the defibrillator pads in place just in case those numbers drop again. Is the oxygenation still running at full speed?"

"Yes, Doctor," Brandi said.

Eva pulled the blankets farther down the bed. "The patient's temperature is ninety-seven degrees. We need to bring it down to somewhere between eighty-nine and ninety-three to prevent possible brain damage."

"Rian," Clark said, "grab some cooling pads. Those will help lower her temperature quickly." He turned to Eva. "Great work, Dr. Gordon."

"Same to you, Dr. Malone," she said, resisting the urge to embrace him as tears of relief burned her eyes. "Once the patient is transferred to the ICU, I'm thinking she should be placed in a medically induced coma to allow time for her body to recover."

"I agree. I'd also like to get those CT scans done as soon as possible so we'll know the extent of her injuries."

"Doctors?" Brandi called out. "The patient's vitals are continuing to normalize. Should I begin preparing for a transfer to the ICU?"

Clark blew an exhausted exhale, nodding his head. "Yes, please. Thank you, Nurse Bennett." He turned to Eva. "Today was a tough one. I'm glad you were here, working alongside me."

"So am I. But I'm sure you would have done just fine without me."

He gave her hand a squeeze. "Maybe. Thank goodness I didn't have to find out."

Once the patient had been transported to the ICU, Eva joined Clark at the surgical sink.

"I am exhausted," she sighed before leaning over and whispering, "I cannot wait to slip out of these scrubs and in between the sheets with you. Dinner and drinks at my place tonight?"

"Mmm, that sounds nice…"

"I was thinking about whipping up a teriyaki-glazed chicken stir-fry, some spicy garlic edamame, sautéed French green beans—"

"But I can't," Clark interrupted.

Eva's hands froze underneath the stream of water. "I'm sorry. You what?"

"I can't get together with you tonight. I have plans."

"Uh…" Eva uttered. "Okay."

She waited for him to elaborate. He didn't. Instead, Clark backed away from the sink.

"Thanks again for today," he told her. "You were amazing in there. See you in the morning?"

She forced a nod. "Yep. See you tomorrow."

Clark turned his attention toward the rest of the team. "Great job today, everyone. I appreciate all the hard work and quick thinking." And with that, he exited the emergency room.

Eva just stood there, watching him leave.

"You okay?" Brandi asked, her gaze drifting from Clark's back to Eva's baffled expression.

"I'm fine. It's just…it's been a long day. I was looking forward to hanging out with Clark tonight, but apparently he has other plans."

"Well, Leo and I are going to the Oasis to grab drinks tonight. Why don't you join us?"

"Thanks, but I'll pass. I don't wanna disrupt your evening. You two go on and have a good time. I'll be fine."

"Are you sure?"

"I'm positive," Eva lied.

After the cavalier brush-off from Clark, she was far from fine.

CHAPTER THIRTEEN

"HAVE YOU HEARD the news? Your ex-fiancé won the election," Amanda said, her tone as dry as the Mojave Desert.

"Yeah, I know."

Eva's cell pinged loudly in her ear once again. Ever since Kyle had been declared the winner of Iowa's senatorial race last night, her phone had been blowing up.

"Everyone knows that Kyle and I aren't together anymore. I don't know why they feel the need to reach out with congratulatory calls and messages."

"Maybe that's their way of trying to bring you two back together."

"Starting with my very own mother. *And* his. Not only have they both called to inform me of the win, but according to my cousin, they're ready to resume the wedding planning."

"Okay, now they're going way too far."

Eva plopped down on the couch and slipped on her sneakers. It was her day off, and she'd decided to make it all about her. A nice run in the park, a little shopping, a few rounds of blackjack at Aria followed by a Cantonese lobster dinner at Catch. Since she'd been in Vegas, most of her days had been spent inside Fremont General's emergency room, while the nights had been dedicated to Clark. But Clark had been pulling away from her recently, and Eva figured she should dedicate more of it to herself.

"Look, enough about Kyle," Amanda said. "How are things going between you and Clark?"

"Um...they're cool. I guess..."

"Just cool, you guess? Well, that doesn't sound very convincing."

"Listen, there's something I need to tell you. And just know that I didn't mention it sooner because I didn't want you to make a bigger deal out of it than what it is."

"Okay, I'm listening."

Eva leaned against the back of the couch and squeezed her eyes shut. "Clark and I have been sleeping together."

"I knew it!" Amanda screamed so loudly that Eva almost dropped the phone. "The way you kept disappearing at night and not taking my calls, then acting all coy when I asked about him. Why would you withhold something like that from me?"

"Because I didn't want you to get your hopes up! It's nothing. Just a friends-with-benefits type of situation that's going to end once my temp assignment is over."

"But if I know you like I think I do," Amanda said, "I'm assuming the feelings you've always had for Clark have intensified, haven't they?"

"Yes." Eva stood and began pacing the floor. "Not to mention the sex is *amazing.* Ever since Clark and I opened up to each other about everything that went down in the past and started over fresh, I've wanted to see where things would go between us. Explore something deeper. But he seems to be against any sort of commitment. Clark is the one who insisted we keep things casual in the first place. Instead of us getting closer as time goes on, he's actually been keeping me more at an emotional distance. And I don't know why, but whenever I try to talk about anything meaningful, he brushes me off."

"And you haven't pressed the issue about wanting more?"

Eva schlepped over to the mirror and pulled her hair into a high ponytail, then swiped on a coat of clear lip gloss. "I haven't. I guess I just assumed it would happen naturally. You know how close Clark and I were back in the day. Maybe that had me convinced he'd eventually change his mind and want something more, too. Clearly I was wrong. And that's fine. I won't be in Las Vegas forever. I'll just focus on finishing out my assignment then get back home to the real world."

Huffing into the phone, Amanda replied, "Easier said than done, my friend. I think you and Clark feel the exact same way about each other, but neither of you are willing to admit it. And you know how men are. Once they've been hurt, it's hard for them to bounce back. He's afraid. Convince him that you won't run away this time. The man loves you. Don't let this second chance pass you by. If you do, I promise you'll regret it."

Eva grabbed her keys and headed for the door, ignoring the pangs of frustration rattling her rib cage. "One thing you're right about is that I hurt Clark before, and I don't think he'll ever let that go. Maybe keeping his guard up while dating around is his way of getting back at me. Whatever the case may be, I'm not about to try to force a man to want me. I refused to do it with Kyle, and I won't do it with Clark. And on that note, I love you, but I need to get this run in to clear my head."

"I love you, too. And I hear what you're saying. But please, just take what I'm saying into consideration before you completely write Clark off."

"I'll think about it. Bye."

Eva disconnected the call and headed down to the lobby. When the elevator doors opened, she saw someone standing at the concierge's desk behind a huge bouquet of pink peonies.

"Aww, how sweet," she whispered, her tongue stinging with envy.

"I'm not sure of the apartment number," a familiar voice said, "but the name is Eva Gordon. *Dr.* Eva Gordon."

She stopped so abruptly that the soles of her sneakers almost sent her crashing to the floor.

"What's *my* name?" the man asked the concierge. "Senator Kyle Benson."

Eva's stomach dropped to her knees. She quickly pivoted, rushing back toward the elevators. On the way there, she skidded across the freshly polished floors, grabbing hold of the couch's armrest before almost hitting the marble tiles.

Footsteps charged in her direction. "Dr. Gordon?" the concierge asked. "Are you all right?"

Kyle was right behind him. "Hey, there's my girl!"

She stood, straightening her bright pink tank top. "I'm fine, Mr. Jackson. Thank you. Kyle, what in the world are you doing here?"

"What do you mean? I'm here to celebrate my senatorial win with my future wife!"

Mr. Jackson's expression wrinkled with bewilderment. "I will, um… I'll give you two some privacy," he uttered before returning to the front desk. He'd gotten to know Clark quite well during his frequent visits to the building. Eva could only imagine what the concierge was thinking. In that moment, however, his opinion was the least of her concerns.

Kyle approached with open arms. She studied his face, noticing that the stress of the election had completely dissipated. Gone were the dark circles surrounding his eyes and hunched shoulders plagued with the weight of the campaign. He appeared brighter. Lighter on his feet as he flashed her a genuine, carefree smile.

Pressing his lips somewhere between Eva's cheek and mouth, then stepping away, Kyle oozed confidence as he straightened his perfectly tailored gray blazer.

"But before you start interrogating me," Kyle said, "here's a question for you. What in the world are *you* doing here? In Las Vegas of all places. Oh, and on a side note, I shouldn't have had to find out from your mother that you'd moved across the country."

"First of all, I didn't move here. I accepted a three-month assignment at Fremont General Hospital. Secondly, why would I go out of my way to inform you of anything? You broke off our engagement to focus on your campaign, remember? I figured you'd be too busy to care where I went."

"Come on, E. That was just a break, not a *breakup*. You knew we'd get back together once I won the election."

"I didn't know that, actually."

"The time apart was obviously worth it, because you're standing before the new senator of Iowa! And where am I right now, when I should be back home celebrating with my people? I'm here, with you. Because *you're* the only one who I really wanted to share this moment with."

The air thickened around Eva as Kyle led her toward the front desk. When he reached for the floral arrangement, she spun a full turn, suddenly anxious to escape the lobby.

"Eva, what's wrong? Are you okay?"

"I just… I need some air."

She hurried through revolving doors and headed straight to the neighboring coffee shop.

"Sir!" Kyle called out to the concierge. "Can you please keep an eye on those flowers for me?"

His hard-soled oxford shoes clicked along the pavement as he ran after Eva.

"Baby," he panted, grabbing hold of her. "Talk to me. I know this must be a lot, me popping up unannounced."

"Ya think?" she shot back. "I'm overwhelmed, to say the least. We haven't spoken since that night at Chateau Eilean. So, yes. I'm gonna need a minute."

Raising his hands in surrender, Kyle backed off. "I understand."

Eva allowed him to open the café's frosted glass door. She

stepped inside, cool air settling into her damp skin as the rich aroma of roasted coffee beans floated through the air. The rustic shop usually served as a place of calm after a long day at the hospital. But today, there was nothing the low lighting, neutral color palette and lush plants could do to soothe her chaotic mind.

She approached the counter and ordered an iced black coffee. Kyle told the barista to make it two and rushed to pay for their drinks.

"Look," he said, following her to the end of the bar. "Just hear me out. I am beyond sorry for the way I handled things back in Black Willow. You have no idea how many nights I've spent wishing I could turn back time and change what I did. I shouldn't have allowed my campaign to take over and in the process, given up on us. I will forever regret it. Winning that election doesn't mean as much to me as I thought it would, because I don't have you by my side."

Eva stared at him blankly, as if she couldn't quite comprehend his words. Never had Kyle spoken to her with that much heart. And in the five years they were together, she couldn't even remember a time when he'd apologized for anything.

"Despite the fact that I'm still angry with you," she said, "I can appreciate you saying that. So…thank you."

After the barista handed them their drinks, Kyle pointed to the outdoor patio. "It's a beautiful day. Why don't we sit outside and talk?"

They settled in at a table facing her building. Kyle stared into the lobby and waved, giving the concierge a thumbs-up. "Just making sure he doesn't let anybody touch your flower arrangement. Does it look familiar?"

"It does, ironically. That display is very similar to one of the options I'd chosen for our wedding."

Kyle leaned back, his lips spreading into a toothy smile. "Yeah, I know."

"What do you mean, you *know*? You couldn't have remembered a thing about our wedding plans considering you weren't interested in them."

"Welp, obviously I was. Because I remember you showing me something that looked just like the arrangement sitting on your concierge's desk."

Confusion pounded inside Eva's head. Who was this smooth-talking man with the self-assured gleam? Kyle the politician always knew how to turn it on for the people. The charm. The warmth. The wit. Until now, Eva hadn't realized just how distant he'd become toward her behind closed doors. In this moment, however, he lit up the entire patio, exuding love and redemption.

Don't fall for it...

Sliding his chair closer to hers, Kyle said, "I can only imagine how eager you are to return to Black Willow."

"Hmm, I don't know. I'm really enjoying my time here in Las Vegas. The weather is great, there's always something to do, and working at Fremont General has been really rewarding. I've learned so much while treating patients with conditions I never thought I'd face."

Talk of the hospital brought on thoughts of Clark. Where was he? Who was he with? What were they doing? An image of him lying in bed with another woman flashed through her head. Eva squeezed her eyes shut, hoping the pressure would dissolve the visual.

"I can understand that," Kyle continued. "I love a good challenge, too. But this place isn't you, Eva. This town reeks of alcohol and marijuana. Ringing slot machines and cheap sex. A distinguished, intelligent, classy woman like you doesn't belong here."

"Let me stop you right there. You can't speak on this city as if it's just some seedy underworld. Las Vegas has plenty to offer other than drinking, gambling and partying. It is a hub for economic development. The job market is booming, the technological endeavors are flourishing, the educational, social service and health care systems are advancing—"

Gently placing his hand over hers, Kyle interjected, "Listen to me, honey. That's not what I'm saying. The point is, this place isn't Black Willow. You're a huge part of our hometown and a pillar of the community. Your patients miss you. Your family misses you. More importantly, *I* miss you. Things will be good between us again now that the pressure is off me."

Eva slid her hand out from underneath Kyle's grasp. "You can't just assume that. Now you've won the election, it's time for the real work to begin. Who's to say you won't leave me again when things get tough? Because they will, you know."

Kyle turned away, blowing an exasperated sigh.

"What's gonna happen when a bill you're pushing doesn't get passed? Or a federal judge you're supporting doesn't get appointed? With all the Senate sessions, meetings with constituents, committee hearings and the list goes on, your workload is going to be extremely hectic."

"I know, I know. Leave all that up to me, Eva. I can handle it. And I can handle us. Now, when is this little temp thing you're doing going to be over so you can come back home, take over as my first lady, and put the wedding plans back in motion?"

She fell back against her chair in shock. "Do you really think us getting back together is going to be that easy?"

"Why wouldn't it be?"

Eva rolled her eyes, her head swiveling in the opposite direction. A familiar-looking car appeared in the near distance. It was a midnight-blue Mercedes, pulling out of her building's driveway.

"Wait, is that…?" she whispered. After a brief moment, she muttered, "Oh, hell!" and crouched down underneath the table.

Kyle stood and reached inside his pocket. "Listen, sweetheart. How about I show you just how easy this can be rather than tell you?"

He got down on one knee as Eva stooped in front of him, peering over his shoulder.

"Eva," he continued before pulling out a small black velvet box.

"Wh—what is that?" she asked her eyes wide. "What are you doing?"

He opened it, revealing a huge princess-cut solitaire so brilliant that it set off light beams underneath the bright Las Vegas sun.

"It's a new engagement ring," Kyle said. "To represent our new start. Come on, babe," he crooned, taking her hand in his. "It's me and you against the world. Or Iowa at least. Dr. Eva Gordon, will you accept my proposal once again and marry me?"

The piercing squeal of tire treads screeched in front of the coffee shop. Eva turned toward the curb. There, staring her dead in the face through the windshield, was Clark.

Her knees shook as she attempted to stand. She looked on in horror as Clark tore off his sunglasses with a sneer so contemptuous that it sent chills straight through her.

Kyle was too busy slipping the ring on her finger to notice a thing.

It's not what you think! she tried to call out.

But her vocal cords were numb with shock. Grabbing Kyle by the shoulders, she rasped, "Help me up!"

Instead, he pulled her closer. She fell into him, involuntarily wrapping her arms around his back as she struggled not to tumble to the ground.

"I knew you'd come around, baby," Kyle gushed, embracing her tightly. "I *knew* you'd come around!" He pulled her up, raising her left hand in the air and yelling, "We're getting married, people. We're getting married! *Whoo!*"

The small crowd sitting around them broke into applause.

"Will you please let me go!" Eva gritted out after finally finding her voice. She wiggled away from Kyle and jetted toward the curb. But it was too late. Clark had already pulled off.

Kyle approached with his phone in hand and began snapping photos of her. "I cannot wait to send these pics to our moms. They are gonna be ecstatic. I need to call the *Black Willow Herald*, too, and let them know that the wedding is back on. The news will be on the front page tomorrow. Turn around and face me, E. And smile!"

Eva staggered into the street, barely hearing a word Kyle was saying. She was too busy watching Clark speed off into the distance.

CHAPTER FOURTEEN

CLARK STARED AT his reflection in Posh Fit Gym's mirror, heaving as he lifted a fifty-pound dumbbell over his head. The anger pulsating through his veins had him seeing double. He squeezed his eyes shut, pushing past the burn of his sixth set of reps while hoping the pain would numb his feelings.

Leo, who was laid out on the floor next to Clark, had been stretching his calves for the past twenty minutes. Wiggling onto his side, he panted, "So let me get this straight. You and Eva agreed to see other people if you wanted to, but you have yet to go out with anyone else, even if she thinks you have?"

"Yes. Because I haven't come across anyone who I'm interested in dating."

"Or maybe it's because you can't get Eva out of your head. She's the only woman you want. The sooner you can admit that yourself, the better off you'll be."

"Like I said," Clark huffed, increasing the speed on his bicep curls, "no one has caught my attention."

"Is that the story we're going with?"

"Yes. Because it's the truth. Look, while you're so busy grilling me, why don't you admit to whatever's going on between you and Brandi?"

Leo rolled back over and pulled his knees into his chest. "Brandi and I are cool. We're hanging out. Enjoying each other's company. You know what I mean?"

"So you two are dating."

"I didn't say all that. We're simply going with the flow. Now, have we shared a kiss or two? Yeah, we have."

"Okay then!" Clark said, tossing him a high five. "I like you two together—"

"Hold up, see, now you're going too far. Brandi and I are not officially together. And by the way, this conversation never happened. I promised her I'd keep things under wraps. Now, back to you. I'd like to know why you decided to stop by Eva's place without calling first."

"Dude, I told you that she and her ex got back together, and *that's* what you're focusing on?"

"All I'm saying is that when you roll up on someone unannounced, you've got to expect the unexpected. And maybe what you *think* you saw wasn't what you *actually* saw."

"Wait...*what*?" Clark shouted, cringing at the abrupt outburst. His eyes roamed the immediate area. No one was standing close enough to hear him lose his usual cool. "What I saw was him proposing, and the two of them hugging it out."

"That's impossible. Because last I heard, Eva couldn't stand the man. He's the main reason why she left Black Willow. Why would she take him back so easily?"

Clark dropped the dumbbells onto the floor, oblivious to the sonic boom that erupted from the crash. An urge to overexert himself took over. He jumped high in the air then hit the mat, releasing a series of burpees. "Because he's the new state senator of Iowa. And as we both know, Eva is a parentpleaser. That's what they want. And I guess being with a stiff robot who's all about his image works for her, too."

"Well, you weren't presenting her with a better offer, so..." Leo flipped over on to his stomach and attempted to lift his head and chest up off the mat. "Check out my new yoga move. Upward facing dog. See, while you're over there killing yourself, I'm partaking in a much more effective workout that won't ruin my joints and—" He paused, dropped back down and pointed over at Clark. "Wait, how do you even know that Eva's ex won the election?"

Clark responded with a grunt as he broke into a set of jumping jacks.

"Aww, come on, man! Please tell me you haven't gone back to your old ways. Are you using the internet to stalk Eva's life again?"

When Clark failed to reply once again, Leo rolled his eyes.

"Listen. As your best friend, I'm not gonna lie here and tell you what you wanna hear. I'm gonna tell you what you *need* to hear. This is all your fault."

"*My* fault?"

"Yes, *your* fault! You continue to let your past, not to mention old fears, get in the way of your future happiness. Your feelings for Eva haven't changed since med school. You may have suppressed them over the years, but they exploded the day she showed up at Fremont General. And how do you handle it? By coming at her with that dumb *no strings attached* rule. I don't think either of you really wanted that, but for whatever reason you both agreed to it. And look at you now. In denial and drowning your sorrows in sweat."

Exhausted both mentally and physically, Clark plopped down onto a nearby weight bench. He grabbed a towel and wiped his face, then bit into it in frustration. "Eva is an intelligent, outspoken woman. If she wanted more, she would've said that. I honestly think she sees this whole Las Vegas experience for exactly what it is—a temporary assignment. She's here to learn all she can and have a good time. Once the three months are up, she'll go back to her life in Black Willow and walk down the aisle with that clown."

"Here's a thought. Why don't you just ask her what's really going on?"

"Nope," Clark uttered defiantly, hitting the floor and cranking out a set of push-ups. "Absolutely not. When it comes down to it, Eva owes me nothing. We weren't in an exclusive relationship. If she wants me to know what's happening, she'll tell me."

That's what his mouth said. But when thoughts of Eva marrying another man rushed through his mind, Clark became sick to his stomach. The clean slate they'd established was getting muddier by the minute.

Grabbing his water bottle, Leo took a long drink and said, "Let me ask you this again. Why *did* you go over to Eva's?"

Clark acted as if he hadn't heard him, instead focusing on the floor as he pulled his right hand behind his back and pushed down with his left.

"Oh, feel free to stay silent while you show out with the one-handed push-ups. I already know the answer. You went there to tell her how you feel. Confess that you don't want to be with anyone but her. But then you saw Eva with her ex and backed off. So what now? Are you just gonna let her walk out of your life once again without putting up a fight?"

"That's exactly what I'm gonna do. You know why? Because some things never change. Eva showed me who she was back in the day. A *runner*. She ran during med school because she was afraid to give us a chance. Ran from Black Willow when she couldn't face the heat after her relationship ended with a man she never really loved in the first place. And now she's gonna run back home when she's done here and pick right back up where she left off. How would I look trying to stop her when she's proven once again that I'm not the one for her?"

"But for the time being, Eva is still here. So stop ignoring your feelings. And drop that ridiculous *no strings attached* plan. The only reason you set it up in the first place was to avoid getting hurt. And in the end, you *still* got hurt."

Clark flinched underneath the sting of Leo's words. He racked his brain for a snappy response but came up empty. Because his friend was absolutely right.

* * *

Clark threw on his lab coat and rushed down the hallway. He was two minutes shy of being late for handoffs thanks to Leo, who'd insisted on ordering a second breakfast to go before leaving the restaurant.

After checking the schedule, Clark was relieved to see that he was on duty with Dr. Abrams instead of Eva. He knocked on the conference room door and headed inside. "Dr. Beal! I am so sorry I'm late—"

Clark stopped mid-sentence. There, sitting across from Dr. Beal, was Eva.

What in the hell are you doing here?

He swallowed the urge to blurt the first words that came to mind and cleared his throat, slowly closing the door behind him.

Pull it together. You are not that young, vulnerable med school student anymore. Fremont General is your house. Handle yourself accordingly.

"Dr. Gordon," he said, his tone laced with feigned indifference. "Good morning. I thought you were off today."

"Good morning, Dr. Malone. I was called in at the last minute. Dr. Abrams had to leave town unexpectedly, so I'm filling in for him."

Her cool tone was unnerving. Clark walked stiffly toward the chair next to Dr. Beal, his eyes darting in every direction except Eva's.

"No worries, Dr. Malone," Dr. Beal said. "I was just updating Dr. Gordon on a very complicated patient who checked into the ER last night. His name is Flex Cuttington, and he's a professional bodybuilder."

"Hence the name," Clark said wryly.

Eva, emitting that adorable giggle she knew drove him crazy, added, "I said the same thing. Check out this photo I found of him online."

She slid her cell phone across the table. Clark caught it, eyeing the shredded, deeply tanned man with bulging oiled-up muscles standing onstage in a front double biceps pose.

"Wow..." Clark rasped. "He is huge. Does the man have time to do anything else besides work out? From the looks of him, he lives in the gym."

"Yeah, well, don't give him too much credit for time spent on the weight machines," Dr. Beal replied. "Mr. Cuttington owes plenty of this muscle mass to the black-market androgen and anabolic steroids he's been injecting into his delts, biceps, quads and glutes."

"Trenbolone, Superdrol and methyltrienolone to be exact," Eva interjected.

"Oh, no. Three of the most dangerous steroids out there, especially if they're administered incorrectly." Clark slid Eva's phone back to her. Before doing so, the thought of swiping through her text messages and call log crossed his mind, just to see how much she'd been communicating with Kyle. He thrust the distasteful thought away. He'd never do that.

When she caught her cell, their eyes met briefly. He waited for those dazzling hazel specks to shoot him a look of defiance. One that said she'd gotten the best of him yet again. That she had beaten him at his own game. A game for which he'd set the rules. But they didn't. Instead, Eva's gaze was soft. Open. Wide with defenselessness. Which left him confused.

Don't fall for it. Do not allow this beguiling woman's charms to take you down again.

Shifting his focus back to their patient, Clark asked, "So what brought Mr. Cuttington into the ER?"

"Well, he's preparing for a national bodybuilding competition," Dr. Beal responded. "In doing so, he's been stacking all three of the steroids that Dr. Gordon mentioned."

"Wait, you mean to tell me he's been shooting trenbolone, Superdrol and methyltrienolone at the same time?"

"Yes. And what's even more alarming is that he wasn't under any sort of dosage supervision. So he'd been using his own judgment when administering the injections. Now I will give Mr. Cuttington credit for doing some online research on the recommended dosages. However, since he wanted to bulk up quickly for that competition, he'd decided to triple the suggested amounts. After suffering two seizures and a racing heartbeat, his wife urged him to come to the hospital."

"He's lucky that didn't kill him," Clark said while reviewing the patient's chart. "I see here what the patient was hoping that method would do for him. The trenbolone was used to gain muscle and burn fat faster, Superdrol to retain lean muscle tissue and build stamina, and methyltrienolone to increase testosterone production and provide quick visible enhancements."

Eva slid a set of photos and CT scans toward Clark. "That was his plan. But as a result of his misuse, he's suffered a number of illnesses and injuries."

"And that's due to the dangerous combination of all three steroids, the high dosages he'd been administering, as well as the prolonged use of them," Dr. Beal chimed in.

Studying the photos of Mr. Cuttington, Clark noticed several open wounds on his shoulders, biceps, thighs and buttocks. Some were yellow and loose, with fluid oozing from the centers. Others were black, the tissue appearing thick and leathery.

"So the patient was injecting steroids directly into the muscles he was looking to build," Clark commented, "which caused skin necrosis."

"Exactly. We treated the wounds by first removing the dead tissue, then using hyperbaric oxygen therapy to speed up the healing process and improve organ function. I've been monitoring his blood pressure and heart rate as they're both running high, managing them with intravenous metoprolol."

"What dosage are you administering?"

Dr. Beal pushed his rimless bifocals up the bridge of his nose while thumbing through his notebook. "Let's see. I know I wrote that information down somewhere in here…"

"I recorded it earlier when we reviewed the patient's medical care plan," Eva said.

As she scrolled through the Notes app on her phone, Clark glanced down at her left hand. It was ringless.

She must've left it at home so as not to draw attention to herself.

Smart move. Clark wouldn't have been able to even look at her had she flaunted her rekindled engagement in his face.

"Here it is," she continued. "When the patient first arrived in the ER, Dr. Beal administered a five-milliliter bolus injection three times over the course of fifteen minutes. Once the patient's blood pressure stabilized, it was recommended that he begin taking one hundred milligram tablets twice daily."

"Thank you, Dr. Gordon," Dr. Beal said. "As for the seizures, I treated them with an intravenous infusion of levetiracetam."

"And what was the dosage on that?" Clark asked.

"Um…" Dr. Beal uttered, once again paging through his notebook.

"Ten milliliters," Eva said, "mixed with one hundred milliliters of sodium chloride. We're still waiting for the lab results from Mr. Cuttington's endocrine panel. My guess is that his extreme steroid use has wreaked havoc on his hormones. Oh, and after the infusion of levetiracetam, the patient was prescribed the same medication in pill form. One thousand milligrams, twice daily."

Dr. Beal gave Eva a nod of thanks before taking a long sip of coffee from his *Best Doctor Dad Ever* mug. "As you two can probably tell, it's been a long night. Plus, I'm coming off a twenty-four-hour shift. Once again, thank you for that, Dr.

Gordon. You are beyond impressive, and it has really been a pleasure working with you."

She smiled, those pretty lips setting off a massive explosion below Clark's belt. Dr. Beal was right about her. Eva was extraordinary. Always present. And never rattled. Even in anger, Clark had no choice but to finally admit that he was as much in love with her now as he'd ever been. And with that came the realization that he never should've diminished their reconnection to a casual fling.

"I appreciate that, Dr. Beal," she responded humbly. "Thank you."

Shifting in his chair, Clark shuffled the papers in his hands. "I can imagine you're exhausted, Dr. Beal, so we won't hold you much longer. I'm looking over the patient's blood test, imaging and biopsy results, and they're showing kidney and liver damage. Have you established a treatment plan for those issues?"

"I have. Regarding the kidney damage, Mr. Cuttington has developed focal segmental glomerulosclerosis. I explained to him that this scarring within his kidneys is a direct result of the excessive steroid usage, and that it can be reversed if he discontinues use. I'm treating the damage with losartan to reduce the protein in his urine."

"Good," Clark added. "That'll help lower his blood pressure, too, along with the metoprolol."

"That's right. I'm also giving him atorvastatin to lower his cholesterol, which clocked in at two hundred and ninety-six, and furosemide to prevent water retention and swelling."

Leaning back in his chair, Dr. Beal closed his eyes and emitted a long sigh.

"You all right, Doc?" Clark asked.

"Yep. Just slowly drifting off into the abyss."

Eva gave Dr. Beal's arm a sympathetic pat, then passed a chart to Clark. "The patient is in stage two liver failure. The fibrosis is moderate since the scarred tissue hasn't replaced an excessive amount of healthy tissue. Dr. Beal explained to Mr. Cunningham that fibrosis is treatable as long as he discontinues use of the steroids. The furosemide he's taking for the kidney damage will also treat the liver as it'll remove excess fluid from the body. It's been recommended that the patient limit his salt intake, implement a healthy diet plan rich in vitamins D, E, C and B, and take a multivitamin daily."

"Got it," Clark said while rigorously jotting down notes. "Sounds like an excellent plan to me."

Dr. Beal burst into a round of applause. "Dr. Gordon, you are a rock star. I'm so glad you're here with Dr. Malone for this complicated handoff." He nudged Clark's shoulder, then said to her, "Are you *sure* you can't stick around Fremont General after your temporary assignment is over? We sure could use someone of your caliber around here permanently."

"Thank you, Dr. Beal. But unfortunately, no. I haven't been asked to stay. Plus, I hear my family and the townspeople back in Black Willow miss me terribly."

Her words crumbled the wall of protection Clark had built around his heart. He'd tried hard to follow the rules they'd both agreed to. Keep his emotions at bay. Not catch feelings. And let their brief fling go once Eva's time in Las Vegas was up. But instead, he had completely failed to do any of that and fallen in love all over again.

When it was all said and done, Clark didn't want to see her leave. Especially on rocky terms. It felt like their last few months of med school all over again. Only this time, the pain was somehow even more excruciating. Eva was going back to a man who didn't deserve her rather than stay in Las Vegas and give the two of them a real chance.

Maybe it's time to risk it all and fight for the only woman you've ever really wanted...

Clark, suddenly growing hot with confusion, pushed away from the table. "Are we done here, Dr. Beal?"

"I think so. Dr. Gordon can catch you up on the rest of the patients' cases, none of which are as extreme as Mr. Cuttington's. And *I* can go home and get some rest."

"Sounds good," Clark told him before hopping up and headed toward the door.

"Wait, Dr. Malone?" Eva said.

He stopped in the doorway, refusing to turn around. "Yes?"

"Would you mind hanging back for a few minutes? I need to speak with you."

Feeling as though he might catch fire, Clark fanned himself with Mr. Cuttington's test results. "I'm actually late for a meeting. Why don't we reconvene inside the ER?"

Before she could respond, he charged out of the room and headed straight to Leo's office.

CHAPTER FIFTEEN

Month three

"ARE YOU SURE Clark's not gonna be here?" Eva asked Brandi for the fourth time.

"Yes, Eva. I'm positive. Tonight is for us girls only. No boys allowed."

Unconvinced, Eva followed her inside the Oasis. "Mmm-hmm. We'll see. I'm only asking because Clark does not want to see me. He's managed to remain professional at work, but underneath it all, I can tell he'd rather eat thumbtacks than be in my presence."

"What makes you think that?"

"Well, he's avoided me at every opportunity, and he's refused to speak to me privately. He hasn't returned my phone calls or responded to my texts. Honestly, I just don't think he's interested anymore, and he wasn't even before Kyle arrived. Maybe this fling was all he needed to get closure from our past. Once I'm gone, he'll probably go right back to playing the field."

"Ha! I highly doubt that. But just to ease your mind, I swear to you that Clark will not be here."

As the pair squeezed through the crowd in search of an empty table, Eva was reminded of the first day she'd hung out there with Brandi, Leo and Clark. That same tsunami of emotions swirled through her head. Only this time, she wasn't fretting over her and Clark's past. Instead she was drowning in the murky waters of their present. How in the hell had she and Clark managed to make such a mess of their situation once again?

Why are you asking yourself questions that you already know the answers to?

Both she and Clark had mishandled their fling from day one. She'd wanted more than just a casual hookup but refused to speak up after he'd laid the ground rules. And from what Eva had gathered, he saw her as nothing more than a woman on the rebound he could enjoy a commitment-free fling with, who wouldn't put any demands on him beyond great sex. The old Clark never would've settled for an emotionless hookup, knowing there was so much more between them. But these days he seemed content being a player with no attachments. Eva knew this way of life would never bring him true happiness. Nevertheless, she felt she had no choice but to accept his wishes, just as he'd accepted hers back in the day.

Reconnecting with Clark had been magical. There was no denying their organic bond and fiery chemistry. Despite never having said the words, he'd made her feel loved. Yet through it all, he'd refused to break their agreement and open up emotionally. So she'd continued to follow his lead and do the same.

Now here they were, ending on a bitter note the second time around.

Suddenly, Eva was overcome by the urge to leave. Go back to her apartment and break down in a hot, soothing bath. Or maybe even start packing so that the moment her assignment was over, she could jet back to Black Willow.

"Is this good?" Brandi asked, pointing to an empty table.

"This is fine."

Right after they sat down and placed their order, Brandi got straight to it. "So, what's the final verdict on you and Clark?"

"Bottom line? This was just a fling that was stamped with

an expiration date from the very beginning. And now our time is almost up. He'll go his way and I'll go mine. Now can we please change the subject and officially kick off our girls' night?"

Brandi glanced down at Eva's left hand. "Yes. We can. But before we do, can I ask just one more question?"

"I'm listening," Eva said before shoving a chicken nacho doused in cheese and salsa inside her mouth.

"What's the deal with you and your ex? I mean, I know he came here and proposed. Are you really gonna go back home and marry him?"

"I hadn't planned on it."

"But you're open to giving him another chance? To seeing where the relationship might go?"

"Honestly, no. I just haven't had a chance to tell Kyle that yet. I've tried calling, but I guess he's been so busy with work that he hasn't had a chance to call back. Maybe he's avoiding me because he knows what's coming. But we're done. And when I return to Black Willow, I'll just have to weather the storm of our breakup."

Brandi's eyes narrowed as she studied the bar's entrance. "Oh, *damn*."

"Oh, damn, what?"

Eva pivoted in her chair. Craning her neck, she noticed Leo dancing his way through the crowd.

"What is Leo doing here?"

"I have no idea. I did tell him we'd be here, but only because I didn't want him showing up with Clark. I made it very clear that he should stay away, and he and I would get together later."

"That's all right," Eva said, turning back around and taking a sip of her drink. "I don't mind Leo joining us. He's always a fun time. And I think it's cute how he can't seem to stay away from you—"

"Hello, ladies," a deep, all-too-familiar voice said behind

her that didn't belong to Leo. "I didn't expect to see you two here. I wonder who set *this* up."

A knot of nausea bounced inside the pit of Eva's stomach. *Clark.*

She sat stiffly in her seat, her hands already trembling with anxiety.

"What's up, my good people?" Leo boomed, plopping down in the chair next to Brandi's. "What are we drinking?"

"How about *I* start with the questions," Brandi retorted. "What are you doing here, Leo? Didn't I tell you that Eva and I made plans for just the two of us, and that we'd hang out later?"

"Yeah, you did. But my man Clark here mentioned that he wanted to grab a beer after work because we had such a long day. So I figured, *hey*, why not stop by our favorite spot? Where everybody knows our name? And they're always glad we came?"

"That's not exactly how it happened," Clark interjected, hovering over the chair next to Eva's as if waiting for an invitation to sit down. "You told me that—"

"Who cares about all the irrelevant little details?" Leo interrupted. "What matters most is that the gang's all here now! I see you two already have your drinks. Clark, I'll go grab us a couple of vodka martinis. Brandi, why don't you come and help me carry them back to the table?"

"You've got two hands. Why can't you go by your—"

Before she could finish, Leo grabbed her by the waist and pulled her away from the table.

And then there were two.

From the corner of her eye, Eva noticed Clark's fingers tapping the back of the chair next to hers.

"Do you mind if have a seat?" he finally asked.

"Not at all."

Her cool tone was a complete contradiction to the flaming nerves burning inside her throat.

"How's that old-fashioned?" he asked.

"It's good. Would you like a taste?"

Now why in the hell did you ask him that?

Eva squeezed her glass, mad that she'd already dropped her chilly facade. But then she glanced over at him and saw a slight smile on his face, highlighting that deep dimple in his left cheek.

Okay, maybe Clark's come in peace tonight.

"No, thanks. I'll wait for Leo to get back with my drink."

He glanced down at her left hand, then back up at her.

"Where's your ring?"

"What ring?"

"The ring that the senator proposed to you with when he came to town."

"It's...um...back at the apartment."

"So when is the wedding?"

"There isn't going to be a wedding."

"Really?" Clark slid his chair closer to Eva's. "From the looks of things when I saw you two together, it seemed as if you'd accepted his proposal."

"Well, looks can be deceiving. Because I didn't."

"So you shot him down? Told him no?"

Eva squirmed underneath Clark's intense gaze. "Put it this way... I didn't tell him yes."

Raising his head toward the ceiling, Clark blinked rapidly, as if his next question was buried within the copper tin tiles. "But you didn't actually tell him no either."

"Not yet. But I will," she snapped.

"Are you sure? Because I know how badly your parents want you to be with someone like him."

"My parents want me to be happy," Eva shot back.

"And being a part of Black Willow's high society, on a senator's arm, wouldn't make you happy? Because after all, you didn't turn down Kyle's proposal and send him home with that ring in his suitcase. Which would leave the door open for you two to get married," he said pointedly.

"What do you care, Clark? You've been pulling away from me emotionally over the past few weeks. Since all you seemed to want me for in the first place was sex, why are you so concerned now with who wants to marry me?"

"*Eva*. None of that is—"

"And we're back!" Leo proclaimed, interrupting the pair. He handed Clark a drink, then rejoined them at the table along with Brandi. "What'd we miss?"

"Nothing," Eva and Clark declared in unison.

"I.e. a hell of a lot," Leo said drily.

The DJ turned down the music and hopped on the mic.

"Hello, hello, hello, my party people!" he crooned.

Eva took several sips of her drink, glad for the interruption. The heated exchange between her and Clark had brought on a mist of sweat. She grabbed a napkin and dabbed at her neck.

"You missed a spot," Clark said, running his fingertip along the edge of her throat.

Eva gazed at him. His expression was just as surprised as hers at his involuntary action. Their sexual chemistry was clearly still ever present and beyond palpable, despite their heated argument.

She pressed her thighs together as the sensation of his skin tickled her most sensitive spot.

Don't do this. Do not let this man get the best of you...

"Welcome to Benny B.'s Raging Eighties Dance Party!" the DJ continued. "I'll be playing some of the greatest hits of the decade while you good people tear up the dance floor. Now, drink up, eat up, tip these hardworking bartenders well and, most importantly, have a good time. Let's *go*!"

Janet Jackson's "The Pleasure Principle" blared through the speakers. The crowd roared, their bodies bumping into one another as they rushed the dance floor.

Without saying a word, Leo turned to Brandi and held out his hand.

"You know Janet is my all-time favorite," she said to Eva. "Do you mind?"

"No, of course not. Go on. Have fun."

That's what her mouth said. But Eva's mind buzzed with worry at the thought of Clark starting back up once they were alone again.

"So," he began the moment Leo and Brandi were out of earshot.

Here we go...

"Your time here in Las Vegas is coming to an end soon."

"Yep. It is."

"How do you feel about that?"

Eva knew what he was doing. Probing her. Baiting her. Trying to analyze her mindset. If she told him the truth, would her feelings simply feed into his ego? Make him feel as though he'd finally conquered his biggest challenge? She hated their back-and-forth battles. The tit-for-tat struggle for power. Their unwillingness to be the first to show vulnerability and reveal their true emotions.

"How do I feel about it?" Eva repeated. "Bittersweet." There. Just enough to chew on without putting it all on the line. "How do you feel about it?"

"The same. Bittersweet."

Touché.

Tonight, they were both playing a mental game of chess, not checkers.

Eva watched as Clark took a sip of his drink. Déjà vu teased her brain as she'd studied that mouth so many times before. The way his soft, full lips skimmed the edge of the glass. His long, strong, flexible fingers reaching down and pulling the toothpick from the rim. Sliding it between his lips. Sucking the olive and chewing it slowly. He knew she was watching. And he made sure to put on a show.

"How's your drink?" she asked.

"Good. Would you like to taste it?"

"Sure."

Rather than hand her the glass, Clark reached over and held it to her lips. She took a sip. When he pulled it away, vodka trickled down his index finger. He ran it along her bottom lip. She licked it right before the alcohol dribbled down her chin.

Oh, he's not playing fair...

Clark placed the glass down and pulled in a long breath of air. "Eva, can I be honest with you about something?"

"Of course." Her muscles tensed as she braced herself. Was he finally going to profess his feelings for her?

"I don't like all this tension between us. To put it bluntly, I've been miserable because of it. I don't want to fight with you anymore. Since your time left here is limited, let's just call a truce. End things on a high note. Enjoy the rest of your stay in Vegas, then commit to maintaining some semblance of a friendship once you return to Black Willow."

It wasn't quite what Eva had expected to hear. She wanted Clark to fight for her. To ask for more. To tell her that he was done with his serial dating ways and was ready to commit to her. But Eva knew Clark didn't have that in him. So she had no choice but to accept the limitations of what he was able to give her.

"I don't want to fight with you anymore either," she told him. "Honestly, I was ecstatic when you and I reestablished our friendship. And the intimate moments we've shared have been nothing short of amazing. We both agreed to remain open, have fun and enjoy each other's company. Which we did. But then we allowed our emotions to get the best of us. And that's when things got...*complicated*. For the part I played in that, I apologize."

Clark leaned in and placed a tender kiss on her lips. "Thank you for that. And for whatever part I played, I apologize, too."

Despite feeling devastated that this was likely their ending, Eva was glad to have finally healed their years-long rift and made memories that she would forever cherish.

"So, we're good?" she asked, holding out her hand.

"We're good."

He took Eva's hand and pulled her close, then slid his hand into her hair. She gasped, shocked that he was showing such a public display of affection. Pressing his mouth against hers, he slipped his tongue between her lips while gently massaging her scalp. The euphoric sensation had her contemplating sneaking him inside the bathroom to finish what he'd started.

"You wanna get out of here?" he whispered in her ear, his tongue lightly nuzzling her lobe.

"Absolutely."

No sooner than the response was out of her mouth, Eva felt Clark's phone vibrate against her thigh. Flashbacks of their first night at the Oasis, when he'd rushed out to meet up with another woman, deflated her swelling excitement. She slowly moved away and drained her glass, anticipating him remembering he'd already made other plans.

Clark pulled the phone from his pocket. Eva's gaze couldn't help but to drift toward the screen. She held on to the edge of the table as he swiped open the home page. Would it be a text? A missed call? A message alert from one of his dating apps?

A list of notifications appeared. The latest one that had just come in was at the very top. A white box with the red letter "E" skirted the left side of the screen. To the right of it was a breaking news headline.

You are being ridiculous, Eva told herself, chomping down on a piece of ice in shame.

Clark put the phone away and stood, holding out his hand. "Shall we?"

"Yes."

They made their way toward the door, peering at the dance floor in search of Leo and Brandi. When the foursome made eye contact, Eva and Clark pointed at the exit then waved goodbye, prompting Brandi and Leo to wave back.

Eva felt as though she were starring in her very own movie as Clark whisked her straight to his car. While she may well be heading for heartbreak, Eva decided to simply enjoy the ride before the inevitable crash.

By the time Eva and Clark landed in his bed, there were no words left to be said. The pair lay together, taking their time while gently caressing each other. Eva soaked up the moment knowing they'd never get it back. Peering up at Clark, she saw him in a different light that glowed with a newfound appreciation. He was so special, and she'd always regret not seeing that years ago. But she knew now she had done too much damage to his trust for things to ever to work out between them.

Clark parted Eva's legs, then nestled his body between them. Holding her arms above her head, their fingers instinctively intertwining. Their lips met, their tongues danced, then went deeper.

Their naked bodies turned in unison. His erection pressed against her, slipping, sliding, teasing. She rolled her hips, throbbing as the tip circled her opening.

"Uh-uh," Clark grunted. "Not yet. I want to relish every moment of this."

The words melted her body underneath his touch. His spell. His prowess. Her moans vibrated against his neck. She bit down, wanting to savor the moment as well but growing impatient to the point of fatigue. He slid down the bed, his tongue trailing her body along the way, from her lips to her ears, her neck to her breasts. He grazed her nipples with his teeth, causing her breathing to quicken.

"You've got to stop this," she pleaded. "I'm on the verge of exploding."

"I'd love to see it."

She arched her back, her nails skimming his scalp, her hands massaging his broad shoulders and smooth, bulging biceps. Having no mercy, he continued toward the edge of the bed. Eva closed her eyes, the sensation of his mouth covering every inch of her body as he devoured the sensitive skin on her stomach, her hips, in between her thighs.

Trembling with expectation, she spread her legs farther apart. He threw them over his shoulders. His face disappeared as he reached up and teased her nipples with his fingertips. She ground her hips to the rhythm of his tongue sliding up and down, in and out. When it stroked upward and caressed her nub, his fingers took its place, slowly gliding inside her.

Eva gripped the sides of his face, unable to hold back the guttural scream that released from deep within. She shivered uncontrollably as he gripped her hips, his mouth remaining firmly between her legs.

"I can't do this anymore," she groaned, locking her hands underneath his arms and pulling him up.

This time, he obliged. Their lips met again. He pulled her toward him, finally slipping inside. She sighed into his mouth, surrendering her entire body to Clark. Pouring everything within her into that moment. Her arms clutched his back while her legs straddled his neck. She thrashed against him and when he went deeper, she pushed back harder, the pleasure escalating with every move.

Clark's thrusts slowly intensified. Eva clenched her muscles in response, relishing every inch of his length while licking his sweat from her lips. His head rose from her breasts. Their eyes met. Emotions poured from his gaze. She could feel the bliss. The desire. And sense the regret.

But behind the pleasure was a hint of sadness. She felt that, too. In the back of their minds lay the constant reminder that her departure was imminent. Time had become a thief of joy, transforming the thought of home into a notion of dread.

Clark's arms tightened around her. His embrace dissolved the angst that invaded the moment. He brought her to a peak as she closed her eyes, her body stiffening, then trembling. When he called out her name she released, biting into his neck as he exploded inside her, ending their night on the highest note yet.

CHAPTER SIXTEEN

Eva stirred slightly as sunlight burned her eyelids. She squinted, briefly forgetting where she was.

Still at Clark's place, in his bed...

Once her blurred vision cleared, she saw him sauntering toward her, fully dressed.

"Good morning, beautiful," he said, pressing his lips against hers.

She wrapped her fingers around his neck, contemplating tearing off his clothes. "Me, beautiful? In all my tousled-haired, smeared-makeup glory?"

"Yes, you, in all of that."

"Why are you already up and dressed instead of lying in bed next to me?"

"Mmm," Clark moaned. "As much as I'd love to be doing just that, I have a community service event to go to. My fraternity brothers and I are hosting a clothing drive at the Earl's House men's shelter."

"You know, I love a man who can help the less fortunate in his free time, when he isn't on the clock saving lives."

"Excuse me, but did I just hear you say the L-word?"

"I don't know. Did you?"

"Yeah, I believe I did."

While waiting tensely to see where he was going with that, Eva's cell phone buzzed. Clark grabbed it off the nightstand.

"Uh-oh," he uttered drily. "Look who it is, FaceTiming you while you're laid up at your secret lover's house. Your mother."

Eva snatched the phone and quickly declined the video chat.

"What are you doing? You should've picked up. Told your mom I said hello and found out what she wanted. You never know. Something could be wrong."

"Trust me, nothing is wrong. She's probably calling to harass me about putting the wedding plans back in motion. And the last thing I need her to see is me sprawled out naked in some man's bed."

The moment the words were out of her mouth, Eva regretted them. Especially when she felt the warmth drain from Clark's body. He stood rigidly, shoving his keys inside his pocket.

"Wait," she uttered. "I didn't mean it like that. I already told you I did not accept Kyle's proposal."

"But you didn't tell him no either, did you?"

"Come on, Clark. I was in shock! The last thing I expected was for Kyle to pop up in Las Vegas and ask me to marry him."

His mouth compressed. "When it comes down to it, what would your parents prefer? For you to marry Kyle, or to continue sleeping with me?"

Eva couldn't lie to him, so she remained silent.

"Exactly," Clark said coolly. "Still living for everybody except yourself."

Eva hopped out of bed and threw on her clothes, acting as if she hadn't heard him. But she had, loud and clear. She could sense his mind flipping through their past, recalling how determined she'd been in school to please her parents and thinking they were the reason she didn't move forward with him. Nothing she said was going to convince him he was wrong about her.

Clark's words from last night popped into her mind.

Since your time here is limited, let's just call a truce. Enjoy the rest of your stay in Las Vegas, then commit to

maintaining some semblance of a friendship once you re-
turn to Black Willow.

Eva wanted nothing more than to do just that. But some-how, she and Clark had managed to hit an emotional roadblock at every turn. And she knew why. Their walls of protection were still standing tall. Neither of them had been willing to let their guard down and reveal their whole selves. The taste of pain they'd both endured during this tumultuous fling was enough to deter any admission that could make them vulner-able. Fear overrode honesty. They were both running hot, re-luctant to test the other's flame.

Clark's lack of trust in her was still apparent, and it still stung. It felt as if he'd always have an issue with her parents and Kyle. Eva was almost ready to give up on him altogether considering he didn't seem to believe in them as a couple. Walking away with what was left of her heart intact felt like the right thing to do, rather than trying to repeatedly make the impossible happen.

But when she looked up at him and saw his somber expres-sion, and the sadness in his eyes, Eva knew she couldn't leave things this way.

"Do you have time to grab coffee before your event?" she asked, hoping the olive branch would somehow smooth things over.

Barely glancing at his watch, Clark replied, "No, I'm ac-tually running late. I was supposed to be at the shelter over thirty minutes ago. But you were sleeping so well that I didn't want to wake you."

His thoughtfulness made her chest pull tight as her mind immediately went to Kyle. He would've woken her up two hours early if it meant being on time for an event.

"How about getting together later?" she pressed. "Maybe for lunch, or an early dinner?"

"Lunch won't work because we're serving food at the shelter from noon to three. I'll get back to you on dinner. The rest of my day is still up in the air."

In other words, he's really not trying that hard to see me despite what he said about making the most of the rest of my time here.

The ride back to Eva's building was silent for the most part, except for the R&B music playing in the background. As soon as Clark pulled into the driveway Eva swung open the door.

"Thanks," she said, her heart practically pounding out of her chest with sadness and loss. "I guess I'll um...see you at the hospital."

"Yep. See you there."

After Clark sped off, Eva stared up at her building's cold mirrored windows. The last thing she wanted to do was sit inside her apartment alone with her thoughts. Instead, she headed over to the coffee shop and treated herself to a strawberry Frappuccino. The outdoor patio was empty, so she took a seat in the sun, catching the last bits of morning rays before they transformed into beaming afternoon scorchers.

She looked out at the palm leaves swaying from the majestic treetops. The morning smog had lifted, leaving a clear view of the Spring Mountains' spectacular peaks in the distance.

I'm going to miss this, she thought as images of Black Willow's flat land and bulky white oaks sprang to mind.

The moment was disrupted by an incoming FaceTime call. Without looking, Eva already knew who it was. A rumble of dread lurched through her stomach as she tapped the accept button. She put on a forced smile when her mother's face appeared, all the while thinking, *If she starts going in about Kyle and the wedding, I'm hanging up.*

Times like this made her regret being born with the parent-pleasing gene. She appreciated how her father's work as a family practitioner had motivated her to become a doctor. But she should've drawn the line when her bougie mother, who'd wanted a better life for her only child than the one she'd had, had continued on that path a little too rigidly.

"Wilson!" her mother called out. "It's Eva. Come and say hello!"

"I'm on my way!"

Her mother ran a French-manicured hand along the edges of her silverish gray pixie cut, clearly staring at her own image rather than Eva.

"Hello, Mom."

"Hello, my love," she replied, her matte red lips blowing air kisses at the screen. "How do you think our new house is looking? Did Valerie and I do a fabulous job with the decorating or what?"

"Yes, you two did." Eva pulled the screen closer as her mother scanned the living room.

Her parents had moved into the ranch style home a few months ago after her mother had insisted on selling the tri-level house they'd owned for almost thirty years, declaring she could no longer climb staircases that resembled Mount Everest.

"Do you like all of the new pieces?" her mother continued, pointing toward acrylic accent tables, a tufted beige sofa and a white sheepskin rug.

"Yes, Mother, everything is beautiful. Where's Dad? I thought he was coming out."

"I can hear him bopping around here somewhere. I'll go to him since he refuses to come to us."

The minute her mother stepped inside their sleek white kitchen, her father appeared. "There's my girl!" he cried.

"Hey, Dad! It's so good to see your face. How are you doing?"

"Great, other than trying to keep your mother from spending all my money. How's it going out there in the Wild, Wild West?"

"Really well. I'm enjoying the challenging work, the excitement of the city, the amazing people—"

"And when is this assignment of yours going to be over again?" her mother interrupted.

Eva's father wrapped his arm around her. "The same time it's always been scheduled to end, Iris. At the end of the month. Now, let's not get started on this again."

"Who's getting started, Wilson? I'm just trying to have a conversation with our daughter."

He gave her chin an affectionate squeeze. Eva smiled softly as she watched them stare lovingly at each other. Her father may be graying a bit at the temples, and her mother crinkling around the eyes. But their passion for each other never seemed to fade, even after all these years.

This is what I want. What I should be working toward...

"I'm glad to hear things are going well, honey," her father said. "I knew that working in a big-city ER would be an invaluable experience for you."

"Thanks, Dad. It really has been."

Her mother pulled the phone in her direction. "I'm glad, too, hon. It just seems like you've been gone forever. I'm ready for my daughter to come back home. We all are. Black Willow is where you belong. You've given enough of yourself to Las Vegas. And let's be honest. That place isn't really *you*, now, is it?"

"What do you mean by that?"

"What I mean is, you're a class act, Eva. An intelligent, dignified woman who was raised to be an outstanding leader within the Black Willow community. Your talents are far better served right here at home. Not across the country in some desert party city."

"You've been talking to Kyle again, haven't you?"

A twist of her mother's lips was all it took for Eva to guess the answer. *Yes.*

"You know, Mom, not only has Las Vegas made me a better doctor, but it's made me a better person. I was just telling a wonderful new friend I made here how I've opened up to so many things, done some exploratory work on myself, come to terms with what I want out of life. And to be honest, my aspirations are beginning to shift."

Her mother turned to her father, mumbling, "What exactly is she trying to tell us?"

"I'm not one hundred percent sure. But whatever it is, I like the sound of it."

"I'll tell you what, honey," her mother continued. "When you come home, you can show all the townspeople how much you've grown, then *really* put the icing on the cake by putting your wedding back on the calendar. Let them know that you and Kyle are back together and better than ever."

"But Kyle and I are not back together. And why should we be? I couldn't imagine being in love with someone, then dumping them over the pressures of my career. Dad, did you ever consider leaving Mom when things got tough during medical school? Or while you were struggling to open your own practice?"

"No. Not for a second."

"I rest my case."

Her mother handed the phone to her father with a pout, then poured two glasses of mimosas. "I never could get through to that child…"

Eva picked at the paint chipping along the edge of her wrought iron chair, thinking back on her evening with Clark, then remembering his reaction when her mother called that morning. She shouldn't have held off on sharing with her parents how Clark had been the highlight of her trip.

"You know," Eva began, "I actually reconnected with an old friend during my stay here."

"Really?" her mother asked. "Who?"

"Clark Malone."

A warm breeze of satisfaction blew over her at the sound of

his name. Eva knew she was too damn old to be so concerned with what her parents thought.

Her mother stared into space while tapping her fingernail against the counter. "Clark Malone, Clark Malone..." she uttered, as if repeating his name would help jog her memory. "That doesn't ring a bell. Wilson, do you remember a Clark Malone?"

"Didn't you two attend medical school together?" he asked.

"Yes, we did."

"Yeah, I remember him. I always liked that kid. If I can recall correctly, you two were pretty good friends, but then you lost touch. What is he up to these days?"

"He's an ER doctor at Fremont General."

"Oh, is he?" her father asked, his head nodding with approval.

Her mother grabbed the phone and shoved it close to her face. "Hold on, Eva. Is that what this trip was really about? You running off to Las Vegas to get together with someone from your past?"

"No, Mom, not at all. I had no idea Clark was even living in Vegas, let alone working at the hospital. But having him here to show me the ropes and adjust to the city has been great. Really great."

With a dismissive wave of her hand, her mother replied, "Well I'm glad you've had a colleague there to assist you. But now that this assignment is coming to an end, it's time to start focusing on your return to Black Willow and how you're going to get back with—"

"Clark isn't just some colleague," Eva interrupted defiantly. "He is a friend. A very close friend..." As her voice trailed off, Eva realized that she'd had enough for one day. "You know, I'm sitting out in this hot sun, and I've got some things I need to take care of back at the apartment. So I'm gonna go."

"Okay," her mother responded. "But before you do, please just let me say this."

Here it was. The moment Eva had been dreading, when her mother would endorse Kyle as if their relationship was yet another campaign and he was running to win her back.

"Iris," her father said, "our daughter has things to do. Why don't we hang up before she gets sunburned?"

"I'll just be a minute. Eva, listen to me, sweetheart. Kyle flew all the way out to Las Vegas, right after he won the election no less, to apologize and propose again with that gorgeous new ring. I know he hurt you, but he was under so much pressure during that intense campaign. Please, at least consider giving him another chance. He's a good man, and I don't want you to miss out on a wonderful life—"

"Eva," her father interjected, "your mother and I want you to do whatever makes you happy. If that means giving Kyle another chance, fine. If it doesn't, that's fine, too. In the meantime, enjoy the rest of your days in Las Vegas, and we will talk to you soon."

Eva blew him a kiss, grateful for his understanding.

"Any parting words, Iris?" he asked her mother.

"Now you already know the answer to that. Eva, I want nothing more than for you to be happy. And I'm sorry if I'm being a little pushy. But as your mother, I cannot help but think I know what's best for you. However, like your father said, if marrying Kyle isn't in your future, then I'll just have to accept that. We love you, miss you, and can't wait for you to come home."

"Thank you. I love you, too. Oh, and before I forget, Clark told me to tell you both hello."

"Who?" her mother chirped.

Right before her father said, "Please tell Dr. Malone we said hello, and congratulations on all his success."

"I will. Talk soon."

Eva disconnected the video chat and immediately composed a text to Clark.

Just spoke with my parents. Told them you said hello. They said hello back, and congratulations on all your success.

While it was clear that things weren't going to work out between them, Eva couldn't shake the need to prove to Clark that he wasn't some taboo secret she was keeping from her parents. Within seconds, he responded.

Please thank them for me. That means a lot. More than you know.

The reply gave her a slight glimmer of hope that maybe, just maybe, things between them could still be salvaged.

CHAPTER SEVENTEEN

CLARK SETTLED IN at a table inside the physician's lounge with his iced green tea and spinach breakfast wrap in hand. The moment he pulled out his cell phone and began scrolling the apps, Eva came walking through the door.

Remorse throbbed inside his chest as he watched her approach the coffee station. Eva's time at Fremont General was coming to an end. While her stay had endured its fair share of ups and downs, he hated how when it came to them, she'd be leaving on a low note. How had they managed to fumble their friendship once again? For his part, Clark's intention of keeping things casual and holding back his feelings had blown up in his face. And now he had no clue where they stood.

He and Eva hadn't spoken outside of work since their last text message exchange, when she'd shared her parents' greeting. The fact that she'd mentioned him to them did give some semblance of him hope. And now, as he watched her chatting with a group of doctors, he wondered if she'd notice him sitting there, and come join him if he asked.

Even in her white coat and scrubs, Eva appeared beautiful and graceful. Everyone inside the lounge greeted her warmly, asking how she'd enjoyed her time at the hospital and when her assignment would end.

"Soon," Clark heard her tell one of the physicians. "Very soon…"

Hearing that response sent a mouthful of tea down the

wrong pipe. Clark pounded his chest and cleared his throat, struggling to prevent a fit of coughs. The commotion caught the attention of several physicians, Eva included.

Clark's skin burned with embarrassment as he nodded, letting them all know he was okay. When he and Eva locked eyes, she gave a small wave. Her tentative smile prompted him to gesture the empty chair next to him. As she sauntered over, the remorse swirling inside his chest settled into a wave of excitement.

"Hey, good morning," he said.

"Good morning. How are you?"

If her breathy tone was any indication of how she was feeling, Eva was just as nervous as he was.

"Hanging in there. You know…"

"Yeah, I do know." Eva fiddled with the lid on her cup, her head tilting to one side. "I'm not used to seeing you here in the mornings. You're usually hanging out in the cafeteria or the ER conference room."

"I know. I wanted to do a little cleanup on my phone, and I'm doing it in here because the cafeteria is so noisy and the conference room is in use." Clark left out the part where he was hoping to run into Eva since she usually stopped by the lounge most mornings.

Eva peered down at his phone screen. "What's going on with your cell? Are you running out of memory? Or is it freezing up?"

"No, nothing like that. Just getting rid of the stuff that no longer serves me."

As Eva looked on, Clark's first instinct was to hide the phone. But considering she was the main reason for the cleanup, he didn't bother.

"Wait a minute," she said, nudging his arm. "Did I just see you delete the Two of Hearts dating app?"

"Yes, you did," he confirmed as he continued clicking the *X* hovering over several other apps.

"Oh, and Swipe Right Tonight and Struck by Cupid's Arrow are getting the axe, too?

"Yep. Gone."

"So what brought on this?"

Clark set his cell to the side and looked her in the eye. "Honestly? They weren't doing me any good. I wasn't getting anything out of juggling a bunch of different women, then running away when things got serious. That was just my way of masking the underlying issues I hadn't faced regarding my past. The heartbreaks that I never dealt with. Then when you showed up here in Vegas, and we got involved again, I was forced to confront that pain. Last time I ran around it. This time I'm going through it. Dealing with it head-on until I heal. I can't do that if I'm focusing on a bunch of frivolous, casual hookups."

Clark blew a long exhale after finally releasing that heavy burden. He'd surprised himself after sharing all that with Eva. But it was the truth, and she deserved to hear it before she left. Plus, if he was planning on doing things differently in the future, expressing how he felt without fear was a good place to start.

"Wow," Eva uttered, watching him intently. "I, um… I didn't expect you to say that. Thank you for being so open with me. That's actually wonderful to hear, Clark. And no matter what comes of us, I do care about you a great deal. I want you to be happy. But that won't happen until you heal. So hearing you say you're working toward that is really amazing. You'll be a better man for it."

"Thanks, Eva. That's my hope."

After taking a long sip of coffee, she asked, "So, where do things stand with us?"

"Well, your assignment ends in a couple of weeks. And at

this point, I have nothing to lose. So I feel perfectly at peace telling you that I love you, Eva. And I wish you weren't leaving. I hate the idea of you going back to Black Willow and even considering marrying Kyle. I know I messed up by letting fear get in the way and diminishing our relationship to a casual hookup. We could've spent this time together working toward building something real. If I could go back and do things differently, I would. But I can't. So I'm forced to deal with my mistakes and hope that we can still salvage our friendship."

Falling against the back of her chair, Eva gazed at Clark through wide eyes. "I—I don't even know what to say to that. You love me?"

"I do. Very much. But I also know that you have some unfinished business back in Iowa, and I don't wanna get in the way of that. You need to be clear on what you want. If that's me, then you have got to tell Kyle that it's over for good and give him that ring back." Clark reached over and slid her hand in his. "I really want to try to make something of us, Eva. And I don't care if there's fifteen hundred miles between us. That's just a plane ride away."

Eva sat straight up, locking her fingers with Clark's. "You know what? I—"

The beep of the hospital intercom filled the lounge, interrupting her mid-sentence.

"Dr. Malone, please report to the emergency room. Dr. Malone to the emergency room."

"Dammit," Clark groaned, glancing at his watch. "I had thirty minutes left until my day was scheduled to begin. Listen, let's continue this conversation right after I check into the ER and find out what's going on."

She sighed in frustration as he shot out the door. She'd wanted to say, *I love you, too, Clark.*

But now she'd have to wait.

* * *

An hour later, Eva's entire body was buzzing with joy as she exited the physicians' on-call room. She shouldn't have been this happy after telling Kyle that they were done considering the news had upset him. But in the back of her mind, all Eva could think about was the fact that Clark had just professed his love for her, even if he didn't know her feelings yet. There wasn't enough begging in the world Kyle could have done, which he'd certainly tried, to make her go back to him. She was moving on to better things.

After hanging up from him, Eva had called her parents to let them know that she had officially broken things off with Kyle for good. Her mother immediately began to unravel. But her father stopped the meltdown before it could really start, preventing her from ticking off all the reasons why Eva was making a mistake. Eva quickly interjected during the moment of silence, letting them both know how unhappy she'd been with Kyle, and that something more than just a friendship had sparked between her and Clark since she'd arrived in Las Vegas.

"Wait, what is that supposed to mean?" her mother had shrieked into the phone.

Once again, Eva's father came to her rescue, silencing her mother as Eva explained all the wonderful traits Clark brought to the table. "Not only that, but we're genuinely in love," she told her parents.

After a long silence, her mom asked, "Are you happy?" to which Eva replied, "Very."

Another extended pause ensued before her mother finally said, "Well, that's all that matters."

Eva checked her cell to see if Clark had reached out, then headed straight to the ER to find him. She rushed through the trauma units, operating rooms and observation areas. He was nowhere to be found. He wasn't inside the conference room, and neither Brandi nor Leo had seen him.

Just as Eva grabbed her phone to text him, it rang.

She eyed the screen, hoping it was Clark. Eva came to a grinding halt when Susan Piper's name appeared, the hospital administrator. That was odd considering she hadn't heard from Susan since the day she began her temporary assignment.

"Good morning, Dr. Gordon speaking."

"Good morning, Dr. Gordon. Susan Piper here. Do you have a free moment to stop by my office? I need to speak with you about something. It's urgent."

Eva's stomach dropped to her knees. "I do. I'll head there right now."

"Great. See you shortly."

What could be so wrong that I'm being called to the administrator's office?

After arriving on the third floor, Eva shuffled down the hallway, her teeth clenching to the rhythm of her clicking heels. One knock on the door and Susan called out, "Come in!"

Eva opened it slowly, sticking her head in first before entering.

"Please have a seat, Dr. Gordon."

I'm being let go early. She's going to send me back to Black Willow today, before I can even digest what just happened with Clark.

"Dr. Gordon, I just received word that Dr. Abrams will be leaving the hospital. His wife has accepted a position as the Caribbean Tourism Organization's new human resources director. So they'll be moving to Barbados. Soon."

Is this what I think it is? Eva asked herself, growing lightheaded with anticipation as she stared across the desk.

"You have done an exceptional job here at Fremont General, Dr. Gordon. And I have received nothing but glowing feedback on your performance. Primarily from your former medical school classmate, Dr. Malone."

Wreathing her hands together, Eva rocked back in her chair, taking in the moment as it slowly sank in. "That is so nice to hear, Susan. Thank you."

"No, thank *you*. For all that you've done. And with that being said, we would like to offer you a permanent position here in the ER."

"Really?" Eva breathed, clutching her chest.

"Absolutely. I know it's a lot to think about. Las Vegas is a long way from Iowa. Your family is there, your friends. And I'm sure the staff at the Black Willow Medical Clinic would hate to see you go. But you seem to be enjoying your time here, and you've adjusted to our bustling emergency room beautifully. So, just think about it. Dr. Abrams isn't leaving for another few weeks, and I haven't even begun putting together a package for you. I just wanted to let you know what was happening so that you could consider it."

"You know what, Susan? Actually, it isn't a lot to think about. I haven't just enjoyed my time here at Fremont General, I've loved it. The people I've met, the things I've learned, the challenges I've faced. I came to Las Vegas looking for an escape and ended up finding a home. So I don't need time to think about it. I accept the offer."

"Wonderful!" Susan said, pressing her hands together. "I expect to have your package together within the next couple of days. Of course the salary will be competitive, and negotiable. But we'll work all that out. Until then, welcome aboard!"

"Thank you so much," Eva said, barely able to contain herself as she stood. "I look forward to the next steps."

"As do I. Thank you, Dr. Gordon."

Eva shot out of Susan's office and ran toward the elevator, texting Clark along the way. When she reached the first floor and rounded the corner, he appeared, almost knocking her to the floor.

"Sorry!" he exclaimed, grabbing her arms and lifting her up.

"I have been looking all over for you!" Eva exclaimed. "You will not *believe* all the new developments I have to share with you."

"Really? New developments since I last saw you about an hour ago?"

"Yes! Now let's go find someplace quiet so we can talk."

"Follow me."

Clark led Eva inside an empty consultation room. They sat close to each another on the burgundy tweed love seat, the energy between them vibrating at a feverish pitch.

"I must tell you—" Eva began before Clark interrupted her.

"Wait, before you start, I realized there were a few things I forgot to mention earlier when we spoke. Do you mind if I go first?"

"No, of course not," Eva lied, her knees bouncing impatiently as she was dying to share her news. Both the job offer and, more importantly, how much she loved him.

Clark took her hands in his. "I owe you the real explanation as to why I first suggested we only kept things casual between us. It had a lot to do with how you'd turned me down during med school. That rejection made me feel as if I wasn't good enough for you. And when I think about the man you were going to marry, I realize that I'm nothing like him. I'm not some stuffy politician from your hometown. The whole Black Willow pedigree means a lot to your parents, and I know how much their opinion means to you. So I figured you'd be more concerned with making them happy than making me happy."

Tears began trickling from Eva's eyes before words could escape her lips. As she opened her mouth to speak, Clark silenced her once again.

"Please, before you respond, just let me say that what we have is special. This is a once-in-a-lifetime kind of love. The kind of love that you deserve. From what you've told me, Kyle is not even close to being good enough for you. You'd be doing yourself a disservice giving him another chance. And I'm not just saying that because I want to be with you. I'm saying that because it's true. You're a good woman, Eva. You deserve the world. And I want to be the man to give it to you."

"Thank you, Clark. You deserve the same. And I *am* the woman who can give it to you. Because I love you, too. I was so confused when you suggested we keep things casual. But you were adamant, and I knew you had your reasons, so I just went along with it. That wasn't necessarily a bad thing, either. Because it gave me a chance to realize that you're the one for me. You always have been. Kyle isn't half the man that you are, and I can assure you that I will never go back to him. As a matter of fact, I just spoke to him and told him that."

"You did? When?"

"Right before I ran into you. So he is completely out of the picture. As for my parents, I spoke with them as well, letting them know that Kyle and I are done and there will definitely be no wedding."

"Did your mother faint?"

"Almost. But she eventually rebounded. Then when I told her and my father about us—"

"Hold on," Clark said, grabbing his head. "Now I think *I* might faint. You told your parents about us?"

"Yes, I did."

"What did they say?"

"Well, my father was fine with it. As for my mother, it took her a minute to come around. But eventually, she did. I convinced them both that you're an amazing man. And they reiterated that they just want me to be happy."

"I'm going to see to it that you are," Clark murmured, leaning in for a kiss.

Pressing her hands against his chest, Eva stopped him. "Wait. I have one more thing to share with you."

"Okay, let's hear it."

"I was just offered a permanent position here at Fremont General."

He leaped from the couch and pulled Eva to her feet. "What? *And?* Did you accept it?"

"I sure did."

Clark wrapped her up in a tight embrace, lifting her off the floor. "That is fantastic, Eva! You should've told me that the minute that door closed!"

"How could I after you insisted on talking first?"

"You make a good point." Clark paused, slowly lowering Eva. "You do know that everybody back in Black Willow will be devastated by this news, don't you?"

"I don't know about *devastated*. But I do think they'll be sad to see me go, for sure. However, just like my parents, they'd want me to do whatever makes me happy. So if that means moving to Vegas to take on this exciting new opportunity and be with the love of my life, then I'm sure I'll have their blessing."

"Mmm, the love of your life. I like the sound of that." Clark paused, his eyes drifting from Eva down to the pale gray carpeting. "Listen, I'm all for you moving to Las Vegas permanently, taking the job here at the hospital and us being together. But if we're really gonna do this, and I mean do it the right way, then I'm going to have to lay some ground rules."

Her body went limp within his embrace. "Here we go with these damn ground rules again. What is it going to be this time?"

"Well, obviously you'll no longer be my hookup buddy. But I don't want you to be my girlfriend, either."

"So what exactly am I going to be?"

"This time around, I want you to be my wife."

The air suddenly left the room. Eva stood there, frozen, her vision blurring as Clark got down on one knee. He took her left hand in his and kissed her ring finger.

"Now I know I'm not doing this the right way. This should've been planned out, our families and friends should be here, and I should have a stunning diamond ring to slip on your finger. But I'm hoping that my love for you will override all of that. At least for the time being. Eva Gordon, will you marry me?"

"Yes. Yes!" she squealed happily, pulling him up and jumping into his arms.

"Finally," he murmured in between kisses, "I got my girl back."

"Yes, you did. Thank you for being so patient with me, Clark. And for understanding that I needed time for my head and heart to align. I cannot wait to begin this new adventure with you. I love you, Clark Malone."

"I love you, too, Eva Gordon."

EPILOGUE

Six months later

EVA RELAXED HER head against the pillow and took a deep breath. "This feels so weird, being on the other side of things."

"I know it does," Clark agreed. "But this side of things looks good on you."

She looked up from the hospital bed at him and smiled, loving his newfound glow.

"Well," Dr. Hall said, turning their attention back to the monitor. "It looks like you're about thirteen weeks along, and according to the ultrasound, you're having a baby girl."

Tears of joy sprang from Eva's eyes as Clark leaned down and embraced her.

"Exactly what I wanted," he said huskily.

Eva chuckled, caressing his face before saying, "Stop lying. You know you wanted a boy!"

"That is *not* true. I'm happy either way. But this just means we'll have to keep trying…"

"For now, why don't we just focus on the bundle of joy we've got coming?" she suggested while focusing on the tiny gray image on the screen.

Life in Las Vegas had been a whirlwind ever since Eva had accepted the full-time position at Fremont General. After saying her goodbyes and selling her loft back in Black Willow, she'd packed up her things and moved into Clark's townhome. Then they'd found out about the baby, which had prompted them to host an intimate wedding ceremony for family and close friends at the Wynn. It was the first time they'd seen each other's parents since medical school. Eva was so pleased when hers welcomed Clark into the family with open arms. Her mother had become so ecstatic about the union and pregnancy that it was as if Kyle never existed. As for Clark's parents, they'd always been kind and accepting of Eva. It was as if no time had passed between them.

"Have you two thought of any baby names yet?" Dr. Hall asked.

"Of course I have," Eva said. "I love Simone, Nina, Devon, Eden...there are so many that I'm thinking of."

"What about you, Dr. Malone?"

"Honestly, I'm fine with whatever my wife chooses."

"Really? So you're not going to throw any names into the ring?"

"Doctor," Clark said, "I'm so happy to have this woman back in my life that she can pretty much do whatever she wants."

"Aww," Eva and Dr. Hall sighed in unison.

Dr. Hall pointed at Eva and said, "He's a keeper."

"Trust me, I know. Which is why I'm never letting him go."

The tears that had pooled along the rims of Eva's eyes slowly trickled down her cheeks. She still had trouble grasping how drastically things had changed within less than a year. From arriving in Las Vegas with a broken heart to falling in love with Clark, their second-chance romance was one for the books.

"Can you believe this?" he whispered, resting his hand against her belly. "That we're married, and pregnant, and getting to spend the rest of our lives together?"

"No, I cannot. It feels like a dream. There was a time when I never thought I'd find contentment. But this...this is far more than I could've ever hoped for. This is the ultimate happily-ever-after."

* * * * *

COMING SOON!

We really hope you enjoyed reading this book.
If you're looking for more romance
be sure to head to the shops when
new books are available on

Thursday 15th February

To see which titles are coming soon, please visit

millsandboon.co.uk/nextmonth

MILLS & BOON

MILLS & BOON ®

Coming next month

RESISTING THE OFF-LIMITS PAEDIATRICIAN
Kate MacGuire

John glanced her way as he waited in line.

He gave her a little nod. What that meant, she couldn't say, but it unleashed a flurry of goosebumps down her back. She smiled in return, then dove for her water glass to relieve her parched throat. Why was she so nervous about this lunch? She'd completed dozens of assignments as a traveling doctor. Meeting new people, fitting in—it was all old news to her. So this edgy feeling she had around John made no sense.

It was also annoying, because she had some ideas for helping Angel get her testing done faster. She needed to stay focused if she was going to get past John's territorial tendencies, not stutter her way through her speech because of nerves.

Reflexively she groped through her handbag until her fingers found her lipstick and compact. She flipped it open to check her appearance and was just about to freshen her lipstick when she paused.

What are you doing, Char?

Her gaze shifted from the mirror to John, who had made it to the order counter and was oblivious to her gaze. He was a solidly built man, that was for sure, with a cool, streetwise vibe. The woman taking his order was giving him lots of big smiles while twirling a strand of her hair. Even at this distance, it was obvious she was flirting.

Charlotte could see the appeal. John was a strong, attractive man, with a no-nonsense attitude that could make a girl feel a bit invincible by his side.

Her gaze shifted back to her mirror. Was that what she was doing too? Flirting a little with her attractive, vigilant colleague?

She paused to consider that scenario, then felt a rush of heat as she realised it was true. She snapped her compact shut. No need to give anyone the wrong idea—including herself. She had one simple rule when it came to romance on the road, designed to keep her career intact and her reputation stellar. *No. Dating. Coworkers.* As a traveling doctor, she needed excellent recommendations to secure her next assignment. She couldn't afford loose ends, bad breakups, or misunderstandings in her line of work.

So John could keep that stacked body of his on his side of the clinic—because romance was not in the cards.

Don't miss
RESISTING THE OFF-LIMITS PAEDIATRICIAN
Kate MacGuire

Available next month
millsandboon.co.uk

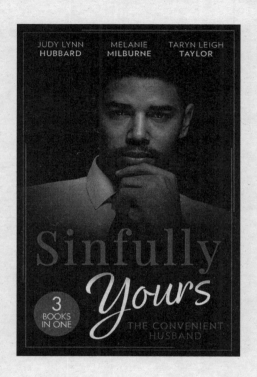

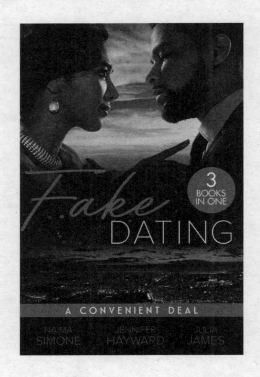

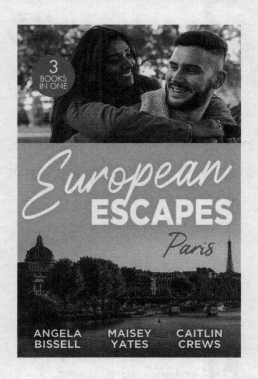

LET'S TALK
Romance

For exclusive extracts, competitions and special offers, find us online:

f MillsandBoon

X @MillsandBoon

⊙ @MillsandBoonUK

♪ @MillsandBoonUK

Get in touch on 01413 063 232

MILLS & BOON

THE HEART OF ROMANCE

A ROMANCE FOR EVERY READER

MODERN
Prepare to be swept off your feet by sophisticated, sexy and seductive heroes, in some of the world's most glamourous and romantic locations, where power and passion collide.

HISTORICAL
Escape with historical heroes from time gone by. Whether your passion is for wicked Regency Rakes, muscled Vikings or rugged Highlanders, awaken the romance of the past.

MEDICAL
Set your pulse racing with dedicated, delectable doctors in the high-pressure world of medicine, where emotions run high and passion, comfort and love are the best medicine.

True Love
Celebrate true love with tender stories of heartfelt romance, from the rush of falling in love to the joy a new baby can bring, and a focus on the emotional heart of a relationship.

HEROES
The excitement of a gripping thriller, with intense romance at its heart. Resourceful, true-to-life women and strong, fearless men face danger and desire - a killer combination!

 **afterglow BOOKS**
From showing up to glowing up, these characters are on the path to leading their best lives and finding romance along the way – with plenty of sizzling spice!

To see which titles are coming soon, please visit

millsandboon.co.uk/nextmonth